Peak Season

EMILY HARRISON

BENEATH
THE ASH
PUBLISHING

Formatted with Vellum

For Jeff, my anchor, my soulmate, my Harley Nash. You sat beside me in the quiet hours, night after night, while I built this world from nothing. You never complained, never wavered, you just stayed, steady and sure, the way you always do. You were the first to hold this story in your hands, the first to believe in it, the first to believe in me. This book carries your fingerprints as much as mine, and every word is a love letter back to you.

Foreword

Peak Season is a story about healing, found family, and falling in love when you least expect it, but it also deals with heavier themes, including emotional abuse, coercive control, trauma, and a scene of attempted sexual assault (non-graphic, but emotionally intense). Please read with care.

This book is intended for readers 18+ due to mature language, adult themes, and explicit sexual content.

CHAPTER 1
Inbound
LOLA

The plane jerks and my stomach drops like it's trying to ghost my body.

Over the speaker, an aggressively chirpy flight attendant says, "Ladies and gentlemen, the captain has turned on the seatbelt sign," like that's supposed to be comforting.

We're all going to die, but at least we'll be neatly buckled in when we do.

It's mid-November, and the sky is the kind of grey that makes everything feel paused. The Alps are down there somewhere, jagged and waiting, like a mouth full of teeth I don't want to fall into. I press my boots flat to the floor, grip the armrests, and try not to cry, or puke, or both. I didn't think leaving England would feel like this, like my bones were trying to crawl out of my skin. There's no one next to me to grab, no one to pretend I'm not absolutely shitting myself, so I pray to a God I haven't believed in since my mum died when I was eleven, that the plane won't crash.

I'm not ready to die in the sky, not yet. I haven't even kissed a stranger on a mountain or made bad choices in a bar yet, I haven't done anything.

A kid across the aisle throws up into a paper bag. His mum rubs his back like it's just another Tuesday. The woman beside them fans herself with the in-flight magazine. The guy behind me snores like he's on a beach instead of bouncing through air pockets over the Alps. The cabin reeks of sour cream flavoured pretzels, recycled air, and that silent kind of panic people pretend isn't real. The air's too hot and too cold at once, everyone's pretending they're fine, and none of us are.

Another shudder, sharper, a rattle that zings through the overhead bins. I lock my jaw and stare at the safety card like the little cartoon man knows what to do when the sky decides it hates you. My palms sweat and I flex my fingers, release, flex again. Counting breaths, four in, four out, picture the ground, the pavement, a front door that sticks in winter. The heavy key in my pocket, anything that says, you're allowed to be alive.

The pilot crackles on, calm voice, we're on the final approach into Grenoble, apparently there are light crosswinds, I'd hate to know what heavy crosswinds feel like then. He tells the cabin crew to prepare for landing, I look at the wing through the oval window, the lights are blinking evenly, the metal looks steady, everything's pretending to be calm, even as the sky throws punches at its own reflection.

The plane dips again, a woman up front makes a noise that's almost a laugh, almost a sob. The kid whispers, I hate it, I hate it, I hate it, and his mum murmurs, almost there, sweetheart, nearly there, like a spell. I borrow it because we're almost there, Lola, nearly there, I tell myself on repeat.

I pick up the TikTok recommended paperback book I've been trying unsuccessfully to read, and hold it against my chest, tightly like it's some kind of shield. The girl across the aisle gives me a sympathetic look when I catch her looking at me. Of course I pretend not to notice, I don't want sympathy, I just need the ground.

When we hit the runway with a bump it ripples through my spine. The tyres scream, the engines roar, the flaps bite air. Then I thank that God again for gravity, just breathe and count my heartbeats until they stop feeling like punches.

The bell dings and I hear seatbelts snap open. People spring up like survival is a race, but I stay put until the aisle thins, because being trampled to death after not dying in the sky would be the worst plot twist ever.

Grenoble airport is cramped, loud, and smells faintly of wet wool and burnt coffee. There are low ceilings, tired lighting and the automatic doors keep sighing open and letting in a slap of cold that bites my cheeks. I fight my way to baggage claim, scanning the belt like I'm on a mission, my army brat training kicks in, spot the target, move fast, stand your ground. My scuffed pink suitcase slides into view and I hook my hand through the handle in one clean grab.

The Powder White rep's easy to find, she has a white fleece, the obligatory clipboard, and a thousand-yard stare of someone who's answered the same question a hundred times. She's holding up a sign like it's the last shred of her patience.

"Hi," I say, aiming for competent. "I'm looking for Harley Nash?"

She barely looks up and tells me in her thick Scottish accent, "Out the doors, turn left, bus four-two-seven, about ten buses down. Tall, black hair, he's in uniform."

"Thanks." The word hits the top of her auburn-haired head, and she's already onto the next person.

Outside, the wind feels like knives straight through my jeans, and my hair becomes a weapon against my own face whipping my cheeks and stopping me from being able to see. Coaches idle in a long line, drivers smoking, snow grit crunching under boots. The light is flat winter grey, everything desaturated like someone turned the world to low power mode. I drag my case along the row until I find bus four-two-seven.

No Harley.

Figures, he's probably off being interesting somewhere else. Then I see him.

He moves down the pavement like he knows people are watching, black trousers, white fleece pushed to the elbows, two full sleeves of tattoos, dark ink wrapping strong forearms. Black hair just messy enough to look intentional, he's watching a brunette climb the steps like she's the only person in the world.

"What's the name, babe?" he says when I reach him, eyes flicking to his clipboard.

The babe sticks in my spine, ugh, we've never met. Instant familiarity, tossed out like confetti, I don't show it, but it grates.

"Lola. I'm working with Powder White this season."

He glances up, his eyes are a similar blue to the sea in the Caribbean, the kind that makes you check if you're imagining it. He doesn't comment, just grabs my suitcase like it weighs nothing. "You can ride up front with me."

No greeting, no wink, no smile, just the faintest curve of his mouth that says he doesn't need any of it.

The bus is warm when I climb aboard, which is light relief to the freezing cold outside. The driver nods at me professionally, and I take the front passenger seat. Harley stands with one foot braced against the step, reads a laminated sheet into a handheld mic which includes a snow report. Fresh dusting overnight, cloud pushing in by late afternoon, dinner times, childcare sign-ups. Instructions not to leave wet boots in corridors, his voice is steady, low, built to carry without shouting.

He doesn't look at me once.

The city slips to fields, the fields to valleys, a river runs alongside us. Villages flicker past, shutters shut, smoke lifting thinly from chimneys, dogs barking in the quiet of the journey. The bus starts to climb in earnest, hairpin turns, there are chorus's of oohs and nervous laughs, I don't look, because I don't want to think of falling off the edge of the mountain before I've even got there. Someone makes a joke about life insurance, someone else asks if crampons are a thing you can rent, what?

A little girl behind me drops a mitten, I twist, pick it up, and pass it back. Her mum mouths thank you and when I turn back to face forward I catch Harley watching me in the windscreen reflection, quickly dropping his gaze to the clipboard like I misread it.

Towards the end of the coach ride, he moves down the aisle while we crawl, checking on people, pointing out landmarks, answering questions with patience that doesn't feel fake. Stopping to smile at the brunette he was ogling earlier, and to my surprise it lands soft not sleazy. I hate that I notice the difference, I hate that he has a difference.

The resort opens up ahead like a cinematic set unveiling itself, It's beautiful, chair lifts are carving lines through the sky, chalets are stacked, glowing orange, warmly-lit. Pistes criss-crossing like someone stitched the mountain with white thread. I press my palm to the glass and breathe out so it fogs, I made it, I actually made it.

❄

We pull up outside the hotel, a 1970s time capsule trying to be cozy, it's brown carpets in vomit swirls, dim lighting that wants to be warm and isn't quite. Harley hauls my suitcase to the entrance and points inside.

"Scarlett's expecting you."

"Thanks," I say, even though I'd like to knock the curve off his mouth with my fist and see if he flinches.

Inside is absolute chaos with a system, staff in white fleeces slip past each other like a dance. Radios crackle, kids cannon through the lobby, wild with sugar and altitude. A man in an expensive looking jacket complains about missing skis like someone stole a limb. I stand off to the side because I know better than to plant myself in the flow.

Behind the desk, a blonde woman with a sharp bob jabs at a computer screen like she can will it into order, so I wait patiently, but she doesn't look up. I keep waiting until eventually she looks at me, but not seeing me.

"Name," she barks eventually, eyes still on the list.

"Lola Maxwell."

She frowns a scroll and then another. "Are you sure you're booked in here?"

"I'm not a guest, I'm here to work, I'm supposed to ask for Scarlett."

She looks up and something flickers. "That's me. Sorry,

transfer day, welcome to the madness." The smile clicks onto her face neat and real. She's already dialling as she talks. "Hang tight. I'll get someone to show you the ropes. We'll chat after the welcome meeting."

"I'll take her," a voice says. Of course it's Harley.

Scarlett's relief is visible. "Thanks, Nash." She vanishes toward a fresh fire to put out.

By this point Harley is quite acquainted with my suitcase and he lifts it already moving. "Thanks, I guess," I mutter.

He smirks like that's a language he's fluent in, angling towards a narrow door I thought was a broom cupboard that is supposed to be a lift when it actually looks like a vertical coffin.

"I don't think." I start, but he's already shoved my suitcase in, then himself, then me.

I'm pressed up against his back, there's no space, no room to breathe. My pulse hammers anyway, heat radiates off him and he smells clean and human up close. My pulse jumps so hard it feels like he can see it on my neck.

"This isn't regulation safe," I say, which is not what I meant to say, but my brain mouths off when my body is busy.

He chuckles, It sounds unpractised. "Five seconds, tops."

The doors slide shut, his hip brushes my stomach, my heart is beating everywhere in my body except in my chest. I can feel it in my ears, in my head... The lift hums up one floor, two, three, slow enough to notice the numbers as they glow.

We stop on the staff-only floor and the doors gasp open to a corridor that smells like laundry and pine cleaner. Stepping out first, he gives me space to breathe. He leads me to the last room on the left right next to the fire door.

"Your suite, m'lady."

Pulling the handle down I walk in and stop at the window. The view hits me like a soft punch, the peaks are layered and look endless. There are lifts dragging chairs through white air and a horizon that doesn't know how to end. The room's small and clean, but it's big enough for a double bed and a desk with a mirror hanging above it. The radiator ticks like it's thinking about cooperating, it feels warm and cozy and I take a breath to steady myself.

"Wow," I say, softer than I mean to. "That view's insane."

Harley fills the doorway, too much, but somehow not enough.

"You good here?"

I turn and let him see I'm scared and here anyway. "Yeah. I think I am."

He nods once, and something twists low in my stomach. I ignore it, so does he. "Cool," he says. "I'll come back in an hour."

"Okay, Harley, see you in a bit." And the way his name fits in my mouth feels like a choice I'm going to keep making.

He closes the door with a soft click and the room goes quiet in a way that makes me aware of every small sound. I hear a radio crackle down the hall when I walk over to touch the window with two fingers like the mountain might hum back and for the first time since the plane, I let myself smile.

This job's going to be trouble, the kind I think I want.

❄

Harley

She seems so soft, not emotionally, that's still under review. Physically pressed up behind me in a lift that should count as a hazard, her hips brushed mine. Breath hitched, she smelled a lot like coconuts.

Lola Maxwell.

Outside airport arrivals, she was easy to spot, the wind had caught her blonde curly hair and tangled it across her face, but she didn't fix it, she just walked like she didn't care who saw. No fake tan, no lipstick, no obvious effort to impress. She looked pale, like she hadn't eaten much or slept properly in a while, but her eyes were sharp and alert. The kind of girl who watches everything and keeps her mouth shut until she's sure what's safe. Beautiful yet understated, in short, a fucking knock out.

She didn't say much on the drive up, sat near the front, hands clenched in her lap, eyes fixed on the window. I watched her in the mirror for a bit, long enough to see she wasn't just zoning out. She was tracking, every curve of the road, every noise, every person around her.

Some girl dropped a mitten behind her. Lola picked it up, handed it back like it was nothing. Didn't look for thanks, didn't smile, just did it and turned forward again. That stuck with me more than it should've.

She didn't ask the questions, most of them do. Where are we staying? Do we get ski passes? What's the drinking age here? Lola just listened, took it all in and stayed quiet, not shy, something else, maybe controlled.

When we reached the hotel, she stepped off the coach with her head high like she was bracing for impact. I carried her suitcase in, pointed her towards Scarlett, and left it at that.

I figured that'd be it for the night, but then for some unknown reason, I told Scarlett I'd be her buddy and show her to her room.

She didn't argue, so I just grabbed her suitcase again and led her to the lift. She hesitated, just a beat, and I nearly offered to take the stairs, but she followed.

It's not a big lift, we've nicknamed it the 'coffin lift', so you know it's not exactly built for comfort. I felt her behind me, light, small and stiff with nerves. Her breathing changed halfway up, like she was trying to slow it down.

She didn't say much, neither did I. I dropped her off at the fire-door room, standard for new hires. Door sticks, radiator clicks, the mattress isn't great, but the view's solid, mountain straight out the window.

She stood at the glass like she was trying to memorise it. Said "wow" under her breath, softly like she hadn't meant to.

I didn't comment, just watched her take it in, then stepped back out before she turned around.

Back in my room, next door, I dropped the clipboard on the desk and sat on the edge of the bed. Ran through my list, sauna's still down. Scarlett wants guest numbers by seven. The Statham's need a cot, dinner timings, childcare schedule, all standard, nothing I can't handle.

Still, my head wasn't in it, I kept seeing her in that lift, breathing like she was trying not to panic. I've seen that before, in guests, in new staff, in kids on the slopes when they realise the hill's steeper than they thought, it's not fear, exactly, it's restraint.

I started scribbling on the kit list, added extra gloves. Almost wrote her name next to the XS, caught myself, crossed it out, didn't rewrite it.

Then the radio crackled, Scarlett wanted a final headcount, confirmation on the cot, someone to take the two late arrivals on the town walk, said front desk was slammed and the new girl didn't have her uniform yet.

I pressed the button. "Copy, the cot's in, I'll take the extras."

I kept my voice even, just as I've learned to do. Checking the time on my watch, I'm a couple of minutes early when I knock on her door, so not like me, and when she opens it quickly, it's almost as though she'd been on her way out already.

She'd changed, nothing dramatic, just a different jacket, hair pulled back, still looked a little pale, still watching me too closely.

"Ready?" I asked. Kept it light.

She nodded. "Ready."

We walked side by side down the corridor, I didn't look at her, didn't need to, I could feel her there, holding herself tight, like she didn't want to take up too much space. Not my problem, she's staff, new, a stranger.

I've got a job to do, and it doesn't involve getting distracted by someone else who's barely walked through the door. Still, there was something about the way she moved beside me. Like she hadn't made her mind up yet. Like she was giving this place a chance to disappoint her, most people come to the mountain for fun. Lola looked like she came up to breathe, and I didn't like how quickly I noticed that.

CHAPTER 2
Orientation Hangover
LOLA

The welcome meeting's done, thankfully. I sat through it because apparently staff count as "guests" when you're brand new. Scarlett, the manager, did her whole serious speech about skiing rules, and that "Powder White has a strict no off-piste policy. Last year a guest ignored the signs and we nearly lost him to a slide." Everyone laughed like it was a joke, but Harley didn't, his jaw locked tight, and I couldn't stop thinking, had he been there?

By the time Harley and I leave the chalet hotel, my boots are soaked through, every step producing that cold squelch you only get when snow melts into places you'd rather it didn't. My fingers ache inside my gloves, the air has that hard blue quality that says mid-November is here to bite. The sky slides toward indigo, and every breath scrapes my throat and leaves a thin ache behind.

We've barely made it down the street when Harley loops his arm through mine, my face scrunches when I look across at him. It looks casual but it doesn't feel casual. His brows pull together in a frown.

"Don't want you falling over on my conscience okay?"

"Okay, but I'm perfectly capable of looking after myself," I mutter, giving in anyway, even if a tiny part of me hopes he isn't just doing this because we're "buddies."

Butterflies erupt in my stomach at the press of his body, twice in one day. His forearm is solid, his touch sure, and it does something to my balance that has nothing to do with the snow. I pretend it's nothing, but my chest tightens and my thoughts scatter.

He's warmth wrapped in cold. His hand hooks around my arm when my steps falter on the packed slush. The tug is gentle but grounding, pulling me back before I can slip. I steady myself, pretending it's just the pavement beneath me that's unstable, not my head. When I glance up, Harley's watching me, brows slightly raised, his full lips curved into a smirk.

"See," he says, smug as hell.

The welcome night out, that's what they called it at the meeting, like a tradition and a dare. New staff get dragged to the local bar on the first night and thrown straight in before they learn where the fire exits are. Harley's my Powder White buddy, the one assigned to help me get settled, so technically he has to stick with me, and hasn't looked thrilled about it all day. To be fair, I haven't made it easy, I have been a bit prickly since the airport. I blame the nerves, and maybe the trauma of surviving Ryanair with my soul intact.

The Red Frog sits a ten-minute walk away, a squat timber building hunched under a soft heap of snow. The windows are lit with a red glow that pulses against the night, like the whole place is breathing and slightly drunk. A line of boards and skis lean along the wall under a canopy, their edges puckered with old scrapes. Someone's strung fairy lights over the doorway and the bulbs click when the wind nudges them.

Inside, heat slaps my cheeks, the room's full and loud. Coats are thrown over chair backs in messy piles, wet boots steam on the stone floor. The music is a steady thump that climbs up through my soles and into my ribs. The air's thick with spilled beer, citrus sour from old wedges, a ribbon of woodsmoke that sneaks in every time the door opens. Bodies move with the lazy confidence of people who've already decided tomorrow can look after itself.

Harley eases me into the crush and starts the parade of names. I try to hang on to them, but they slide off as fast as he says them. I catch Jack's name, mostly because he's right in front of me. Tidy features, light brown hair he keeps pushing off his forehead when he smiles. Tall, but not Harley tall. I'm five-three, and Harley's got to have a good foot on me. Jack's maybe half a head shorter. His shirt's crisp, his aftershave clean. He stands closer than he needs to when he talks, the kind of habit that probably works on plenty of girls. Apparently, I'll be joining his team, the wait staff crew. He presses a palm to his chest and says, "Welcome aboard." I nod and try to look like I belong.

I recognise Sarah, the Scottish head nanny, from the airport. She appears now with a pint in one hand and that same grin, the distracted rep no longer so distracted. Auburn hair, soft eyes that miss nothing. Her gaze drops to Harley's arm still looped through mine, and her brows shoot so high they nearly leave her face. That grin turns sly. She's already writing the story.

She clinks her glass to mine and murmurs, "First night, you'll be fine."

I believe her for about five seconds, which is more belief than I usually hand out.

Across the room I'm introduced to Imogen, beautiful, tall, with long brown sleek hair, she's with Niko near the fruit machine, laughing at something he's showing her on his phone. Her laugh is low, amused without effort. She's front of house like Tyler and Niko, one of the senior ones, and she wears certainty like a good coat. She looks over and gives me a neat nod, friendly but distant, then lets the room swallow her again. Fair enough, I'm new, not a bet anyone wants to make yet.

We slide deeper into the crowd, and that's when I notice the man behind the bar. I don't know him, and he doesn't seem like the type who needs me to. Then his gaze cuts to me.

"First week?" he calls over the music.

"Yeah," I say, and my voice decides to be shy without warning.

"Welcome to the Red Frog," he says, already reaching for a bottle, already pouring with his attention split the way a good bartender's is. The welcome lands anyway, heavier than the syllables, and I store it because it feels like a permission slip I didn't know I needed. His accent throws me, American, I think. Then the edges soften, a hint of French in the vowels that doesn't match the flag in my head. Canadian, maybe, I wouldn't bet money on it, but it sits there, a little puzzle, warming the word welcome after the fact.

Harley leans closer so I can hear him over the bass, his mouth grazing the shell of my ear. "That's Zane," he says, nodding toward the man behind the bar. "He owns the place."

I follow his gaze. The guy's tall, broad, sleeves rolled up to his elbows, dark ink wraps his forearms. His dark hair's cropped short, silver peppering his temples. He moves with the kind of economy that comes from doing the same thing a thousand times, no wasted motion, no raised voice, but everyone around him tunes in anyway.

"You know him?" I ask, leaning in so I don't have to shout.

"Yeah," Harley says, a low chuckle curling under the word. "Everyone does."

He hesitates, and for Harley that's... new. Finally, he tips his chin toward the bar. "Used to play ice hockey. He was a big deal back in Canada, fast, brutal, captain at twenty-three, Olympic medals, magazines, all of it. Then there was... an incident, a fucked-up fight on the ice, someone got hurt bad. He walked away, vanished for years, then showed up here and built the Frog out of nothing."

I blink, letting the story slot into place as I study Zane's easy authority behind the bar. "So he left all that for... this?"

Harley smirks, but it doesn't reach his eyes. "Didn't leave, he got shoved. The team wanted silence, he wanted truth. Guess you don't get to have both."

Something in his tone makes me file that away under things I probably shouldn't forget.

Zane glances up like he feels us talking about him, catches Harley's eye, and tips his chin in the smallest greeting. His gaze cuts to me for half a second, sharp and assessing, like he's reading me faster than I can think, and then he's back to pouring drinks without a word.

Before I can say anything else, the temperature in the room shifts.

A woman walks in, tall and deliberate, blonde hair sliced sharp to her shoulders, every inch curated. The crowd doesn't part for her, she just slides into it like she owns the air.

Harley sees her, pivots towards her, and suddenly I'm not sure he remembers I exist.

Tyler materialises at my elbow, leaning in close enough for his breath to warm my ear. "That's Sophie," he says, and the name lands like it's supposed to stick.

She's already air-kissing Jack and Sarah, murmuring something that makes Sarah roll her eyes, before sliding onto a barstool like she was designed for it. Harley's gaze hooks on her for a beat too long, and then his hand slips from my arm, leaving space for Jack to move in next to me.

"I'll get you a drink," he says, already moving, not bothering to ask what I want.

I stand there, trying to be invisible, but my shoulders creep up anyway, cold settling somewhere it doesn't belong.

"Vodka cranberry, right?" He holds it out, half a smile in place.

"Yeah," I say, surprised enough to forget how to be cool. "How'd you know?"

He shrugs. "You look like a cranberry girl."

I don't know what that means, but I take the drink anyway and swallow too quickly. It hits the empty space in my stomach and radiates a slow heat, producing a comforting buzz. Jack talks, he's good at it, and I float in and out of listening while my eyes stray toward the bar. Sophie's fingers brush Harley's waist like she owns the space. Her laugh follows, loud and deliberate, territorial. And I hate how my stomach twists. Like it matters, like he's mine.

Maybe the discomfort is hunger, maybe it's jealousy. Maybe it's that I've never done this before. Not the season part or the letting go part.

Back home, feelings were contraband. Dad ran the house like a base, no raised voices, no softness, no crying. After the funeral he got quieter, started polishing his boots more. Heating up the one room we used, drinking his tea, and staring past me like I was a shadow he forgot to salute.

Eighteen couldn't come quick enough, so when it did, I packed a suitcase and booked a flight. I called it a gap year because calling it escape sounded too honest.

And here I am, in France. The Alps. In a bar that smells like effort, spilled beer and the sugar rush of hope people bring to new places. I hold my drink like it's a flotation device and practice breathing in time with the bass.

Niko drifts over at some point, his grin already halfway to trouble. He's got a French accent, warm and low, like butter on a fire. "Hello again, new one," he says.

"Hello," I say.

"If anyone gives you grief, you tell me, and I'll distract them with my face." He winks like he knows exactly how much it works and still manages to keep it sweet.

"Noted," I say. "Thanks."

"Don't thank him yet," Tyler calls from my left. He's leaning on the bar, talking to two girls. He tips his chin at me. "He says that to everyone."

"Jealous," Niko says without heat.

"Always," Tyler says, and the girls laugh, and I'm weirdly relieved at how easy the banter sits between them.

Another tall brooding man is on the far side of the bar with a pint, watching the room with the quiet focus of someone who can see ten seconds into the future. Harley introduces him almost offhandedly. "That's Ash. Old friend. Runs the ski team. Don't let him scare you, he's a soft touch underneath." Ash lifts his glass at me once, a small welcome that feels bigger because it isn't loud. I lift my vodka cranberry back. We don't need to speak for it to count.

By the time my second double disappears, my edges have blurred enough that the music gets inside my bones without asking. Sarah drags me and Jack toward the small square of floor that's trying to be a dance area. A Kylie Minogue track kicks in and I discover that my hips remember it even if my head doesn't. We dance like we meant to end up here, laughing loud enough that a couple of people turn to look. For a moment I let myself be the girl who isn't eighteen with everything to prove, who isn't pretending to be a braver version of herself. I let the heat and noise sand down the sharp parts.

Harley's watching, I can feel it like a line of current across my skin. It isn't possessive, it isn't distant either. It's a weight, steady and impossible to ignore. I look back and don't look away. He holds my gaze for a beat and then someone says something to him and the moment slips, but the weight doesn't.

A man I don't know slides behind me with the slippery ease of someone who's done this before. His hands land on my hips like they belong there and my body goes rigid on instinct. The laugh dies in my mouth.

Before I find my voice, before I can step forward or turn and say any of the things already queuing at the back of my teeth, I'm pulled away, Harley's grip closes around my wrist, and I'm free of the stranger's hands so quickly it makes my stomach flip.

Harley plants himself between me and the man, his face is a storm front. His voice doesn't rise, but it cuts through the music like it was designed for it.

"Touch her again and you'll be drinking through a straw. Clear?"

The man tries a laugh, looks at his mates for approval he doesn't get. "She didn't say no."

Harley takes a step closer, not explosive, just inevitable. "She froze, that's a no, learn it."

The man lifts his hands in surrender, melting into the crowd like he knows when he's beaten. The nearest tables act like they weren't watching, like this isn't gossip by morning. The music keeps going, ruthless and loud.

Harley turns, checks my face, and something like relief slips over his features so fast I almost miss it. Then his jaw tightens and he swings toward Jack.

"What was that? You were right there." His words land hard, flat, no room for argument.

Jack blinks, surprised and defensive. "She didn't look bothered."

"She froze," Harley says again, sharper now. "Use your head."

Jack folds his arms. "I figured you had her covered."

"She's new, it's your job too to watch out for her."

"She's not yours," Jack says, and there's something under it that's small and ugly.

"She's mine to look after," Harley says, and that something in me that's been tight since the airport pulls tighter and then loosens in the same second. I don't know whether to be angry or grateful. I think I'm both.

I slide between them before they do something we all regret. Heat climbs my throat and stains my cheeks.

"Stop it, both of you," I say, and my voice is steady enough to surprise me.

Harley's eyes cut to me. "I'm your buddy. This is what I'm supposed to do."

"Well stop doing it like you own me," I say, the sentence landing with a thud that makes the space around us wobble.

"Relax, babe, I don't own you, but I'd probably treat you better if I did."

"You think you're charming, but it's not landing with me."

Harley's smirk fades.

Silence floods in, and Jack looks away first. Sarah's by my side the next second, like she teleported, pressing a cool glass into my palm I don't remember asking for. Her eyes flick between the two of them and then back to me.

"You all right?" she asks over the music.

"Yeah," I say. I'm not sure if it's true yet. I want it to be.

Across the bar, Zane catches Harley's eye again. It isn't a glare but it's not approval either. It's a look that says, handle your side and I'll handle mine. He gives the smallest nod back, and the tension steps down a notch.

Someone suggests calling it a night and the group exhales like they'd all been holding the same breath. No one argues. Coats get tugged from chair backs, glasses drained, the low hum of good-byes starting up around us. Niko brushes past, tapping the brim of an imaginary hat with a grin that promises trouble for another day. Imogen catches my eye and mouths, *see you*, and it hits me like passing a test I didn't know I was taking. Tyler leans in to whisper something to his girls that makes them laugh before sending them off. Across the room, Ash's gaze finds mine. He gives one small nod, quiet, certain, like I've just cleared some unspoken checkpoint.

Outside, the cold shocks my lungs and clears a corner of my head I'd abandoned to noise. Snow squeaks underfoot on the pavement. The lamps along the street slice the night into warm circles. We walk in small groups stretching and closing as people jostle and joke.

Harley stays beside me, but he doesn't try to take my arm again, and when we hit a slick patch his hand finds my elbow without thinking. He steadies me, but lets go quickly. A few steps later he does it again, he doesn't speak, which feels kinder than anything he could say. The silence between us isn't empty. It just feels full of the things we're not ready to say out loud.

Jack drifts on my other side for a while giving me a sideways look. "You good?"

"I will be," I say, keeping my eyes forward. There's a flicker of something like an apology in his expression, but he swallows it and coughs into his fist, then speeds up to talk to Tyler.

We follow the curve of the road back to the chalet hotel. The windows are lit and honey warm against the night. The automatic doors breathe open and the lobby air folds around us. My cheeks prickle with the temperature change. Everyone scatters with the easy choreography of people who know the building by heart.

Harley and I end up at the staff lift. He hits the button and stares at the numbers above the doors like maybe they'll move faster if he wills them to. The lift arrives with a soft groan, and we step inside. It's cramped, the walls holding the leftover heat and noise from everyone who's passed through tonight.

He stands just far enough away to be polite and just close enough that my skin prickles. The doors close and we start to rise.

"You didn't have to fight my fight," I say into the small space. My voice sounds softer than I meant it to.

He looks at me then, properly, like he's counting the freckles on my nose. "I didn't fight it," he says. "I ended it."

I don't know what to do with that, so I just nod, the lift dings, and the doors part.

We step out into the staff corridor, past multiple closed doors and the scuffs on the skirting from seasons of bags. He walks me to my door, the fire exit at the end hums gently with cold air.

He asks for my number, taps it into his phone, then hits call. My mobile buzzes in my pocket. He smirks. "Now you've got mine. Text me if you need anything."

"Night, Lola," he says, my name low and careful.

"Night," I say. I stop with my hand on the handle. "Thank you," I add, and I'm not sure whether I mean for the drink I never got from him, or for the way he put himself between me and a pair of hands that didn't belong on me, maybe it was both.

He nods once, that same small, compact gesture he used all night when something mattered. He looks like he might say more, he doesn't, he steps back, and the space between us expands by degrees until it feels like a hallway again and not a wire strung tight.

I go inside and rest my forehead against the door for a second, listening to the low hum of the radiator and the faint groan of the lift somewhere down the hall. My pulse is finally slowing, so I kick off my boots and peel off my socks, letting the heat settle into my toes.

I cross to the window, the mountain is a bulk of shadow and silver where the lamps catch it. The lifts are still and hanging, chairs like punctuation marks on a line. Somewhere out there the first run of the season is waiting, edges sharp, snow still holding its breath. I press my fingertips to the glass, it's cold, clean and doesn't care who I was before I got here.

My phone buzzes on the bedside table. It looks as though I've been added to the staff group chat 'Snowjob Squad'. Yes that's actually what they call it. Niko swears he came up with it sober, which somehow makes it worse.

Sarah: You okay, hon?

Me: Yes, thank you.

Niko: Tomorrow, I'll teach you to carry three plates. You'll fail, but you'll look magnificent. I send him a crying laughing emoji in response, and put the phone face down.

Me: Don't you work front of house Niko?

Niko: Oui Mademoiselle. But I'm wasted there.... Sigh

Imogen: Go to bed Niko, you're on shift at six am!

Niko: Battle axe!

At this point I decide to put my phone on do not disturb, this feels like it could spiral. Sitting on the edge of the bed for a long minute I let the quiet climb into me. The night still hums in my legs from the music. My cheeks are warm from the walk and the words I said that I didn't rehearse.

Harley walks beside me in my head like a memory that's already rooted. The way his hand found my elbow without asking permission. The way his voice went soft after it went sharp. The way he stood between me and a stranger because he decided that was his job for tonight, It's ridiculous, and it's real at the same time.

After a quick shower, I slide under the duvet, it smells faintly of detergent, warm and clean. I switch off the lamp and let the dark settle around me.

Tomorrow there'll be trays and name badges and the practicalities of learning to be the version of myself that works here. There'll be Sophie with her polished laugh and the quiet ache in my chest I'll pretend I don't feel. There'll be Jack with his neat hair and the friendliness he wears like a uniform. There'll be Niko's jokes and Tyler's sideways grins and Imogen's measured nods. There'll be Ash's steady watchfulness and Zane's small welcomes that mean more than they look like.

For now there's this, a bed that isn't mine yet, a mountain outside the glass. A hot thread of annoyance and attraction I don't know how to hold at the same time. And a promise I make to myself in the dark, I will not be furniture, I will not be a shadow someone forgets to salute. I'll be here and I'll take up the space I'm given and then some.

Sleep comes slow, but when it lands, it lands hard. The last thing I feel is the echo of a steady hand at my elbow, and the last thing I see behind my eyelids is a pair of blue eyes that didn't look away when I looked back.

CHAPTER 3
Chaos Theory
LOLA

My first morning and the floor's already tilting, not literally, but my brain doesn't know the difference.

The Powder White training pack made it all look charming, smiling instructors, tray angles, customer tone. Easy. But there's no bullet point for this. For the sound of plates crashing, espresso machines groaning, kids whining about toast like it's a personal betrayal. My name badge is crooked again, I straighten it, it slips, I do it again, and again. Like it'll hold me together if I press hard enough.

Tray on my left palm, elbow tucked, wrist neutral, fingers loose. I repeat Jack's words in my head like a mantra. Relax or the tray will punish you, he said that three times, like he knew I wouldn't. My right hand twitches anyway, like it doesn't trust my left to do the job alone.

Someone shouts for oat milk. Someone else asks if the eggs are organic. A toddler screams at full volume because a sausage rolled off their plate and now apparently life is over.

The floor near the coffee station is sticky, my boots squeak with every step like they're laughing at me. I'm ninety percent sure table five wanted oat milk, but my brain's glitching, flicking through flashcards it hasn't learned yet, trying to find the right answer with the wrong system. I gamble on oat and take one step before...

"You look like you're two seconds from hurling that tray at someone's head," says a voice just behind my shoulder, it's Jack.

He slides into my space like he's always belonged there. That boy-next-door kind of pretty, crisp shirt, chestnut hair, polite smirk like he borrowed it from a toothpaste ad. Everyone else sees safe, I see someone who knows he's safe-looking, and uses it.

"Want me to fake a complaint so Scarlett tells you to take a break?"

"I'd rather you tell me where the hell the teaspoons went."

He grins and opens a drawer I've checked twice. Produces a stack of clean silverware like it's a party trick. "Level two cutlery unlock. You're welcome."

"Do I need a password?"

"Just taste in coworkers."

He winks. I don't return it, but I follow him anyway. Rhythm is better than panic, and he's moving like someone who's done this enough to glide through the noise without it touching him.

We fall into a pattern, I clear, he resets. I refill water, he folds napkins with surgical precision. He slides between tables without brushing a single chair. He knows what guests need before they do, laughs with a table of guys in matching salopettes, calms a frazzled mum with one line. It doesn't make me feel capable, but it keeps me from drowning.

For now, that's enough.

Noise ramps up fast. Heat from the pendant lights, steam off mugs, chairs scraping across tile. Someone's crying about burnt toast. Someone else is losing their shit about ski school times. A woman at table nine is staring at her eggs like they personally offended her.

Then Jack whistles, two sharp notes, and my body reacts before I think. I sidestep just in time. A blur flies past me. Kid. Mitten. Panic. He slips. Goes down hard. Arms flailing, face scrunched like he knows what's coming and can't stop it.

"All good, mate?" Jack's already crouched. Checks for blood.

Slides the mitten back on the kid's hand like he's knighting him. Says something I can't hear, but the kid walks back taller. Braver.

Jack stands, tosses me a look like it's nothing.

"See? It's not us against the chaos. We are the chaos. You just have to dance with it."

"Feels like the chaos forgot to buy me a drink first." I tell him.

He grins. "It always does before nine."

The lunch shift builds quick, noise stacking on noise. Voices rise, cutlery crashes and the bell at the pass won't quit, sharp enough to set my teeth on edge.

I'm halfway through polishing a glass when Niko appears, gliding through reception like the laws of physics don't apply to him. He's all cheekbones and mischief, grinning like he's just solved a crime and wants praise for it.

"Bonjour, new one," he says, like I've been summoned rather than greeted. His hand drifts casually toward the side station. I watch him pluck a breadstick without breaking stride.

A small boy at table four gasps, scandalised.

Niko gasps louder, returning the breadstick with a dramatic flourish. Then he reaches behind the boy's ear and pulls out a second one like he's performing at a five-year-old's birthday party.

The table bursts into laughter. The parents try to look stern and fail instantly.

He winks at me like he's saying, you're welcome, then slips out without bumping a single chair.

I blink after him, vaguely stunned.

"What the hell was that?" I mutter. "Does he... do that a lot?"

"All the time. He's basically our emotional support chaos."

"Is he actually employed?"

"Unclear."

We share a look. I almost smile. Almost.

Two tables over, a woman raises a single finger like she's filing a formal complaint with the universe.

"This is supposed to be gluten free," she says, stabbing a piece of bread with visible disdain.

"It is," I say, calmly. "From the separate batch. Prepped in the GF station in the kitchen."

"It doesn't look gluten free."

I keep my tone soft, but firm. "It's the flour blend. Buckwheat base. We can bring rice crackers if you'd prefer."

She stares at me a beat too long. Testing. Then recalibrates.

"That won't be necessary."

I nod once and move. I don't exhale until I'm two tables away.

Jack sidles past. "Handled."

"Yeah."

"You did good."

I don't answer. But something in my chest loosens. Just a little.

A toddler starts screaming because someone took away his pancakes. A dad drops a fork into his own boot. A knife clatters. My tray skims past a guest's puffer jacket and tips slightly.

I freeze.

Then a hand, steady, warm, slides under the rim. Two fingers. Just enough to level it.

"Careful," Tyler says, quietly.

He doesn't grab it, doesn't make a show. Just steadies, confirms I'm not about to crumble, and lets go.

"I've got it," I say, breath catching.

He nods once. "You're fine."

Then he's gone again. Back to reception, back to his rhythm.

I breathe through it. Stack plates. Pour water. Reset knives with blades turned inward. Fold napkins with corners sharp enough to cut someone.

But my brain's getting foggy. I miscount a table, deliver the wrong plate. The woman at nine snaps like I've committed a federal crime. Scarlett's head swivels in my direction like a hawk with a clipboard.

Before she can speak, Jack's there.

"Sorry, my mistake," he says smoothly. Swaps the plate, resets the mood, walks away with zero fallout.

Scarlett moves on and I'm left blinking at the gap where disaster should've been.

We meet in the service corridor a few minutes later. Bell still tapping, heat rising through the kitchen vents.

Jack leans against the wall like he's on a break in a cologne ad.

"You didn't have to do that," I say. "Take the hit."

"You looked like you were about to cry."

"I wasn't."

His gaze skims over me. "Sure."

It lands somewhere between dismissive and disappointed. The quiet turns sharp. Too quiet to be comfortable.

"You should keep your head down," he says. "Especially with guys like Harley."

My spine snaps straight. "What's that supposed to mean?"

"He's good at letting people think there's more going on than there is."

"And you're... warning me?"

"I'm just saying." Jack shifts, eyes flicking sideways, then back. "You're new. He's not."

I stare at him, every muscle in my face trying to stay calm.

"I'm not stupid."

"Didn't say you were."

I'm topping up a water jug at table nine when the mood in the room changes. Not loud. Not obvious. Just... different.

It starts as a shift in pace. A few heads turn. Someone laughs, louder than they need to. I look up.

Harley Nash walks through the dining room like he doesn't notice the attention. His white Powder White fleece is unzipped at the collar, sleeves shoved up just enough to flash the ink on his forearms. Black hair messed up like he's just pulled off a beanie. His boots are wet, his walk is quiet and controlled. Like he's holding something back and doing a really fucking good job of it.

He doesn't scan the room, doesn't need to. His eyes land on me like it's accidental, but it isn't. That blue? It hits hard. Sharp and cold and impossibly steady.

I freeze for half a second. Not dramatic. Just enough for Jack to notice.

"You keep looking at him like that," Jack says, voice low, "people are going to start talking."

I blink. "I wasn't."

"You were."

I stack the glasses faster than necessary. "He was just walking past."

"Yeah. And now he's not." Jack's eyes cut across the room, then back to me. "Don't let it go to your head. That's kind of his thing."

"What is?"

"Making people feel seen. Doesn't mean he actually sees them."

I pause, one hand still on the tray. "You sound like you know him well."

Jack shrugs. "I know enough."

He doesn't say anything else. Doesn't need to. The silence is loaded.

I pretend it doesn't get under my skin.

❄

Service winds down like a car with the handbrake half on. Plates disappear, voices fade. The service bell finally stops its relentless tapping. My hands are raw from all the washing. My boots feel fused to my feet. But I'm still standing. Still moving.

I collect a pile of cutlery, reset two tables, refill the water carafes for next service. Small things. Easy wins. Control where I can find it.

Jack reappears at my side, sets a glass of water down in front of me.

"You didn't crash," he says. "Most new starters cry in a freezer their first week."

I wipe my hands on my apron. "You keep saying that like it's a compliment."

"It is." His smile is smaller now. Not for show. "You did good."

Before I can answer, movement pulls at the corner of my vision.

Harley's back. This time with Ash beside him, taller, broader, quieter. Ash walks like he belongs in any room he enters, but he's not the one I can't stop glancing at.

Harley's talking to him, something low, unreadable. His head tips back slightly, a half-laugh at something Ash mutters. Then, without warning, Harley looks at me again.

Not a smirk. Not a leer. Just a look. Long, sharp, unflinching.

Like he sees something and doesn't know what to do with it yet.

Something in my chest tugs tight. Jack sees it. Of course he sees it.

"Keep your head down," he says again, quieter this time. "With him."

I turn to him. "That's twice now. You want to tell me what your problem is?"

He doesn't blink. "I've worked with Harley for two seasons. I've seen what happens."

"To who?"

"To girls who think he's more than what he shows."

My mouth pulls tight. I should walk away. But something in me wants to stand my ground.

"Thanks for the concern," I say, voice clipped. "But I can handle myself."

Jack's jaw twitches. Just slightly. Then he smiles like the conversation never happened.

"Sure you can."

Scarlett ghosts through again, eyes scanning the dining room like she's doing a headcount in her sleep. She stops beside me.

"You did well," she says, tone flat but not unkind. "You'll be faster tomorrow."

"I'll wear thicker socks."

"That too." She looks over her shoulder, already turning. "And sleep. You'll need it."

I clock out and head for the stairs. The weight in my legs feels earned. The ache behind my eyes does too.

Halfway up the corridor, I catch my reflection in the mirror.

I look like a girl rebuilding herself one table at a time.

Not whole. Not yet. But trying.

And that counts for something.

❄

Upstairs, the staff corridor is too warm and too quiet. Someone's door bangs shut down the hall. Voices drift through the walls. The overhead light flickers, struggling to stay awake.

My phone buzzes with a message from Snowjob Squad.

Sarah: You smashed it Lola. Amazing first day!

She was the one who did my laundry yesterday without being asked. Left a biscuit by the kettle like it wasn't a big deal.

Me: Yeah. Thank you.

The chat pings again.

Jack: Tomorrow I'll teach you to carry four plates. You'll probably fall though :)

Me: Rude.

Tyler: Tray from table ten survived.

Me: Barely.

I smile at the phone screen longer than I should. Not because it's funny. But because it's something. A thread. A pulse.

Outside my door, I hear footsteps, steady, unhurried. I crack it open slightly. Niko's passing, dancing slightly to music only he can hear. He's already waving before I say anything.

"You survived," he says, voice cheerful but quiet. "Some people don't. They go home and pretend they meant to."

"I only wanted to cry once," I say, leaning against the doorframe. "That feels like restraint."

He grins. "That is restraint."

"Tyler said I handled table ten like a pro."

"That's high praise." Niko lowers his voice like it's a secret. "Tyler barely speaks to most new people."

"I don't think he even looked at me."

"Exactly." He starts walking again, throws a wink over his shoulder. "That's his version of flirting."

"I'm serious."

"So am I."

His door clicks shut two down from mine. Quiet again.

There's a pause. Then I see Tyler at the end of the corridor, where he's double-checking the fire exit. He doesn't look at me. Just keeps inspecting the handle.

"Hey Tyler, you okay?"

"Oh hey, Lo, good, you?"

"Jack said I should keep my head down," I tell him.

"Jack says a lot of things."

My fingers tighten on the doorframe. "How do I know who to listen to?"

"You don't," he says, calmly. "But you'll figure out who's worth hearing."

He gives the handle one last pull, ticks something on his clipboard, and walks away without waiting for a response.

I go inside, the air in my room is still, warm. I drop my phone on the pillow, pull the duvet halfway up and sink into it. My legs are sore. My thoughts are slower now, less sharp around the edges.

Tomorrow I'll still be new. But not this new. And that matters.

That's how it works here. Inch by inch. Table by table. Name by name.

CHAPTER 4

The Head Bartender

LOLA

It starts with a tray of hot chocolates and a screaming child.

I'm halfway across the dining room with three mugs stacked precariously in each hand when the shriek goes off like a fire alarm. My whole body jolts, and the top mug wobbles. I freeze mid-step, one foot in the air, praying the marshmallows don't go flying.

They don't, but the child is still shrieking.

"Clementine! For God's sake," a posh mum hisses, gripping her daughter's arm like she's seconds from full-blown meltdown. "That's enough."

Clementine, maybe five, dressed head-to-toe in a highlighter-pink ski gear, doesn't stop. She launches herself onto a dining room chair like she's auditioning for a West End tragedy.

"I want the blue cup!"

I clutch the tray tighter and plaster on a smile that feels like it's been stitched to my face.

"Coming through," I mutter, weaving past a cluster of teenagers draped across a table, legs sticking out like a tripwire. One of them knocks over a bottle of Fanta and doesn't even blink. Great. Now the sole of my boot sticks slightly to the floor.

It's a mess tonight.

Half the guests are still in the dining room despite the dinner shift ending half an hour ago. Coats hang from every hook, boots pile up in corners, and the fire's working overtime. The noise is relentless, loud laughing, clinking glasses and someone shouting for a second round of drinks. A woman in designer snow boots is arguing with her partner about where they left their lift passes, and he swears he left them in the boot room, she's convinced they were stolen. Someone else is asking if the kitchen has almond milk hot chocolate, and I'm seconds from quitting.

I reach the table, drop off the hot chocolates without incident, and pivot to bolt back to the kitchen, but stop dead. She's already halfway across the room, a wine bottle in one hand and a corkscrew in the other. Tall, blonde high ponytail. Her lips are painted the kind of red that's so sharp it could cut glass.

Sophie Whitmore, Infamous and Le Grenier royalty. And apparently Harley Nash's past, judging by how fast he stormed across the bar last night. She's not wearing a name tag, like the rest of us, and exudes this easy, assertive walk like she owns the world and we're just living in it. Heads turn, and even the kitchen porter, mid-step, watches her. It's almost as though she's walking in slow- mo.

She doesn't acknowledge anyone, just glides through making a beeline for the bar, then hops behind it like she never left, and pulls a glass from the rack.

"I see Sophie's back," someone mutters behind me. I can't look away. Thirty seconds, that's all it takes for her to uncork the wine, pour a perfect measure, and hand it to a man who didn't even speak. He stares at her like he's forgotten how his tongue works.

Sophie smiles, closed-mouth, practiced.

Someone taps me on the shoulder and I flinch, when I turn abruptly I see Imogen.

"You good?" she says, already knowing the answer, then, dry, "Ah. You've seen her."

"That's Sophie Whitmore, head bartender. She wasn't going to come back to Le Grenier this year, but Scarlett couldn't find a decent replacement, so all but begged her to come back."

I breathe out, slowly. "She's... kind of terrifying."

Imogen laughs. "She's worse when she likes you. Come on, you need to reset the dessert station, I'll help you. Niko and Tyler have reception covered."

She slips her arm through mine and walks to the other side of the room.

"I'm sure you noticed Harley's face when he walked into the Frog the other night, "Imogen says, voice low, while we stack spoons.

My gut tightens. "I did, but what's going on there?"

She shrugs. "It's a whole thing, if you want my advice you'll stay out of it."

I don't push, not yet. Then we hear glass shatter out front.

"I've got it," I say too fast, ducking through the kitchen door to grab the dustpan and brush.

When I return a few minutes later having had to hunt down said dustpan and brush, the lounge has cooled off slightly, there's less yelling and more contented drinking. I look up and see Sophie's still behind the bar, wiping down counters like she's been doing it her whole life. It looks methodical, like an exact art. I crouch to gather the glass and when I stand, she's staring at me.

"You must be Lola?" She drawls. Her voice reminds me of smoke, smooth, with an edge.

"Yeah it's my first season."

Her head tilts and scans me, just like the dinosaurs do in Jurassic Park.

"You work front of house?"

"No I'm a waitress, I work with Jack."

She nods once. "Do us all a favour and don't leave trays in the corridor, or anywhere they shouldn't be for that matter. There are kids running through, and Scarlett's already sick of risk assessments."

My cheeks flush and I don't respond.

Back at the dessert station where Imogen is stacking mini eclairs on a silver tray, she turns to me and raises one beautifully plucked eyebrow. "Did she give you the warm welcome yet?"

"She warned me about the tray thing."

"Classic Sophie, don't worry, if she didn't say anything, then you'd be in trouble."

I wring my hands, the whole encounter leaves something lodged in my chest. Like I've just been measured and found... underwhelming. A flash of my dad's voice skims through my mind, all gravel and disdain, *Don't expect people to like you just because you try hard, Lola, that's not how the world works.*

The rest of the shift bleeds into itself, plates, wine orders, Imogen's sarcastic commentary, Niko waltzes through at some point singing badly to early 2000s hits, this seems normal for them, until I'm untying my apron from my waist and catch sight of movement through the bar door.

"Ready ?" Imogen asks.

"Yeah."

"Are you alright?"

"I'm just tired."

She gives me a look that tells me she doesn't believe me, but doesn't call me on it.

We go up to the fourth floor to our respective rooms to ditch our uniforms and change into comfy clothes. I'm out first wearing my black leggings and slouchy pink jumper, my blonde curls pulled up in a claw clip. I knock on Imogen's door a few rooms down from mine, and she joins me still looking like the Goddess she is, sleek, glossy, long, brown hair still in place from this morning, tight dark blue jeans and her green off-the-shoulder jumper. I make a mental note to try and up my game from now on, I probably won't though.

"Let's get down there before all the good seats are gone," she says

"The good seats?"

"Yeah, Ash always steals the big brown leather armchair. I'm sure he thinks it's his throne or something," she sighs.

In the corridor just before we walk into the staff lounge I feel a flicker of apprehension in my stomach. I don't want to see Harley and Sophie together, but I also need to remember I'm still the newbie and known him a week, we've actually barely spoken. I don't even like him, I mean, I do, but not like, like him. Not like some clingy girl who needs reassurance from a boy who can't even be arsed to say hi in a hallway. God, maybe I do like him, what is wrong with me?

We walk in and Imogen's still talking about some guest who asked her if mulled wine counts as one of your five-a-day, but I'm not really listening.

At the end of corridor, voices carry.

"That's the third time you've turned me down this week." I hear Sophie say sternly.

I freeze and Imogen bumps into me. Harley's voice follows, low and even. "Take the hint, Whitmore."

"You alright?" She asks again for probably the tenth time today.

I purse my lips then lie. "I'm fine."

We keep walking, but slower now. The kind of slow that means we're absolutely eavesdropping and don't even care.

Inside the lounge, Sophie laughs, dry, but a little tight around the edges. "Since when do you need space? You practically lived in my bed last season."

Silence. A beat too long.

"I'm not that guy anymore," Harley says.

It hits harder than it should.

"Come on, you don't want to get caught listening to that circus," Imogen says.

But I do, God, I do. Still, I follow her inside.

Later, we're both curled on the battered brown leather sofa in the staff lounge, and I'm pretending to scroll through Instagram on my phone. Imogen's got her boots up on the table and I've got a tension headache I can't shake.

Harley walks over to the cupboard, above the sink and grabs a protein bar.

Imogen doesn't look up. "So," she says, casual as anything. "Sophie back for good?"

Harley glances at her face unreadable. "Looks like it."

"Are you two picking up where you left off or what?"

His eyes flicker over to me once, but back to Imogen in a blink and snorts. "No."

"Are you sure, Harls? She seems to think otherwise."

His jaw ticks. "She thinks a lot of things."

Imogen raises an eyebrow, then glances at me like she's saying, See? Told you.

Harley takes a bite, chews in silence, then, with a sigh, "I didn't ask her to come back."

Imogen shrugs. "Didn't say you did."

He looks at me again, quick, sharp. Then answers Imogen.

"You didn't have to."

The air goes still.

"Alright, easy." Imogen lifts a hand. "I'm just asking. Lola's new. Sophie's not exactly warm and fuzzy. Just try and keep her from eating her alive will you."

Harley softens a fraction. "Sophie's not my problem anymore."

He looks at me. "You're alright aren't you Lola?" he says, pointing the protein bar at me with a wink.

I glance at Imogen, trying not to hold my breath.

"Yep, all good." My voice comes out too breathy, so I duck back to my phone, cheeks heating.

"Good, well, don't forget you've got my number if you need anything."

I jerk my head up again.

"Yeah, I'm still your buddy, babe," he adds, mouth curling into a smirk.

Then he just leaves without waiting for a reply.

The second the door swings shut, Imogen's head whips toward me. "You're still my favourite, but that was hot."

I let out a breath I didn't realise I was holding.

She laughs. "Drink?"

"Yes please, and something strong. And preferably something that doesn't taste like kitchen bleach."

We both collapse back into the sofa, and I tuck my legs underneath me letting myself sink into the cushions.

"Hey," she says after a moment. "You do know he's not seeing her, right?"

"Yeah," I lie. "It's just a lot. The shift, the new faces, the everything."

She nudges me with her foot. "You're doing fine, better than fine. Sophie might be a hurricane, but you're unshakeable."

I shake my head. "You didn't see my hands shaking when she looked at me."

"Please. That's half the staff. Sophie just acts like she's MI5."

I smile despite myself. "Thanks."

She picks up her phone. "Snowjob Squad's already blowing up. Looks like Niko took a picture of Harley's face when Sophie walked in this evening, and sent it in the group with the caption, 'Big Yikcs.'"

I snort, pulling my own phone out and for a second, it feels a little bit like I could belong here.

CHAPTER 5
All Hands on Deck
LOLA

The breakfast room is louder than usual, which is saying something. Cutlery taps, scrapes and clatters, mugs touch down, chairs screech across the floor a little too hard. The coffee machine breathes like a dragon. Outside, fat flakes drift past the windows, lazy at first. Then thick and insistent, as if the mountain shook a duvet and told winter to get serious.

I'm parked at the drinks station with heavy water jugs. The glass lip catches thin ribbons of light that move when I move, and watching that little shimmer is stupidly soothing. I keep my breathing level and count each jug as I finish it. One, lid on. Two, wipe the condensation. Three, rotate the spout toward the room so no one drips it on their sleeve and moans about it later. Little rituals help, the world sits still when my hands have a task.

"Morning, Lo," Jack calls from the juice station, easy and bright. His sleeves are rolled, his smile set to charming, and he's chatting to a pair of uni girls who are pretending they don't see him flex each time he lifts the orange juice. "You on the long one today?"

"Looks like it," I say. "Lucky me."

"Lucky them," he fires back, and the uni girls turn in perfect tandem like sunflowers. He winks at one of them. The girl goes pink and hides behind her hair.

Niko dances through the tables with a tray of pastries, somehow avoiding three different small children without braking. "Eyes on the carbs, not the boy," he says to the uni girls, gentle and amused.

Tyler slips in from the lobby and drops a hand on Niko's shoulder to steady the tray. Tall, calm, steady. He gives me a nod that says he's seen every detail in this room and none of it's a problem. He disappears toward reception, where he lives like a lighthouse, always blinking slow and sure even when the sea is messy.

Sarah is crouched by a little girl in pink salopettes, tying a bow with careful fingers, listening like the kid is giving her the weather report for the soul. The mum mouths a thank you. Sarah smiles back and touches the child's shoulder in a way that says you are safe here. It softens something in my chest. I like knowing she's around.

I'm aligning the jugs, making the glass rims line up like beads on a string, when Scarlett's voice breaks over the clatter.

"Lola, do you have a minute?"

I look up from the water jugs. Scarlett stands in the doorway, pink in the cheeks, hair a little too tousled for this early in the day.

I pause. "Everything okay?"

"There's flu going round. Couple of hosts are out for the week."

I wince. "Yikes. Hope it's not serious."

She exhales, pinching the bridge of her nose. "I need you to step up. Just for a few days. Hosting."

My breath catches. Hosting?

"I, yeah. Sure. Of course."

Before I can ask what that actually means, her phone buzzes and she's already answering it. "Go see Niko," she says, waving a hand as she walks off. "He'll get you sorted."

Cool. No pressure or anything.

I untie my apron and roll my shoulders, trying to shake off the nerves. I fold it into something that looks neat enough and shove it under the bar. My notepad's in my pocket where it always is. I tap it once, out of habit, like I can anchor myself with something familiar.

Reception's buzzing when I arrive. Niko's multitasking like a machine, phone between his shoulder and chin, iPad open on a dozen screens.

He catches my eye and grins. "Host squad, eh? You're levelling up."

"Scarlett voluntold me," I mutter.

He drops the call and waves me over. "You'll be fine. You've already got the best people skills in the building."

I raise a brow.

"Trust me," he says, handing me a sheet. "Mingle with guests, oversee tea, and tonight..." He pauses for dramatic effect. "Welcome meeting."

I freeze. "Wait, the welcome meeting?"

"It's a slide deck and a microphone, Lo. Not the Royal Variety."

I still look like I'm about to bolt. So he grabs his phone. "Hold up, I'll get Imogen to cover and run you through the flow myself. We'll even find you a cute uniform."

True to form, Imogen saunters in two minutes later, arching a brow. "So who died and made Lola Queen of Front of House?"

"Flu, bébé," Niko says, deadpan. "It's coming for all of us."

She smirks and leans over the iPad. "Let's make sure Sarah sees the rota so she can plan night cover. I'd like to get through this week with everyone still standing."

After a whirlwind intro, I'm at reception helping with checkouts. Harley's outside, all tight white fleece and wind-blown hair, loading guests onto coaches like he was born doing it.

It's stupid how attractive that is.

"You're drooling," Niko mutters under his breath.

I snap out of it, cheeks hot. "I'm going to check on the housekeeping team."

"Five minutes," Tyler says, eyes on the arrivals screen. His voice is a bass note under the lobby noise, steady and cool. "Then back here. I want you to run the first three questions on the desk. I'll be right next to you."

I nod. The promise lands like a hand on my spine. I can do a first three if he is there.

The next twenty minutes stretch and snap and stretch again. Niko gives me the front of house crash course while Tyler shows, quietly, how to move so guests don't feel blocked by the desk. Stand a little to the side. Turn your body toward them like they are the point. Let your hands be visible. Tell them what you're doing as you click. It removes the mystery. Imogen appears and disappears like a magic trick, leaving the kind of advice that could live in a book. Smile with your eyes, not just your mouth. If you don't know an answer, don't guess. Never point. Always show.

A couple comes to the desk to ask about ski passes. My brain scrambles, then goes blank. Tyler leans in, places one finger on the right button, doesn't touch the keyboard, just guides the air. "Click there," he says, quiet enough that only I hear. "Say it back to them."

I do. I hear my own voice sound like a person who knows things. The couple thanks me like I just unlocked their holiday. It hands me a tiny hit of relief. I could chase that all day.

I check the printed arrivals list and practice the welcome script under my breath. Hello and welcome to Le Grenier, I'm Lola, can I take your surname and your booking reference, thank you, I will just find your room, here are your lift passes, breakfast is from seven-thirty to nine-thirty, lunch is twelve-thirty to two, dinner is at seven, the spa's on the lower ground floor, towels are in your room, please ask me anything at all. I speak it in a low mumble and edit as I go. My pen scribbles in my notepad. If I keep the sentence clean, my nerves do not chew it.

Through the glass, the coaches are back and turning in. A hiss of brakes, a door folding open, voices at once. I catch a flash of a white fleece and dark hair, and my mind tags it before I can stop it.

Harley.

He lifts a suitcase one-handed and slides it out of the hold like it's easy. He speaks to a little boy, at the door of the coach, drops to the kid's eye level and shows him how to hold the rail, then gives the mum a nod that says I see you. He looks up and catches my eye through the glass. It's a fraction of a second, not even a thing, but my stomach does a neat flip, then keeps falling.

The lobby seems smaller. The noise swells. The new arrivals push through the doors with their wheeled cases and flushed faces and cold noses. Laughing, calling to each other, asking where things are, breathing out the kind of energy that rolls right over a small person like a wave.

I glance at the iPad. Tabs. Lists. Names. The words refuse to settle. My chest tightens. My breath turns thin.

Then my phone buzzes, Snowjob Squad blasts on the desk with a short message from Niko that might as well be a siren.

Niko: ALL HANDS ON DECK

And suddenly the air disappears.

My lungs squeeze. The floor tilts.

The hum of the lobby becomes a roar.

Too much. I back out of reception, trying to keep it together, trying to breathe. Outside. I need outside.

The cold hits me like a slap, and I take it gratefully. Stumble to a bench, sit and grip the edge.

My Apple Watch flashes. 131 bpm, shit.

Panic rises like floodwater, fast and merciless. My chest locks up. Vision tunnels. I blink hard, counting my breaths. It's like trying to tame a wildfire with a teaspoon.

I hear my name being called, but it sounds like it's being said in a different frequency. "Lola?"

Harley's voice cuts through the static like it's wired to my heartbeat. I don't lift my head, but I feel him kneel in front of me.

"Hey," he says gently. "Talk to me."

I can't. My throat's a closed door.

"Okay. Just nod if you're having a panic attack."

I nod once.

"Right," he murmurs, shifting closer. "We've got this. I'm going to help you lower your head. I'm here, yeah?"

His hand cups the back of my neck, warm and steady, guiding me forward. His other hand presses to my spine firm, calming.

"Good girl," he breathes. "Breathe in with me four seconds."

I try. Fail.

"Again. In, two, three, four, hold it two, three, four. Out, two, three, four. That's it," he praises me. He guides me through the breathing exercise for another few minutes.

His voice is so calm, soothing, so close. I grip the edge of the bench harder, grounding myself in him.

"Lo," he whispers, his lips almost at my ear. "You've done harder things than this. You're braver than you know."

It's all he needs to say when tears sting my eyes and start to fall shortly after. I hate that he's seeing me like this. Messy. Weak. Wrecked.

"I'm fucking this up," I whisper through my tears.

"No, you're human." His tone is fierce now. "You're allowed to need someone."

I look up, finally. His face is stormy with worry, his piercing blue eyes dark and locked on my hazel ones.

"You scared the shit out of me," he admits. Which only makes me feel worse than I already do.

"I didn't want to ruin today."

"You didn't. You're doing everything right." He takes my wrist, checks the watch. "164. Jesus, Lo. You must feel like your heart's trying to escape your chest."

I nod. I do.

Harley takes his fleece off leaving him only wearing a long-sleeved white t-shirt and wraps it around my shoulders. When I protest, he sits down next to me, his knee touching mine, and just says "You're not alone," his voice barely a whisper. "You hear me?"

I nod again, and something in my chest cracks.

His presence steadies me. My heartbeat ticks lower. 150. Then 140. Breath by breath, I come back to myself.

"Just stay like this for another minute, okay? Let me hold this moment steady for you."

And I do.

The lobby door opens partway. Tyler is there, careful not to crowd. He sees the scene in a second and gives a small nod that says I'll catch the spill inside. He holds the door with his foot for a pair of teenage boys dragging skis, answers a question without taking his eyes off me, then mouths take your time at Harley. The door closes again. The cold keeps my skin awake. Harley's breathing steadies mine.

My mind slides back into place slowly, like plates after a tremor. I count four in, hold two, four out. Harley's hand stays at the back of my neck. I realise his palm is big enough to cover the worst of my shaking. The thought is ridiculous and steadying at the same time.

Another guest drifts outside to take a photo of the peaks and stumbles a little when she sees us. Harley doesn't turn. He speaks without looking up, calm and kind. "One minute and we'll be right with you." The woman nods, murmurs sorry, and goes back in with the picture she wanted. My humiliation spikes, then fades. People cry. The world doesn't end.

I breathe and breathe again, then feel the bench under me. I feel the sting in my palms where I've gripped the edge too hard. The watch number dips another notch.

When I can speak without my throat catching, I manage, "Okay."

Harley slides his hand away from my neck like he is removing a pressure dressing. He doesn't make it a moment. He just gets to his feet, slow, eyes checking my face for real signs, not polite ones. I nod. He believes me.

"You realise half the lobby was watching?" he murmurs, mouth twitching like he can't help himself.

I groan. "Relax, Lo. I'll tell them you're more trouble than you're worth."

"Good. Maybe they'll stay out of my way then."

He chuckles, low and real. "Somehow I doubt it."

By the time I come back inside, I've wiped my eyes, smoothed my hair, and handed Harley back his fleece with a soft thank-you I hope says more than my words can.

The lobby's bustling again. The second coach has just pulled up, and guests are spilling in with their wheeled suitcases and red noses.

I slip behind the desk, my name badge now clipped to my new front-of-house uniform, still crisp from Niko's magic laundry touch.

Tyler gives me a two second look. Not pity. A check. I nod once. He turns to the next guest and lets me stand beside him so I can echo his cadence. Niko moves like a conductor, sending a family toward the lifts, a couple toward the bar, a group of teenage boys toward the boot room with a gentle warning to walk, not skate, unless they want to meet our manager's wrath on their first day.

"Ready?" Tyler asks, quietly.

"Yes," I say. It surprises me that it's true.

"Run the next two," he says. "I'll fill any gaps."

The next two are a middle aged couple with a booking note about a birthday, and a trio of friends who want rooms close together. I manage both without dropping the thread. I find the birthday, circle it on the paper copy, add it to the system, and ask what cake they want so the kitchen can plan. I juggle the trio's rooms so they are close and promise robes will be in each wardrobe by the time they unpack. When I hand over keycards, my hands don't shake.

Across the lobby, Harley comes in with a final armful of hand luggage. He hasn't put his fleece back on and his shirt is clinging to his forearms, the curve of muscle there is ridiculous. I shouldn't notice it. My eyes notice anyway. He sets the bags down, checks the chalkboard for coach times, and looks over. Not long. Not loaded with meaning. Just a look to check the weather of my face. I keep my posture open and my hands easy on the desk. He reads it. The sharp line between his brows softens. He gives me a tiny, warm smile that barely reaches his mouth but lands heat at the back of my ribs. Then he turns away and is talking to a dad about the safest run for the youngest child. He's back to work and so am I.

We hit a rhythm. Questions land and I field them. Where are the towels. In your room. Breakfast times. Seven-thirty to nine-thirty. Dinner. Seven, second sitting at eight if needed. Where to rent a helmet for a teenager who swears he doesn't need one. Downstairs, and yes, you do. Spa access. Lower ground floor, turn left at the framed black and white photo of the avalanche that will scare you into reading the safety guide. Lift passes. Here's your envelope, sign here. Robes. I'll have them brought up. The room is cold. The thermostat is on the wall behind the curtain, the one that blends in, flip it to twenty and wait ten minutes. The child is hungry. There are biscuits in the jar by the tea station, yes you can take two, your mother will forgive you. The boy in the blue hat is trying to lift a suitcase that is bigger than him. Harley's already crossing the lobby to take it from him with a grin.

Jack appears at the edge of the desk and leans his elbow on the wood. He watches me finish with a family and gives a little clap that reads as a clap and also doesn't. "Look at you. Reception Goddess."

"Polish the halo," Niko says, cheerfully. "She's flying."

"Who knew you could talk and type at the same time," Jack says, smiling, but there is a little bit of bite under it. "Guess that's what they like up here."

I don't know what to do with that, so I hand him the printout for bar pre-orders and say, "Can you take these to the bar and let Sophie know the big group wants the welcome fizz on ice by five. She'll want time."

He lifts the pages, glances over them, then drops them back on the desk. "I'm on juice duty for another ten minutes. I'll grab them later."

"Now would be better," Niko says, lighter than light but with steel under it. "Sophie can't chill time."

Jack flicks his gaze to Niko, then to me. He smiles again. It looks tight. "Fine." He takes the printouts and heads for the bar without a goodbye.

Tyler breathes out through his nose and shakes his head once, more at the air than at Jack. He slides a chocolate from the drawer to my side of the desk like a magician. "Sugar," he says. "Trust me." I pop it in my mouth and feel my brain thank him.

The big group arrives. They come in like a storm, all at once, laughing and rolling suitcases and asking over each other. Imogen materialises and does that thing where she splits a crowd with a smile and a hand gesture, then directs them to lounge, desk, lift, tea. Tyler handles the spokesperson. I take the spillover. Niko floats and plugs any hole that opens.

"Welcome to Le Grenier," I say, again and again, and it sounds natural by the fifth time and almost warm by the tenth. "I'm Lola. Let me grab your booking. Can I take your surname and your reference. Perfect. Here we are. Let me talk you through the basics while I print your keycards. Breakfast, dinner, spa. Any questions now, or do you want to come back after you have seen your rooms." My body finds the rhythm. When the printer chews a card, I smile and keep talking. When the pen doesn't write, I swap it for another without the blank panic that used to swallow me whole.

Across the lobby, Harley reappears in the doorway after stashing the last suitcase. He rests one shoulder against the frame like he's giving his knees a second. The wind lifts his hair and then drops it. He looks at me for the length of two heartbeats. He doesn't hide that he's watching. The corner of his mouth tips up into a smile again. Then he is gone again, swallowed by the day.

Jack drifts back toward the desk once the big group is settled and the lobby calms to a low buzz. He sets the bar sheets down with a light thud and nods toward me. "You still alive, then."

"Just," I say. I make my voice friendly because it costs nothing.

"Imogen will be thrilled you are a natural," he says. The words are sweet. The tone is not. He tips his head and adds, "You must have had a good teacher."

"I had three," I say. "Tyler, Niko, and Imogen."

He looks past me toward the door. "And Harley," he says, like a card turned face up. "I saw him walk you outside."

Niko's head lifts. His eyes flick average and then sharp. "He walked her nowhere," he says, smooth as cream. "He saw a teammate needed a minute and he gave it. That's all."

Jack's smile doesn't move. "Sure," he says. "Teamwork." He plucks a spare keycard from the stack and flips it between his fingers. "Didn't know hosting came with concierge service."

"Jack," Tyler says, quiet, and the single syllable is a line on the ground.

Jack puts the card down. He laughs and pretends he doesn't feel the line. "Relax. I am happy for her." He lifts his hands. "Promotion day. Balloons. Confetti."

"Please take the welcome deck to the lounge," Imogen says as she approaches, unbothered by the tension even though she has clocked every particle of it. She puts a tablet into his chest lightly. "The projector is plugged in and I need you to test the sound."

Jack takes the tablet and strolls out to the lounge like there was never a line.

"Ignore the noise," Imogen murmurs to me without looking away from the screen she is scrolling. "We work, we smile, we let the children sulk outside. How are you feeling?"

"Better," I say. "Thanks to the breathing thing."

Niko leans in and bumps my shoulder with his. "She's flying," he says, pleased.

The afternoon slips into the kind of rhythm that makes time move faster. We field lost gloves, a complaint about a draft that is actually a window left open, a request to book a birthday dinner in town. Tyler calls the restaurant, then hands me the phone like I won't spontaneously combust. "I don't speak French," I hiss. "You'll be fine." I'm not. The woman on the other end says something elegant and incomprehensible. I make a noise that sounds like *"Oui?"* Somehow, she laughs and says *"of course."* When I hang up, I give Tyler the finger. He grins like a proud dad.

I take a quick break in the staff corridor, lean my head on the cool wall, and breathe in for four, hold for four, out for four. My watch says a number that doesn't make me want to cry. I drink water and feel it hit the empty places. When I go back out, the lobby looks less like a storm and more like a lake with small waves. Manageable.

A family of five swoops toward the desk in a cluster of voices. The dad asks three questions at once. The mum smiles apologetically while trying to keep the youngest from dragging a suitcase over his own foot. The teen daughter keeps saying I'm fine. Tyler peels the dad with a calm hand gesture and answers him point by point. I crouch to the youngest and show him how to hold the case so it doesn't bite his ankle. Niko makes the teen laugh by asking her to rate our lobby playlist out of ten. Imogen appears with a stack of kids' spa times and hands the mum a slip. We do it like a dance. The family leaves smiling and a little less scattered.

Harley walks past the desk with a stack of folded high-vis vests and a clipboard he probably stole from Scarlett's office. He doesn't stop. Doesn't speak. Glances over at me once, registers that I'm standing tall with my shoulders down and my voice level, and that almost-smile warms like a small sun. I feel it for several minutes after he's gone. It doesn't distract me. It anchors me.

By late afternoon, the lobby calms to a soft murmur. The fire in the lounge is going, which makes the air smell like wood and comfort. Sophie sends a message from the bar that I read on the iPad to say the welcome fizz is chilled and the glasses are polished within an inch of their life, which is exactly how she wants them.

Tyler stands at the printer, feeding it fresh paper. He tears off a sheet and hands it to me. "You've done six hours without a miss," he says, matter of fact, like he's reporting the weather. "Not everyone manages that on their first day."

"Not everyone has you standing at their shoulder," I say.

He considers that for one beat. "Maybe not. Still counts." He looks back at the screen. "Welcome meeting at six. You'll shadow tonight, not lead. Watch how Niko handles the big group questions. Watch Imogen when someone tries to dominate the room. You'll learn as much from what they don't say as what they do."

"Got it."

"Drink water," he adds, which is the kind of instruction that should annoy me and somehow doesn't when he says it.

I drink. He's right. Of course he is.

Jack reappears at the printer with a stack of menus and slides them into the tray a little too hard. He doesn't look at me, and I've officially seen a side of him I'm not that fond of.

CHAPTER 6

The Journal and the Knock

LOLA

It's past midnight and my body knows it. The kind of heavy that settles in your bones, not your muscles. The kind of tired where your brain goes quiet, like it's moving through mud. When my heart spikes like that, it always hits later. My brain crashes. Muscles heavy, thoughts slow, chest tight like it hasn't let go yet. I act fine so no one asks, but inside, I'm still bracing for impact.

The chalet hotel's finally quiet. Proper quiet. Just the soft hum of the heating, the tick of pipes, the creak of the floor settling after a long day. Outside, the noise from the bar has faded to nothing. Everyone's gone to bed or found someone to keep them up.

I'm curled on my bed, knees to chest, duvet wrapped tight. It's not comfort, it's armour. The lamp flickers like it's about to give up. My phone's face up beside me, screen dark. I roll onto my side. My uniform's still slung over the chair, badge clipped to the lapel. *Lola.* It looks like it belongs to someone else. Someone who fits.

I reach under my pillow and pull out my journal.

Not the new one I pretended I'd start this season with fresh pages and a fresh brain. The old one. The one from home. The one with the soft brown leather and the thin scratch on the back where I caught it on the zip of my bag. My brother's name is on the first page in block capitals, Liam, written with a felt tip when we were kids and he decided he wanted to be the kind of boy who kept secrets and scores in a book. He gave it to me the year he left for training, told me to write the stuff I wouldn't say out loud. I wrote two entries and hid it. After he died, I found it at the back of my wardrobe. I didn't touch it for months. When I finally did, the pages were stiff with guilt and something else that dried into the paper and never left.

I open to a clean page. It feels wrong to cover the neatness. I write the date in the top corner. It looks too neat, like I'm pretending I'm tidy.

My hand shakes a little, a tiny tremor that shows up when my body is still catching up to what happened, when the day's been loud and the night finally lets me hear myself.

I write anyway. Not pretty. Not careful. Just honest.

Jack let me down.

The words sit there like they're waiting to be argued with. I drop my pen for a second and watch the ink gloss, then dry. The sentence is small on the page and still somehow too big. I swallow, pick up the pen again, and keep going.

I thought he was my friend.

There's a pause where the tip of the pen rests on the paper and leaves a tiny dot like a freckle. I didn't want to write the next line, but it pushes through.

But people always seem to resent you when you stop needing them the way they want you to.

I sit back against the pillows and let that sit with me. It feels like I'm being a bit dramatic, so I argue with myself in my head for a second. He was having a bad day. He didn't mean it like that. He didn't say anything that cruel. He was just surprised. And then the other voice, the one that sounds like me when I don't care about being liked, says, He knew exactly what he was doing. He wanted you small again.

My throat tightens. I add another line before I can flinch away from it.

I don't feel safe with him anymore.

That one slices in its own quiet way. Not a scream. Just a clean cut that bleeds after.

It isn't even about Jack. Not fully. It's about me letting myself believe someone could just... care. Without deciding that being needed equals being owed. I'm mad at him for how he looked at me today, like my improvement cost him something he should have kept. I'm mad at myself for being surprised.

I turn the page. The paper crackles, too loud in the stillness. I start again on a clean sheet. The last one's done what it needed to. This one's for something else.

I miss home.

Not the place. The version of me I was before I started trying to make everyone else comfortable.

I stare at that for a long second. I don't know if it's true, but it sounds like it could be. I'm not even sure what version I mean. The kid who used to sit on the kitchen counter and eat cereal from the box while Mum danced to the radio. The girl who believed in being loved without auditioning. The sister who was sure that if Liam was in the room, she would be fine. The part of me that stopped performing and just... existed. I don't know if she's still in here. I don't know if I'd recognise her if she walked right up to me.

The tears arrive with no warning. One moment my eyes are dry, the next there's a film over the words and I'm blinking them back, and then they spill without fuss. I press the back of my hand to my mouth because that's how you keep sound in your chest. I fold forward as if I can physically keep every feeling tucked inside my ribs if I curl small enough.

For a second I wish I was outside. Not in the cold exactly, but under a sky that doesn't have a ceiling. The stars on a clear night here look like they were poured rather than placed, like the dark is full and alive. Tonight it's snowing, so the sky is a blank, but the idea of outside still loosens something in my spine. I breathe in and out.

There's a knock at the door. Soft. Careful. Like whoever's on the other side isn't sure I want to hear it.

I freeze and hold my breath, maybe it was nothing.

Another knock, same gentleness, no urgency, still real.

I wipe my face with my sleeve and pull my duvet straight like that matters. I stand and catch sight of myself in the little mirror above the desk. My hair's a wild mess of waves and frizz. My eyes are red around the corners. I'm in an old sweatshirt and joggers that have been washed so many times the colours have faded. I don't look like a girl who should open the door to anyone, but I open it anyway.

My eyes land on Harley, grey joggers, Powder White fleece zipped up, black hair still damp at the ends like he showered not long ago. There's a shadow of stubble across his jaw that makes him look older, or maybe just more tired. His blue eyes are careful, like he's approaching a skittish horse and he doesn't want to spook it.

"Can I come in?" he asks. Voice low.

I nod and step back, he slips inside and closes the door behind him. That quiet competence that always makes me weirdly aware of how big he is in small rooms.

He takes a slow look around, orienting himself, his eyes drift to the desk, the chair, and the bed that I very obviously just climbed out of despite my attempt to straighten it up. His gaze finally lands on the journal on the duvet. He doesn't comment, just drags the desk chair a little closer to the bed and lowers himself into it, elbows on his knees, hands loose, body tipped forward a bit like he's ready to move if he needs to.

"I saw you walk away earlier," he says. "From Jack."

I sit on the edge of the bed and pick at a stray thread on the duvet cover. He doesn't move closer. He doesn't push the silence full of words. He lets it breathe. After a few beats, he tries again.

"You looked... hurt," he says. "Not angry. Just... gutted."

I nod and stare at the floor. The carpet is that beige that every hotel thinks looks expensive. There's a tiny stain near the skirting board shaped like a comma.

"I thought he was different," I say. The words feel like chewing something stale. "I thought maybe he gave a shit. But I think he just liked it better when I needed him. He liked having the upper hand."

Harley stays quiet.

"I get it," I mutter. "People don't like it when you change the rules. Makes them uncomfortable."

"You didn't do anything wrong," he says.

I nod like I agree. I don't. Not yet. There's that old reflex that says I should have been softer, smaller, sweeter, whatever would have kept the peace. He hears the lie in my nod. I don't know how, but he does.

"You didn't," he says again, firmer. Using a tone that doesn't invite debate.

My throat tightens like a hand is there. I swallow around it.

"I know what it's like," he says, eyes on mine for a brief second and then back to a point on the floor between us, "to outgrow the version of yourself someone else needs you to be."

That lands straight in my ribs and stays there. He's not offering a story. Not trying to compare pain. Just... being with it. And somehow, it unclenches something in my chest I hadn't even realised was tight.

He shifts forward and reaches out one hand, slower than his usual movements, careful enough that I can see the decision happen. He doesn't touch me. He lets his hand hover, palm up, an offer. I take it.

His hand is warm and the size difference makes my knuckles look small. He doesn't squeeze. He doesn't rub his thumb over my skin. He just lets me hold on. It isn't romantic. It's practical. It's a rope.

"You don't have to explain it to me," he says. His eyes drop to our hands like he's giving me privacy while he's still here. "I just wanted you to know someone saw it."

Something in me cracks where it needed to. Not the kind that breaks you. The kind that lets the pressure out. I breathe a little easier.

"You always this good at showing up the exact moment I'm falling apart?" I ask. I try to make it a joke and almost manage it.

His mouth twitches at the corner. "Only for you, apparently."

It makes heat climb my neck and I hate that I like it. I let go of his hand because I don't trust where that heat goes if I hold on. He doesn't reach for me again. He leans back a little and lets the space grow back.

My phone lights up on the duvet next to me. The screen shows the name before I can flip it. Dad.

My stomach knots like someone's tightened a strap around it. It's like my body knew who it would be and braced before I did. I press the side button to black the screen and shove the phone under my pillow as if he can see me if his name is facing the room.

Harley saw it. Of course he did. He notices everything. His eyebrows pull together just a little. He doesn't do the too-much face. Just concern without intrusion.

"You alright?" he asks.

I nod. It's a lie. We both know. He doesn't call me on it. He lets the lie sit there while the truth gathers its courage.

"Does he message a lot?" he asks after a few seconds, not pushing, just turning a question into a door I can open if I want.

"Not really," I say. Then I sigh. "Only when he wants something. Or wants to remind me I've disappointed him somehow."

Harley doesn't say, I'm sure he loves you. He doesn't say, he means well. He doesn't say, that's just how some dad's are. He stays quiet and it's the kind of quiet that lets me keep going.

"He was in the army," I say. "Very rigid. Discipline. Obedience. Loyalty. All those words that sound noble when you're not the one they're being used on. He thinks feelings are weak. Hates that I talk back. Hates that I left. Hates that I don't call him sir."

Harley's jaw flexes once like he bit on something hard.

"He's never hit me," I add, too fast, like the absence of bruises is proof I'm exaggerating. "He just... everything is control. Every conversation feels like I'm being graded. And if I fail, it's silence for days. Or he flips it and makes me the villain. Says I'm ungrateful. Says I'm an embarrassment."

The last word tastes dirty. I want to spit it out. I stare at the carpet comma and focus on not crying again.

"That's not love, Lola," he says gently. "That's ownership."

It knocks my breath a little. Not because I haven't thought it. Because I haven't let myself say it. Hearing it spoken makes it more real.

"Yeah," I say, my voice small. "I know. It's just... hard to unlearn it when it's all you've known."

He nods. The nod is slow and steady, like he's counting the seconds with me.

"You write about him?" he asks, tipping his chin toward the journal.

"Sometimes."

"You ever write about me?"

I blink at him. There's no cocky edge. No smirk. He sounds like he's asking if it rained earlier. Just curious.

"Maybe," I say.

"Was it bad?" One corner of his mouth lifts like he's giving me the option to take the piss if I want.

"No."

He nods and takes that like a win. It makes me smile.

We sit in a quiet that isn't awkward. The lamp flickers. The corridor stays silent. Somewhere outside, snow taps the glass lightly where the wind shifts it. Harley's presence settles the air in the room. Not because he's doing anything. Because he's not.

"You did well today," he says after a while. "After."

The word hangs there with the weight of everything we're not recapping. The bench. His hand on my neck. My heart fighting the air and then finally letting the air back in.

"Tyler helped," I say. "And Niko. And Imogen. I didn't drown. They made sure I didn't."

"You didn't drown," he echoes. "You swam."

It's a simple line and it warms me a stupid amount. I look at my journal and fight the urge to write that down.

He shifts like he's going to stand. Then he settles again.

There's a thought he's arguing with and I can see it in the line of his shoulders.

"I should go," he says finally.

The words hit a space in my chest that's still sore and I react before I think. "You can stay," I blurt. "If you want. We don't have to talk. We could watch something. Or sleep. I've got an extra blanket." I hear myself and cringe at the way the hope pokes out like an elbow.

He doesn't make me feel stupid. He just holds my gaze and lets me see the decision. "Not tonight," he says. There's softness to his words. "I don't want to do this wrong. And right now, I might."

I nod. "Okay."

He stands and the room feels smaller for a second, like he takes oxygen with him when he moves. He steps toward the door and puts a hand on the handle.

"I'm here if you need me," he says.

It's simple. It's not a promise bigger than he can keep. It's not a vow. It's just real.

He opens the door and leaves without waiting for me to say anything back. The corridor swallows him in two steps, quiet as he came.

I sit for a long time after he's gone. I don't cry. I don't write. I let the quiet be a thing I don't try to fix.

The silence isn't empty. It's full of the weight of what wasn't said and the relief that I didn't have to say it. I press my palm to my chest and wait for the thud to even out. It does. Not because I forced it. Because it wanted to.

I reach under my pillow and take out my phone. The screen lights my face and I swipe to the message thread I wish I could delete without deleting the part of me that still answers. Dad's name sits above a couple of texts from earlier. I don't open them. I don't need the words to feel the tone. I press my thumb against the screen until the menu pops up and I stare at the options I've never used. Mute. Hide alerts. Block this caller.

I don't press anything. Not tonight. It feels like making a decision while my hands still shake would be cheating. I turn the phone face down and let it exist without being a threat.

I pick up my journal. The page I left open reads like a girl trying to explain herself. Neat words. Careful lines.

I add a new one. Messier.

I'm not his version of me.

Not anymore.

I stare at that until it stops buzzing. I add one more sentence because I want something to hold.

Today I swam.

I close the journal and slide it under the pillow again like a secret I want close to my ear in case I forget it by morning.

I lie down on my side and pull the duvet to my chin. The radiator clicks once and then settles. Somewhere down the hall a door opens and closes gently. The mountain is a quiet giant beyond the wall. I close my eyes and let my mind do that floaty thing where thoughts come like bubbles and pop without turning into sentences.

I'm half asleep when the memory of his hand at the back of my neck slides in. Not the heat of it. The steadiness. The way he counted without hurry. The way he let me decide when to speak and when to stay quiet. The way he didn't mistake softness for weakness.

I don't know what to do with that yet. So I do nothing. I let it live there.

Sleep comes in small pieces and then all at once.

❄

I wake before dawn to the soft thud of snow slipping off the eaves. My body feels used up and loose, like I ran and then slept in a hammock. I blink at the ceiling for a second, then check my watch. The number is low and calm. The kind of resting heart rate that feels like a gift rather than a number you have to work for.

My phone is a quiet brick on the bedside table. I don't touch it yet. I'm not ready to face any words from a man who taught me to read the tone before the sentence.

I sit up slow and the room tilts just a bit. I pad to the ensuite and splash water on my face. It's cold enough to make me inhale through my teeth. I brush my hair into some kind of submission and pull it into a messy knot that will fall down by lunch anyway. I pull on tights, then my uniform, clip my badge on last, a small ritual to say I'm someone today.

The corridor is cold on my ankles. I walk quiet past the closed doors and down the back stairs. The staff kitchen smells like toast and coffee already because Sarah is always ten minutes ahead of need. She stands by the kettle pouring hot water into a teapot. She looks up, reads my face, and gives me a smile that doesn't ask for anything.

"You okay, lassie?" she asks.

"Yeah," I say.

She nods. "Tea first."

I wrap my hands around the mug she offers to me and let the heat sit in my fingers. I'm not a tea person at home. I am here. The steam warms my nose. My chest settles one notch further.

"How's your dad?" she asks. She doesn't look at me when she says it, like she's giving me privacy inside the question.

I huff a breath that isn't a laugh. "Still himself."

"Hmm." It's a sound that holds a universe of opinion and restraint. "You don't have to answer the phone."

I've had a few heart to hearts with her and Imogen over the weeks I've been here in the Alps about my dad, and them being older and seemingly wiser have helped more than they know.

"I know."

"Good." She pours the last of the water and sets the kettle back. "Imogen said you were a superstar on reception yesterday."

"Harley helped," I say. "Tyler, Niko and Imogen too."

"So did you," she says simply. "You let yourself be helped. That's harder than it looks."

I let that land. It softens my shoulders. I didn't expect a

morning pep talk, and I didn't know I needed it. I lift the mug and take a sip. It's strong and a little sweet.

"Eat something," she adds, already turning toward a stack of plates. "There's toast over there."

I eat toast because Sarah told me to and because she's always right. By the time I head toward reception, the day has started moving under me like a conveyor belt. Not running, not dragging. Just carrying.

Niko is at the desk in a sweater that probably cost more than my phone and a grin that says he's already charmed three guests and a delivery driver. Tyler stands beside him going through everything for the day, pen tapping in that steady rhythm of his.

"Look who survived," Niko sings. "My star."

I roll my eyes and lean on the desk. "Please never call me that again."

"I'll call you worse," he says cheerfully. He tips his chin toward the lounge. "You got a fan last night."

I follow his look and find Harley across the room talking to Ash, hands moving as he explains something. He glances over like he felt it and his gaze meets mine for half a heartbeat. The warm, tiny smile shows up again. It's quieter in the morning light. It still lands where it did last night.

"Don't start," I tell Niko without looking at him.

"Didn't say a word," he says, all wide eyes and fake innocence. "Still not saying one. Not until at least eleven. Then I'll say too many and get told to shut up."

"Be nice," Tyler murmurs, eyes still on the iPad.

"I'm an angel," Niko says.

"Hmm," Tyler says, and I hear the edges of a laugh that he's hiding out of principle.

Jack walks in through the bar door with a crate of glasses. He sees me and something flickers across his face, fast, unreadable. He sets the crate down harder than necessary and nods without looking at me properly. Not hello. Not nothing. Just a warning not to ask.

"Morning," I say.

“Morning,” he says. He pushes a stray glass into place and doesn’t look up again.

The air between us is different now. Not cold. Just thinner. Like something’s gone missing and neither of us wants to name it. I don’t try to fix it. I don’t owe him that.

Guests start trickling down. I take the first question before Tyler can. Nail it. Then the second, just to keep moving.

Tyler glances over, gives a small nod, then goes back to the iPad like nothing ever shifted. It isn’t. But it can be.

By mid-morning I’ve answered six different versions of the same question about lift passes and only wanted to scream internally once. I take that as growth.

I pull my phone from my pocket and open the messages. The thread with Dad is there with the two texts from last night.

Dad: Are you ignoring me

Dad: Call me

No please. No question mark. No context. Just a command and an accusation I’m supposed to correct. My thumb hovers over the reply box the way it always does. I close the thread and open settings. I scroll without hurrying. Mute. Hide alerts. Block.

I press mute.

I don’t owe him a reply. Not tonight. Not ever, if I don’t want to. He doesn’t get to hijack my sleep just because he’s bored and holding a phone.

I slide the phone into my pocket and straighten up. Out in the lobby, Harley’s at the far end with a group of guests, talking them through the green runs. He gestures with one hand like he’s sketching the slope from memory. Then he sees me, and that small, quiet smile pulls at his mouth again.

I smile back, take my place at the desk, and clip my badge straight. The day moves. My heart keeps going. That’s enough.

And for the first time since I got here, the version of me that doesn’t apologise for taking up space sticks around long enough to feel real.

CHAPTER 7
Stars and Other Things That Matter

LOLA

The cold hits like a slap the second I step outside. The decking's slick under my boots, the air sharp enough to sting my nose, but it's better than being inside. The lounge is packed tonight, staff and guests both too warm, too loud, too many voices talking over each other. My head can't keep up with any of it, not when everything already feels too big, too fast, too much.

I grip the railing, leaning forward until my fingertips go numb against the ice-cold wood. The slopes stretch out below, half-buried under darkness now, just faint outlines of tracks zigzagging down through the trees. They look quiet, untouched. I wish I felt the same. But I don't.

Every time I stop moving, the guilt creeps in, this dull, heavy throb I can't shake. I left without saying goodbye properly. Ignored Dad's calls. Haven't replied to his messages. I told myself coming here was a fresh start, but it doesn't feel like one. It feels like I ran away and left a hole behind me.

And then there's Harley.

I haven't been able to stop thinking about that night, the hallway, the panic attack, his hands steadying me when I couldn't breathe. I thought maybe it'd change something between us, that it'd make him softer with me somehow. But he's been distant ever since. Back to clipped answers, unreadable looks, like none of it even happened. And I don't know why that bothers me so much, but it does.

The door behind me creaks open, letting a burst of warmth and noise spill out onto the decking before it slams shut again. Heavy boots on the boards. I know it's him before I even turn, it's almost like I summoned him with my thoughts.

Harley comes to lean on the railing beside me, close enough that I can feel the heat radiating off him even in the freezing air. He doesn't say anything at first, just stares out at the dark slopes like they've got secrets written all over them. His shoulders are tense beneath his jacket, jaw set like he's holding something back.

The silence stretches, thick and loaded, until I can't take it anymore.

"What?" I ask, softer than I mean to.

His gaze doesn't shift from the view. "You looked like you were about to bolt."

My eyebrows knit. "What?"

"Inside," he says finally, glancing sideways at me. "You looked like you couldn't breathe."

For a second, my throat feels tight, like I've been caught out. I grip the railing harder. "I'm fine."

"Sure you are," he says, quietly, almost flat, like he doesn't believe me but isn't going to push it either.

We stand there like that for a moment, side by side, both staring out at the slopes, neither of us saying the thing we're really thinking. It's not comfortable, but it's not exactly uncomfortable either. Just... charged. Like something's there, waiting, but neither of us is ready to reach for it yet.

He shifts his weight, elbows resting on the railing now, breath clouding in the cold. I glance at him from the corner of my eye, trying to read his expression, but it's pointless. Harley's impossible like that.

"You don't have to keep checking on me," I say, aiming for casual and failing.

His mouth twitches like I just gave him a private joke. "Wasn't."

I huff out a short laugh, more defensive than amused. "Right."

That earns me a sideways glance, sharp and brief, like he's trying to decide if I'm worth replying to. Finally, he mutters, "Just making sure you're not freezing your arse off, Maxwell."

My lips twitch despite myself. "I've survived worse."

"Yeah?" There's the faintest trace of interest in his voice now. "Like what?"

I hesitate, my fingers tightening on the railing, and for a second I consider telling him. About my home in Aldershot, more about my Dad, about the house where silence meant danger if you broke it. But the words get stuck somewhere in my throat, and I just shrug instead.

"Doesn't matter."

His gaze lingers for a second too long, like he knows there's more but decides not to push. He just nods once and looks back at the slopes.

The quiet stretches again, but this time it feels... different. Softer. Like neither of us minds it.

I glance at him again, and this time I notice little things I hadn't before, the slope of his nose, the sharp line of his jaw, the way the faint glow from the lodge lights catches in his hair. Stupid things. Things I shouldn't be noticing, not when he barely talks to me half the time. I wonder if Sophie ever saw this version of him. If she did, I hate her for it.

His eyes flick sideways, catching me looking. His mouth curves. "Careful, Lo, you carry on staring at me like that and I'll start thinking you're into me."

My stomach jolts, heat rushing where I don't want it. I roll my eyes so hard it nearly hurts. "Don't flatter yourself." Although, you're not what I expected.

His face scrunches. "Yeah?"

"You're... quieter than I thought you'd be."

That gets his attention. He turns fully to face me now, one eyebrow lifting. "Quieter?"

I nod, instantly regretting opening my mouth. "You've got this... reputation, right? Everyone talks about you. The snow-boards-slash ski God, the party guy, whatever. But you're... not loud. Not really."

He studies me like I'm some puzzle he didn't plan on solving tonight, then lets out a low chuckle that's more breath than sound. "People say a lot of shit. Doesn't mean it's true."

"You don't seem to care either way," I say before I can stop myself.

That earns me a look, the unreadable kind, weighty, like he's deciding something and doesn't want me to know what. "Maybe I don't," he says finally, his voice low, measured. "Or maybe I just stopped giving a fuck a long time ago."

The answer sits heavily between us, and for a second, I want to ask. About when, about why, about what he's carrying that makes him sound like that. But his shoulders tense the tiniest bit, and I get the sense he wouldn't tell me even if I asked.

So instead, I just nod, hugging my arms tighter around myself, pretending the cold's the reason for the shiver running through me.

Behind us, the decking door creaks open again, letting laughter spill out from the lounge. Someone calls Harley's name, but he doesn't move. Doesn't even turn around. His jaw flexes, and I wonder if he's avoiding them, or avoiding something else entirely.

"Nice necklace," he says after a beat, casual on purpose. "You wear it every day."

My hand lifts before I think about it, fingers brushing the little silver star. "Yeah."

"Where's it from?"

"My mum," I say, barely above a whisper. "She gave it to me before she died. Said it was for looking up... that even when every-thing feels heavy, there's always something brighter out there."

There's a ghost of a smile on his lips. "She sounds like someone worth listening to."

"She was." My voice does a strange soft thing. I clear my throat. "I try to look up. Some days I forget."

"I used to sleep under the stars," he says. "Not because I wanted to. Just... didn't always have a roof."

A beat passes. "I'd stare up and count anyway. Gave me something to do when everything else felt shit."

The words come without weight in his voice, which makes them heavier in the air between us. I turn toward him because not looking would feel like disrespect.

"You were on the street?"

He exhales like he's decided to stop dodging for a minute.

"Foster care roulette," he says. "Some nights it was safer not to go back."

I freeze. The words land heavy and I wasn't ready for them.

"Harley..." I say his name, quietly. Like I don't know if I'm allowed.

He shrugs, eyes still on some middle distance I can't reach. "It was what it was."

He hesitates, rubbing his thumb over the railing like he's deciding how much to give away.

"There was this one place," he says finally. "He used to lock me in the attic if I came home late. No windows. No light. Called it my quiet room."

"That's awful."

He shrugs, like it's just something he's learned to do.

"You figure out ways to cope. Counting helped, stars helped, not much else did."

I want to reach for him but I don't. Instead I say, "Guess that's why you're always looking out for everyone else."

His eyes find mine, steady and unreadable. For a second I think he'll deflect. He doesn't. "Maybe. Or maybe I just don't want anyone else to feel like that kid in the attic."

"What happened to your family?" I ask, my hands tensing on

the railing. He notices and just when I don't think he'll answer, he says.

"My mum died of an overdose when I was five. Never knew my dad."

For a second, I just stare at him, like the words need time to sink in. Jesus. I thought my story was heavy, but his... it hits different. And it's not a competition, it never was, but something in my chest twists hard.

"I'm sorry," I manage, and it feels small. Too small for everything he's been through. My heart aches for little Harley, carrying all that alone.

For a while neither of us speaks. I can hear the wind cutting through the trees, my heart still trying to find its rhythm. The silence settles between us, heavier than the cold, warmer than it should be. One of those rare moments where it feels like everything's being said without a single word.

The silence is interrupted when the lounge door bumps, letting out a leak of warmth and sound. Tyler walks out with a bucket and that blank face people always read as kind.

"Watch the ice by the mat when you come in," he says. "You two good?"

"We're good," Harley says.

"Fine," I say at the same time, and Tyler's mouth softens like he's satisfied by that answer from both of us.

When the door closes again, Harley's attention returns to me like a touch I can feel without contact.

"You have a dangerous smile, makes people think they matter."

"I don't know what that means."

"It means it makes people want to earn it."

"You trying to earn it?"

He holds my gaze. "I'm trying not to waste it."

My chest tightens in a good way and I nudge his knee with mine to keep the moment from swallowing me. "You know, for someone so mysterious, you're really bad at keeping people from wanting to know more."

"And you're terrible at minding your own business."

"That's literally my best quality."

"Wouldn't call it your best," he says, eyes doing a slow once-over that warms me through my coat. "But it's up there."

I laugh before I can help it. The sound comes out softer than I meant.

Harley touches his ear where an earpiece would be if he wore one, his gaze tracks the slope like he's mapping a way out even from the railing.

"You always do that?" I ask.

"What."

"Scan the world for exits."

"Yeah." He doesn't pretend not to know what I mean. "Less exhausting than the alternative."

"I get that." My phone buzzes in my pocket, a small vibration with a big weight. I hesitate, but don't look at the screen. I know the name attached to it. He sees the movement, then looks away, not pushing. The respect in that choice is louder than any question.

"Got a day off coming up?" he asks.

"Yeah, tomorrow I have a half day."

"You'll actually take it?"

"That's the rumour, I might sleep till my bones stop humming."

"Sleep helps." He nods toward the slope. "So does moving."

"You offering a training montage?"

"Not today." He says, accompanied by a half smile. "Tomorrow I'll race you to the spruce line."

"You'd win."

"Probably."

"You're supposed to pretend I have a chance."

"I don't lie to people I like." The words land between us and neither of us looks away.

Before I can decide what to do with that, the door edges open again. Imogen steps halfway out, hair sleek and dark against her coat, eyes already drinking in everything.

"Lola, when you come in, can you grab the guest welcome cards? New arrivals at six," she says. "Harley, Scarlett wants you to check the south run. Patrol reported a drift."

"Copy," he says, voice sliding into work mode.

Imogen's gaze lingers on my face. "You warm enough?"

"I'm fine."

She softens. "Okay." She goes back inside, taking a puff of warmth with her.

"She's good at her job," Harley says.

"She's good at everything," I say honestly.

Two teenage boys duck under the railing to take a shortcut, then freeze when Tyler appears on the other side of the window with a look that says turn around. They backtrack with red cheeks. I laugh before I can stop it. Harley's mouth moves like he wants to smile again.

"What," I ask.

"Nothing."

"Tell me."

"You laughing sounds like relief."

"You're annoying."

His answering smile tells me he accepts that like a compliment.

"What did you want to be when you were little?" I ask.

"Tall."

"You're impossible."

"I wanted to be fast," he says, relenting. "Didn't matter how. Trainers, wheels, engine. Just fast."

"And now?"

"Now? Just... still. Without losing my mind."

There it is, the soft target inside the armour, it hits me low. I nod like I'm not bleeding empathy on the decking.

A cluster of guests drifts out, arguing in polite voices about the shuttle. One leans over the rail. "Does the bus stop by the bakery?"

Harley points across the car park. "Every thirty minutes. Blue sign. If the driver looks like he hates his life, you're in the right place."

They laugh, thank him and shuffle off in a tangle of expensive zips.

"You're good with them," I say.

"With who."

"People. Kids. The ones who talk too loud. The ones who panic."

"I'm good at spotting what hurts and getting there before it spreads."

"You sound like a medic."

"I feel like one some days."

"What about you," he asks, turning it back on me. "What did you want to be?"

"Brave."

"You are." He says it like a fact, not flattery.

"I don't feel it."

"That's not the measure, Lo."

My throat goes tight and I pick up a lock of hair and start twisting around my finger.

Harley's watching me again. It feels like standing under a warm light.

"Do you hate talking about your mum?" he asks, quietly.

"I don't hate it. I just never know if people want the real answer."

"I do."

"That's because you get it, people don't usually lose their mums as young as we did." I say simply. "She made normal things feel like rituals. A cup of tea was connection, not a drink. A walk was together, not exercise. She made cheap days feel rich." I grin as the memories flood my insides wrapping around my ribs.

"Sounds familiar," he says.

"Don't."

"What."

"Don't make me cry on the decking."

He tips his head back like he's reading something on the sky.

Snow sticks to his lashes and he doesn't blink it off. My stomach does something stupid.

"Come on," he says after a moment, grabbing my hand, making heat pool low in my stomach. "Walk with me. To the end and back. Warm your feet."

"I'm not a pensioner."

"Prove it."

I let him tug me along, close enough that the heat from his coat seeps into mine. The boards creak beneath us. In the car park, a shuttle hisses and a family bursts out, kids and bags everywhere. One little boy's clinging to a stuffed dinosaur like his whole world depends on it.

We reach the edge of the decking where the snow banks in a neat ridge and stops. The sky feels lower here, like it's leaning in. We sit on the bench, the wood is cold through my coat.

"You'll have to teach me some time... the counting I mean," I say. "But only if you want." I tack on feeling a bit silly.

He looks at me like I handed him something fragile.

"The way you do it."

"It's easier at night, but you can practice any time. Pick a spot, fix your eyes and just let everything else blur."

I pick a patch just over the roof. "Okay."

"Five things you can see without moving your eyes."

"The roof edge, the antenna, the big spruce, the slope sign, that cloud that looks like a fish."

"Four things you can hear."

"The shuttle idling, plates clinking, someone laughing in the bar, your coat when you breathe."

He smiles, quick and real. "Three things you can feel."

"Cold ankles, the bench imprinting my thighs, my heart beating in my chest."

"Two things you can smell."

"Coffee, snow."

"Onc thing you can taste."

"The hot chocolate, I had just before I came out here"

"See," he says. "You're here."

The words hit low and true. The counting's not about stars, like I thought it would be. It's about surviving the minutes between bad and better.

"Thanks," I say, rough around the edges.

He doesn't reply. He knocks his shoulder against mine, gently, and we turn back.

Inside, Scarlett's voice carries through the open door. "Team meeting at eight, bring your brains." There's a chorus of dramatic groans in answer. The wind shifts and sends a flurry across the decking. A flake lands on my wrist and melts like a sigh. He watches it like my wrist is more interesting than the sky, then looks away.

"What scares you the most," he asks, "right now?"

"That I'll make one decision because I'm tired and it'll follow me forever."

"What's the decision trying to be?"

"To shut the world out and call it peace."

He nods. "I get that."

"What scares you?"

"The mountain. It's the only thing you can't fight back, and that I'll need someone and not know how to be good at it."

My chest goes tight. "You're better at it than you think."

He doesn't answer, he doesn't need to. The look is enough, It lands and stays.

"Do you ever want to go back and tell little you anything?" I ask.

"He wouldn't listen." The corner of his mouth tips. "I'd try anyway. Sleep when you can, accept help from people who don't make you pay for it, stop packing a bag every time someone raises their voice."

I swallow. "I'd tell her she doesn't have to be perfect to be loved."

He looks at me. "Who told you that."

"No one, everyone. The world."

"Then the world can be wrong."

It should be cheesy, it isn't. Not with his face open like that.

I pat the bench under me. "I should go in before Imogen has me filling welcome cards with my tears."

"Yeah," he says, but he doesn't move, neither do I.

A beat. Two. The kind of silence that says more than most people manage in an hour.

I shift and my knee brushes his. It isn't an invitation. It feels like one anyway.

He doesn't flinch, but leans a fraction towards me, I hold my breath.

He leans in, but stops short, his breath warm against my cheek like a kiss he's still deciding on. He doesn't close the gap, and I don't bridge it. But we both feel it.

The radio crackles. Scarlett, "Harley, you heading out?"

He lifts the radio from his pocket. "South run. Ten minutes."

"Copy. Lola, after cards, help Imogen with the tasting table. Group booking who think artisan means expensive."

"On it," I answer with a grimace.

Harley stands, stretches, the way a cat does when it's decided to get up and stalk something.

He nudges the chain with the back of his fingers. It's stupid how much it feels like more than it is.

"Keep looking up," he says.

"Only if you count with me."

"Deal."

He heads for the door, pauses, looks back like he's leaving something important behind and wants to make sure it'll still be here when he returns. I hold his gaze, which hopefully tells him I'm not going anywhere and follow him inside.

The main lounge is a controlled mess of staff and guests moving around each other in the practiced choreography of a place that lives and dies by timing. I slide behind the bar and snag the stack of welcome cards from under the till. The tiny desk by the window is mine for the next chunk of time.

Imogen appears with a clipboard and a pen tucked behind one ear. "Thanks, love. Keep the handwriting friendly but not flirty. They're British."

"I can do crisp and competent," I say.

"You can do warm and terrifying," she says, with a soft smile, "which is better." She scans the room, then lowers her voice. "You look steadier."

"Yeah." I don't explain and she doesn't need me to.

I write the first dozen cards. Welcome to Le Grenier. Breakfast from seven-thirty. Boots in the boot room, not the corridor unless you want Tyler's haunted stare. I print clearly, add a line or two when the names make me think they'll appreciate it. Mr and Mrs Fletcher, happy anniversary, we hid the good pastries. The little things make a day feel personal.

I finish the last welcome card and stack them by the register. As Scarlett requested, I plate a tray of hangover food for room fourteen and carry it upstairs dodging a stag in a novelty ski hat who apologises with the sincerity of a man who thinks apologies are foreplay. I leave the tray with a polite knock and a note about hydration.

When I get back, the radio crackles. "South run's clear," Harley says, calm and efficient. "Drift's manageable. Edge markers need resetting."

"Copy," Scarlett replies. "Reset and come back in. We've got a group asking for private lessons who think discount means two for one."

"On my way."

Something loosens in my chest that I didn't know was held. I don't need to see him to feel the shift when he's near. It's like someone steady put a hand on the wheel.

I'm standing by the window gazing at the snow again, when I see Harley walking at the bottom of the slope with a couple of guests who seem to be laughing at something he said. Tyler joins me for a second. "He's good with them," he says.

"Yeah, he is, I told him that earlier." I agree.

"Good with you too." He says it like a neutral weather report and moves on before I can answer.

Then he comes inside, and my eyes blur everyone else out of the lobby.

“How’d it go?” I ask, trying to sound casual and landing somewhere near eager.

“All sorted now.”

“Good.” I pretend to adjust a stack of coasters so I don’t beam at him like a lighthouse.

“You good?” he asks.

“Yeah.” I try to sound breezy and probably sound like I swallowed a bee.

“You keeping your half day tomorrow?” he asks.

“Yeah. I might disappear to the quiet path behind the spruce line. Tyler says the wind’s calmer there.”

He nods like he already mapped it.“Take spikes. The corner near the sign ices over.”

“You telling me to be careful?”

“Always.” His voice goes softer. “Text if you need help.”

I smile in response and answer “I will”.

❄

Dinner smells start leaking from the kitchen, the kind that make even staff hover for a taste. Imogen floats past with a new rota and a smile she swaps in for guests.

The evening crowd begins to build. Zane’s name gets tossed around again, the Red Frog pulling like a tide on locals and staff with energy left. I could go, but the idea of noise on top of noise makes my skin feel thin.

Harley must see it on my face. “Skip it tonight,” he says. “Take the quiet.”

“You skipping too?”

“Yeah.” He rubs his jaw, like he’s thinking through something he won’t say. “I’ve got early patrol.”

A new kind of quiet settles between us. Not the empty kind. The charged, patient kind that knows it’s holding something.

Scarlett calls out shift changes, the board gets updated, people swap places like cards shuffling into a new hand. I land at reception for the last hour of check-ins and the kind of questions that start with, sorry to bother you but. Harley drifts to the lobby to walk the perimeter with Tyler and check the boots that have been abandoned near the radiator. He comes back with a child's glove, tiny and blue, and sets it on the counter in front of me like a mission completed.

"Lost and found," he says.

"Found and found," I say back.

He leans on the counter. "You ready?"

"For what."

"Counting."

My chest loosens. "Yeah."

We wait until the flow of guests thins. I lock the drawer. Imogen takes the keys for a late arrival and gives me a nod that feels like a hug from far away.

We step back onto the decking. Night has arrived for real. The sky's so dark it feels like it could rub off on you. The snow's smoothed out, like no one's touched it in hours.

He points up. "Pick your spot."

I pick the edge of the roof, the faint smear of cloud, the dark cut of the spruce, the blinking light on the antenna, the single bright point that might be a star or a plane pretending. I fix my eyes and let the rest blur.

We go through the motions again in the same order as he taught me earlier. He squeezes my hand once, lets go, and walks inside like it didn't mean anything. Which makes it mean more. I sit for another minute and do the exercise by myself, five, four, three, two, one, just to prove I can. It makes the world the size of a moment I can hold.

Back inside, my heart's loud in the good way. I get what Mum meant now, about looking up. I'm doing it. And he's right there, counting with me.

CHAPTER 8

'Twas the week before Xmas

LOLA

It's our first proper full day off in weeks, me, Imogen, and Sarah, and somehow we've escaped the chalet hotel without anyone yelling about towels, transfers, or the sacred disappearance of rosé. The shuttle drops us on Magic Avenue for the End of Year Celebration parade and for a second it feels like we stepped into a snow globe someone keeps shaking. The roofs wear white, strings of fairy lights stitch the buildings together like they're holding hands. Somewhere a bell rings with that neat, well-behaved sound only rich villages and postcards manage.

The Christmas market looks as though it goes on for miles and miles down the avenue. The stalls glow like lanterns. Steam lifts off copper pots and one stand sells spiced mulled wine, the woman behind it wrapped in a red scarf scattered with tiny snowflakes. Another stall piles sugared almonds into paper cones and hands them over like tiny heaters. A third has candied orange slices that catch the weak sun and look like stained glass you could eat. A violinist plays Silent Night slow and deliberate, the way a careful person might step across ice.

It's stunning, and I fall in love with it instantly.

"Right," Sarah announces, yanking her beanie down while a curl springs free anyway. "First stop, food. Second, hot chocolate.

Third, unfiltered gossip. Questions welcome, critiques will be ignored."

"Fourth," Imogen says, eyes on a rack of knitted socks. "You making a tit of yourself in front of ski patrol again?"

"I'm aiming higher this year," Sarah says. "Paramedics only, ski patrol is so last season."

I laugh, and a little of the weight loosens.

We follow the smell of pastry to a pretzel stand, the pretzels look indecent, huge, coated in glossy butter, the salt crystals look like tiny planets. The man behind the counter looks as though he just stepped out from his day job as a circus ringmaster. He's wearing a red tail coat, black top hat and a handlebar moustache. We don't buy any though, just breathe the amazing scent of them into our lungs, because Imogen, our resident event planner, booked us a table in a little restaurant she tells me I just have to try.

A kid in a blue snowsuit spins with both arms out and almost knocks into a display of Christmas decorations. His mum catches him just in time and shoots us an apologetic look. I grin back, a reflex I'm learning here. People bump, you keep moving.

We drift to the cocoa stand, the man running it reminds me of a retired wizard. He stirs a long wooden spoon in an old copper pot and pours thick chocolate into cups dropping two marshmallows on top like he's blessing them. The first sip is a full-body exhale, my shoulders immediately go down without permission.

Imogen watches me over her cup. "You're doing that thing again."

"What thing?"

"The silent spiral." She tips her head the way she does when she wants me to cut the performance. "Spill."

"I'm just tired, but happy," I insist, because that's the easy answer. I look into the cup like it might give me a better one. "Okay, I'm not just tired."

Sarah rubs my arm, but Imogen doesn't push. She just waits and lets the space exist. It feels like a safe pocket in a noisy market.

"I think I'm in a weird place," I confess finally. "With someone."

"Harley," Sarah says, no hesitation.

I blink. "That obvious."

"He looks at you like he's seconds from falling," Imogen says.

I take my woolly hat off shoving it in my pocket. "It's complicated. And there's something else I haven't told anyone."

They go still the way people do when something wild sits on their palm and they don't want to scare it.

"I haven't slept with him," I say. "I haven't slept with... anyone."

Nothing in either of their faces turns smug or surprised, the quiet that lands is soft.

"Thanks for saying it," Imogen says, and it's not nothing, hearing it put like that.

"I feel late," I admit. "Like there was a sign-up sheet and I never got the link. Like I'm outside the party looking for the door."

"There's no deadline," Imogen says. "No checklist, no prize for pushing through fear. Anyone worth sharing it with will treat it like an honour."

The words knock at a locked place under my ribs, I don't open the door yet.

"I'm scared," I say. It sounds young even to my own ears.

"Of course you are," she says. "It's a big thing."

"It feels like I've got a neon sign over my head that says inexperienced and terrified."

"You don't," she says gently. "You've got a sign that says careful with what matters. That's not a flaw, that's a boundary."

The violinist switches to O Come All Ye Faithful and somehow sharing my secret with these two amazing women, lifts another layer from my chest, which makes me smile. Sarah clears her throat.

"Mine was back home in Edinburgh in the back of a Ford Fiesta with a guy called Zach," she says. "He cried after."

"What."

"Yeah, he sobbed like a toddler."

I snort cocoa and cough it back down. Imogen actually wheezes and has to pretend she didn't. Sarah looks proud of herself for making us laugh.

We loop the market more slowly, a stall of handmade candles lures us in. The woman talks about wicks like no one's ever lit one before. Imogen buys one that smells like pine and Sarah picks one called Midnight Snowstorm, which seems to annoy her. I pick up a tiny tin labelled Library and put it down again because it smells like my Mum reading under a lamp while I did my homework at the kitchen table. The memory is soft and bright; it hurts and heals at the same time. I inhale it once more and leave the tin for a stranger to buy.

We stop at a table with thin silver chains and charms, stars, tiny skis, a mountain outline. My fingers go to my own necklace without thinking.

"Nice necklace," Harley had said that time on the deck. *"You wear it every day."*

I rub the edge with my thumb and the movement settles me like a hand on my back.

A little boy at a wooden toy stand can't decide between a red or green truck. He keeps picking one up, then the other, face serious with the work of choosing joy. His dad laughs and says pick with your eyes closed. The boy squeezes his eyes shut and stands there too long with both hands hovering. I laugh too, and he peeks one eye at me, guilty and delighted.

At the edge of the market, I spot a stall selling picture frames, some cheap, some cracked, some trying too hard. I walk over when one catches my eye. Pale wood, a little weathered, like it's held something important before. I don't overthink it. Just picture the photo I brought with me, the one of Liam and me taken the week before his deployment. I'm sixteen, he's nineteen, in uniform and trying to look brave. I'm not smiling in it. He is. It's the last one we ever took. I buy the frame, tuck it in my bag like it might fall apart if I hold it too long, and rejoin the girls before I say something stupid like *I miss him* out loud.

The girls chat animatedly at the side of a small rink that has been set up on a deck with a low rail. A dozen kids shuffle on rental skates like penguins. A teenager who thinks he's hot stuff glides too close and wipes out in a smooth split, he pops up and bows. Everyone claps, and I find myself clapping too.

When we reach the restaurant, the windows are fogged. The roof is held up with wooden beams like old ship rigging. The door shuts and the warm air moves over my face, everything inside glows yellow and soft. The counter holds tarts and quiches and little stacks of sugar like treasure. The waitress finds our reservation and leads us over to a corner booth with cushions that have probably heard decades of gossip.

We order like people who decided to be decadent for an hour from the smiley waitress. Croque-Monsieur. Quiche. Carafes of coffee and small bowls of hot chocolate with thick cream. A plate of pastries appears because Sarah is persuasive when hungry.

Imogen sets her cup down and looks at me in that steady way she has. "Now tell us the truth about the weird place."

"I just... want it to be with someone who actually sees me. Not some idea. Just, me. The real me."

"Then you already know the shape of it," she says.

"And I want it to be safe," I say. "But not boring."

"Safety isn't the opposite of heat," she says. "It's the thing that lets you stop performing and actually feel it."

Sarah chews, swallows, shrugs. "It's better if you can just let go. That's my big life lesson, apparently."

Imogen flicks a crumb at her. "Here's the deal, protection first. Location matters, somewhere that doesn't scream 'my mum might walk in.' And if he's any good for you, he'll go slow. If he doesn't, punch him in the throat and call me. I'll bring wine."

I laugh with them, clutching my mug like it's proof my hands don't shake. Snacks, hydration, coffee ratios, it's so ordinary I almost forget what's twisting inside me. Almost. Because under all their jokes, I can hear it, they want me safe. And the thought sneaks in before I can stop it, safe doesn't sound like Harley, but wanted does.

On our way back to the chalet hotel we pass a novelty stall. Imogen finds a snowman hat with button eyes and a carrot nose and sticks it on my head, she laughs so hard that snot comes out of her nose.

"Get this for Harley," she says when she recovers.

"No," I say, tugging it off. "You deliver it."

"He'll be thrilled," she says, which is her code for I'm doing it anyway. She buys it and hands it to me as if I agreed.

Sarah finds socks that say GIRLS WHO SLAY SKI SEASON and buys three pairs without consulting us. "Unity," she says. "In fuzzy form."

The staff lounge is chaos, all elbows and voices, and I can't help wondering who's actually running the chalet if half the crew's hiding in here. Blankets lie in heaps, casualties of staff naps and hangovers. Within arm's reach there are at least three abandoned chocolates, half-eaten and melting into their wrappers. Hygiene's optional in here. Tyler and Niko are sprawled on the beanbags arguing about whether Die Hard counts as a Christmas movie. Tyler says no, because rules. Niko says yes, because vibes. Ash perches on the arm of the sofa like a smug cat, watching them like he's above it all.

Harley's lying on a mountain of pillows, arguing with Ash about Love Actually like it personally offended him.

"I'm just saying," he says, pointing a popcorn bag at him. "It's emotional hostage taking dressed as festive cheer."

"It's a classic," Ash says. "You're dead inside."

"Possibly," Harley says. "It's still manipulative."

I step into the room; his eyes find me and he offers a small smile. The look lands like a hand on my pulse, steady and sure. I move toward the cushions and sit beside him. Our knees touch and he shifts just enough to make room for me and not an inch more. He doesn't reach, doesn't crowd, just watches my face the way people watch the first five seconds of a snowfall, to see if it'll stick.

"We brought you a present," I say.

His mouth curls. "Should I be scared?"

Imogen tosses the snowman hat at his chest. "Deeply."

He catches it, looks at it, looks at me and a grin edges in. "This is revenge for the mistletoe thing, isn't it."

"No comment," I say, and make the mistake of noticing the way his shirt stretches across his shoulders when he laughs. I look away at once and pretend the remote control is fascinating.

Sarah falls into the other side of the cushion pile and starts a running commentary on the film options. Niko disappears and returns with a bowl of clementines and a declaration that vitamin C is sexy. Ash snags one and throws another to Harley with a lazy arc. Harley catches it one handed without looking. Of course he does.

The noise breaks up into little pockets of chatter. Scarlett comes into the room, she and Imogen discuss tomorrow's rota with the kind of diplomacy usually reserved for peace talks.

Harley leans a little closer and drops his voice like this is just for me. "You good."

"I am," I say, and for once the answer is true.

"Market was decent?" he asks.

"Good cocoa," I say. "And Sarah revealed a backseat tragedy."

"I don't want to know," he says, then adds, "I do, but later."

"You'll regret it."

"I regret most things," he says softly.

Ash elbows him like brothers do when the tone shifts. "Tell her Love Actually is manipulative again."

Harley tosses a clementine at his head with tender accuracy, he catches it and pretends it hurt.

Imogen slides into the cushion pile and shoves the hat at Harley again. "Wear it."

"I'm an adult," he says, The hat goes on his head anyway because she makes it look inevitable, button eyes stare at me. The carrot nose points slightly off centre. He looks ridiculous and somehow even more dangerous, which is unfair.

"Stunning," I say. "Terrifying."

He tips an imaginary brim. "Ma'am."

The film goes on, the room settles, so I lean back and let the edges of the day soften. At some point I notice my body isn't braced for impact. My breath comes steady. That used to be rare. Maybe it still is. I let myself have it anyway.

My phone buzzes. I pretend I don't notice. Harley does. "What, ignoring all your other boyfriends for me?"

I snort. "Yeah, that's exactly it."

But the way he looks at me makes the joke feel less like a joke.

Niko announces, holding up his phone. "Snowjob Squad, Lola edition. Favourite market stall, hit us. Jack and Sophie are missing out."

I roll my eyes and type.

Me: Wizard cocoa.

Niko: Correct answer.

Tyler: Incorrect. The waffle stand.

Imogen: The sock stall saved our souls.

Sarah: Paramedics were unavailable for flirting. I consider this a structural failure of the market.

Harley sends nothing. He never hits the chat unless it's necessary. I don't look at him to see if he's reading. I can feel the weight of not needing to know.

Sarah falls asleep and snores into a cushion like a small chainsaw. Imogen puts a blanket over her even while calling her a disgrace. The film ends and more arguments flare about the best Christmas film. Someone says The Holiday, someone else says Elf, Tyler says It's A Wonderful Life in that dry way that makes everyone groan because of course he does. Ash quotes something emotional in a deadpan voice and ruins it.

I slip out to the corridor seeking air for less than five minutes and lean my head against the cool wall. The quiet out here is the building's real voice. Pipes, radiators. The sound of footsteps. I check my phone and see Dad's name twice, then a third time, then the little red number in the corner like a warning siren. I mute the thread and put the phone away. Not a forever decision, just a tonight decision.

The door opens and Harley steps out. His eyes hit mine, and something in him eases before he moves closer.

"You good," he asks again softer.

"I am," I say. "I muted him."

"Ahhh," he says, raising a brow. "So the text wasn't from a desperate ex then. Your Dad?" he asks.

I nod once.

"Do you want me to walk you up later," he asks.

"Okay," I say, and pretend that's all I want when it isn't.

We go back in. Everything's the same. The hat's still there. I don't know if I want to laugh or cry, so I pick laugh and save cry for later.

Imogen kicks off charades because she's a menace. Ash refuses until she threatens to text his sister, then caves with a glare that promises revenge. Tyler turns out to be freakishly good at it, doing Titanic with two fingers and a doomed expression that makes us all yell it at once. Niko follows with Mamma Mia like he's been training for the role his whole life. Then Harley pulls a slip, reads it, and shakes his head like he already regrets being alive. He frowns, does that tight little smile, taps his chest and points toward an invisible arrivals board. Ash groans out "Love Actually," then immediately swears he hates himself.

Harley points at Ash with satisfaction, then at me like he knew I'd appreciate the petty.

I do.

Later, people peel off to bed in ones and twos. Niko collects mugs, Tyler rewinds the extension cable he will take out again in the morning and puts it in the exact place it lives. Sarah kisses my cheek and says unity in fuzzy form and points at the sock packet like we made a pact with cotton. Imogen squeezes my hand and doesn't say anything. She doesn't need to, she looks at my face like it's proof I'm doing better, clearer, more natural.

Harley waits while I help Tyler stack the last glasses on a tray. He doesn't hover, he doesn't vanish, just leans on the doorframe his t-shirt riding up showing his six pack. I unconsciously wipe my mouth with the back of my hand, and he smirks pulling it down to his waistband when he sees me looking. Shit. When I turn to leave he falls into step at my shoulder.

The service corridor's quiet except for the echo of laughter drifting down the back stairs, cold air clinging to the walls. At my door, he halts, like he's reached an invisible line neither of us is sure we should cross.

"Night, Lo," he says shoving his hands into the front pockets of his jeans.

"Do you like your hat?" I ask.

"It's powerful," he says nudging the carrot nose with one finger.

"Sleep," I tell him.

He tips his chin. "Text if you need to."

"I will," I say, and I mean it.

He doesn't move for a second, like he's making a note in a file only he can see. Then he steps back and walks away quietly. He never pushes. I stand at my door, hand on the handle, and watch him slip into the room next to mine.

Inside, the room holds its small, honest warmth. I put the socks on the chair. The star at my neck is cool under my fingers, I drop onto the bed and breathe. I don't cry, don't write in my journal, I just let my mind float like those flakes in the square that took their time arriving and then decided to stay.

My phone is a small brick face down on the desk. I'll respond to my dad when I'm ready. I drink water and get ready for bed.

Tonight, I'll let the version of me that doesn't apologise for wanting to feel safe stay. I curl under the duvet and think about nothing in particular until the nothing becomes sleep. The last thing I see are the socks on the chair, staring at the ceiling like it knows a secret. The last thing I feel is the ghost of a knee against mine, steady and unhurried, like a promise that doesn't need words yet.

CHAPTER 9

Love and Missing

LOLA

I wake before everyone else.

The sun hasn't even thought about showing up yet, just a pale blue bruise bleeding into the edge of the sky. The kind of early where the air feels thick, like it's holding something back. The chalet hotel's dead quiet, that heavy, padded kind of silence that makes you want to move slower so you don't disturb it. Just stillness.

I pull a jumper over my pyjama top, the wool scratchy at the cuffs, and grab my UGG boots on the way out. I don't put them on yet. Instead, I pad barefoot into the hall, the boards are icy under my feet, biting until my toes curl. The cold steadies me. At least this is a choice I get to make, unlike everything else. It's my second Christmas morning without Liam's name in my phone.

I don't go looking for it, but it's there anyway, like muscle memory. Two years ago we'd swapped voice notes before breakfast. His came with the background noise of base camp, wind whipping at the mic, someone shouting off to the side, and his voice cutting through, warm and rough. "Turkey's crap, tell Dad to stop being a dick." A laugh at the end like he knew he'd made my day just by being himself.

I move past the bar, fairy lights still glowing in their lazy loop, past reception where the counter's empty but smells faintly of polish from last night, until I reach the little nook behind the staff lounge. It's small and out of the way, and the window there frames the dark line of trees and the pale slope that'll wake up when the sun hits it.

I drop onto the sofa and pull my knees to my chest. The leather's cold through the flannel of my PJs. I press my heels into the seat, enough that it aches in a satisfying, grounding way. The air smells of laundry soap from the dryers and the ghost of woodsmoke drifting in from the lounge.

I let my eyes sting without letting the tears fall. Not yet.

He'd have loved this. The chaos, the bad jokes, the paper crowns sliding down people's foreheads. He'd have been up first, stealing bacon from the pan, winding everyone up before coffee. Flirting with Imogen until she told him to piss off, then making her laugh five minutes later. Getting Tyler to do shots by ten. Calling me "Lolly Lola" in front of everyone just to see me glare. He'd tell me these reindeer PJs make me look like a Christmas disaster and then keep smiling like he couldn't believe he got to have a sister like me.

The lump in my throat swells until I can't swallow it down. I rest my forehead on my knees.

A memory slides in uninvited, us as kids, creeping downstairs before Mum was up. Me in one of his old T-shirts, him in socks that didn't match. The two of us whispering like we were in some spy mission as we tried to peek at the presents without touching them. He'd swat my hand away every time I reached, like it was his job to keep me out of trouble and also the one daring me into it. Mum would come in with bed hair and a Santa mug, pretending she hadn't been listening from the stairs. Liam would always get the first present open because I let him.

I lift my head and look out at the dark trees. My voice is a whisper I'm not sure is sound at all. "Merry Christmas, Liam."

For a second, in the stillness, I feel him. Or maybe I just want to. Either way, I stay there, curled up on that sofa, letting the grief settle like snow instead of trying to sweep it away.

I stay there until the quiet changes. It's subtle at first, the faint creak of a door, the shuffle of socks on the hall floor, a low laugh that could only belong to Tyler before coffee.

By the time I wander into the staff lounge, the room's halfway awake. Someone's dragged the tinsel off the dartboard and looped it around the curtain pole. The little plastic tree's leaning worse than last night, its crooked gold star about one sneeze away from falling. Mugs of hot chocolate, the real kind, thick and heavy with cream are scattered across the coffee table between scraps of wrapping paper.

Everyone's still in pyjamas and jumpers, hair rumpled, faces soft in the morning light. Niko's wearing an offensively festive robe, red velvet with white trim like he mugged Father Christmas in the hallway. Imogen's got her hair piled on top of her head, strands already trying to escape.

Ash stands by the pile of gifts like he's hosting some low-budget awards show.

"Tyler, from Imogen," he calls, tossing a badly wrapped box across the table.

"Harley, from Lola."

My stomach tightens. My hands twitch like they're looking for something to hold.

Harley's in the corner, long-sleeved tee pushed to his elbows, tattoos curling across his forearms. His hair's damp, like he barely towel-dried it, and his blue eyes cut through the chatter when he looks up at me. He glances at the tag, then back to me. No smile. Just that steady look that makes it hard to breathe right.

He tears the paper slowly, like he's not in a rush to get it over with. Opens the box.

The dog tag and silver chain sit there on black velvet. The front is engraved *2009*, the year his mum died. On the back, four words: *Still standing. Still here.*

His thumb skims over the engraving once, twice. The muscle in his jaw jumps once before he smooths it out. The room noise dulls, just for me, and I wonder if anyone else notices how still he's gone. He doesn't say a word, doesn't need to. When his gaze meets mine again, there's something heavy in it.

Out of the corner of my eye, I catch Imogen pausing mid-sip of tea. Niko raises his brows at Tyler, who pretends to study his present but isn't fooling anyone. Sophie's chewing her lip like she's trying not to scowl. Even Sarah, who's usually unflappable, tilts her head like she's seeing something she didn't expect.

Tyler clears his throat, cutting the tension.

"Alright, Nash. You opening hers or what?"

Harley blinks, like the rest of them reappear all at once. He stands, shoves a hand in the pocket of his joggers, and comes over to me.

The box he hands me is wrapped in deep green paper, tied with gold twine. His voice is low. "Here. Hope you like them."

I open it carefully, like the paper might matter later. The lid clicks open, and inside are delicate gold huggie earrings. One has a tiny star charm.

"You remembered," I say before I can stop myself.

He shrugs, a faint curve to his mouth. "You told me about your mum's star necklace. Thought you should have something that matches."

For a second, I'm caught between wanting to laugh and wanting to cry. "My ears aren't even pierced."

"That's why there's a voucher inside," he says. "Figured you might want to do it here with Imogen and Sarah for backup. Or not. Just thought... if anyone deserves to shine, it's you."

Something in me wants to step back, make a joke, break the eye contact before it pins me down. My old reflex, don't give them the whole truth. Keep it light. But I hold still.

"Oh for God's sake," Sophie groans. "I swear I just got a cavity. Do you two even hear yourselves?"

Niko laughs. Tyler makes a gagging sound. Imogen chucks a cushion at Tyler's head. Jack just looks at the floor like there's something fascinating in the carpet fibres.

After breakfast, Harley pulls me aside in the corridor as everyone peels off to get ready for work.

"You okay?" he murmurs, voice low enough that it barely carries.

I swallow. “Yeah. You?”

“Yeah.” His hand comes up, slow and deliberate, tucking a strand of my hair behind my ear. Then he leans in and brushes his lips against mine, just once, light enough to leave me reeling.

I blink up at him, my heart thundering.

“I didn’t say thank you for my present,” he admits softly. “Was a bit... overwhelmed.”

My mouth curves without meaning to. “I didn’t either, for the same reason.” I blow out a shaky breath, and he still hasn’t stepped back. We’re just... there, caught in it, eyes locked like we’re both holding something we’re not ready to say out loud.

“I loved them,” I whisper. “Thank you.”

His gaze drops briefly to my mouth, and I have to drag myself back to reality before I do something stupid, like pull him into the nearest storage cupboard. “I should go get changed,” I say, forcing a breathless little laugh. “If I’m late, Imogen’ll have my head. Literally.”

He nods once, thumb brushing against my jaw before he lets his hand fall. “See you later, yeah?”

“Yeah,” I breathe, softer than I mean to.

❄

Christmas or not, we’re still on shift. The lodge doesn’t pause for holidays, plates still need carrying, glasses refilled, faces smiling until my cheeks ache. By midday the whole thing blurs into one long performance, me laughing at jokes I don’t even catch.

By the time dinner’s over and the guests wobble back to their rooms, full of wine and fondue and their own self-satisfaction, the rest of us collapse into the lounge like we might never get up again. My feet are screaming, my back’s a tight knot, and if someone asks me for *one more thing*, I’m actually walking straight into the snow barefoot and letting hypothermia decide my fate.

The board games come out and the mood shifts instantly, the exhaustion from dinner dissolving into low-grade chaos. Someone spikes the hot chocolate with Baileys, Sophie, obviously, and the first mug hits harder than expected. Before long, the Uno tournament kicks off and the yelling follows.

Accusations of cheating fly like snowballs. Tyler and Niko are locked in a death match over whether a draw four can be stacked, both swearing they've read the official rules. Imogen, pretending to be above it all, sips her spiked chocolate with the calm of a queen… right before she plays the dirtiest hand of the night.

It's ridiculous. Loud. Messy. But for once, it's the safe kind of chaos, the kind that doesn't demand anything from me except to just… be here.

I slip out onto the decking when the noise gets thick.

The cold hits hard, sharp enough to make my eyes water. My breath comes out in visible bursts, hanging in the air before the wind steals them. The railing's metal bites into my palms. Snowflakes drift in lazy spirals, settling on the wooden boards and in my hair.

The door opens behind me, soft and certain.

Like he's my magnet, Harley steps out, closing the door quietly. His breath plumes in front of him as he comes to lean beside me. We don't say anything at first. The snow settles into his lashes, tiny white sparks against the dark.

Silence folds around us, thick with things unsaid.

His hand covers mine on the railing, thumb brushing once. The warmth of his skin against the metal bite is a shock.

He leans in, forehead almost to mine, and every old reflex in me says to retreat.

"I'm scared," I whisper.

"Of what?"

"This. You. Me. All of it."

His eyes close briefly, like my words hit him somewhere unguarded. When they open, they're softer. "Me too."

"I don't want to mess this up," I add.

"You won't," he says, and there's a small tremor in his voice now, like keeping it even costs him. "And if you do, I'll still be here."

The stars are faint behind the snow clouds, but it feels like the night's holding the two of us in place.

For the first time in a long time, I don't feel alone.

❄

It's Boxing Day, and I'm back on shift when I bump right into Niko in the lobby.

"My star returns," he says.

"Don't start," I tell him, but I'm smiling.

He kisses the air near my cheek and steals the crust of the toast I'm carrying. "Miserable," he says, and grins when I try to smack his hand.

Tyler slides in behind him with the iPad under his arm and a face that says he's already checked three schedules and solved two problems in his head. "Morning," he says. His voice is still sticky with sleep.

"Morning," I say.

Imogen appears with a scarf looped around her neck even though we're inside. She bumps her shoulder against mine as she reaches for a mug. "You look rested," she says in a low voice only for me.

"I feel rested," I say. It's true and also fragile. I hold it like a glass thing I want to keep.

She nods like she already knew. "After shift, come with me to town," she says. "We'll pierce those ears. Voucher redemption day."

I laugh before I can help it. "You're not coming near me with a needle."

"I won't do it," she says, lips twitching. "I'll hold your hand and talk rubbish while someone qualified makes holes in your head."

"Tempting," I say, and mean it more than I thought I would.

The room fills and the day begins to stack itself. We speak in short, efficient sentences. Milk delivery at nine. Coach at ten. Two families want early lift passes. The Belgian group needs gluten free for dinner. The coffee machine cries for attention. We move around each other like we've practiced, and we have.

On my way for my break, I pass the big lounge window. The slope is waking up, the first lights of the lift swinging like stars on a line. For a heartbeat my chest pinches with that child memory again. Me and Liam in the half light, socks sliding on carpet, whispering about whether Santa had eaten the mince pie. Mum catching us and laughing with her hand over her mouth. His hand tugging mine, his palm warm, his whisper loud enough to get us caught on purpose. The picture is bright and then gone. I keep walking before I can step into the hole it leaves.

Back on reception, Niko has his customer service smile on that looks real because it is, and Tyler's pen taps a quiet beat on the wood. I slide into place and the next guest arrives like a cue. It's a steady stream. We juggle keys, questions and maps and the phone that rings like a small alarm every time I start to breathe.

The earring voucher sits in my pocket, the card warm from my leg. I touch it when I think too hard, like it's a lucky coin. His other gift sits under my skin in a different way, the idea that someone looked at me and found hope in the view. It makes me want to stand up straighter at the desk. It makes me soften when a woman with red hands asks the same question three times. It makes my voice steady when a dad huffs at his child and I imagine the sound my own father's words make in my ear. I don't carry it. Not right now.

By late morning the desk hits that quiet patch where the late risers are still finding socks. Imogen leans on the counter and watches me with the look of a cat who knows there's cream somewhere.

"So," she says.

"So what," I say, without looking up.

"The earrings," she says.

"What about them," I say, but it comes out softer than I mean.

"He did good," she says.

"He did," I say.

Her mouth curves. "You going to pretend you don't want me to hold your hand," she says. "Or are we skipping to the part where you let me book this in for lunch, and then you swear at me for thirty seconds while I tell you a story about a man who tried to propose with a Haribo ring."

I snort before I can stop myself. "Book it," I say, and her eyes brighten like it's her birthday.

Guests start to pool at the doors, zipped and padded and clumsy with gear. Harley walks in from outside, the kind of stride that says the day is already under his skin. Snow catches in his hair like confetti that forgot the party ended. He's talking to Ash, hands describing a run in the air, shoulders loose in a way that makes something in me ease without permission.

He looks over, like he felt the look before he saw it. The small smile surfaces, that quiet one that belongs to mornings and empty corridors. It lands in my chest in the same place it landed last night. I give it back without thinking, a soft thing, a yes without words. He tips his chin, then turns back to his conversation, the line of his mouth still set like he has a secret he's willing to keep for the both of us.

Lunch comes fast. Imogen forgets to forget about the piercings and drags me to town in a gap between guest needs.

The shop smells like alcohol wipes and cheap perfume. The girl behind the counter is bored and kind. I sit in a chair that has seen too many teenagers dare each other to be brave and squeeze Imogen's fingers like the world might fall through the floor. The sting is bright and quick and makes my eyes water on reflex. The second ear is worse because I know how much it'll hurt. I laugh at myself while I am crying, which is a talent I didn't know I had.

Imogen dabs at my eyes like I'm a flower that needs tending. "You survived," she says. "You look beautiful. You always did. Now strangers will be forced to admit it out loud."

Back at the chalet, the afternoon runs on rails. A family returns with a ski boot emergency. I kneel on the floor and help a child untangle a strap while her mother says sorry five times. The child's face is red from the cold and she tells me she fell but it wasn't scary, it was like a game. I think about falling and all the times it was a game until it wasn't. I tell her she's brave in the way that doesn't sound like a line.

Footsteps stop at the doorway. Harley leans on the frame, one shoulder propped, hands in his pockets. His eyes do a quick check of my face and then settle on my ears.

"You got your ears pierced," he says walking over to stand in front of me now.

"Yeah, I didn't really have much of a choice, Imogen made the appointment and dragged me," I say grinning.

"They look beautiful on you, Lo," his breath hitching for a second. "Did it hurt?"

"Like a motherfucker," I say, giggling. "But only for a beat," I reassure him.

He smiles again. "I knew they'd look good. I have to get back out to the slopes, so I'll catch you later, yeah?"

And then he's gone, and I can breathe again, because that boy knocks the air right out of me when he smiles at me like that. But I'm not naïve. I know nothing is fixed forever because of one snowy night, a pair of earrings and a word that lit a lamp inside my chest. I know my dad will text again and the old reflex will flare and I'll have to choose myself more than once. I know Jack will find a way to be a problem. I know grief is patient. I also know this. I'm allowed to feel held without proof. I am allowed to let hope sit next to fear and not kick it off the bench.

I breathe in. I breathe out. I do my job. I let love and missing sit side by side without fighting. I'm still standing. I'm still here.

CHAPTER 10

First Tracks

HARLEY

I spot them before I'm even through the doorway.

Lola's curled into the corner of the staff lounge sofa, legs tucked under her, cheeks still flushed from the morning shift. There's a pen twisting endlessly between her fingers, like her body's restless even when her head's somewhere else entirely. But her eyes flick toward Jack every so often.

And he's leaning in. Too close. Wearing that smug, grease-slick smile he saves for girls who haven't figured out yet what's underneath it.

I already know what he's doing before I even hear him speak.

"I could take you out on a green this week," Jack says, voice pitched low like he thinks he's charming. "Easy slope. Just one-on-one. I've done it loads."

The muscles in my jaw tick once, hard. I stop by the kettle, let the whistle of steam fill the pause, and watch. I want to see what *she* does.

Lola doesn't flinch. She just raises a brow without even looking straight at him. "You mean teach me to ski?"

Smart girl.

Jack shrugs, tries for casual, but his eyes are already checking to see if she's buying it. "Yeah, why not?"

"You're not allowed to instruct though, right?" she says, head tilting, voice soft but edged. "Don't we have, like, professionals for that?"

There it is, the stumble. He hesitates for half a beat too long.

"I mean... it's not like your buddy's going to volunteer."

That's my cue.

I turn, leaning against the counter, mug dangling loosely from my fingers like I've got all the time in the world. "I am, actually."

Both their heads snap my way. Jack's smirk twitches into something meaner, tighter.

Lola grins, just a little, and I feel that stupid, sharp rush in my chest, the one I keep pretending I don't notice. "Aren't you too busy off-piste in the bowls?"

I shrug, deliberately casual. "I've got time tomorrow morning. Eight o'clock, if you're up for it. Staff sessions count under the buddy system if cleared through Scarlett. I'll take you."

She blinks, surprised, but she doesn't hesitate. "Okay."

Jack makes a sound like he's swallowed a sneer. I don't give him the satisfaction of a second look.

Because he doesn't get a look at all. Not at her. Not at what's mine.

The next morning, she's already outside the boot room before I even get there, bouncing lightly on her toes to keep warm. The sun's still low, a pale smear over the ridge line, the air sharp enough to bite skin.

She's dressed in a black one-piece ski suit that cinches at her waist, the kind that looks like it was designed with *her* in mind and no one else. My cock stirs instantly, a low, tight ache pressing against my briefs, and I have to drag in a breath to steady myself.

Her blonde curls spill over her shoulders in loose waves, catching the faint morning light, and she's grinning like she's been waiting for this all week. God, she's radiant. Not in an obvious way, it's subtler than that, the kind that creeps under your skin and lodges there before you even realise what's happening.

She doesn't notice the way I slow my steps, taking her in, burning the picture into my brain like I'll need it later. There's something about seeing her here, waiting for *me*, bundled up against the cold, cheeks pink, eyes bright and clear, it hits me square in the chest before it hits anywhere lower.

She's a fucking vision. And she's mine for the morning.

"Hey," she says.

"Hey. You ready?"

"As I'll ever be." She drags her teeth across her bottom lip, and I have to clear my throat before my brain continues down the wrong track.

Inside, the boot room smells like wax, cold metal, and damp nylon. I pull skis from the rack, measure them against her shoulder, then grab a helmet.

"What size boot are you?" I ask, already crouching by the shelf.

She tells me, still chattering through rapid-fire questions about bindings and flex, like if she keeps talking, she won't have space to second-guess herself.

When I help her buckle the boots, her knee brushes my thigh. She doesn't seem to notice. I do. She smells faintly of shampoo and cold air, sharp and clean, and it cuts straight through me. The kind of scent that lodges in your chest, refuses to leave, makes you wonder how close you'd have to get to breathe it in properly. My palms stay steady, but my pulse doesn't.

Outside, the slope's washed in pink light from the sunrise. The snow's fresh, untouched except for the groomer tracks. Every breath leaves a plume of white in the air. She points and giggles at the "Avalanche Risk" sign and jokes nervously.

"Those aren't jokes, Lo. Snow doesn't care if you're ready, one crack in the wrong place and it all comes down."

She blows out a long breath and grimaces.

"You sure about this?" I ask, bending to adjust her bindings.

"Nope," she says, grinning "But I'm here."

I run her through the button lift first. "Hold it between your legs; don't sit on it. Keep your skis straight. Let it pull you, don't fight it."

She laughs nervously. "You make it sound dirty."

I roll my eyes, but my mouth twitches. "Focus, Maxwell."

She nearly slips on the first try and lets out a startled yelp, but catches herself. Gritty. I like that.

At the top, the run spreads wide and soft, a beginner's dream. I talk her through stance again, "knees bent, weight forward, hands where you can see them," then glide backwards, showing her.

"Pizza to slow down," I call out. "Pressure on the inside edges, eyes forward, knees soft."

She pushes off, stiff as a board, arms locked. The scrape of her skis is rough and uneven, setting my teeth on edge.

"Relax!" I shout. "Let the skis do the work."

"I hate this already!"

"You'll hate it more if you fight it."

Something in her clicks. Her weight evens, shoulders loosen, and she stumbles into a rhythm. She even manages a turn. A laugh breaks out of her, bright, breathless, cheeks pink from the cold and the rush. It punches straight through me. I want to hear it again. I want to be the reason for it.

Then, in a blink, it's gone. Her left ski catches on a ridge with a brutal jerk, yanking her off balance. The tips cross, and she slams down hard, the crack of impact shuddering up my spine.

"Lo!"

I'm at her side in seconds, ripping out of my bindings and throwing myself into the snow. She's curled around her ankle, breath sawn short, face contorted. My stomach drops. Stupid. I should've held her longer, drilled her slower, kept her safe. I put her on this slope, and now she's on the ground because of me.

"Talk to me," I say, hands already moving to check her.

"I think it's twisted. Shit. Ow."

I pop her binding, ease the boot off carefully. There's swelling, but no obvious break.

"This is my fault," she says.

"What?"

"I pushed too hard, I knew I wasn't ready."

"No, this is on me."

"I was doing fine, I almost had it."

“And I let you hit that ridge alone, I should’ve been closer.”

“Harley.”

“Don’t,” I cut in. “I said I’d keep you safe.”

And just like that, I’m somewhere else, five years ago, concrete steps, my foster brother Robbie’s small body crumpled at the bottom, one leg bent wrong. The sound of the fall, that wet, final thud, has lived in my bones ever since. I was supposed to be watching him, supposed to stop it. The same cold weight settles in my chest now.

She tries to push herself upright. “Let me stand.”

“Nope.”

“Harley, I can walk.”

“I’m carrying you.”

“You don’t have to.”

“Let me help.”

“This is ridiculous. I hate being fussed over, I’m fine.”

“I know you’re not made of glass,” I say, softer now. “But you’re hurt, and I care, so let me, okay?”

Her eyes search mine, weighing the words. Then she sighs. “Fine. But only because it’s freezing.”

She’s lighter than I expect when I lift her, but the trust in the gesture is heavy. Her breath ghosts against my collar, uneven. She hooks her fingers into my jacket I’m sure without thinking, and I keep my stride steady through the snow. Over her shoulder, I catch movement, Jack, standing at the bottom of the slope, watching. He thinks I’m playing hero. He doesn’t know it’s the guilt that’s been riding my back since I was five.

“I radioed Ash to grab your gear,” I tell her. “We’ll get you to Scarlett.”

She rests her cheek against me, and for once, she doesn’t fill the silence. Doesn’t crack a joke, just holds on.

“You’re alright,” I murmur, low enough for only her to hear. “I’ve got you.”

And in my head, *Not again. Not ever.*

❄

I carry her through the service entrance because it's faster and warmer. Lola's fingers are still bunched in my jacket, every time I step she tightens, then eases, like she's syncing her breath to my stride.

Scarlett's already waiting by the boot room, arms folded over her white fleece, reading glasses low on her nose like she can glare better from behind them.

"What happened?" she asks, voice clipped.

"Green run. Ridge caught her left ski. Looks like a sprain," I say, easing Lola onto the bench. "Swelling, but it's not bent out of shape."

Scarlett crouches, hands practised and gentle. "Lola, I'm going to check your ankle. Tell me where it hurts the most." She works her fingers carefully along the joint, tests how far it moves. "Mm. Ligament strain, most likely. Good news, it's not broken. Bad news, you're off your feet for a couple of days."

Lola exhales through her nose. "Love that for me."

Scarlett's mouth tugs. "We'll ice it, wrap it, keep it up. Physio can see you at four."

Sophie appears in the doorway with a tray she clearly isn't supposed to be balancing, eyes flicking from Lola to me and back again. The smile she puts on is sweet with a sour aftertaste.

"Oh no, poor Lola," she sings, way too bright. "First lesson and already a damsel rescue. How... cinematic."

Scarlett doesn't look up. "Sophie, put the tray down before you decorate the floor."

Sophie sets it on the boot bench and leans a shoulder into the frame. "So, Harley, playing beginner instructor now? Thought you preferred the scary stuff."

"It was a staff session," I say, keeping my voice even. "Cleared through Scarlett."

Scarlett glances up. "It was. And he reported it properly. Thank you."

There's motion behind Sophie, Jack, hovering with that not-hovering posture, hands in pockets, jaw tight. He takes in Lola's ankle, the ice pack Scarlett has already wrapped, and gives me a look like he wants to sharpen it on something.

"You alright?" he asks Lola, tone soft, eyes not soft.

"I'll live," she says, wryly. "My pride's more bruised than my ankle."

Sophie's mouth curls. "At least you had a strong pair of arms to fall into."

"Enough," Scarlett says, not loud, just final. She tapes the elastic wrap with efficient snaps. "Lola, keep that ankle up."

Jack clears his throat. "If staff need instruction, they should probably ask someone who isn't... distracted."

"Which you're not," Scarlett says, still mild. "And this was an approved buddy session. If you've got a process concern, email me. Don't loiter in doorways."

Sophie snorts, a quick, delighted sound she tries to smother in a cough.

Jack's eyes flash. He looks back to Lola, softer again. "If you need anything..."

"I'm good," Lola says, gentle but firm. "Thanks."

He nods, doesn't move. Scarlett raises an eyebrow, teacher-sharp, until he peels off, shoulder brushing mine on purpose.

Sophie lingers. "Do you want me to... fluff your pillows?" She laughs at her own joke, then to me: "Hero of the nursery slopes. Cute."

"Don't you have a bar to run, Sophie," Scarlett says.

"On my way," she chirps, perfume trailing.

When it's just us again, Scarlett softens. "You did fine," she tells me, which from her is practically a medal. "Accidents happen, even on greens."

"Still my line to hold," I mutter.

Her eyes warm, then shutter. "Hold it by sticking to protocol, which you did. Now, both of you, out of my boot room. Lola needs a sofa, not a bench. Harley, grab two pillows from housekeeping and set her up in the lounge. Elevation, ice, paracetamol. I'll check on her in an hour."

Lola salutes. "Aye aye."

Scarlett almost smiles. "Don't make me regret being nice."

❄

I lift her carefully, her arm tight around my neck, and carry her into the lounge. The place is quiet, just the low hum of the heaters and muffled voices drifting from the kitchen. I ease her down onto the sofa, slide the pillows under her calf, adjusting until her knee's slightly bent, ankle high. She winces, then exhales, settling.

I crouch, fingers ghosting the edge of the wrap, checking it hasn't pinched. Up close, I can see the fine shake in her hands, the stubborn line of her mouth. She hates this, being still, being looked after. Hates it and endures anyway.

"You don't have to hover," she says, watching my face.

"I know," I say. I don't move.

I stand at last. Lola's gaze tugs at me, an elastic I feel in my chest. "I'll swing back after last lift," I tell her.

"You don't need to."

"I know," I say again. "I want to."

Something loosens in her eyes. She nods. "Okay."

I step into the corridor's colder air. Voices from the lounge ripple toward me, Niko complaining about the coffee grind, Tyler insisting he's using the wrong setting, Ash laughing at both of them. Normal sounds. Good ones.

❄

I slam the door behind me harder than I mean to. I've had the whole day to reflect and it hasn't got easier. The silence greets me like an accusation. My hoodie's still on the back of the chair, boots drying by the wall, gloves stiff on the radiator, everything's in its place, but none of it feels like mine. The air's dry and faintly metallic, like it's been sitting still all day. My chest feels too tight for the space.

I lean against the door and close my eyes. My palms press flat to the wood, fingertips buzzing with leftover adrenaline.

She was smiling, beaming, her cheeks were pink from the cold, her laugh bouncing off the mountain, and then she wasn't. One second she was upright, fearless, almost graceful, the next, folded in the snow like a broken thing.

I should've seen the ridge, should've stayed closer. Should've said something, anything, I was too busy staring at how fucking perfect she looked in that ski suit, thinking about the way she bit her lip, the way she made me feel like I was thirteen and clean again. Like I hadn't been dragging shame behind me like a second skin since I was ten.

I drop onto the edge of my bed, elbows on my knees, forehead resting in my hands.

The mattress groans under me, springs protesting like even it doesn't want me here.

What the hell was I thinking?

Trying to be her hero? Playing instructor like I've got some kind of magic touch that makes me less of a fuck-up? I never should've let her get on that lift. My leg bounces without me realising, heel thumping a dull rhythm into the floorboards.

There's a knock. I ignore it. Of course the door opens anyway.

"Jesus," Imogen mutters as she steps in, tossing my snowboard against the wall with more care than she's pretending to have. "You left this like a total amateur. If Niko had gotten to it first, it'd be neon green by now."

"I could have been naked," I deadpan.

She smirks and walks further in without waiting. She swings my chair around, straddles it backwards, chin resting on her crossed arms, her nails tap against the wood in a slow, even rhythm, like she's keeping herself from saying something too soon.

"Alright, tragic prince. You brooding in here all night, or just until your next existential crisis?"

"Go away, Im."

"Nope. Try again."

She studies me, that unreadable look on her face she saves for when she's worried but too proud to say it. The jumper she's wearing hangs off one shoulder, her hair scraped into a bun, understated, calm, anchoring.

"She shouldn't have gotten hurt," I mutter.

"She fell on a beginner slope."

"I was meant to be watching."

"She's not made of glass."

"She looked at me like it was her fault."

"She's also not an idiot."

"She trusted me."

Imogen sighs. "And she still does. Jesus, Harley, she sprained her ankle, she didn't die in your arms."

I rub my eyes. The skin under them burns, gritty with wind and exhaustion. "I said I'd keep her safe."

"You did. You got her down the slope, called for Ash, carried her back like she was a bloody Disney princess. You didn't leave her there to be nibbled on by bears."

I huff. Not a laugh, but close.

Silence wraps around us again, not hostile now, just familiar. Like she's waiting for me to get there on my own.

"I was five," I blurt out.

Her gaze flicks up.

"My mum OD'd. I found her, I thought... I thought if I held her hand long enough she'd stay."

Imogen doesn't speak. Just listens, her jaw shifts once, a muscle ticking there before she stills it.

"She was still breathing when I got there, and I sat there for hours, holding on, talking to her. Thinking if I just didn't let go..."

I swallow hard.

"But she died, right there on the kitchen floor."

For a split second, I hear the soft *whumpf* of Lola's skis catching, the same cold dread flooding my chest, the same useless lunge forward.

Imogen's still now, not frozen, just quiet, holding space for me, much the same as I did a few weeks ago for Lola when she had her panic attack.

"And as you know after that, it was just bouncing, Foster home to foster home. Nobody wanted the junkie's kid, nobody wanted me."

I don't realise I'm gripping my hands until I see the red marks.

"Until Ash found me."

More silence.

"And today," I say slowly, "for a second, when she hit the ground, I felt five again."

Imogen gets up, walks over, and without asking, wraps her arms around me. She smells like vanilla and something sharp, expensive. Her hug is all elbows and grip.

"I've known you for two bloody years, Harls. You could've told me sooner." Her voice is soft but firm, like she's daring me to argue. "I'm here for you. Always."

Something in my chest tightens, then shifts. I nod, not trusting myself to speak.

"She's not your mum," she says into my shoulder. "And you're not that kid anymore."

I press my face into her jumper and just breathe.

"She's got a sprained ankle. That's it, you didn't fail her, you didn't fail anyone."

"She looked at me like I let her down."

"She was embarrassed, vulnerable, probably in pain. You've been there."

I close my eyes.

"You can't control everything, Harley. That's not love, that's fear in a leather jacket."

A breath escapes me, it's shaky.

"She's going to be fine," Imogen says again. "But you? You need to stop trying to rewrite your own history by fixing someone else's."

I stare at the floor. "You should do this for a living."

"I do," she deadpans. "It's called being the only emotionally literate one in the chalet."

That gets a real breath from me. Almost a laugh.

She steps back. "Alright, I've hit my quota of emotional labour. Go check on her or go to bed, but either way, stop sitting in here like the ghost of boyfriend's past."

"Thanks, Im."

She heads to the door, then pauses and glances back. "Next time you want to spiral into trauma, try doing it in your own head, not out loud, people can hear you."

I flip her off. She grins in response, tosses a middle finger back, then leaves.

The door clicks shut. I sit there, breathing, until the quiet stops feeling heavy.

My fingers curl around the edge of the bedspread, grounding in the rough weave.

I think about Lola, her laugh, her stubbornness. The way she tried to argue with me even while she was hurt.

I didn't save my mum, but I can protect her.

Next time, I will.

CHAPTER 11

Big Dreams and Bigger Plans

HARLEY

Imogen told me once I needed something bigger than guilt to live for. She'd said it over coffee in the Sunship staff lounge, hair still wet from an early dip, eyes on me like she could see every crack I thought I'd covered.

At the time, I shrugged her off, but it stuck. Got in my ribs and stayed there, because she wasn't wrong. That's all it's been, the weight of my past and the not knowing where the hell to go after it.

And then there was Mateo.

Last summer, Sunship,

He'd shown up late to water sports training, skinny as hell, wetsuit half-zipped, muttering apologies in broken English. He was sixteen, maybe seventeen. From Madrid, and a foster kid, like me. Scarlett told me later he'd barely scraped the application process but they took him anyway because Sunship needed warm bodies in peak season.

He'd been nervous, kept wiping his palms on the thighs of his wetsuit like the ocean was scarier than anything he'd faced before. I told him to grab a paddle board, meet me at the dock.

He fell in five times before we even left the shallows. But the sixth time, he stayed up. Ten minutes later he was grinning like he'd won the World Cup.

Later in the season, I found him by the bar, telling some guests' kids how to balance, how to trust their legs, he didn't notice me watching. He also didn't notice the way the younger ones lit up when he called them "pro."

When the guests left at the end of their stay, one of the parents slipped me a thank-you card. Inside was a note. *Tell Mateo he's got something, we'd hire him in a heartbeat.*

When I told him, he went quiet, blinked fast, then he said, "No one's ever said anything like that to me before."

I've been thinking about it ever since.

Tonight my thoughts are too loud, so I grab the notebook I've been scribbling ideas in since forever, scoop up my laptop and head down to the lounge.

Ash is already slumped in his usual armchair, legs thrown wide, hoodie pulled halfway over his face, a bag of crisps resting on his stomach. Niko's here too, curled up on the beanbag with a mug of something, scrolling on his phone. They both look up as I enter.

"Jesus," Ash says, squinting, "Tell me that's not a laptop."

"It's a laptop."

"You doing admin now? Shall I fetch your clipboard and highlighters?"

"Already have them," I mutter, flipping it open.

Niko snorts. "Mate. It's midnight."

"Business course deadline. Don't get excited."

Ash peers over. "What's the topic? How to Build Your Unicorn Brand and Manifest a Maserati?"

I roll my eyes. "Something like that."

They quiet as I pull up the tabs, slides, videos, budget templates. The cheesy American dude with the square jaw and suspiciously white teeth plays on mute while I pull out my notes.

Ash leans in, frowning. "Is this... serious?"

"Yeah, been thinking about it since last summer," I say. "You remember those gap year kids Scarlett hired for the Sunship backup crew? The ones with zero experience on the water, but turned out better than half the full-timers?"

Niko perks up. "That Aussie girl who sorted the linen cupboard in, like, two hours? Total legend."

"And that Spanish guy, Mateo," I add. "Didn't speak much English, but by the end he was leading the kids' club. He was a proper natural with them."

Ash nods, getting it now. "You're talking about a pipeline."

"Exactly, a real programme. We bring in young people from underrepresented places, different backgrounds. Train them, give them roles, and let them leave with experience, references, actual skills. Ski instructing, front-of-house, chalet management. Summer stuff too, paddle boarding, boat crew, lifeguarding."

Niko lowers his mug. "You want to build something for them."

I nod. "Foundation, maybe. Summer and winter placements. Bring kids out here, train them up in resort life, Ski, snowboard, water sports. Certify them, set them up with contacts and show them how there's a life outside the postcode they got handed."

Ash straightens. "That's not just a passion project, that's a whole movement."

"It's not about movements, it's about one kid at a time."

Niko tips his mug toward me. "That's the kind of thinking that got me onto the courts. One coach. One racket."

I tap a page in my notebook. "Just need a working name, but I do have a few grant leads and potentially business mentorship through the course. I'm thinking we run a pilot with Sunship this summer."

Ash grins. "Oh, we're taking over the world now, are we?"

"Yeah, starting with Ibiza."

Niko smirks. "Harley's House of Ski and Sin."

"Please stop."

"Fine," Ash says. "Sunship Youth Foundation, it's boring, but marketable."

I scribble it down anyway.

Ash props his chin on his fist. "You doing this for you?"

I glance up. "Yeah."

Not for a girl, not for redemption. Just... because I want something that fucking lasts.

Ash watches me like he knows exactly what I'm not saying.

"Then make it count."

Niko nudges a highlighter toward me. "Here. For your spreadsheets."

"No thanks, I have my own."

We fall into easy silence again, broken only by the soft clack of my keyboard. Plans forming, slowly, tangibly for once, the future isn't some shapeless thing I'm bracing for. It's something I'm carving into shape.

Ash yawns. "If you make me write a business plan, I'm out."

"You're on mentorship."

"Better."

Niko raises a brow. "And I get what? Tennis coach-slash-event planner?"

I grin. "You're already halfway there."

Ash props a pillow behind his head. "Alright, dreamer, build your empire, but if you name it anything involving puns, I'm burning your laptop."

Niko snorts, flicking snow from his jacket. "Yeah, no 'Ski-cess' or 'Slope Squad.' Please. Spare us."

I grin despite myself. "Wouldn't dream of it."

Ash lifts an eyebrow. "Then what, Harls? You've got the idea, niche resorts, guided freeride, proper coaching, tech to match. But company names are like tattoos. You can't half-arse it."

I pace the length of the room, feeling the plan in my chest like a thing that's been waiting to be told out loud. "I want something that says movement. Breaking out. Not just another booking app or gear hire. This is about the line you take when you decide to go somewhere different. The line you break to make your own run."

Niko whistles. "Nice. Sounds dramatic. You after a TED Talk or a business plan?"

"Both," I say. "And I want it to be simple. Catchy. Honest."

Ash sits up, folds one leg over the other. "Honest is good."

Niko laughs. "Break Point?"

I shake my head. "Sounds like a crisis hotline."

"Break Track?" Ash offers. "Break Trail?"

"Trail is too pastoral. We're not carving picnic paths." I shrug. "Break Line."

There's a beat, not just because the words land, but because they land exactly right.

"Break Line?" Niko repeats, testing it. It's short. It snaps.

"Think about it," I say, leaning forward. "There's the ski line, the route you pick down a run. A good line says who you are. Then there's the line you break when you stop doing what everyone expects. Break the line between people who deserve access and places that gatekeep it. Break the line in the industry where 'this is how it's always been done' keeps people out."

Ash's face shifts. He's the one who always makes the idea human. "So it's not just about skiing. It's about changing the rules. Breaking the line that says you need money or contacts or the right surname to get in."

"Exactly." I can feel it now, the name clicking into place like a binding snapping shut. "It's disruptive, but not in the 'burn it all down' way. More like, redraw the map. Give people a new line to follow."

Niko leans back, eyes narrow, considering. "It's gritty. It's clean. It's almost poetic."

"And not a cliche," Ash adds. "No forced metaphor. It works as a verb and a brand. 'We Break Line' sounds like bollocks, but 'Break Line presents', it's solid."

I smirk. "We'll worry about taglines later."

Ash grins, throws the pillow at me and misses. "Right then. Break Line it is, unless one of you comes up with something better and you'll both owe me beers."

Niko raises an imaginary glass. "To Break Line. May it break the things that need breaking and leave the good stuff standing."

I let the name sit in my mouth for a second, taste it. It fits. It pulls at something that's been tight in my ribs since I was a kid, the idea of making a lane where none existed, of carving my own way instead of being pushed off it.

"Okay," I say, quieter. "Break Line."

Ash laughs. "Get ready for the logo requests, mate. Someone will want a mountain with wings."

"Then tell them no wings," I reply. "Simple. Strong. A line you can follow."

We hit the practical after that, the domain, the pitch deck skeleton, who knows someone who knows a lawyer, how we'll test the idea with a winter pop-up. The easy stuff. The stuff that makes the dream real.

But beneath the logistics, the name has done its job. It anchors the idea to something we all feel. A few clumsy jokes later, we're already mapping routes in our heads, talking about the first runs we'd open, the people we'd bring. Break Line is no longer just a name. It's the line we've decided to walk.

❄

The others head up to bed, but my mind is still in overdrive, so I don't go with them. The lounge is too quiet now, and my brain won't let go of it, the idea, the weight behind it, the way Ash looked at me when I said it out loud. So I grab my fleece, shove my laptop in my locker along with the notebook and head down the hill.

The Red Frog looks closed from the outside, so I cup my hands around my face and peer through the window. The lights are off, the are chairs are stacked, but there's a dim light in the back of the bar. I decide to try the front door it's unlocked. I step inside, snow crunching off my boots.

There's no music playing, no voices, just the low hum of the fridges and the faint scrape of glass on wood.

Zane's at the bar alone, his back to me. He keeps touching the same bottle, moving it, moving it back, like standing still might kill him.

I don't say anything yet, just walk in slowly, take the second stool from the end. He doesn't turn, but he knows. He always knows. "You finally gonna say it out loud?" he asks.

I drag a hand through my hair. "That obvious?"

He sets the bottle down and folds his arms, still no eye contact. "You've been walking around all week like something's digging under your ribs."

"Need your take on something."

Zane finally looks at me just once, then turns away and pulls down two tumblers.

"You drinking?" he asks.

"Not tonight, I'm leading an early group in the morning."

"Suit yourself."

He pours some Jack Daniel's. Takes a sip. Waits.

I blow out a breath, scrub a hand through my hair. "It's not just an idea, it's a plan."

He raises a brow.

"I want to set something up. A programme. For kids who didn't get lucky. Foster care, council estates, kids like I was. Bring them out here. Give them a shot."

Zane doesn't speak, doesn't blink, just rests a hand on the bar and lets the silence stretch.

"I don't want to talk about it for two years and do nothing," I go on. "I want to build it. Something real, something that matters."

He takes another sip, another pause. I fidget on the stool, drumming my fingers on the wooden bar in front of me.

"You know what it's gonna cost you?"

"Yeah."

"No you don't."

His voice is low, like he's dragging something out from his own bones.

"It'll take time," he says. "More patience than you've got, more failure than you're ready for. The admin will break your balls, and the first kid who drops out will feel like a knife to your heart."

I swallow hard. "I still want to do it."

Zane's jaw flexes, but nods once, slowly.

"Then write the plan properly, none of this scribbled napkin shit. I want to see structure, numbers, who you're targeting, how you'll find them, what you'll offer that no one else can."

I exhale. "Okay."

But before I can say any more, he lifts a finger and points it at me.

"And I don't mean a pitch deck that sounds good on paper. I mean grit, I want to see what you're building when no one claps for it, when it's three a.m, and you're still fighting for funding. Because that's what it takes."

My jaw tightens, but I nod.

Zane steps out from behind the bar, leans on the wood like he's giving a sermon, and this isn't a conversation.

"I'm not some rich guy with a saviour complex; I don't back things that feel good, I back things that work. You bring me something with backbone, something that won't fall apart the first time some kid ghosts you, and then we talk."

I blink. "So... you're saying maybe."

"I'm saying," he replies, "show me it's not just a ski season fantasy."

I hold his gaze. "Alright."

Zane studies me for a beat longer, but something in his expression shifts, just a fraction.

"Good, because if it holds up..."

Zane slides a card across the bar, not because I don't know his number, I do, but because it's different when it's in print, embossed, the official version. "This isn't mates' rates, Harls. Call me when you're ready to make it real." "And Harley?" he adds as I turn to leave.

I glance back.

"If you do this right, it won't just change their lives, it'll change yours."

"I'm fucking banking on it," I tell him in earnest.

He turns away, starts wiping down the bar like the conversation never happened.

I leave before the emotion gets too obvious, tuck the card into my pocket, zip up my fleece, and head back into the cold.

Whatever comes next, it's not about fixing the past. It's about fucking showing up.

CHAPTER 12

Collision Course

LOLA

By the time midday hits, the front desk is barely holding together. Not the kind with clattering cutlery and spilled soup, that's behind me now. This chaos is quieter, sharper. The kind that hides behind polite smiles, a constantly ringing phone, and the tight coil of dread in my stomach.

I'm at the desk, headset crackling in one ear, juggling three check-ins, two complaints, and one furious guest convinced his boots were swapped in the ski locker. Niko's out back sweet-talking someone on the radio, and I'm left smiling so hard my jaw aches. I should be focused. I'm not.

My eyes keep drifting to the wide windows beyond the lobby, where the slope winds down through thick trees. It's empty, for now, but my brain keeps painting him there... Harley.

Even though I know, thanks to the schedule, he's out on the mountain, guiding some advanced group down a black run with Ash, my traitorous eyes still scan for him. Like maybe he'll appear out of nowhere, shake the snow from his hair, and lean against the counter like he used to. Black brows perfectly framing his ocean-blue eyes, pretending not to watch me. I sigh. He hasn't looked at me in a week. Not once. Not since the accident. Not since I fell during the lesson he insisted on giving me. I'd thought it would be fine. Thought learning from the best meant I'd be safe, that if I froze or panicked, he'd be there, steady, unshakable.

But when my skis crossed on the ice and I went down hard, ankle twisting beneath me, he changed. One second, warm hands and teasing smirks. The next, stone-faced. Cold. Like he'd shut the door from the inside and turned off the lights. And I haven't known how to knock since.

The front desk phone rings for the third time in a row. I don't answer. Tyler appears in the side corridor, wearing the standard black uniform and a grin like he's hosting a party no one else got invited to. "You gonna answer that, or just let Imogen have a stroke?"

I blink. The phone's still ringing, my hands are flat on the desk, useless.

"Sorry," I say quickly, snatching the receiver. "Le Grenier reception, Lola speaking."

The voice on the other end is clipped, irate, something about a missing lift pass and an overcharge on their bar tab. I jot notes, apologise, promise to investigate, then hang up and lean back in the chair like I've just run a marathon.

"You alright?" Tyler asks, stepping behind the desk. His tone is casual, but his eyes aren't.

"I'm fine," I lie, staring at the guest log like it might write itself.

"Mmm." He leans on the counter beside me. "You've got that look again."

"What look?"

"The 'Harley's being a dick and I'm pretending not to care' look."

I glance at him. "Is that a real category, or are you just projecting?"

He smirks. "I invented the category."

Before I can answer, a woman in high-end ski gear strides up to the desk, platinum hair, expensive sunglasses perched on her head. She's got that slow, predatory grace rich women seem to be born with.

I stand. "Hi there, can I help you?"

She adjusts her gloves and studies me. "Yes, actually. My room's too warm and no one's returned my call."

"I'll sort it," I say quickly, typing the name she gives me into the system.

She watches me for a beat too long. Then says, quietly, "He's not worth it."

I look up. "Sorry?"

"Whoever he is," she says, her voice soft now. "You've got that look, sweetheart. The kind that says someone you care about just stopped showing up."

I swallow. Hard.

Before I can reply, Tyler swoops in with his clipboard. "Room 306, right? I'll call maintenance now."

She gives him a polite smile and walks off, but I just stand there, heat crawling up my neck.

"Are you alright?" Tyler asks again, but gentler this time.

I shake my head. "I just... I need a minute."

The shift's almost done when Jack corners me behind the front desk, brushing croissant crumbs from the front of his shirt.

"Hey," he says, casual as anything. "You wanna grab lunch tomorrow?"

I raise an eyebrow.

"Nothing formal. Just the crêperie by the lifts. Chill vibes, hot chocolate with whipped cream. Maybe a ski run after?"

I hesitate. "I don't know," I say, already inventing excuses I don't feel like using.

"Come on, Lo." He steps closer, not quite invading my space, but close enough to notice. "You can't let one little fall put you off, I'm not Harley, I won't push you too far."

That last line lands hard. Too deliberate.

I bite the inside of my cheek. I don't want this. But I'm tired of waiting for someone who won't even look at me. Like I'm stuck holding something fragile Harley dropped without warning.

"Alright," I say. "Lunch. Maybe something easy on the slopes after."

Jack grins, boy-next-door charming. "Deal."

But as he walks off, whistling, I already know I've made a mistake.

❄

I'm tucked into a corner of the staff bar, half-watching the others while nursing the world's least inspiring Coke. Jack's somewhere in the middle of it all, gesturing wildly, telling a story I'm sure he's inflated for drama. It should make me laugh. It doesn't.

Tyler slides into the seat beside me like he's been waiting for the moment all night.

"Hey Lo."

He's all effortless charm, olive skin still glowing from the afternoon sun, green eyes catching the low light, dark curls perfectly tousled in that I didn't try, still won kind of way. The gold chain at his neck flashes as he leans back, legs stretched out like he owns the floor.

I raise my glass slightly. "Hey."

He grins. "So, big date tomorrow?"

I freeze. "It's not a date."

"Sure," he says, amused. "Just lunch, on the mountain. With the guy who keeps calling you Lo like it's a term of endearment."

"It's not like that," I say, sharper than I mean to. "It's skiing, that's it."

Tyler tilts his head. "You planning on telling Harls that?"

That knocks the breath from me.

I recover fast. "He hasn't spoken to me in a week, pretty sure he doesn't care."

Tyler's smile fades, just slightly. "Then you'd be wrong. Dead wrong. Do you know him at all?"

I frown. "Then why is he acting like I don't exist?"

"Because he's stubborn, and proud. And pissed at himself for letting you get close."

He says it casually, but the weight of it lands like a dropped brick.

"I don't get it," I murmur. "He shut down. I was the one who fell, I was the one who got hurt."

Tyler nods slowly. "And that's exactly why."

I stare at him.

"He blames himself, Lola. Doesn't know how to deal with it, so he shuts off before anyone can blame him out loud. It's textbook Harley Nash."

"I didn't blame him."

"I know that, you know that. But he doesn't believe it, not really."

Tyler hesitates, then adds, "And this ski thing with Jack. It's not just about the slopes. It's about the fact that Jack isn't just some mate from work, he's interested. Everyone can see it, so will Harley. You skiing with Jack, will hit him in two places, protective instinct, and jealousy."

I say nothing, because everything in my chest is suddenly tight and confused and heavy.

"Look," Tyler continues, quieter now. "He's not your boyfriend. I get that. But he is your buddy in your very first season at Powder White at eighteen years old no less. That meant something. To him, that was trust, when he doesn't do that for anyone. And then you get hurt and now, instead of coming to him, you're going out there with Jack. To Harley, it won't just be 'not a date,' it will be rejection."

I try to swallow what feels like glass stabbing my throat. I take a long drink of my Coke. Tyler shifts forward, dropping the act for just a second.

"You're allowed to ski with whoever you want. But when he finds out it's Jack..."

I nod in understanding, slowly.

"Trust me, I've known him for three years, he's gonna lose his fucking mind."

My head shoots up to look at him. "You think I should cancel?"

"I think," Tyler says, rising to his feet. "You should ask yourself if you're doing it to move forward... or to get a reaction."

Then he winks. "Either way, he's gonna give you one."

And with that, he disappears into the bar crowd, leaving me cold, still, and suddenly not so sure I want tomorrow to come.

❄

I regret it the second I click into my skis. The slope isn't beginner-level, no matter what Jack promised. The incline is sharp, slick patches of ice scattered like traps waiting to swallow me whole. But I'm already here, already strapped in, and Jack's watching. I can't back out now.

"You ready?" he shouts over the wind.

"Not really!" I yell back, but I push off anyway.

It takes less than a minute to go badly.

My balance wobbles first, then my footing goes, and suddenly my body twists the wrong way. The world tilts, snow blurring white and grey as I slide. My scream catches in my throat as my hip smacks the ground and I skid until I finally stop with a bone-rattling thud.

For a second, I can't breathe. Everything burns. Everything aches.

Then I hear it.

"Lola!"

Of course it's Harley. Like I manifested him here with every reckless thought.

He's off his board in seconds, with one binding unstrapped, legs cutting through the snow. There's no hesitation, just raw, unfiltered panic. Ash shouts something behind him, but Harley doesn't slow down, doesn't look anywhere but me.

By the time he drops to his knees in front of me, my tears have already started, hot and messy against frozen cheeks.

"For fuck's sake, Lo," he says, his voice is sharp, frantic. "Are you hurt?" His hands are already on me, brushing snow from my jacket, checking limbs, finding my wrist, my ankle, my hip, searching for damage with a precision that makes my chest ache. "Where? Tell me."

"I twisted my wrist," I manage through ragged sobs. "My ankle again… and I think I hit my hip."

His jaw locks, breath hissing out like he's trying not to explode. "Can you move?"

"I… think so."

He tears his gloves off, cupping my face, his thumbs wiping my tears without thinking. His voice softens, breaking under something deeper than panic. "I've got you, Lo. I've got you."

And God, in the moment he means it.

He eases me upright, steadying me with careful hands, but when he looks past me and sees Jack finally making his way down the slope, something in him snaps.

"You absolute fucking idiot," Harley barks, standing to his full height. "This isn't a beginner run!"

"She said she was fine," Jack shoots back, palms raised, trying for innocence.

"You're not qualified to judge that!" Harley growls, and closes the distance in two strides, fists tangled in Jack's jacket before anyone can react. "You want a disciplinary?"

Ash wedges himself between them, firm but calm, like he's done this before. "Harley. Enough. I've got this."

Harley hesitates, shoulders heaving, chest rising and falling like he's holding himself together by a thread. But he lets go, barely.

Ash turns to Jack. "Inside. Now. You're lucky she fell where she did. Further up and the snow's unstable as hell."

Jack glares at us, mutters something under his breath, and trudges off.

Harley doesn't move. He's still breathing hard, fists flexing, like he hasn't fully decided not to go after him again.

I reach for his sleeve, my hand trembling. "I'm okay," I whisper, needing him to hear it.

His head drops, eyes locking on mine, tender and furious all at once. “You shouldn’t have been out there,” he says, low and tight, like he’s swallowing something sharper.

“I know.” My throat aches, tears slipping hot and helpless down my cheeks.

His jaw works, breath coming rough, like he’s holding back a hundred other words. “I would’ve killed him,” he says, softer but no less deadly. “If you’d been seriously hurt.”

“I know,” I whisper again, but it doesn’t land.

He pushes a hand through his hair, fingers locking behind his neck like he’s trying to hold himself together. His chest rises and falls too fast, like he’s still on the edge of going after Jack. He looks past me, up at the slope, jaw tight enough to crack.

“Go inside, Lo,” he mutters finally.

I hesitate, but his eyes are already elsewhere, locked on the mountain, on everything unsaid between us. He doesn’t look at me again, doesn’t follow me, just stands there in the snow, fists clenching and unclenching like he’s trying to bleed the anger out through his hands.

I limp toward the chalet, throat raw, heart hammering, knowing one thing for sure.

Harley Nash is nowhere close to done with this.

CHAPTER 13
The Line between us
HARLEY

I knock and wait for her voice, but the second I hear it, I shove the door open like I've got a right to be here. Courtesy and impulse colliding, because I'm not thinking straight.

My chest's a war drum. My jaw's clenched so tight it aches. She's sitting on the edge of the bed, foot bandaged again, jumper sleeves pulled down past her hands, and she looks up at me like I'm the last person she wants to see.

"Don't you dare start," she warns.

Too late.

"What the fuck were you thinking?" I snap.

She stands, winces, but doesn't sit back down. "Excuse me?"

"You went skiing with him? After what happened the first time? With your ankle still healing?"

Her eyes narrow. "Wow. Not even pretending to check if I'm okay first?"

"I thought I was going to find your body on that slope."

She laughs, but it's sharp and defensive. "It was a beginner's slope, not a cliff edge."

"You don't need a cliff to end up in hospital."

She snorts. "Thanks for the imagery."

"I'm serious, Lola. Do you even understand how reckless that was?"

"I know, I literally told you on the slope, but I wasn't alone."

"Oh, right. Jack the idiot waiter is your bodyguard now?"

She steps forward, shoulders squared. "He was trying to help."

"He's not qualified. You're not ready. What the hell was the plan, Lola? Just wing it until you snapped the other ankle too?"

She folds her arms. "It was my decision."

"It was a stupid decision."

"Jack's been sniffing around you since the moment you showed up," I snap before I can stop myself.

"Don't tell me you didn't see it."

That hits harder than I intended. Her mouth tightens, and for a second, she looks like she might cry again. But she doesn't. She just turns away and limps a step toward the window.

"You don't know what it's like," she mutters.

I blink. "What?"

"You don't know what it's like to feel like you're just... stuck. Like every move you make, someone's watching, judging, waiting for you to fail."

My voice lowers. "You think I don't know that feeling?"

"You act like you don't."

I pace, trying to shake the rage off, but it won't go. Not when I can still see her on the slope, twisted, scared, in pain. Not when the memory of that fall is playing on a loop in my head.

"You think I want to spend my days wondering if I'll find you crumpled in the snow again?"

Lola crosses her arms tighter, voice shaking with anger. "You don't get to swoop in when it suits you and act like you've got some claim on me. You're not my fucking boyfriend, Harley. And you sure as hell don't get to play protective when you've spent the past week pretending I don't exist."

I freeze.

She swallows. "You barely even like me, remember?" she whispers, like it costs her to say it.

That one lands like a gut punch.

"Don't say that," I manage.

"It's true. You avoid me half the time. You talk to everyone else like you're alive, and I get what? Cold glances and one-word answers?"

"You think that's because I don't like you?"

She lifts her chin. "What else am I supposed to think?"

I take a breath, but it's like trying to breathe through smoke.

"I've been trying to stay the fuck away because I like you," I say, voice rough. "Because I can't think straight when I'm around you, and it scares the shit out of me."

She blinks and something shifts behind her eyes, not softness. Not yet, just confusion. Hurt, maybe a little hope trying to survive.

I drop my voice. "I thought I was over this. Over needing people. But then you..."

My throat catches. I force the words out.

"You're not easy to walk away from."

She looks down at her bandaged ankle. Her lip trembles, and I hate myself for being part of the reason.

"You don't get to explode at me like this and then throw a confession at my feet," she says quietly.

I flinch, because she's not wrong.

"I know."

"And you don't get to act like you care only when I'm in pieces."

"I know that too."

"I needed support today, not a lecture."

"I was scared."

Her eyes flash up. "Of what?"

"Of losing you before I ever had the chance to," I say, then cut myself off.

She sees it, the truth I can't say yet.

I run a hand down my face, and breathe like it hurts. "I fucked this up again."

Lola presses her lips together. I can see the war behind her eyes, trust me or don't. Stay or go.

"I thought you saw me," she says. "I thought for once I wasn't invisible."

"I do see you, Lo. I see everything."

She shakes her head. "Then why are you so good at making me feel like I don't matter?"

I step forward. "Because you matter too much."

"Then show me."

"I don't know how."

She lets out a sound, half laugh, half cry, and sits down heavily on the bed. "That's not good enough, Harley."

I sit across from her on the bed, not too close, though. My voice is quieter now. "When I was a kid, every time I got close to someone, they either left or used me. So I stopped letting anyone in and that worked for a long time."

"And now?"

"Now you're here. And I don't want to fuck this up, but I already have."

She watches me for a long moment. "Then fix it."

I nod once, an apology, a promise.

"I will."

She doesn't say anything else. Just sits there on the edge of the bed, hands folded in her lap like she's trying to hold herself together. I don't know what the fuck to do with my hands. Or my mouth. Or my entire existence. For a second, I think she's going to tell me to leave. She doesn't, so I stay.

The silence stretches, heavy but not hostile, not anymore. Just... tired. Like neither of us has the energy left to pretend we're okay. She shifts slightly, wincing as she adjusts her ankle. I start to move, to help, then stop myself. She notices.

"You can sit properly, you know," she murmurs, not looking at me.

I stay put and wait a beat.

"Do you want me to go?" I ask, voice low.

She doesn't answer right away. Then. "I don't know."

Fair enough. I rub my thumb across the seam of my jeans, staring at the wall behind her like it's got answers written on it. "I didn't mean to yell like that."

"You did," she says, but it's not cruel. Just honest.

"Yeah. I did."

Another pause, then, softer, "I do dumb shit when I'm scared."

She finally looks at me, and it's not anger in her eyes now. It's something that might be forgiveness. Or might just be exhaustion.

"Yeah, you said... me too," she says. "But not of falling."

My chest tightens. I lean forward, pushing my elbows on my knees, voice like sandpaper. "Do you want me to stay? Just for a bit? To keep you company?"

She hesitates. I have no clue what I'm doing. I'm still fucking this up. I'm not articulate. I want her to say she wants me to stay, because fuck, I want to stay here in this room with her. I need to make this better. I don't want her to think I'm angry with her; I'm angry with Jack for treating her like a toy. I'm angry at myself for not being able to tell her how I really feel.

Then she nods, small. Barely there, but it's enough.

I shift slightly, angling toward her now, not too close, not touching, just there. The kind of silence that used to make me crawl out of my skin doesn't feel so loud anymore. It feels... necessary.

We sit like that for a while. Just two people who broke something, trying to figure out if they've got the guts to rebuild it.

Eventually, she leans back on the pillows, eyes fluttering shut like the fight's finally drained out of her. I don't move, I don't dare. I just sit there, watching her breathe, praying this isn't the last time she lets me get close.

CHAPTER 14

Smuggled Joy

LOLA

I'm not sure what time it is. The curtains are still half drawn, but pale light slips through the edges, painting soft grey shapes across the carpet. My eyes sting. My body feels bruised in places that haven't even been touched.

Harley's still here.

He's lying on his side beside me, one arm flung over his eyes like the light's too much, boots kicked off sometime in the night, his whole body stretched out like he meant to stay awake and lost the battle. There's a careful gap between us, but not much. Just enough that I'd only have to lean a little closer to breathe the same air.

And the fact that he stayed, that he's *here*, burns more than anything he said last night.

I shift carefully, testing my ankle. It throbs in warning, but the bandage holds. I loosen and retie it, wincing with every tug, like even the sound of Velcro might wake him.

He doesn't stir.

I look at him again, and something in my chest squeezes tight. He's different like this. Softer. Without the smirk, without the defences, he looks younger, not unscarred, but less weighed down by whatever he's carrying. His jaw isn't clenched, his fists are loose, though there's still a faint crease between his brows like even in sleep he can't completely let go.

Before I can stop myself, my hand moves. I brush a strand of hair from his forehead with the lightest touch, holding my breath. He doesn't move. My fingers hesitate, then I trace the line of his jaw, slow and careful, before sliding up to smooth the crease between his brows.

That's when his breathing shifts.

His arm drops from his face, lashes fluttering as his eyes blink open, deep blue and heavy with sleep, locking on mine instantly, like he was already half-aware I was there.

For a second, neither of us says anything.

Then his gaze drops, from my face to my hand, still suspended an inch from his skin, and back up again. His voice is low and rough, cracked from sleep.

"Morning," he murmurs.

I swallow hard, my throat dry. "Morning."

His brows pull together slightly. "What were you just doing?"

Heat hits the back of my neck. "I wasn't, I was just..." I hesitate, fumbling for something less humiliating. "Your hair was in your face."

One corner of his mouth lifts, not quite a smile, but close enough to make my stomach twist. "Right," he says softly, still watching me too closely. "Just my hair."

I glance away, tucking my hands under the duvet like I can hide the evidence. "You were frowning in your sleep. Thought I'd... fix it."

There's a pause, and then his voice drops even lower, almost a rumble. "Did I look that bad?"

I chance a look at him. "No," I whisper before I can stop myself. "You looked... peaceful. It was nice."

Something flickers across his face at that, something unguarded, there and gone again.

He shifts beside me. The duvet rustles as he stretches. His eyes sweep the room, slow and curious, until they land on the photo frame I set on the bedside table a few days ago. The smile fades from his face.

"Who's that?" he asks softly, voice still sleep-rough.

I follow his gaze. The picture is of me and Liam, just before his deployment. I was sixteen, he was nineteen. His arm is slung over my shoulder, our heads tilted together, matching smirks caught in that one good shot before everything changed.

"My brother," I say quietly. "Liam."

Harley doesn't say anything right away. He just nods, eyes fixed on the image like it's giving him a piece of the puzzle he didn't know was missing.

"You look like you idolised him," he murmurs.

"I did." My throat tightens, but I keep my voice level. "He died in Afghanistan. Army patrol, roadside bomb."

Harley's gaze lifts to mine, something sharp and protective flashing behind it. "Shit. Lola, I'm..."

"It was years ago," I cut in, fast, like if I don't I'll drown. "But yeah. He was... everything."

There's a long pause. He doesn't say he understands. He doesn't say sorry again. Just sits there with it, with me. And somehow, that helps more.

For a moment, it feels like the quiet stretches between us, warm and fragile, and then he exhales slowly, rubbing a hand over his face. "About last night," he says finally, voice rougher now, words heavier. "I was... I shouldn't have yelled at you like that."

I blink, caught off guard by the softness in his tone. "You were scared," I say quietly, more an observation than forgiveness.

"Yeah," he admits, his gaze finding mine again. There's no smirk this time, no armour. "Scared out of my fucking mind, Lo. But that's no excuse."

Something twists low in my chest at the way he says it. "I shouldn't have gone with Jack," I admit, my voice barely above a whisper. "I wasn't thinking."

His jaw works, and for a second, I think he's going to argue. But instead, he just nods, slow and deliberate. "Guess we both fucked up," he says quietly.

"Guess we did."

The silence that follows is different now, less tense, but somehow more dangerous, because there's something in his eyes I can't name.

He sits up slowly, dragging a hand through his hair, but his gaze doesn't leave mine.

"Lo…" He exhales sharply, as if he wants to say more, but bites it back. He shakes his head, jaw tightening, and mutters instead, "I should go before I make this more complicated than it already is."

"More complicated?" I echo, unable to hide the edge in my voice.

His eyes lock on mine, sharp now despite the sleepiness clinging to him. "You have no idea," he says quietly.

My breath catches, but before I can ask, he's on his feet, pulling on his boots without looking at me.

"Get some rest," he says finally, softer this time, like he's smoothing out the roughness he just showed me. And then he's gone, the door clicking shut behind him, leaving the air in the room charged and unsteady.

❄

I'm halfway through rewatching *To All the Boys I've Loved Before* for the third time when the door bursts open without warning.

"Delivery for Madame Misery!" Niko announces in an outrageous French accent, arms full of snacks, DVDs, and what looks suspiciously like a bottle of wine wrapped in a scarf.

Behind him, Sarah steps in like she owns the place, already kicking off her boots.

I blink at them. "What… what is happening?"

Sarah flops onto the bed and wrinkles her nose immediately. "Why does it smell like boy in here?"

I go rigid. "It doesn't."

Niko leans in theatrically, inhales, then recoils. "Oh, it absolutely does. Eau de Masculine Angst with top notes of pine and bad decisions."

Sarah smirks. "Is that... Lynx Africa? Jesus."

"I hate you both," I mutter, snatching the crisp bag off my lap to hide the blush I can feel crawling up my neck.

Sarah grins. "So who was here, hmm? You don't strike me as the type to sweat out teenage angst solo."

"I had a visitor," I mumble.

Niko's eyes go wide. "Was it him?"

"Shut up."

Sarah gasps, delighted. "It was totally him."

"I swear to God..."

"Oh my God, did you cuddle?"

I bury my face in the crisp bag. "You're both banned. Get out of my room."

"Don't be silly 'bébé,' we're totally here for it, but now we're staging an emotional intervention," Niko says, smirking.

Sarah grins. "Scarlett told us you were under house arrest for a week. So naturally, we've decided to break you out. Spiritually, if not physically."

"Also, she said you looked like you were halfway to writing Wuthering Heights 2: Alpine Misery," Niko adds, flopping into the desk chair. "So here we are."

I try to glare, but I'm smiling before I can stop myself. "You guys really don't have to..."

Sarah cuts me off with a deadpan stare. "You're banned from saying thank you or apologising tonight. We're here. We love you. Shut up and eat your crisps."

My throat tightens in that annoying, unexpected way. I blink it back.

"What's the wine situation?" I ask, to cover it.

Niko winks. "Illegal and badly concealed."

Sarah pulls the scarf free with a flourish and holds up a cheap bottle of white. "Also, tragically room temperature."

"We'll live," I murmur, finally leaning back against the

pillows. "Please tell me you brought wine glasses. I only have the glass for my toothbrush in the bathroom."

Niko produces three glasses with a flourish from his bag, lines them up on my desk and fills them to the brim, handing one to me and one to Sarah. "We brought Easy A. Bit of chaotic good energy, by the way."

Sarah nudges me. "And I'm crashing here tonight, so you don't get any ideas about watching sad girl TikToks at two a.m."

"I don't do that," I lie.

Niko just grins. "No judgment. But we're here now. And tomorrow, if you're up for it, we thought we'd sneak into town for lunch. You know, smuggle you out before the regime notices."

I blink. "You're serious?"

"Deadly," Sarah says. "We'll get pizza. You'll hobble dramatically. Niko will flirt with the waitress for a discount. It'll be perfect."

I laugh a real one, for the first time all week. My ankle still throbs, and my chest still aches with the weight of everything I don't understand about Harley Nash... but for now, it's quieter.

I nod. "Okay. Tomorrow. Let's do it."

Niko lifts his crisp bag like a champagne glass. "To freedom."

"To carbs," Sarah adds.

"To not spiralling alone," I say, the words catching at the edges of my throat. My fingers curl tighter around the stem of my glass, and for just a second, I don't feel like the sad girl they're trying to fix. I feel seen.

They both glance at me and this time, they don't joke.

Just smile. Like they've got me.

❄

True to their word, the next afternoon starts like a heist.

Sarah distracts one of the receptionists with some elaborate story about lost guest luggage. Niko wheels me out in one of the hotel's spare luggage carts, blankets stuffed around my legs for disguise, and Tyler meets us at the corner like we're fleeing an international incident.

"Nice form," he says, lifting his sunglasses to smirk down at me. "Could've used a fake passport and a fake moustache, though."

I flip him off. He grins like I've made his day. By the time we reach the town square, I'm out of the cart and limping along with a borrowed crutch and about fifteen layers of smug encouragement from my so-called friends.

"You're like a wounded gazelle," Niko declares. "Graceful, but also very tragic."

"I hate you," I mutter, but the truth is, I've missed this. Noise, distraction, brightness. People who see me.

The restaurant's low-lit and heavy with the smell of garlic and cheese, the kind that clings to your clothes and makes everything feel a little softer than it is. We claim a corner booth, order enough food for ten people, and pretend we're not on a time limit. Tyler orders four Aperol spritzes the moment we sit down.

"Don't give me that look," he says when I raise an eyebrow. "A promise is a promise. You deserve at least one drink with a stupid straw before you die of boredom back at the chalet."

Sarah snorts. "Lola? Bored? Nah, she's got Harley Nash's mood swings to keep her entertained."

I groan, dropping my face into my hands. "Do not start."

Niko leans in with a wicked grin. "We didn't start. He did. With that look. You know the one."

The one from the decking. After the fight. The one that cracked something open and left it bleeding.

Sarah imitates Harley's scowl perfectly, folding her arms. "I'm brooding because I have feelings and no idea what to do with them. Let me lift something heavy to cope."

I'm laughing so hard I nearly knock over the spritz.

"You guys are awful."

Tyler leans back, arms stretched over the booth. "He's not awful. He's just... like a broken smoke alarm. Always going off, even when there's no fire."

I raise a brow at that.

"Look," he continues, a little softer now. "He's my mate. But he doesn't know how to handle someone like you."

I tilt my head. "Someone like me?"

"Someone who actually matters to him," he says.

That silences the table for a beat. Even Sarah looks surprised.

Tyler shrugs, unfazed. "I've seen the way he watches you when he thinks no one's looking. It's not casual. It's like he's waiting for you to disappear."

Something twists deep in my chest.

"Then why does he act like I don't matter sometimes?" I whisper.

"Because he's never had anything to lose before," Tyler says. "And that makes you terrifying."

Niko reaches across and squeezes my hand. "And also powerful."

I smile, but it's faint. "You lot really know how to cheer a girl up."

Sarah raises her spritz. "To terrifying women."

We all clink glasses.

And for a moment, in this cosy booth with Aperol in one hand and good people on all sides, I forget the bruise on my ankle, the ache in my chest, and the boy who won't stop running from both.

❄

I'm still warm from the cocktails and laughter, cheeks tingling from the cold and my friends' ridiculous jokes. But as soon as we step through the staff entrance, the mood changes. The air feels stiff. Niko's smile falters. Sarah slows beside me. Voices leak out of the office at the far end of the corridor. Scarlett's. And Ash's.

"...two weeks' suspension," Scarlett says, clipped and final. "We've got guests complaining, two documented injuries, and no qualifications. It's non-negotiable."

Ash's tone is lower, calmer. "He thought he was helping. He didn't mean to..."

"Intent doesn't override policy," Scarlett snaps. "He lied about giving her a lesson. That's gross misconduct. We're lucky she wasn't more seriously hurt. And since when have you been in Jack's corner?"

My stomach flips. Sarah sees my face and touches my arm gently. "Lo..."

"I didn't know," I whisper.

Niko frowns. "We didn't want to ruin today."

"He asked me," I say numbly. "I said yes."

They all look at me, Niko, Sarah, even Tyler who's leaning against the stairwell with a dark look in his eyes.

"He's still responsible," Tyler mutters. "He shouldn't have taken you up there."

"He was trying to be kind," I fire back. "He thought he was helping."

"And now he's suspended."

I blink hard. "I didn't mean for that to happen."

No one says anything. I turn away before they can try to reassure me. My chest is tight, my ankle throbs like it's echoing the guilt inside me, and the cocktails in my stomach suddenly feel sour.

I thought I was finally standing on my own. Instead, I knocked someone else off their feet.

❄

I'm back in my room curled under the duvet with the TV playing something I'm not watching. The laughter from earlier has faded. Niko, Sarah and Tyler left hours ago. The silence now feels like a punishment.

The knock is soft. Not urgent. Not hesitant. Just... steady.

I drag myself up and crack the door open. Ash stands there, hands in his jacket pockets, dark stubble catching the hallway light. His expression is unreadable, as always, but his eyes are kind.

"Can I come in?"

I hesitate, just for a second, then nod. Too tired to pretend I don't need the company. He doesn't sit; just stands there for a second, scanning the room like he's weighing something.

"You look better," he says gentle but steady. "Colour in your cheeks again. That's good."

"I just found out Jack got suspended," I say, not bothering to dance around it.

Ash nods. "I figured you might've."

I swallow. "Scarlett was right, wasn't she? He shouldn't have taken me out. It's my fault."

"Stop that," Ash says calmly. Not cruel, just matter-of-fact. "Your injury's not your fault. His decision to teach you off-book? That's on him."

"But I agreed to go with him."

"And he shouldn't have asked you. He only did it because he wanted to impress you. Or help you. Or maybe both. Doesn't change the fact that it was his call."

I don't reply. I just stare at the frayed edge of my duvet cover, picking at it. My knees pull to my chest like I'm trying to hold myself together.

Ash watches me, waits, then says,

"Lola... you've turned Harley inside out."

That catches me completely off guard.

"What?" I frown.

"He doesn't know who he is around you. That scares him, which means, yeah, he's going to pull back, act cold, misdirect like a magician at a kids' party."

"I noticed," I mutter, folding my arms.

Ash finally sits. The desk chair creaks under him, and he leans forward on his knees like a coach at half-time.

"I met Harley when he was twelve," he says. "Pissed off. Barely speaking. He wouldn't let anyone get close to him. Not properly."

I stay quiet. There's a lump forming in my throat again.

"He's had sex with women he didn't care about. He's cared

about people he never let in. You're the first person he's let affect him. That's not small. That's not casual. That's seismic."

I don't say anything, just pull my knees tighter, like it'll hold me together better.

My voice is hoarse. "Then why push me away?"

"Because he's terrified of hurting you. Of screwing it up. And because people like Harley… we get used to surviving. Not building."

Something shifts in my chest. Like he's cracked open a window I didn't realise was there.

"You think he cares?" I ask quietly.

Ash looks at me like I've just asked if snow falls in the Alps.

"Lola, he's breaking. He hasn't said it out loud because saying it makes it real. But he's never cared about anyone like this. And he doesn't know how to be someone who deserves it."

I blink fast, chest too tight to hold it all.

"I don't want to be a project," I whisper. "I don't want to be another thing he fails at."

Ash stands, moves to the door, then turns back and says the softest thing I've heard all week.

"Then don't be. Just… remind him what it feels like to be good."

The door clicks shut behind him.

I don't move. Just sit there, knees hugged to my chest, heart thudding like it's waiting for something that hasn't arrived yet.

He's breaking.

Ash said it like a fact, like it explains everything, Harley's silences, his sudden heat, his way of looking at me like I'm the only thing he doesn't want to ruin.

And maybe… maybe it means I'm not imagining this.

Maybe I'm not the only one waiting.

CHAPTER 15
Clean Break
HARLEY

I didn't even want to come here.

But guilt's louder than pride, and I owed her the truth. No more blurred lines. No more ghosts in the rear-view mirror. No more excuses. Sophie was a chapter I should've closed months ago, and I didn't. So now I'm here, trying to stitch up something I let rot.

She slides into the seat across from me like she's walking into a date. Hair curled, cleavage framed in a neckline designed to get her whatever she wants, and that smirk, the one that always meant trouble, dialled up to dangerous.

She already looks like she knows how tonight ends.

"Didn't think you'd ever text again," she says, flicking her hair off her shoulder like a weapon.

I rub the back of my neck, jaw grinding. "Didn't call you here for that."

Her grin sharpens, all confidence and venom. "Sure, sure. We'll talk first, and then I'll remind you what it feels like to come undone in my mouth."

I exhale slowly. "Sophie."

She leans forward, eyes locked on mine, voice low. "You think I forgot how you taste when you're worked up? The sounds you make?"

Fucking hell.

"Stop." My voice is flat. Final.

She pauses. Not because she's shocked, but because she's calculating. And then her mouth twists.

There she is. Caustic at the core.

"Wow," she says, folding her arms. "That's the tone now?"

I nod once. "I'm done. With us. With whatever the fuck that was. I should've said it sooner, but I'm saying it now. We haven't been a thing since last year and you know that."

She sits back, scoffing. "Oh, how noble."

"I'm not here to be noble. I'm here to end it."

Her mouth hardens. "Let me guess, this has nothing to do with Princess Lola? The girl you've been making moon eyes at since orientation?"

My spine goes rigid. "She's got nothing to do with this."

"Bullshit," she snaps. "You haven't looked twice at me in months. And now you wanna play the honourable card? Please."

I push my chair back slowly, blood hot under my skin. "I'm not going to do this with you. I'm trying to be decent, even if it's late. We were friends with benefits. Let's not rewrite the past. You were fucking other people, so was I. We both knew what this was."

Her laugh is cold. "You're not decent, Harley. You're just dressing it up now, trying on the costume to impress your latest conquest."

My jaw clenches. But I don't bite.

I stand. "Goodnight, Sophie."

I've barely taken two steps when the door opens.

Three silhouettes in the doorway, backlit by streetlight and snow.

And one of them is her.

Lola.

Her eyes lock on mine.

I see it all in her face, confusion, betrayal, heartbreak, fury. It hits like a fucking freight train.

She doesn't speak. Just turns on her heel.

"Lola!"

But she's already gone.

I shove through bodies and tables, ignoring Sophie's voice behind me, venom curling in the air.

Outside, the cold bites hard. I spot her up the road, moving fast. Sarah and Imogen are chasing her, trying to talk her down.

"Lola!"

She doesn't stop.

I take one step toward her, then freeze. Sophie's voice drips from the doorway like poison.

"So much for being decent."

I don't answer. I won't give her the satisfaction.

Because everything I tried to fix just shattered anyway.

❄

I don't remember walking home.

The wind bit hard. My hands stayed fists the whole way. Every step louder in my skull than the last. My breath refused to come right. My ribs ached. My brain spun.

Now I'm pacing my room, chest burning, thoughts slamming into each other like fists in a cage.

I should've ended it sooner. Should've told Lola. Should've made it clear that Sophie was history. Instead, I let the lines blur and the silence grow, and Lola walked straight into the one scene that would break her trust completely.

The tick of the wall clock mocks me. I see her face every time I blink.

❄

There's a knock on the door. I yank it open without thinking, hope clawing up my throat, but it's not her. It's Ash. His hands are in his pockets, his face unreadable.

"She's not speaking to anyone," he says, no preamble.

My throat's raw. "Is she okay?"

"She's hurt."

The words slice deep.

"She thought she saw something that wasn't there."

I nod. "Then I'll tell her."

Ash raises a brow. "So go."

"I don't think she'll listen, though, I shouted after her. She heard me, I know she did, I saw her shoulders slump."

He shrugs. "Then make her listen."

I stare at him like he's lost the plot. "You think this is about convincing her I didn't fuck Sophie? She saw me with her. It doesn't matter if I was breaking it off. All she saw was me, sitting with a girl I never explained, looking exactly like the guy she was afraid I'd be."

Ash leans against the doorframe. "Do you love her yet?"

My heart stutters.

"That's not the point."

"It's exactly the point. Because if you do, you'll fight for it. If you don't, walk away. But don't stand here whining like a kicked puppy while she spirals."

I drag both hands through my hair. "I don't know how to fix it."

"Then fight like hell for it."

My chest tightens. "She thinks I'm still fucking Sophie."

"Then prove you're not. Prove you're not that guy."

"I don't even know who I am anymore."

Ash's voice softens. "Then figure it out. Fast. Because Lola? She's not going to wait around while you decide if you're worth the risk."

❄

I don't sleep. Her voice echoes in my skull, the look in her eyes. The way she turned, like I'd already answered every question she hadn't asked yet, like she knew.

The next morning, I can't stay still.

I go looking for her. She's not at reception. Scarlett's there instead, so I hover like an idiot.

"Have you seen Lola?"

She glances up. "Tried her room?"

"Yeah, no answer."

Scarlett's face softens. "She'll be okay. Maybe. You might not be."

Fair.

I check the lounge, kitchen, staff corridor... nothing.

Back in my room, I stare at the door. My knuckles itch and my ribs burn.

What if she never speaks to me again? What if I broke something that can't be put back?

❄

By the time evening rolls around, I'm pacing like a caged tiger.

Imogen's curled up in the staff lounge, reading. She doesn't even look up.

"Come to beg forgiveness?" she mutters.

"Something like that."

"She's not in the mood, Harls. Sarah and I both tried. You're not making it easy for us to convince her you're not that guy."

"Does she hate me?"

Imogen lowers the book and fixes me with a stare. "No; that'd be easier. She's just gutted."

My voice is a whisper. "I didn't sleep with her."

"I know."

"You do?"

Imogen shrugs. "You're a lot of things, but a liar's not one of them. Doesn't mean you didn't hurt her."

"I didn't think she'd show up. I just wanted to end it. Sophie, she's a loose end, that's all."

"And Lola's not?"

I flinch.

"She thinks you've been hiding Sophie because you still wanted her. You weren't, but you didn't tell her either."

"I was scared."

"Of what?"

"That she'd leave."

Imogen's quiet for a beat. "Then be the guy she believes in. Not the one Sophie knew."

I breathe out. "You know where she is?"

"She's in her room now."

"Should I go?"

"Yes, Harls, go before it's too late."

❄

The hallway feels longer than usual. Every step lands like regret. My hand trembles when I knock the first time. Nothing.

I wait. Another knock. Then the door cracks open. And there she is.

Oversized jumper swallowing her frame, curls frizzy and wild, eyes red-rimmed and glassy. Her skin's too pale. Like she hasn't eaten. Like she hasn't slept. Like I've taken whatever light she had left and crushed it.

My stomach drops.

"Can I come in?" I ask, voice low, rough.

She doesn't answer. Just steps back without a word.

The air inside feels heavy. A muted film plays on the TV, the volume off, the subtitles flickering. Her bed's a mess of blankets and tissues. She climbs onto it slowly, pulling her knees to her chest like she's afraid she'll fall apart if she doesn't hold herself together.

I stay standing. I don't want to get too close and startle her.

"I didn't sleep with her," I say.

Nothing.

"I went to end it. That's why I was there. Because I should've done it months ago, and I didn't. And then you walked in at the worst possible moment."

Lola's gaze shifts towards me slowly, her eyes sharp now, wet but burning. "Don't. Don't stand there and talk about timing like it was some cosmic fuck-up. You didn't trip and fall into Sophie's lap, Harley. You made a choice. You kept making choices. And not once did you think I might need to know."

I swallow. "I didn't want to lie to you."

"No you didn't. But you lied by omission. Why didn't you tell me?" she snaps. Her voice cracks. "Why let me start to believe I was safe with you, when you were still hiding her in the background like a backup plan?"

"I wasn't...."

"You were."

She gets off the bed, pacing now. Her voice is rising, splintering. "You kept me at arm's length, then pulled me back in. Again and again. I didn't even know I was falling until it hurt to hit the ground."

My chest caves. "Lo..."

Her eyes flick to mine. "Do you even see what you've done to me?"

I step forward. "Yes. I see it. I see you, and I'm so fucking sorry, Lo"

"You don't see me," she says, breathing hard now. "You see the version of me that fits into your guilt. The girl you think you can protect so you don't have to fix your own shit. And I let you. I let you come in and touch the places no one else gets to touch, and I still don't know if you actually want me or if you're just scared of being alone."

"I want you," I say, ripping both hands through my hair.

"Then why wasn't I worth the truth?" she asks, voice trembling.

I don't have an answer that makes any of this okay. Just the truth.

"Because I don't think I deserve you," I say. "Because every time I start to let myself care, I panic. And I run. Or I hide. Or I fuck it up so bad that there's no way you'll stay, because then at least I'll know I was right about myself."

She stares at me, stricken. "That's not protecting yourself. That's destroying us before we even start."

"I know," I say. "It's fear. But I'm trying. I'm here. I came back. Even though I thought you'd shut me out. Even though I know I don't have a right to ask you for anything."

Lola wraps her arms around herself like she's cold. "I don't trust you."

"I know."

"You make me feel like I'm losing my mind. One minute you're this guy who looks at me like I'm the only person in the world, and the next you're shutting down, disappearing, pushing me out like I'm nothing."

"You're not nothing."

She looks at me, really looks, and I hate the tears on her cheeks. I hate that I put them there.

"I wanted to believe you were different," she whispers. "I needed you to be different."

"I still can be."

She shakes her head. "I don't want promises. I want proof."

I nod. "Then let me stay. Just tonight. I won't touch you if you don't want me to. I won't say another word. But let me be here. Let me prove I'm not walking away this time." I say, needing to be with her.

The silence stretches. I don't beg. I don't plead. I just wait.

Finally, her shoulders fall. She turns back toward the bed, crawling into it like she's exhausted from fighting her own pain. "Fine," she murmurs. "But don't mistake this for forgiveness."

"I won't."

She doesn't look at me when she lifts the blanket.

I take off my trainers, slide in slowly, fully dressed, careful not to crowd her. I lie behind her, leave space, my hand hovering between us in the air like I don't know what to do with it.

After a minute, she shifts back against me. Barely. Her spine meets my chest, and I curl an arm around her waist like I'm holding onto the last chance I'll ever get.

She rests her hand on mine. Not a grip. Not a promise. Just presence. It's not peace. Not yet. But it's something. And this time, I won't fuck it up.

CHAPTER 16
The Morning After
LOLA

The first thing I notice is the heat. A warm, steady weight against my back. The faint, rhythmic rise and fall of someone breathing beside me. And then the slow, inevitable realisation that I'm not alone. Harley's still here. I knew he'd stay. Even before I fell asleep, I knew. But it still hits me in the chest when I open my eyes and he's here.

I blink, squinting against the early morning light seeping through the gap in the curtains. My bedroom is quiet, the movie we fell asleep to long since stopped, the only sound is his breathing and the occasional creak of the old radiator. I shift slightly, careful not to wake him, but his arm tightens around my waist like his body knows I might leave. I freeze. His hand is heavy on my stomach. My heart kicks once, then settles.

I could pretend to still be asleep. Stay curled up in this fragile peace we've built out of broken pieces. But the truth presses against my ribs, sharp and insistent. We need to talk. We can't just skip to the part where everything's okay again for five minutes anyway. But God, it's tempting.

I turn slowly. His face is soft in sleep. The hard lines of his jaw relaxed, lashes casting faint shadows beneath his eyes. His mouth, usually twisted into a smirk or scowl, is open slightly. He looks young. Vulnerable, almost.

And suddenly I hate that I know this version of him. Hate that it's mine to see when the rest of the world only gets the armour.

I watch him for a moment longer, then gently slide out from under his arm. My ankle protests the movement, but I grit my teeth and shuffle across the room, wrapping the jumper tighter around me. The room's cool now, the radiator clicking to life in the corner, but I barely feel it.

By the time I've made it to the mirror, I don't recognise myself. My eyes are puffy. My hair is doing a pretty good impression of a bird's nest. My lips are swollen from sleep and unsaid things. I don't know what I'm doing.

Harley shifts behind me. I see it in the mirror before I hear his voice.

"You okay?"

I nod, then realise he can't see me. "Yeah. Just needed to stretch."

He sits up slowly, rubbing a hand over his face. "Didn't mean to fall asleep again."

I turn, arms crossed over my chest. "But you stayed."

He meets my eyes. "You let me."

The silence between us feels different now. Not empty. Just... waiting.

"What happens now?" I ask.

Harley looks like he wants to say something profound. Instead, he runs a hand through his hair and says, "I have no idea."

A laugh slips out of me. It's small, tired, but real. He watches me, guarded but open. "Do you regret it?" I don't know which part he means. Letting him in. Letting him stay. Letting him see me fall apart.

"No," I say quietly. "But I still don't know if I trust you yet."

He nods like he expected that. Maybe even agrees.

"Then I'll keep showing up until you do."

The words shouldn't make me melt. But they do.

I look down at my hands. "Sarah and Imogen want to take me into town later. Just for a walk. Some air."

His gaze sharpens slightly. "You sure you're up for that?"

I arch a brow. "What, are you my physio now?"

He holds his hands up. "Just asking. I don't want you pushing yourself."

It's annoying. And sweet. And maybe a little bit hot.

I sigh. "I'll be fine."

❄

Harley

"Harley"

She says my name like it's a question I haven't answered yet. And maybe I haven't. Not properly. Not with words. But she's looking at me like she already knows, and fuck, that's dangerous. Because the second I go, I'll go too far.

I scrub a hand down my face and shift to the edge of the bed, trying to remember how to breathe with her words still lodged in my chest.

But then she moves towards me and touches my wrist. Light. Barely there. A brush, not a grip. And it stops me.

"You don't have to go." Her voice is softer now. Tired, but not defensive. She's not pushing. Not pulling. Just... there. Holding space for me I didn't think I deserved.

I turn toward her slowly, eyes dragging over every inch of her face like maybe this'll be the last time I get to.

It's not fair how beautiful she looks right now, creased from sleep, ankle wrapped, eyes still rimmed with the kind of heartbreak I put there. But she's still looking at me like I'm worth staying for. And fuck me, I want to believe her.

Her hand is still resting near mine, close enough I could touch it without trying. So I do. I let my fingers find hers.

She doesn't pull away. Neither do I.

Her eyes search mine like she's trying to read the parts of me I keep buried. And then, God help me, she leans in. It's not fast. It's not even confident. It's hesitant, like she's bracing for me to flinch. But I don't.

I meet her halfway. Her lips brush mine like a whisper, barely-there contact that still manages to gut me. I respond before I know I'm doing it, one hand cupping her jaw, the other catching her hip, pulling her down onto my lap.

And then I'm kissing her. Properly. But when she sighs against my lips, this tiny, breathy sound that curls straight down my spine, my control slips.

I deepen the kiss, tilting her head to mine, my other hand fisting in the duvet like it's the only thing keeping me tethered. She tastes like sleep and want, like everything I've been holding back.

She makes another sound, quiet, helpless, and her fingers slide into my hair, tugging gently, like she needs more of me. I groan into her mouth, and the way she reacts, like it scorches her, makes everything worse. Or better. Or both.

My hand slides under her shirt. Not rushed. Not rough. Just... hungry.

She's warm and soft and arching into my touch like she's been waiting for it, for me. And I swear, the way she gasps when my thumb brushes over her bra makes my cock throb so hard I have to grit my teeth.

Fuck. She's making me lose it. Completely.

She wriggles in my lap, like she's searching for friction. I slide my hand around her ribcage, thumb grazing the edge of lace, and I feel her shiver over me.

Her mouth finds mine again, needy now, like the switch has been flipped. I kiss her back, matching it, losing myself in it, until I realise I'm about five seconds from flipping her to her back, sinking into her and forgetting every reason why I shouldn't.

I pull back. Not far. Just enough.

Her breath catches. She doesn't move away, doesn't cover herself or look embarrassed. She just blinks at me, lips kiss-bitten, eyes dark with whatever we just let loose.

I rest my forehead against hers. Close. Intimate. Still here.

"Lola," I breathe, voice wrecked. "You have no idea what you do to me."

She nods slightly, cheeks flushed. Her fingers are still tangled in my hair, and she doesn't let go.

I stroke her side once, slowly, then kiss her forehead. And then her nose. And then, finally, her mouth. Gently this time. Like a full stop. She exhales against me, and I feel it at the bottom of my stomach.

We stay like that for a long moment. Not talking. Not moving.

Lola's the first to break the silence, sucking in a long breath.

"I need to get ready for work. First day back. If I'm late, Imogen'll smack me," she says with a smile.

"Yeah. I should head out too," I say, reaching up to smooth her wild, beautiful hair behind her ear before kissing her temple.

Reluctantly, I lift her off me and shift off the bed, hooking my arms gently under her arms to lift her to her feet. She lands in front of me, toes sinking into the carpet, her body close, her head level with my heart.

I lean down, press a kiss to her mouth, still warm and swollen from before, then pull her in tighter. Her head rests against my chest, and I breathe her in. Coconut shampoo and something sweeter I haven't found the name for yet.

"I'll see you later, yeah?" I whisper, tipping her chin so she'll meet my eyes. "Don't overdo it when you're out."

She rolls her eyes. "I'm fine, Harley. I went into town last week. My ankle survived. You can stop worrying."

I kiss her one last time. Then cross the room, glance back at her, and grin before slipping out the door to get to work, already counting the hours until I can come back.

❄

Lola

I tug on my uniform and make my way down to reception. My ankle aches with each step, but I force myself to push through. It's been over a week since I worked a shift and I need to feel useful again.

Scarlett raises an eyebrow when she sees me. "Did Imogen clear you for work again?"

"Light duties," I say, lifting my chin.

She doesn't look convinced, but before she can say more, Imogen appears beside me like clockwork. "She's under my watch. Promise."

Scarlett sighs. "Fine. One complaint, and you're off duty again. Got it?"

"Got it."

I settle behind the desk, logging into the system, trying not to notice how slow my fingers feel. Like my brain's buffering. It doesn't take long for the chaos to find us. My lips are still tingling from this morning. I keep thinking about the way his hand slid beneath my clothes like he knew exactly where I needed him.

A guest marches up to the desk, clearly irate, holding up a torn bathrobe like it's evidence in a murder trial and ruins the moment with one sentence.

"This was hanging on the back of the bathroom door," she huffs. "It has a rip the size of my fist. And don't get me started on the shampoo dispenser, it's stuck, I nearly broke my thumb trying to use it."

I blink. "I'm really sorry about that. Let me speak with housekeeping and..."

"And why is the heated towel rail not working? This place isn't cheap, you know."

Before I can find the right tab on the system, Imogen appears beside me again, all composed poise and gentle authority.

"I can log all of this and get maintenance up to check the heating. In the meantime, I'll have housekeeping deliver a replacement robe and replenish your toiletries. Would you like a complimentary drink sent to your room while we sort it out?"

The woman breathes through her nose, appeased but still grumbling. "Fine. Sauvignon Blanc. Cold."

"Of course," Imogen says, already tapping it into her iPad.

The guest leaves, muttering about standards.

I blink. "She was intense."

Imogen shrugs. "We all have our off days. Don't let it get to you."

I exhale. "Thanks."

"Niko and Tyler are taking over reception this evening," she adds. "So we'll go to town, yeah? Breathe. Laugh. Spend money we don't have."

A smile tugs at my lips. "Sarah's coming too."

Imogen grins. "Oh good. She needs it. Her whole week's been kids with colds and a toddler who vomited on her boots."

I grimace. "Poor Sarah."

"She's a saint," Imogen says. "But she's also overdue for some girl time. And a strong cocktail."

Maybe we all are. I nod, and for the first time in days, I feel something close to normal.

Maybe not perfect. But definitely healing.

CHAPTER 17

No More Pretending

LOLA

The lobby is quiet. Too quiet. Like the air itself is still holding its breath after what happened yesterday morning. I'm not.

I've been breathing like a lunatic since it happened, shallow, erratic, totally fucking useless breaths that don't do a thing to settle me.

Because how do you come down from something like that?

His mouth.

His hands.

The way he kissed me like he'd been starving for weeks and I was the first taste of anything real.

I haven't moved much since my shift ended. Just me, a half-finished guest list, and a cup of tea that went cold hours ago. My tights are bunched awkwardly under my skirt. My feet ache in heels I never should've worn. I should go to bed. I don't.

The door creaks open behind me and my spine goes straight.

I don't have to turn. I already know.

The air shifts. Warmer. Denser.

Harley.

He walks in like the storm he is, snow-dusted hoodie pushed back, dark hair damp at the edges, jaw locked like he's still chasing whatever thoughts dragged him out into the night. His ocean-blue eyes find mine instantly. Hold. Burn.

The kiss is there between us, thick and loud and impossible to ignore.

"You shouldn't still be down here," he says, voice low.

I raise my chin. "Neither should you."

He shrugs out of his coat but doesn't look away. Doesn't blink. Just walks toward me like he already knows I'm not going anywhere.

"Niko said you were finishing up alone."

"Well, that's nothing new."

Harley stops on the other side of the desk. Not too close, but close enough that I can smell the cold on his clothes. That soft, sharp alpine scent that always clings to him.

He looks rested, but wired, like his body slept and his mind didn't.

"You okay?" he asks, voice rough.

I hesitate.

"No."

Something flickers in his eyes, regret, maybe. Or guilt. Or something that doesn't have a name.

"Me neither."

The air goes still again. Something stretches between us, not silence, not distance. Just tension. Thick and unsaid and *undeniable.*

He opens his mouth, but I get there first.

"I haven't stopped thinking about yesterday morning."

His jaw tightens. His fingers twitch.

"Neither have I."

I glance down. Swallow. "So now what?"

He moves, fast. Around the desk, in front of me, his hand reaching, not to touch, just to *be there*. Like he's anchoring us both.

"I'm not going to keep pretending that didn't happen," he says, voice wrecked. "Are you?"

I shake my head. "No. I don't want to."

He breathes in like it hurts.

"Come with me."

That's it. No more waiting. No more lines we're pretending not to cross.

And this time? I follow without hesitation.

❄

His mouth's on mine again before the door even clicks shut to his room. No hesitation, no careful buildup, just heat and hunger. His hands slide into my hair, angling my head, fingers tight enough that it borders on rough. My back hits the wall and I gasp, he doesn't apologise.

"Tell me to stop," he growls. Voice wrecked.

I grab the bottom of his t-shirt and yank. "If you stop now, I'll never forgive you."

A sound breaks out of him, half groan, half snarl. I step out of my heels and he lifts me. My thighs wrap around his waist without thought. He carries me like I weigh nothing. The world tilts as he lowers me to the bed, my back hitting the sheets with a soft bounce. There's reverence in the way he looks at me then, like he's not just undressing me, he's unwrapping something precious.

I reach for my blouse buttons, fingers trembling.

"Let me," he says.

I drop my hands and he undoes them slowly, one at a time. Eyes burning like he's memorising my skin, my freckles and the way my throat jumps under his mouth. He doesn't rush when it's open, just brushes the fabric back from my shoulders and looks. His eyes hood and my heart tries to crawl out of my ribs.

"You're beautiful," he whispers. "You know that?"

"I need to tell you something," I say, barely above a whisper.

He stills. "Okay."

"I've never done this before. Not with anyone."

Silence gathers. Heavy.

"Lola." His voice splinters. "You're a virgin?"

"I've kissed people, messed around a little, got myself off. But

I've never..." I bite my lip. "You are the first person I've ever wanted like this. The only one who's ever made me feel like I'm allowed to want."

Something cracks across his face. His hands shake on my waist.

"Fuck," he breathes. "You don't know what that does to me."

He kisses me again, slower now, deeper. Like he wants the taste of this locked in his bones. Then he pulls back enough to look me in the eye.

"Once I start, I'm not stopping unless you tell me to. You say yes and I'm yours and you're mine."

"Yes," I whisper. "I want you."

He peels his t-shirt off and I forget how to breathe. Lean muscle and sharp lines, ink on skin, and I press a hand to his chest like I need proof. "You're unreal."

"And you're overdressed," he murmurs, sliding my blouse the rest of the way off, and kissing down my neck. Every place he touches snaps awake.

"You okay?" he asks against my skin.

"I need more."

That's all he needs. He unclasps my bra with a practised flick and drops it, kneels between my legs and pushes my skirt up around my waist, then looks up at me like a question.

"You're shaking," he says.

"I'm not scared," I whisper. "Just desperate."

He kisses the inside of my thigh. "You're not going to break, I've got you."

He peels my underwear away in a slow drag and parts me with his thumbs, his breath catching.

"Fuck," he says. "You're soaked."

"Because of you."

His mouth finds me and the world shrinks to the shape of his tongue and his hands. It's too much and not enough. Pressure turns into heat that turns into noise I don't recognise as mine. He slides a finger into me and I cry out. He freezes.

"Too much?"

"No," I pant. "I'm just not used to it."

"Then I'll get you used to it."

He slides a second finger inside me, slow, deliberate, curling until my back arches off the mattress.

"Fuck, Harley," I gasp, clutching at the duvet, at his hair, at anything.

"Easy," he murmurs against me, voice rough. "Let me take care of you."

He works me open with patience that borders on cruel, every stroke making my thighs shake harder. I can't keep still, hips rolling helplessly toward his mouth, needing more.

"Please..." The word rips out of me, half-sob, half-prayer.

He hums into me, tongue flattening, unhurried, greedy. "Christ, you taste so good," he says against me, like it's half-confession, half-worship. "Could live here."

The sound and the words together wreck me, pull me tighter, higher, until everything inside me coils to breaking.

"Harley, I, oh God..."

"Don't hold back," he says, mouth slick, steady, relentless. "Give it to me. All of it."

And I do. My climax tears through me, violent and unstoppable, leaving me gasping, clutching, breaking apart under him. His tongue doesn't let go, doesn't ease up, just follows every convulsion, drawing it out until I'm trembling and boneless, wrung dry and undone.

When it finally ebbs, I collapse into the bed, shaking. He licks me through the aftershocks like he can't bear to stop, savouring me as though every drop is sacred.

He kisses his way up my stomach, ribs, throat, slow, deliberate, like he can't get enough. Then he shifts back just long enough to kick off his trainers, his eyes never leaving mine. I reach for the button of his jeans, but his hand closes gently around my wrist, stopping me.

"Let me," he murmurs, voice low, reverent.

I drop my hand. He strips with one practiced movement, jeans and boxers gone in the same breath, and my mouth goes dry.

My eyes drag lower and Holy shit… massive. Thick. Hard already, jutting out like he's been waiting for this all night.

"Is that supposed to fit inside me?" I blurt, eyes wide.

He smiles. "I'll go slow. We'll make it work."

He reaches for the drawer, grabs a condom, and tears it open with shaking hands. He rolls it on, crawls over me, skin hot, solid and shaking with restraint. He fits his cock and drags the tip through my slick entrance and pauses.

"I'm going to go slow," he says. "If it's too much, tell me." He breathes.

"I need you to do it." I say. My voice is small. Honest. "Please."

He places his forehead to mine and pushes in an inch and I gasp, my body clamping around him, instinctively resisting the stretch.

"Lo," he groans, voice breaking. "You're so fucking tight. Are you okay?"

I nod, shaky. "Keep going. Please."

He stills, kisses my temple, then presses another inch deeper. My breath comes in stuttered bursts, my nails scrape down his back. It hurts, but not sharp, more like pressure, like my body's fighting to make space.

"Talk to me," he murmurs. His thumb strokes my cheek, grounding me.

"It's… a lot," I admit, teeth catching my lip. "But I want it. Don't stop."

He eases in a little more, then stops again, chest heaving. I can feel him trembling with the effort of holding back.

"Jesus, Lo, you're squeezing the life out of me," he groans. "Relax for me, breathe with me."

I match his breaths, forcing my body to unclench. The burn eases, turning into a deep ache, heavy but bearable.

"That's it," he whispers. "You're taking me so good, baby."

By the time he bottoms out, I feel stretched to my limit, stuffed full in a way that makes my head spin. I cling to him, overwhelmed.

"Holy shit," I whisper. "You're actually inside me."

He laughs, ragged, forehead dropping to mine. "Yeah, all of me, and I'm never fucking leaving."

He stays still, kissing me softly while my body adjusts. When I finally roll my hips, testing, he sucks in a sharp breath.

"God, you feel... incredible," he chokes. He pulls back a little, pushes in again, slow and deep. The stretch turns into friction, friction into heat, and suddenly I'm gasping.

"Does that feel better?" he asks.

"More," I beg. "Please, Harley."

He finds a rhythm, shallow at first, then deeper, harder, like he's learning me stroke by stroke. Every thrust pushes a whimper out of me, and every whimper seems to drive him closer to the edge.

"Fuck, Lo," he growls. "You're gonna make me lose it."

"Don't," I pant, clutching at him. "Not yet. Just, don't stop."

The ache sharpens into pleasure building slow and relentless until I'm clinging, shuddering, begging, so close I could scream. But I don't break. Not yet.

I sob his name and he curses into my mouth like he's on the edge too. He stills, shaking with restraint, then drives deeper now that my body has learned him. His hand cradles my face. The other grips my hip like he needs the anchor. I wrap my legs around his waist and pull him closer and he groans.

"Tell me what you need," he says, voice ripped up.

"Harder," I whisper. Then, braver, "I can take it. I want all of it."

His rhythm changes, not careless, more like intent. He drags me up the mattress and back down on him. He keeps his mouth on mine so I can breathe with him when I forget how to breathe at all.

"You feel like you were made for me," he pants.

"Then don't ever stop," I say, and mean it like a vow.

He fights it, I can feel it. The way he chases the edge and backs off because he doesn't want to finish before me. I reach for his face and make him look at me.

"It's okay," I whisper. "I want you to, I want to feel you lose it."

His control snaps. The rhythm turns rougher, exquisite, each thrust pulling another sound from me I'll never admit to making. The pleasure coils tight, slow and fierce. When my body clenches around him, he swears. That's what breaks him.

"Fuck, Lola, please," he groans, barely holding on. "Come for me, baby. I need to feel it. Need to feel you lose it around me, please, I need all of you."

The pleasure, is nothing I've ever felt before, it drags me under; it pulses hot and bright, and I have to hold my breath while the waves take me over the edge into the abyss. He follows, a guttural groan against my skin, thrusting hard once more before he shudders and buries his face in my neck. The bed creaks and I hold him because I've never felt closer to a human being in my entire life. Harley's inside me, and all around me, and I never want to let that feeling go. Ever.

For a long minute neither of us moves. I feel the shake in his arms, I feel my pulse thumping against his mouth where it rests on my throat. I'm sore in that good way that means something happened that won't unhappen, I feel fulfilled.

He slips out carefully and kisses my cheek like an apology for leaving my body even for a second. He fists the base of his cock and pulls the condom off with steady hands, ties it off, and tosses it in the bin beside the bed. He tucks a strand of hair behind my ear.

"You okay?" he asks.

I bite my bottom lip. "Better than okay."

He smiles like he doesn't know what to do with that.

I brush my thumb over his lower lip. "Come back here."

He folds over me and I tuck myself under his chest because that's where I've wanted to live for weeks. I breathe him in, sweat, soap, and snow drying in his hair. My body aches, my mind goes quiet, I did it, with him. With the only person who has ever felt like a risk worth taking.

I don't know how long we lie like that. Long enough for my

heartbeat to settle and my skin to cool. Long enough for the stutter in my muscles to turn into something like peace.

I tip his face up with my fingers. "That was everything and more, thank you."

He frowns, stroking two fingers along my throat. "Baby, thank you for trusting me with your first time, I can't tell you how much that meant to me." His lips touch mine slow and wet, and it takes everything in me not to deepen the kiss again with the pulsing need he's ignited deep in my belly.

❄

Harley

She's lying half on top of me, one leg slung over my hip, cheek resting on my chest like it's the only place she belongs, and I'm hoping it is. I've had a lot of sex, fast, rough, meaningless with girls who wanted something to brag about. Girls who only saw the surface, who didn't care about the mess underneath.

But this? This was something else. Lola's breath ghosts over my skin, warm and slow, she's not asleep, not yet, but she's quiet, wrecked, satisfied in a way I've never seen on another human being in my fucking life, and I did that, I got her there.

My hand finds her waist, stroking slow, lazy circles into her bare skin, her skirt's still bunched up around her hips, I never even took it fully off. I was too desperate, too far gone, and now that I've had her? I want her again, badly.

My cock's already stirring against her thigh, and she must feel it because she hums, eyes still closed, and shifts just enough to press against it.

"Already?" she murmurs.

I grin. "You're surprised?"

"You just..." Her voice is thick. Sated. "You literally just came like five minutes ago."

I roll us, gently so she's on her back again, and lean over her with my arms braced on either side of her head.

"Yeah," I say, brushing a kiss over her jaw. "And it wasn't enough."

She laughs, that soft, sleepy sound that does something dangerous to me.

"Are you trying to kill me?"

I kiss her throat. "Maybe."

She looks up at me, eyes glossy but playful. "That was my first time. You remember that, right?"

I smirk. "Yeah, you told me, just before you begged me to ruin you."

Her cheeks flush. I love it. Love knowing I'm the only one who's ever seen her like this, flushed and fucked-out, legs still trembling from what we just did.

"I meant it," she says, quieter now. "I wanted it to be you."

Something tightens in my chest, not fear, not panic, just... Fuck. Gratitude? Awe? That aching, clawing need to protect her from everything?

"Lola."

She blinks up at me. "Yeah?"

I lower my mouth to hers again, slower this time, less heat, more weight, more truth.

"You wrecked me," I whisper. "You have no idea."

Her fingers tangle in my hair. "Good."

That smile, that wicked, shy little smile she gives me when she knows she has the upper hand.

It makes me want to take her again, make her say my name louder, make her come even harder.

I press my hips against her, hard enough that she gasps.

"Round two?" I ask, voice low.

She bites her lip. "You'll have to go slow. I'm."

I catch her chin gently, tipping her face up to mine. "Are you sore, baby?"

"A little," she admits. "Not in a bad way. Just... sensitive."

I nod, brushing my thumb over her bottom lip. "Okay. Then we stop."

But then her eyes shift and something sparks.

"I still want to make you feel good," she says, voice quieter now. "I want to... I want to touch you."

My stomach drops straight through the bed.

"Yeah?" I murmur.

She nods, cheeks flushed, eyes locked on mine. "Will you let me?"

I don't say another word, I just roll onto my back, giving her space.

Sitting up on her knees, her hands go to her skirt and she wriggles out of it, before climbing over me, sliding down my body with slow, deliberate intent. Her hands skim down my chest, and she settles between my thighs like she owns the space, and fuck, she does.

My cock's pulsing against my stomach and she looks down at it with wide eyes and a hungry little smirk.

"No wonder you're cocky."

I huff a laugh. "You saying I've earned it?"

Instead of answering, she wraps her hand around me and hums. "Oh, fuck," I groan, as I nearly lose it.

"Yeah, you have."

"Shit, Lola"

"Relax," she murmurs. "Lie still."

I do, barely, every muscle in my body is pulled tight, straining for her.

Her hand moves slow up and down my shaft, teasing, she leans down and brushes her mouth over the tip.

Then her tongue flicks out to lick the bead of pre-cum that's gathered there. I groan, one arm flung over my face. "Jesus fucking Christ."

She hums around me, taking more of my cock into her mouth, her pace unhurried and cruel in the best way, not deep yet, just thorough, focused, filthy.

"Where the hell did you learn to do that?" I choke.

Then I catch myself, panic rising, I don't want to think of her with anyone else.

"Wait, don't answer that."

She pulls off, lips shining, eyes laughing.

"I listen to smutty audiobooks," she says. "With hot boys and no plot."

I blink. Then let out a shaky laugh and fist the sheets.

"Fuck me."

"Already did," she laughs.

She goes back down on me, and I'm gone, utterly and completely gone.

My hips jerk as her mouth slides deeper, wetter, slower. One hand works the base, the other cradles me, her tongue swirling over the tip.

I groan and reach for her shoulder. "Shit, Lola, I'm gonna come in your mouth if you don't move."

She hums in response and doesn't move.

"Fuck..." My head drops back, throat tight. "Okay. You win. Fucking have me."

She keeps going, deeper, faster, her hand tightens, her mouth sucks harder. I'm unraveling, grip white-knuckled in the sheets.

I lose it with a hoarse, broken groan, body locking up as I come hard down her throat.

She swallows, slow and steady, wipes her mouth, then crawls back up beside me like she didn't just shatter me in the space of a minute.

"Still want round two?" she teases.

I glance down at her, lips swollen, cheeks flushed.

"I think you're the one trying to kill me," I whisper.

"Maybe."

She crawls back over me and I kiss her forehead, her temple, her jaw.

"I'm keeping you now," I murmur. "Don't care what happens next. Fuck, now I know you can take me like that, I'm never letting you go."

'Yeah, okay, Harley," she says, smirking.

Her fingers thread through mine after I pull the sheets over us.

CHAPTER 18

Cold Starts and Clean Slates

LOLA

I step onto the back deck, tea warming in one hand, pastry in the other. The air bites, the snow drifts slow, and calm slips in before I can chase it off. Until the door creaks open behind me. I glance back to find Jack standing there.

He looks different. Not dramatically, same uniform, same boy-next-door face. But there's a weight behind his pale blue eyes now. Less swagger. More... stillness.

He closes the door gently and stands beside me without speaking, just breathing for a second.

"I'm not here to make things awkward," he tells me.

I nod slowly, waiting.

"I was an idiot," he says. "The ski lesson, the flirting, the way I tried to make you choose, all of it. I was so focused on proving something to Harley I forgot you weren't a pawn."

The words hang in the cold between us, turning to fog as we breathe them in.

"I didn't mean for you to get hurt," he adds, quieter. "And I sure as hell didn't mean to hurt you."

I sip my tea, searching his face for bullshit.

"Why now?" I ask.

"Because I've had two weeks with nothing but my own voice

echoing back at me. And I realised I've been a dick. To you, to Harley, to everyone."

He rubs the back of his neck. Classic Jack move.

"I miss having you as a friend," he says. "And I don't mean that in a 'still hoping for more' way. I mean it like... someone who got me, before I screwed it up."

The wind picks up, and I tug my jacket tighter. My breath catches slightly, but not from the cold.

"I appreciated your friendship," I say slowly. "But I won't pretend that didn't shake me. You put me in danger, Jack."

"I know." He swallows hard. "And if that means you never speak to me again, I'll have to deal with that. But I wanted to own it... all of it."

The sincerity in his voice cuts through me, and I look at him, really look at him.

"I think we could be friends," I say. "But it's going to take time, and trust."

Jack exhales like he's been holding that breath since he walked out here. "Fair enough."

Then he smiles, small, sheepish, real. "You can punch me, if it helps."

I shake my head. "Don't tempt me."

He chuckles, then gestures toward the kitchen door. "Guess I'd better earn my place back."

"Guess so."

As he walks inside, something in my chest feels lighter, I haven't forgiven or forgotten. But I'm not festering anymore.

Not everything broken has to stay that way.

❄

We're halfway through afternoon shift when the pod machine behind reception sputters and lets out a low hiss like it's fed up with the season. I press the start button again, there's nothing, just steam and defiance. I could honestly pick it up and chuck it through the window.

Imogen leans in beside me. "It's clogged again. That thing's practically antique."

I groan. "Should I call maintenance?"

"Already did this morning, he said it's on the list. Which is translation for we might fix it by spring."

Sarah appears from the stairwell, rubbing her temple like she's two tantrums away from a breakdown. "One of the four-year-olds has glued her gloves to her face."

Imogen doesn't even blink. "Just another Tuesday."

Sarah sighs. "And a parent asked me if we do themed childcare packages."

"What does that even mean?" I ask.

"They wanted 'Frozen meets Montessori."

I cough on my laugh. "Did you offer to throw in a singing Elsa and some educational trauma?"

"Tempting." She sinks into the bar stool behind reception. "I'm not sure if I want a nap or a drink."

"Both," Imogen says. "With a foot rub and someone else's credit card."

We all chuckle, and the tension in my shoulders finally starts to ease. The chalet feels full again. No longer tight with tension or silence. Just... normal chaos.

Imogen checks the rota. "Niko and Tyler are on the evening shift. You're free to go after this next check-in."

I hesitate. "Are you sure?"

She nods. "Go, you've earned it."

It's snowing again, light and slow, nothing too dramatic. We wait for the shuttle into town, bundled in scarves and coats, laughter curling in the air like smoke.

Sarah nudges me. "You really do seem good."

"Less emotionally feral?" I ask.

She smirks. "I was trying to be nice." Then her tone dips, almost like she didn't mean to say it out loud. "I know what it's like, smiling at strangers when you feel wrecked inside."

I glance at her. "Yeah?"

She shrugs, eyes on the snow. "I used to be a paediatric nurse.

Then I wasn't, lost too many kids, and lost myself somewhere in there."

The air between us shifts, not heavy, just honest.

"I thought I'd end up with a family," she adds, quietly. "Now I work in a ski resort full of kids who aren't mine. Irony's a bitch."

I want to say something profound, but all that comes out is. "You're one the strongest people I know."

She scoffs, smiling without teeth. "Try tiredest. But thanks."

As we walk, my phone buzzes.

Harley: I miss you xx

I snort, typing back quickly.

Me: You saw me this morning xx

Harley: Not the same. I'm hard just thinking about you xx

Harley: Come to mine tonight? xx

Harley: Are you still sore, baby? xx

Sarah leans over my shoulder just as the last message lights up the screen. She groans, dramatically conflicted. "Awwww," she says. Then immediately says, "Yuck."

I laugh, heat crawling up my neck. But I don't hide the smile curling at my lips. I type quickly.

Me: Still a bit sore, I can still feel you when I walk, but I'm hoping you'll make me feel better later. Can't wait to see you xx

A beat later, his reply pops up:

Harley (muscle emoji) xxx

Sarah bumps my shoulder. "He's good for you, even when he's gross."

"Especially when he's gross," I murmur.

And for the rest of the walk, I don't check my phone again. Because I already know, he'll be waiting for me when I get back.

CHAPTER 19

Boot Room Confessions

HARLEY

The boot room's half-dark, one flickering overhead bulb doing its best to light the space. Damp gloves hang like deflated balloons from a drying rack in the corner. The air's thick with the familiar tang of melted snow and whatever's festering in someone's week-old socks. Perfect backdrop for an existential crisis.

I shut the door behind me, slower than I mean to. Not slamming it, but not quiet either. This place has always been strange to me. A kind of in-between. No windows, no clocks, just damp stone walls and the low hum of the boot dryers, like time doesn't quite know what to do in here.

Ash is perched on the bench, feet up on a crate, hood up. He doesn't look up when I walk in.

"Took you long enough," he mutters.

I ignore him and sit opposite, dropping my gloves on the bench beside me. "Didn't realise I was expected."

He finally glances up. "Mate. You've had that dazed I've-been-ruined-by-love look since breakfast."

I roll my eyes, but I don't argue.

He smirks. "So. You and Lola, huh?"

I exhale slowly. "Yeah. Me and Lola."

He nods once, like that's an answer in itself. "About bloody time."

I glance at the far wall, then down at my hands. "It's not casual."

"No shit."

"I mean it. It's... different. She's different."

Ash leans forward, resting his arms on his knees. "Harley, I've known you a long time. I've seen you run from things that were good for you. I've seen you self-destruct when things got too real. But this? This feels like you're trying."

"I am."

He watches me carefully. "Because you want to be better? Or because you think she deserves better?"

"Both."

I rake a hand through my hair. "She makes me feel... like I'm not stuck. Like I could have something else. Something more."

"Because you can," he says simply. "You always could. You just needed someone worth not running from."

I nod, throat tight. "I want to be someone she can count on. Not just the guy who shows up when shit goes wrong."

Ash studies me for a long moment. "Then keep showing up. Every day. Even when it's hard. Especially then."

I lean back, eyes fixed on a scuff mark on the wall. "You always make it sound simple."

"It is. Simple doesn't mean easy."

We sit in silence for a while, the kind that doesn't need filling. Just the hum of the dryer and the occasional groan of the old building settling.

Another pause, then I say, "Zane offered to back Break Line."

Ash sits up straighter. "Wait, seriously?"

"He wants to fund it. Said he believes in giving kids a second shot. He's seen what it's done for me."

"That's huge."

"Yeah."

Ash smirks. "You think there's something going on with him and Scarlett?"

I laugh. "What gave it away? The subtle flirting or the fact she only ever smiles like that around him?"

Ash grins. "Power couple energy."

We both chuckle, the tension bleeding out just a bit.

Ash stands and stretches. "Alright, lover boy. I've got stag lads to wrangle and boots to disinfect."

I shake my head. "Good luck with that."

He heads to the door, then pauses. "Hey, Harley?"

"Yeah?"

"She's good for you. Don't fuck it up."

I nod, serious now. "Trying not to."

The door swings shut. The boot dryers hum. The room goes back to that strange in-between quiet, and for a second I just breathe.

The handle turns again.

Lola slips inside.

She's already in ski pants and a thick jumper, curls barely tamed by a stretched hair tie, jacket swung over her arm. Her cheeks are flushed, maybe from the cold, maybe from what we didn't say when we woke up.

She shuts the door with her hip, then leans back against it, watching me.

"Still up for this lesson?" she asks, casual, too casual.

She doesn't know I've been replaying the way she asked me last night, half-asleep and draped across me, her voice loose with satisfaction. Like it was nothing, like she didn't care if I said yes or no. But I heard the edge under it, the wanting. And I'd decided right then I'd give her that second chance, whether she remembered asking or not.

I stand. "Yeah. Not until I strap your ankle, though."

She starts towards me, chin tilted, already deflecting. "I told you, it's fine."

"Sit," I say.

She hesitates, then obeys, that half-smile ghosting across her lips like she knows exactly what she's doing to me.

She perches on the bench, and I crouch in front of her, and

the moment tilts again, all warm skin and quiet breath and the kind of silence that says we're not ready to talk about it yet.

I peel her sock down. My hands are warm from the dryers, hers are cool from the walk over. The joint's not swollen, not angry, but there's heat under the skin where ligaments got pissed off and haven't forgiven her yet. I press two fingers along the bone to check for tenderness. She hisses, barely. My eyes flick up.

"Is that where it hurts the most?" I ask.

"Yeah, only on the outside," she murmurs. "Not sharp, just a little aggravated. More like it remembers."

"Then we help it forget."

I tear a strip of tape and smooth it across the front of her ankle, anchoring it. My thumb follows after the tape, slow, pressing the adhesive down, heat to help it bond. She watches my hands like they're saying more than my mouth can handle. I work another strip from behind her heel, under the arch, back up the other side. Figure-eight, snug but not choking. Her breath goes shallow when my knuckles brush the soft skin just above the boot line.

"Are you always this bossy?" she asks, pretending, light.

"Only when I care what happens next."

Her eyes catch mine. The air shifts. Not louder. Denser. I could lean in and kiss her now, soft and deep, and the whole world would tilt the way it always does when she opens for me. Instead I keep working, because if I start I won't stop, and we came here to do something else first.

"Lift," I say.

She raises her heel. I loop another strip under the arch and cradle her foot in my palm while I set the tension. She's small. I'm not. The scale difference does something to my chest I don't have words for.

"How's that pressure?" I ask.

"Good," she says. "Feels... supported."

I swallow. "That's the idea."

I smooth the sock back up, slow. My knuckles graze her calf again, and she trembles, barely there. Her jumper rides up an inch when she shifts. Skin flashes at her waist. I keep my eyes on the ankle like I'm a professional and not a man with a pulse.

"Better," I say.

She doesn't move right away. Her gaze drops to my mouth, and climbs back up. She leans in, only a little, like she's testing gravity. I meet her halfway. Our mouths brush. It's more breath than kiss, more promise than answer, but it hits hard anyway. When I pull back, she chases a fraction, eyes half-lidded.

"Come on," I say, voice rougher than it should be. "Let's go make you hate me for being right."

She grins. "Already do."

We suit up in the quick, practised way of people who live out here. Helmets, jackets, goggles and gloves. Skis over shoulders. The corridor out to the snow is a narrow tunnel of cold air and bad fluorescent light. We push through it and step into the white.

The nursery slope sits easy and open under a sky that can't decide if it wants to clear or dump. Soft corduroy lines ripple down the gentle pitch. A cluster of kids in bright bibs are doing their best to imitate a snowplough while their instructor threatens to lose his mind with a smile on his face.

Lola clips into her skis and plants her poles. "I feel stupid," she says.

"You look hot," I say without thinking.

She snorts, eyes on mine over the rim of her goggles. "Focus, Nash."

"Right. Stupidly hot."

She shakes her head, but her shoulders loosen. Good. Fear lives in tension. We need softness.

"Okay," I say, settling my skis. "We start simple. From the beginning again. Weight forward. Think about pressing your shins into the front of your boots. That sets your centre over the balls of your feet, gives you control."

She nods, stance a little too wide.

"Hip width," I say, tapping my pole between her skis. "You're not doing the splits, you're skiing."

"That's rich coming from a man who can barely fit through doorways."

I laugh. "Flatter me later. Show me your snowplough."

She angles the tips of her skis towards each other, heels apart, knees soft.

"Nice. That's your brake and your steering wheel. If you start going faster than you like, pull your toes up and press your heels down. Feel the inside edges bite."

She breathes out, and sets her weight. I ski a few metres down, stop, and face up the slope. "Slide to me. Gently. Let gravity help."

She moves. Wobbly, then steadier. When she gets close, I side-step, and she glides past with a face that is both terrified and proud.

"Good," I say, chasing after her. "Keep your hands forward. Imagine you're holding a tray and you don't want to spill it."

"You're obsessed with trays," she says, adjusting her hands.

"Years of teaching tourists. That one lands."

We stop near the first signpost. She breathes like she ran a mile. I plant my poles and step close enough to fix the angle of her outside ski with the tip of mine.

"Turning left," I say, "means you press a little more on the inside edge of your right ski. Think right big toe. Let it roll onto the edge and the ski will arc. Your left knee follows with a soft inward touch. Don't twist with your upper body. Keep your chest square to the fall line."

"Fall line," she repeats. "I hate that phrase."

"It's honest," I say. "Ready?"

She nods. I push off. She follows. I take a clean arc to the left, letting my hips drive the movement while my upper body stays quiet. She mirrors, late at first, then catches the feel. Her skis scrape when she tries to check speed. I call back, "Toes up a touch. Let the tails drag. That's it."

We snake down the gentle pitch in lazy S's. I talk the whole way. Not because she needs a stream of words to fix her turns, but because if I stop talking, she'll remember to be scared. Snowplough to control speed. Shift to edges to turn. Knees soft. Hips over feet. Eyes up. Look where you want to go, not where you don't want to fall.

At the bottom she plants her poles and doubles over for a second, laughing breathlessly. "I didn't die."

"High bar," I say, grinning. "Lift."

We shuffle to the button lift. She's been on it before. She doesn't look at me for approval, just slides her pole into the rack and catches the plastic disc as it swings round. She hooks it between her legs, leans on it just enough, and lets it pull her. No drama. No scream. Solid.

I take the next one behind her. It jerks my hips as it engages. I set my stance and watch her climb. She keeps her feet relaxed and parallel on the track, shoulders loose, hands forward. Twice she glances back to check I'm there. I am. Always am. I try not to hover with my eyes the way I did before, counting every micro-wobble like it's a countdown to impact. I just watch. She reaches the top, peels off cleanly, and waits to the side, grinning.

When I glide up to her she tips her head. "Still upright."

"Show off."

We set off for another run. I dial it up a notch. "This time, try linking a few turns without dropping back to snowplough. Start in a wedge if you need to, then let the skis drift towards parallel as you come out of each arc. Keep it smooth. Don't force it."

She bites her lip. "I'll try."

"You'll do."

We go. The first turn's late, shaky. The second comes easier, almost by accident. The third she actually earns, weight shifting clean, shoulders holding steady. Her skis carve a truer line, and the run opens under her. She laughs mid-turn, quick and breathless, like she's just shocked herself.

"That one," I say as we slide to a stop. "You felt it."

"I felt it," she says, flushed and bright. "The edge. It... caught. In a good way."

"That's the edge working for you. You let it grip instead of fighting it."

She breathes out like she has been holding that air for months.

We keep at it. Short sections. Stop. One cue. Go. I take her down the left side where the gradient is steady but kind. We play with stance width. Narrower keeps her quicker from edge to edge. Too narrow and she rides a rail. She learns the feel fast because she listens, not just with her ears. She listens with her feet.

On the button lift again, she reaches back and taps the tape on her ankle. "Not bad," she says. "Feels supported."

"Because it is."

"By you," she says, like it's obvious.

I look away at the trees. I've always been good at holding people up when they fall. This is the first time I've had to learn how to not hold so tight they can't move.

Third run. Fourth. On the fifth she beats me to the bottom because I slow to watch and forget to ski. She throws her arms up like she has just won a medal and almost falls over because the celebration messes her balance. I catch her elbow. She steadies. We both laugh.

"Again," she says.

"Again," I echo.

We glide back to the button lift. She hooks the button like a pro and rides up without a wobble. I take the one behind and let the climb give me time to feel what is changing. The first lesson I gave her, I tracked every heartbeat in her face and second-guessed every metre of slope. Today I find myself counting breaths between corrections and leaving the spaces long. She knows when to pull her toes up to slow down. She knows when to allow gravity to carry her and when to say no. She knows the fear and shows up anyway. She is not breakable. She never was. She is just new.

At the top I skate over. "Let's try a shallow traverse to the right," I say. "Stop on a diagonal. Feel the uphill edge hold you. Then step into the next turn. Small step, more like a little release. Let your downhill ski flatten, roll to the new inside edge, and bring the uphill ski with it. No drama."

She squints. "So, magic."

"Physics with better clothes."

We do it. She oversteps the first time and her skis cross. I'm close enough to catch her with a hand under her forearm, nothing heroic, just solid. She resets. The next try she keeps the step tiny and the skis whisper across the snow with that clean sound that makes my bones want to live here forever.

"Better," I say.

"Again."

We add a drill I make beginners hate. Pole drag. It keeps hands forward and weight where it belongs. She complains for the first three metres, then stops complaining because it works. Her upper body calms. Her turns stop starting in her shoulders and start starting where they should, low and quiet.

By the time we call it, she has pink cheeks, loose shoulders, and that look in her eyes that says she remembered her body is hers. It is my favourite look on her. It ruins me.

We step out of our skis and carry them back across the flat to the boot room. The corridor is louder now with returning guests, boots clumping on wet mats, laughter stacked on laughter. She keeps brushing my arm by accident and then not moving away. I keep my hands to myself because I'm trying to be good, which is new and annoying.

Inside, the boot room is warmer than it has any right to be. She sits and peels off her gloves, flexes her fingers, winces once when she points her toes. I unclip her boots and lift her foot to slide it free. The sock's damp where the cuff met the top of the boot. The tape has held.

"How's it feel now?" I ask.

"Tired," she says. "Not angry."

"Good. That's tired we can fix."

I press my thumb into the top of her foot, just behind the toes, and work a slow circle. She sighs, head tipping back against the wall, eyes closing for two beats. When she opens them again she's looking at me like I just proved she can trust me.

"You were less... intense today," she says.

I raise a brow. "Less intense?"

"On the slope. You didn't hover. You watched. You let me mess up without grabbing me."

"I still would have, if you needed it."

"I know," she says. Then, softer, "That's why it worked."

The dryer hums. The bulb flickers. Someone laughs out in the corridor and the sound skates under the door. I rest her heel on my knee and run my fingertips once along the outside of her ankle, checking for any new heat. Nothing screams. Good.

"I'm proud of you," I say.

Her mouth parts, like I gave her something she didn't know she was waiting for.

She swallows. "I'm proud of me too."

I want to kiss her. I want to drag her into my lap and tell her I saw her find the edge and lean into it, and that it did something to me I don't have words for. I do none of that. I set her foot down gently. I strip the tape, and toss it in the bin. I get fresh tape and wrap her again, lighter this time, because I trust what I saw.

"Tomorrow," I say, "we try linking without the wedge at entry. You'll flirt with parallel through the whole turn. We'll keep it shallow. No hero runs."

She smiles. "You want to see me show off."

"I want to see you safe and happy. The showing off is a bonus."

She stands, steps close, and slides her hands into my jacket at the ribs like she knows exactly where I keep the part of me that stops pretending. She rises on her toes and kisses me once, chaste. It's not a kiss that asks for anything. It's a kiss that says she heard me.

When she pulls back, she rests her forehead against mine. "Thank you, coach."

"Any time, Maxwell."

We clean the gear in near silence, me out of habit, her by watching and copying. Skis racked, boots on the dryers, gloves clipped like she's guessing what goes where. She tugs her jumper down, catches me looking, and grins like she knows I'm suffering.

"You coming with me?" she asks, casually.

"In a minute, I just need to see Scarlett. Meet you in your room, okay?"

She nods, hesitates like she might say something else, then just presses two fingers to my jaw and goes.

The room feels colder when she's gone.

I drop to the bench and let the quiet settle. The dryers hum. The overhead bulb still flickers like it's giving up. My heart's louder than both.

I think about the first time I saw her on snow, rigid, pissed off, hating every second. The second time, she was hurt and pretending she wasn't. Today? She leaned into the slope and didn't flinch. Set an edge. Let it carry her.

She didn't need me to hold her up. She just needed to know I was close enough if she reached.

That's the part I keep getting wrong.

Letting go isn't walking away. It's staying steady while she finds her feet.

I blow out a breath. Feel something in my chest shift, not release, not yet. Just a little more space than there was before. Enough for next time.

I grab her gloves. Then head upstairs to find my girl.

CHAPTER 20

Fault Line

HARLEY

It's been two weeks since Lola and I stopped pretending, but I'm feeling unsettled, and the bar's loud tonight, too fucking loud.

Ash is beside me, nursing a pint, halfway through some story about a stag group and a naked snow angel, but I'm not listening, because I'm watching her.

Lola's at the other end of the room, laughing at something Jack's just said. She's wearing that deep green jumper she told me she stole from Imogen, her hair's piled up messily in a bun, like she didn't try, but still looks like a punch to the gut. Her eyes flick to mine across the room, then away just as quickly. That's the third time tonight and my stomach drops.

I've felt it creeping in all day, a shift in her, like she's leaning away, just... distant, measured, careful. And Jack's always there.

He's sitting too close to her, his hand brushing her back as he whispers something in her ear. She grins, and punches his arm playfully, he leans in again and she doesn't stop him. My jaw tightens and I blow out a long aggravated breath.

Ash follows my line of sight. "Uh oh."

"What?"

"You're doing the face."

"What face?"

"The *'I'm about to ruin my own life because I think I'm being replaced'* face."

I down the rest of my drink and stand. "I just need to clear something up."

"Harley," Ash warns. "Don't be a dick."

But I don't listen because there's no talking me down once the red mist descends.

Jack leans closer, his mouth brushing her ear, and my stomach goes molten. I tell myself to breathe, to trust her. But then she laughs, that big laugh she only ever gives me, and something inside me snaps like a ski under pressure and I'm moving.

My voice is sharper than I intend. "Having fun?"

Jack looks up, smug. "Just chatting."

Lola blinks. "Harley..."

I cut her off. "You two look pretty cosy."

Jack smirks. "Jealousy doesn't suit you, mate."

"Just wondering when exactly you decided to start sneaking around with someone else's girl."

Lola's expression shifts instantly. "Excuse me?"

"You think I'm blind?" I spit. "You've been spending a lot of time together lately, laughing and whispering."

Her face goes pale, then flushes red. "Are you serious right now?"

Jack holds up his hands. "Hey, don't drag me into your relationship drama."

"You were already in it the second you started playing second-hand boyfriend," I snap.

Lola's voice cuts through the air like a blade. "*Enough.*"

People are watching now, Niko pauses mid drink, Imogen's eyebrows are halfway to her hairline.

Lola steps closer. "You think I'm *cheating* on you with Jack?"

I don't answer fast enough, so that's the answer.

Her mouth twists like I've slapped her. "Wow."

Jack looks uncomfortable now, finally stepping back.

"I don't believe this," she mutters, voice shaking. "You think I'd do that to you? After everything?"

"I saw the texts, his fucking name popping up every ten minutes on the screen," I spit out. "You were planning something behind my back."

Her eyes blaze. "Yeah. Your *birthday*, you absolute dick."

The room goes quiet and every part of me goes still.

Lola's voice drops, shaking with fury. "We were organising a surprise, Jack was helping me get Scarlett to sign off on the night off. We were trying to do something *nice* for you."

She stares at me like she doesn't recognise me anymore. "But you know what? I'm glad you showed me who you really are before I wasted any more of my time."

Then she turns and walks out straight through the bar, straight out the doors, into the snow. I don't move because I'm rooted to the spot.

Ash comes up beside me, slow and deliberate. "So, just to recap. You accused the girl who *lives in your bed* of cheating on you, *in public*, because you couldn't handle your own feelings."

I don't respond.

He slaps the back of my head. "Nice work, dumbass."

❄

In the privacy of my room, I decide there and then, that I need to make things right. I can't lose her, she's become my everything. The thought of losing her makes my chest hurt. I send her a text, and hold my breath. It remains unread. Fifteen minutes later she pushes open my door and slams it closed behind her without saying a word.

Lola. Stormy-eyed, flushed, her fists curled at her sides. I barely have time to breathe before she's crossing the room, jabbing me in the chest with her finger.

"You don't get to act like that and pretend we didn't mean anything."

My voice is thick, low. "I never said we didn't."

"You acted like it, and you embarrassed the fuck out of me," her voice trembles.

"I was scared Lo, so fucking scared that you'd seen through me." My throat tightens. "I still am."

Her lip quivers, but she doesn't back down. "What, why?"

I step closer. "Because the moment I had you, I knew I'd never be the same, and I didn't know what the hell to do with that."

She stares at me, chest rising, her breath coming in short bursts. She rubs one hand up and down the centre of her chest, like she's trying to keep her heart inside her body.

"Then do something with it now." She pleads.

I don't need more. In one breath, I'm on her. Reaching for her I pull her into my arms, thread my fingers into her hair and kiss her hard. I immediately push my tongue into her mouth and tangle it with hers. My hands grip her hips like I'll fall over without them. It's a clash at first, all teeth and frustration and unsaid shit. But then I feel her body ease into me, soft, real, and anchoring. And I lose everything.

My hands run up her back under her jumper; I pull it over her head. I trace her spine, find the bra clasp, and unhook it one-handed. She lets it drop to the floor with the rest.

Her olive skin's flushed. I can feel goosebumps prickling her arms. I press open mouth kisses to her neck, then her collarbone, then lower, licking the tip of her nipple before sucking it into my mouth. Her gasp is instant. Her fingers tangle in my hair and hold me there like she needs it.

"God," she breathes.

"You're so fucking beautiful," I mutter, moving to the other side, dragging my teeth across the soft skin before licking her clean again.

She whimpers, pressing closer, her legs brushing mine through the thin fabric of her leggings, desperate and restless.

I pull back just enough to look her in the eye. "Tell me you want me."

Her voice is breathy but sure. "I never stopped."

I grab her thighs, and lift her. She weighs nothing, and she wraps her legs around my waist, heat pressing into me. She's small, so small, and I'm suddenly hyperaware of just how much of me there is to fit.

"Bed," she whispers. I carry her to it.

She lies back, curls fanned across the pillow, chest bare, pupils blown wide. My hands go to her waistband, I slide her leggings down slowly, watching her the whole time. She's not wearing any underwear. My breath punches out of me. "Lola."

Her voice is soft, almost embarrassed. "I was getting ready to tell you to fuck off. Then I saw your text. I didn't know what I wanted until I got here."

Christ, what if this is the last time? What if she still walks away when it's over?

I swallow hard. "And now?"

Her eyes meet mine. Steady. "Now I want you."

"Fuck."

I kneel between her legs on the bed, sliding my hands under the backs of her thighs, coaxing them apart as I settle between them. I trace along the crease with one hand, down to where she's already wet, slipping one finger between her folds, she's so warm and slick.

Her whole body jolts. "Harley…"

"Shh." I kiss the inside of her knee. "I've got you."

I slide my fingers through her again, parting her slowly with two fingers now, dragging tight little circles across her clit until her hips lift, searching for more. Then I lower my mouth.

She gasps, choked and high-pitched, as my tongue replaces my fingers, licking slow and deep, soft at first, then harder. Her thighs close around my head and I groan into her.

She tastes like salt and heat and I don't stop until she's shaking.

When she comes, it's with a cry, fingers pulling my hair, spine arched off the bed. I kiss her all the way through it, her thighs trembling around my face. And then I crawl up her body, my mouth grazing her skin, catching the sound of her still-racing breath. I stop when I'm face to face with her.

"Lola," I whisper, my voice sounds thick with need, "I need you to tell me you want more."

Her eyes open, glassy and sure. "I want everything."

I nod, press a kiss to her temple, and reach over for the drawer. I rip the foil, slide the condom on with shaking hands. She watches the whole time, biting her lip.

When I line up, I pause.

"You still good?" I ask, voice low.

She wraps her legs around me, drawing me in. "Don't you dare stop now."

I push in slow. One inch. Then two. She gasps and clutches at my arms, nails digging into muscle.

I freeze. "Too much?"

"No," she breathes, eyes wide. "Just... more careful this time."

I kiss her gently and rest my forehead to hers. "You'll tell me."

She nods.

I move again, inch by inch, giving her time. Letting her adjust. She's impossibly tight around me, hot and slick, I grit my teeth and hold back everything. Finally, I bottom out. She lets out a shaky breath, and I stay still, buried inside her.

"You can move now," she whispers.

I do, slow at first, rolling my hips, letting her feel every inch. She meets me now, fluid, rhythmic, pulling me deeper with each thrust. I catch her mouth with mine, one hand cupping the back of her neck, the other sliding down her thigh to hitch her leg higher around my waist.

Her breath stutters. "God, Harley."

"I know, baby," I whisper into her skin. "I know. You're mine, Lo. I'll never doubt you again. Say you're mine."

"I'm yours, always," her nails digging possessively into my back.

I pant into her mouth. "I can't lose you, not to anyone ever. Come for me baby, I need to feel you." I need her to break for me. I need proof she's still mine.

I feel the little flutters around my cock that let me know she's close, then she shatters again, under me, her body shaking, moan swallowed in my kiss.

Which undoes me, tipping me over the edge into the sweet abyss seconds later, pulsing so very deep inside her, my vision blurs and tunnels at the same time.

When I collapse onto her, breathless, my heart is pounding like I ran up the fucking mountain. We lie there tangled, silent, skin to skin. I kiss her shoulder, still inside her, still trembling.

"Don't go, don't ever fucking go," I gasp.

I told you, Harley. I'm not going anywhere, so don't you dare forget it again. she says, her voice strong.

She reaches up and cups my face with both of her small hands and kisses me slow. And in that moment, I say it, because the feeling is too overwhelming.

"I love you, so fucking much, Lo, I think I've loved you since the moment I laid eyes on you at the airport, your hair whipping around you like a live action Medusa. And then I knew for sure I loved you when you gave me the dog tags at Christmas."

She freezes, for a second. If she doesn't say it back, I'm finished, that's it, game over. Then her eyes soften, and she exhales like she's been holding it in forever.

"I love you too, Harley, so much." She tells me, reaching up to kiss me slow and soft.

And I know it's real, there's no panic, no fear, just the truth of our feelings between us.

We're still tangled. Her skin's warm beneath mine, thighs still curled around my hips, chest flushed, her lips pink from kissing and biting and gasping against mine. I don't move for a long moment. Then I ease out, roll to my side, take care of the condom, and pull her with me half on top of me, her leg slung over my hip, one arm pinned under my back, the other resting across my ribs. Her cheek finds the curve of my shoulder like it was built for her.

Her hair's a mess, curls everywhere, and I run my hand through them anyway, slow and deliberate, like I never want to stop.

She breathes against my collarbone, the smallest sound, so I tip her chin up and make her look at me.

"You're so fucking beautiful, Lola Maxwell."

She blushes, tries to bury her face again, but I don't let her.

"I mean it," I murmur, brushing her damp curls back from her forehead. "You've got no idea what you do to me. I look at you and forget how to act like a normal human."

She smiles faintly, fingertips tracing a line down my chest. "That makes two of us."

"I've been trying to keep it cool, stay professional. Do the right thing." I pause. "But every time you walked past me in that hot little uniform."

She snorts, face flushed.

"I wanted you," I say, soft now. "From the second I met you. But then it got worse."

"Worse?"

"Yeah. You made me care." I tilt her face up again. "Lola, I care about you so much it fucking hurts."

She doesn't say anything right away. Just blinks. And then presses her forehead to my shoulder like she's overwhelmed by it. My hand curves around the back of her head, holding her close.

"I know we're working together. I know it's complicated. But I don't care. I want you in my bed, in my life, wherever I can get you."

"You already have me," she whispers.

That does something to me, something primal.

I pull her tighter into my arms, fitting her head under my chin like I'm trying to fuse us together.

"I'll keep you safe, Lo. No matter what. I don't give a shit who's watching or what rules there are, you're mine now. You get that?"

She nods against my chest, her breath warm where it touches my skin. "I get it."

"And I'll handle the work stuff. I'll keep it professional when we're out there. You don't need to worry anymore, and I'm so sorry about earlier. I was an absolute idiot, and I'll never treat you like that ever again."

She tilts her face to look at me again, and for a moment I see it, the old grief behind her eyes, that quiet ache I've only ever seen in mirrors.

"You don't have to protect me, Harley, and thank you for apologising. But you also don't get to lose me over fucking Jack Pritchard".

"Yeah, I do," I murmur, brushing my thumb along her jaw. "Because no one did that for me. And because I know what it's like to feel alone in a crowd. I won't let you feel that again."

Her throat works like she's swallowing emotion, and then she breathes out a laugh.

"You're really not who I thought you were."

"No?"

"I thought you were all bravado and cocky snowboarder vibes."

I grin. "I am."

"But you're also the guy who made me feel safe, who carried me like I was breakable, even though I'm not."

"You're not breakable," I say, pressing a kiss to her shoulder. "But you are mine. And I take care of what's mine."

She sighs, sinks a little deeper into my arms, like her whole body's softening under the weight of being cared for.

And for the first time in a long time, I feel like I'm not just surviving. I'm actually living. With her.

Light's already seeping through the gap in the curtains when I open my eyes.

She's still here. Still curled into me like she belongs, one bare leg tangled in mine, her hand splayed across my chest like it's instinct. Her curls are everywhere again, and I love it. I could lie here forever just watching her breathe. But time's a bastard. Reality's already clawing at the edge of the silence, service is in an hour, people will start moving, questions will start getting asked. Lola stirs, brow creasing slightly, her fingers curling into my chest. I press a kiss to her forehead.

"Hey," I murmur. "You awake?"

She lifts her head, sleep-heavy eyes blinking at me. She looks soft and messy, flushed from sleep, sex and warmth. My chest hurts just looking at her.

Her voice is quiet. "We should probably get up."

I nod slowly. "Yeah. We probably should."

But neither of us move.

Eventually she pushes herself up, pulling the duvet around her. Her hair's a riot, her skin marked with every place I touched last night. She sees me looking and flushes, but doesn't cover herself.

She smiles. "You're looking at me like I'm a miracle."

"You kind of are."

I sit up, pulling her between my legs, arms sliding around her waist. "I meant it last night. I'm in this. All the way, I love you."

She nods, her fingers brushing my cheek. "I know you are, I love you too, but you do need to trust me, okay?"

"I know baby, I do. I just... in the moment I read it all wrong," I say taking a ragged breath." Please believe me when I say I'll never fuck this up again."

There's a knock on the door and we both jump. There's a pause, then Niko's voice from the other side, lazy and teasing.

"Transfer schedule's changed, Nash. Scarlett wants a briefing before breakfast."

Lola presses her lips together to keep from laughing.

"I hate him," I mutter.

"You don't."

"I really do."

She kisses me, short and sweet. "Go be charming."

I sigh, drag myself out of bed, and start pulling on clothes while she gathers her things.

At the door, I hesitate. "You alright?"

She looks up. "I'm better than alright."

And I believe her.

When I step into the hallway, I feel it, the shift. Something's settled. Something real. She's not just the girl I wanted, she's the girl I'd fight to keep.

CHAPTER 21

Pitches

HARLEY

It's early morning and Lola's curled up in the corner of the staff lounge sofa, bare feet tucked beneath her, notebook balanced on one thigh. She's got a biro in her mouth and her hair's a mess of curls from sleep, half-falling into her eyes. She's wearing one of my old T-shirts, sleeves bunched at her elbows, the hem almost covering her shorts, and there's a blanket pooled around her waist.

She's highlighting something, maybe rota updates. I can't really tell. She looks so small and beautiful I unconsciously tap the centre of my chest and can't believe she's mine for real this time.

I linger in the doorway like a lovesick idiot.

She looks up, and the corners of her mouth curve. "You gonna come in, or just brood from the shadows?"

I scratch the back of my neck, suddenly wishing I'd rehearsed this. "Can I talk to you for a sec, baby?"

She sets her highlighter down and straightens, curious. "Of course. What's going on?"

I slide into the chair opposite her. Try not to fidget; try not to sound like a guy about to ask his girlfriend if she's ever thought about a joint mortgage. This is scarier, somehow.

"I've been thinking about after this," I say, then immediately want to punch myself. Great start.

She smiles again, warm and amused. "That's usually dangerous."

"I'm serious."

"Okay." She leans in, giving me her full attention now. "What about?"

I take a breath. "About after this. After the season. After Ibiza. About… something bigger."

Her brows lift. She doesn't interrupt.

"I've been reading," I admit. "Books. Podcasts. That course I told you about? The business one online? I finished it. And it made me think, what if this job, this life, wasn't just a way out for me. What if we could make it that for other kids too?"

Her eyes sharpen, focused. But she stays quiet.

"I mean kids like me," I go on. "From council estates, from nowhere, who think they'll never get to leave. What if we built something, a real business. A programme. Bring them here, teach them hospitality, ski instructing, lifeguarding, whatever. Help them become like… Ash. Like you."

"Like you," she says softly, coming over to sit in my lap. She strokes her finger along my jaw.

I shake my head. "Like us. A whole crew."

"Harley. That's… incredible."

I finally meet her eyes. "I've already got backing. Zane, Red Frog's Zane, he's in. Financially, hands on. He wants to support it properly. Said it's exactly the kind of thing this place needs."

She blinks, then grins slowly. "Zane? That's amazing."

"He's got reach too. Old contacts in Canada, sponsors. And even some actor friends who invest in charitable projects. This could be huge, Lo."

She reaches for my hand. "And you'd be the one leading it."

I squeeze her fingers. "Not just me. I want you in this too. You've got more heart than half the people I've met in this job. You'd be especially good with the young women. Help shape the whole thing."

Her eyes soften. "You're serious."

"I am."

"And Scarlett?"

I smirk. "Zane reckons she's already half in. Said she's been asking questions about Break Line, wanting to know how it works, what her role would be if she signed on. He thinks she's got her own reasons."

Lola raises an eyebrow. "Her reasons, huh?"

I lean back and grin. "Apparently they've been spending a lot of time in the wine cellar."

Lola laughs, throwing her head back. "Well, damn. I always thought there was something going on there."

I nod. "Same. And now we've got an actual shot at doing something real. Building something from scratch. I've never had that before."

Her fingers tighten around mine where they're already tangled in her lap. "You do now."

I don't say anything for a second. Just watch her. This girl who walked into my life and changed everything without even trying.

Then she speaks. "I love it. Just like I love you."

The way she says it back, quiet, steady, without hesitation, undoes something in me.

"I love you too," I say. And it feels like the first real promise I've ever made.

And for the first time in a long time, I actually believe I can keep it.

❄

The Pitch Part Deux

Harley

Scarlett peers at us from behind her desk, one brow arched.

"So let me get this straight," she says, arms crossed, "you want to build a business that trains disadvantaged young people to work seasonal jobs? Ski hosts, water sports, hospitality, the whole lot?"

Ash and I nod in unison like nervous interns.

"We'd provide the training," Ash says. "We've already got the experience between us. You know how many kids like Harley could've made it if they'd just had someone believe in them?"

Scarlett's expression softens, just a fraction.

"And the framework's already there," I add. "Between Powder White and Sunship. We know the rotations and logistics. Zane's backing it financially, and I've started building out the business plan."

Scarlett tilts her head, eyes flicking with interest. "Zane Beaulieu?" she says, like she doesn't know.

I nod. "He's all in. Said it's exactly the kind of legacy project the Alps needs."

She leans back, expression unreadable now. "I might've heard something."

Ash raises an eyebrow. "You knew?"

Scarlett shrugs. "Zane and I talk."

Ash and I share a glance.

"You... started a business plan?" she asks, refocusing on me.

"I took an online business course," I mumble.

Ash coughs to cover a laugh. Scarlett studies us for a moment longer. Then her expression shifts from sceptical to something else, maybe pride, maybe cautious belief.

"You really want to do this," she says.

"Yes," I tell her. "I want to make sure no kid ever feels like they're stuck just because no one showed them the exit door."

She nods slowly. "It's ambitious. Idealistic. Underfunded. And probably a logistical nightmare."

We wait.

She exhales. "But if anyone's mad enough to pull it off, it's you two. Alright. I'll help however I can."

Ash grins. I exhale.

Lola's waiting just outside the office, pacing. She turns when she sees us.

"Well?" she asks.

Ash grins. "Let's just say... the Godmother of the mountain is in."

She throws her arms around me without hesitation, her breath warm in my ear. “I knew you’d get her on board.”

I hold her tighter than I mean to, because now it’s real.

CHAPTER 22

Blueprints and Backlash

LOLA

It's late, the bar's closed, chairs are stacked, the floors mopped. There's a kind of silence that feels heavy, except for the hum of the cooler and the scratch of Niko's pen against his notebook. God knows what he's writing in it. His best one-liners if I know Niko. We've hijacked a corner booth like teenagers hiding from curfew, with half-eaten pizza boxes spread across the table, mugs of lukewarm coffee, and a pile of scribbled notes that barely make sense outside of this moment.

Ash is pacing, long strides, reminding me of a caged lion in the zoo. Harley's fidgeting with the cap of a pen, clicking it open and shut, over and over, like the sound might drown out the nerves buzzing under his skin. Imogen's got her glasses on, which means we're on the clock, whether Harley likes it or not. Sarah and Tyler sit close but not touching. Tyler with his arms folded, Sarah twisting her ponytail around her fingers.

"Okay," Harley says finally, flipping open his notes. His voice is calm, but I see it, the tightness in his jaw, the twitch in his thumb against the edge of the table.

"The working title," he says. "Break Line."

Imogen cocks her head, sceptical as ever. "Sounds like an avalanche safety manual."

Before Harley can respond, Sarah cuts in. "No, I like it. It's got weight, breaking the cycle, breaking the rules, breaking out. All of it."

Niko grins. "Plus anything that sounds vaguely dangerous fits you Harley."

Harley rolls his eyes; he's listening, absorbing, the way he always does when it matters.

I catch the way his thumb keeps tapping, fast and restless. That's his tell. And I can't stand watching him carry this alone.

"Start from the top, babe," I say softly.

His eyes flick to mine, just for a second, then he clears his throat. "Zane's in. He's already agreed to back the project. We're starting small, pilot phase next winter. Seasonal bootcamps for disadvantaged kids. We bring them here, house them, train them. Give them structure and purpose."

Ash stops pacing. "He's underselling it," he says bluntly. "We've already talked it through, me, him, Niko, Lola. It's not just 'structure.' It's discipline, safety, accountability. I'll run that side." He crosses his arms, solid and immovable. "I've trained bigger groups than this. Trust me, the kids won't walk all over it."

Imogen raises an eyebrow. "And what if they don't want discipline? What if they just want a free holiday?"

"That's where I come in," Niko says, flashing a grin. "They can hate Ash all day, then I'll make them laugh about it, I'll be the person they don't feel judged by. Some of these kids have probably never heard someone tell them they're good at anything, that's my part." He shrugs. "Morale's underrated."

I lean forward, catching Sarah's eye. "It's not about making them perfect. It's about giving them a season where someone believes they can be more than the worst thing that's happened to them." My voice comes out tighter than I meant, because I can feel it, deep in my chest. "That's why I'm in, that's why we're doing this."

There's a tangible ripple around the table.

Imogen finally takes her glasses off. "And you expect us to just... slot ourselves in?"

Ash snorts. "You don't have to do anything, but we'd really appreciate it if you did."

Sarah looks between us, her ponytail twisting tighter around her finger. "I just don't see how it works. Housing, food, equipment, who's paying for all this?"

"Zane's investment gets us the foundation," Harley says. "We've got some early suppliers who've shown interest too. But we'll need to scale. Fundraise. Hustle."

"Wait," Tyler says, voice sharp. "So this is all really happening?"

Harley doesn't flinch. "It's real. The question now is whether we can build the right team to carry it."

The words hang there, heavy in the air.

Sarah leans back, arms crossed now; her expression isn't hostile, just sharp, like she's looking for cracks in the idea. "You make it sound so simple. Bring kids here, house them, keep them fed, entertained, safe. But none of you are social workers. None of you are trained in safeguarding. What happens when one of these kids melts down? Or runs away? Or..." She falters, then steadies herself again. "It's not just skiing and pizza, Harley. You're talking about real responsibility."

Tyler nods, his tone more measured but no less wary. "And what about the resort? You think Powder White is going to let a bunch of kids turn this place into a youth club? That's brand suicide if it goes wrong."

Niko lets out a whistle through his teeth. "Ouch. That's faith, right there."

Ash shoots him a look. "He's not wrong to raise it." He turns back to Sarah and Tyler. "Look, you're not wrong either. It will be hard, it will stretch us, and yeah, it might even fail. But I've led kids younger than this, in worse conditions, with less food and fewer resources, and they still came out stronger on the other side. Structure doesn't have to mean cages; it means boundaries, safety nets, and for some of these kids, that'll be the first time anyone's ever set a boundary because they cared."

The silence after that lands differently, weightier, even Sarah stops twisting her hair.

Harley finally speaks again, voice quieter now. "I'm not saying I've got it all figured out, I don't. But I know what it feels like to grow up without anyone giving a shit whether you make it or not. And if there's even one kid out there who doesn't have to feel that way because of this, then I think it's worth every risk."

My throat tightens at the way his voice cracks on that last word. He doesn't look at me, but I see the way his hand flexes, white-knuckled, around the pen cap.

Imogen clears her throat. "Okay. Let's talk logistics, say Zane doesn't come through, because you know he might not, what then?"

"Then we scale it back," Harley says immediately. "Start small with a handful of kids, maybe three or four. We fundraise, we find local sponsorship, whatever it takes."

Ash stops pacing. He drops into the booth next to Imogen and leans forward, forearms braced on the table. "No one's pretending this is easy, but you've all seen what this season's been, chaos, mistakes. People getting hurt, getting left behind, and yeah, we've all done stupid shit. But we've also seen what it looks like when we pull each other back up. That's what Break Line is an extension of that; a legacy."

His eyes scan the table, and for once even Niko isn't joking. I can feel it building, that ripple that started earlier may not just be hope.

Imogen taps her glasses case against the table. "Fine. But if I'm in, I'm running the admin. I don't want any of you lot messing with legal forms or parental consent slips."

"Noted," Harley says.

"I'm in too," Niko adds. "You know I'm in too, and I'd like to design the team hoodies."

"God help us," Ash mutters.

"Oi. Branding matters."

Tyler exhales, long and slow, rubbing his jaw like he's trying to work the doubt out of it. "Look, I don't hate it. I just... I don't trust it maybe. I've worked too many dead-end jobs to gamble on something built on a 'maybe.'"

Sarah rests her hand over his. "Then maybe it's time we gamble on something bigger." Her voice is quiet, but her eyes are fierce. "Because if Harley's right, and it helps even one kid, then it's already worth it."

The air in the room stills. And one by one, all eyes shift back to Harley. He doesn't move, or blink, just waits.

I squeeze his hand under the table. "You already know my answer."

And then, slowly, Tyler nods. "Fine. I'm in."

Sarah follows immediately. "Me too."

The tension breaks like a dam. Imogen shakes her head with a smile she doesn't even try to hide. Niko punches the air like we've just scored a winning goal. Ash finally sits back, satisfied, like the soldier in him has just won a quiet battle. And Harley, his jaw twitches, but it's not nerves anymore, it's maybe for the first time since I've known him, certainty.

There's an explosion echoing through the valley in the distance and everyone tenses.

No need to worry bébé's the ski patrol are triggering avalanches in a safe way. They sent the area notifications earlier.

We break later than we should, and now everyone's gone to their respective spaces I tell Harley that I'm going to get clean towels and that I'll meet him in our room.

❄

I cut past reception, and stop. Jack's voice carries from the bar hatch, pitched low.

"You'll never guess what Harley's flogging now, some rehab camp for strays. Bring 'em up the mountain, teach 'em to scrub dishes and smile at rich people, and call it salvation."

Sophie's wiping down the chalkboard, the squeak of it scraping a nerve straight through my teeth. She doesn't look over. That's new, she usually meets every conversation head-on.

Jack keeps going. "You should've seen him in there. Big speech, wounded-boy eyes. 'Structure, purpose, community.'" He imitates Harley's voice, badly, and it's so childish it burns. "He's got half the team drinking the Kool-Aid."

I don't realise I've curled my hands into fists until my nails bite my palm.

Sophie sets the chalk down a little too hard. "It's not your call."

He laughs, mean and easy. "Everything's my call when it turns the place into a youth hostel with trauma."

"You don't know the first thing about trauma," she says, still not looking at him. "Or about Harley."

"Please. Harley's a brand, sad eyes, tragic backstory, hero complex. Slap a logo on it, Break Line, was it? And suddenly he's Saint Nash of the Alps." He clicks his tongue. "Give it a month and he'll be recruiting donors at après like it's Comic Relief."

"Jack." Sophie finally turns. It's quiet the way knives are quiet. "Enough."

"What, you're in love with the project now too?" He tips his chin toward the corridor, toward the room we just left. "He's playing them. He's playing her most of all."

He doesn't say my name but I feel it land anyway.

"Watch," he says. "He'll fail. And when he does, he'll have a built-in excuse, 'systemic issues,' 'not enough funding,' 'kids are complicated', and everyone will pat his head and call him brave. Meanwhile we'll be here picking up the pieces when one of his 'second chances' steals a guest's watch."

I taste metal, for a second I see Harley's hands, ink-stained, shaking, on the table while he tried to keep his voice level. I see the way Ash stepped in, how Niko joked because he was nervous, how Imogen measured a mountain of forms in her head and still said yes. I see all of it, tender, messy, real. And then I hear Jack spit on it.

Sophie's voice flattens. "You done?"

Jack shrugs. "Just calling it, some of us live in the real world."

He turns his back like the conversation is over. I step away from the corner before my body makes a decision my brain can't walk back. I won't tell Harley, not yet.

❄

Imogen's still up, curled in the ugly blue armchair that somehow fits her like it was made to fit her. She has a mug balanced on her knee, glasses off, hair loosened from the day. She doesn't startle when I come in, she just looks up like she knew I'd be the one walking through the door.

"What happened?" she asks. Not what's wrong, what happened. It makes it easier to answer.

"Jack." I don't bother sitting first. "I heard him with Sophie just now."

Her face doesn't move at the word *Jack*, but everything in the room tightens around it.

"What did he say?"

I repeat it, Rehab camp, brand, Saint Nash, fail and be forgiven, and the dig at me.

Imogen's jaw sets, hard. She sets the mug down on the windowsill with controlled care, like she refuses to give him the satisfaction of a clatter. "He really said 'brand'?"

"He did." My voice scrapes. "And he meant every word."

"For the record," she says, calm but sharp, "Jack doesn't know life outside a room where he's the loudest voice. He mistakes volume for proof." She tips her chin at the chair. "Sit."

I perch on the arm like a kid about to get told a story and a truth.

Imogen turns towards me. "Listen carefully, what you lot did in there wasn't naive, it was strategic, and it was brave. You started with a maybe and you carved it into a plan, that's how anything worth doing gets born. Jack isn't threatened by the kids, he's threatened by the fact you don't need his permission. And Harley has you, period."

The words find the place in me that's still shaking and stick.

"He said Harley's playing us," I whisper. "That he'll fail."

"Harley might fail," she says, as if that's allowed to live in the air. "We all might; that's why we'll build the boring bits properly. Safeguarding, insurance, rota, catering, transport, the unsexy spine that keeps a good idea upright. That part's mine, I'll make sure we're audit-proof and chaos-resistant, you can quote me."

My throat burns. "He also..." I swallow. "He implied I'm the easiest part, that Harley's... using me."

Imogen's mouth purses. "Jack knows you're the part he can't touch, so he's trying to rot it from the edges." She lets that sit a beat. "Harley's not using you, he's leaning on you. There's a difference. And yes, he'll lean harder than he knows, because this scares him. Your steadiness is going to be part of the work. If you can't hold that, say so now. If you can... then hold it without apologising."

I breathe out, shaky. "I love him and I can hold it and him at the same time."

"Good." She reaches for her tea, rethinks it, and chooses my hand instead, a quick squeeze that says she's got me. "Here's what happens next, you don't engage Jack. You don't dignify his commentary. If he says anything like that to a guest or drops it in front of Scarlett, I'll make sure he's bleaching grout with a toothbrush until the thaw. If he says it to Harley, you tell me first, because I don't want Harley wasting a single ounce of energy on a man whose only talent is erosion."

I laugh, short, unstable, grateful. "You've already thought about all this, haven't you?"

"I think about everything." Her mouth quirks. "It's a sickness."

We sit in the quiet for a moment.

"I thought Jack had changed," I say. "I wanted to believe it."

"Of course you did." Imogen doesn't make me feel stupid for it. "Most of us build our first draft of a person out of hope, editing just takes longer with some men."

"Do I tell Harley?" It feels like the hardest question, even though I already know my answer. "I don't want to load this on him."

"Not tonight," Imogen says. "Maybe not tomorrow, tell him when it's information, not a live grenade. And when you do, anchor it to a plan, not a feeling. 'Here's what he said. Here's what we're doing, here's who's on your side.'" She lifts one shoulder. "Spoiler alert everyone that matters."

I nod. "Thank you."

She stands, smoothing a crease in her skirt that isn't there, armour sliding back on even at this hour. "Go to bed, Lola, you've done enough saving for one night."

As I get up, she adds, almost casually, "And for what it's worth? Break Line is a brilliant name."

I smile. "Sarah said the same."

"Then it's settled." She collects her tea, finally takes a sip, and winces. "Cold. I hate symbolism."

I snort. "Liar. You live for it."

She doesn't deny it. "Goodnight."

"Night."

CHAPTER 23

Dangerous Looks Good On You

LOLA

Upstairs in our room, Harley's sprawled across the bed like he fought a war against the mattress and lost. One arm dangling off the side, his hair's a mess, T-shirt bunched halfway up his stomach. His notebook is trapped under his chest, pages bent, pen still clutched like he fell asleep mid-thought. I stare at him for a few moments, his inked abs are... God; he's so beautiful.

I ease the notebook free, carefully trying not to wake him. His scribbles are messy, half-legible, but my heart clenches anyway. Headings about modules, lists of kids he wants to reach. Words like *purpose* and *structure* underlined twice.

He doesn't even know how much I want him when he's like this, when he has his guard down only for me.

The idea takes root before I can think it through. My pulse spikes as I peel my clothes off slowly, deliberately, until I'm bare in the cool air. Slipping beneath the sheets, I press myself against his warm body.

He doesn't move, but I know he's awake, because his breathing shifts into a lighter, quicker cadence.

I stare at him until his lips twitch.

"Stop burning holes in my face, Maxwell," he murmurs, eyes still shut.

I giggle, busted. "Can't help it. You're too... much."

"Too what?" His voice is gravel, wrecked from sleep.

"You're so hot when you get all serious." I bite my lip. "Like tonight, talking about Break Line, bossing everyone. You don't know what it did to me."

His eyes crack open, blue and sharp even in the dim light. "You're telling me you got turned on by my TED Talk?"

I laugh into his shoulder. "Yes. You're dangerous when you're in charge. Serious CEO energy with tattoos. God help me."

That makes him groan, dragging a hand over his face. "You'll kill me one day."

I press closer, lips brushing his ear. "Maybe."

He shifts onto his back, blinking up at the ceiling like he's buying time, but I catch the second his brain catches up. His body goes taut under the sheets. His gaze flicks down to where I'm pressed against him, then back up, his jaw tightening.

"You're naked." His voice is low, dangerous in that way that makes my stomach flip.

I grin, completely unashamed. "Observant."

"Lola..." There's warning in it, but his hand betrays him, sliding to my hip like it can't resist the gravity of me. His thumb brushes my bare skin, and his eyes squeeze shut. "Fuck."

I nudge his notebook toward the bedside table with a smirk. "I took this hostage, payment required."

He huffs a laugh, but it's strained. "You don't play fair."

"Neither do you," I shoot back, dragging my nails lightly over his chest, just enough to make his muscles twitch. "Do you even know what it does to me when you get that look? When you're in a room and everyone listens because you're too intense not to?"

He shakes his head, almost disbelieving. "You're turned on by me talking logistics."

I kiss the corner of his jaw. "I'm turned on by you, full stop."

His breath hitches, his hand cupping the back of my neck holding me there, but he still doesn't pull me in. He's fighting it, every muscle straining with control.

"You're naked," he repeats, like if he says it again it'll make sense.

"And you're not," I whisper, teeth grazing his ear. "Unfair advantage, don't you think?"

That earns me a groan so deep it vibrates through my whole body.

"Jesus Christ, Lola..."

I giggle into his skin, wicked and breathless. "What?"

"You're playing with fire."

"Maybe I want to get burned."

His eyes snap open then, blue fire catching mine, and for a second I swear the whole room tilts with it.

The second those words leave my mouth, something in him fractures. His restraint, that tight leash he's been holding, just... snaps.

In one motion, Harley rolls, pinning me beneath him, the sheet tangling around our legs. His weight presses me down into the mattress, caging me completely, the look in his eyes is feral.

"You think this is a fucking game?" His voice is a growl, rough, chest heaving.

My laugh comes out shaky, wrecked already. "Kind of?"

"Wrong answer." His mouth crashes against mine, all teeth and tongue and fury. He kisses like he's starving, like I've been tormenting him for hours and he's finally done letting me win.

His hands are everywhere at once, gripping my wrists above my head, sliding down to grab my thigh, hauling it around his hip like he owns every inch of me. I moan against his mouth, arching into him, and he pulls back just enough to rasp, Jesus, you're naked fucking naked under me while I've still got clothes on. Do you have any idea what that does to me?"

"Mm-hmm," I breathe, smug even now.

He snarls, ripping his t-shirt over his head and tossing it somewhere across the room, then grinds down so I can feel just how gone he is for me. I swear, my breath catches at the sight of him, like I forgot he was this beautiful up close. "Not smug anymore, baby, I warned you."

My nails dig into his shoulders. "Warned me about what?"

His hand fists in my hair, yanking my head back enough that his mouth can drag down my throat, biting hard enough to make me gasp. "About how filthy I'll get when you push me like this."

I shiver, writhing under him, completely at his mercy, and he laughs darkly against my skin. "That's it. That's what you wanted, isn't it? To make me lose it, to hear me say the things I shouldn't?"

"Yes," I gasp. "God, yes."

"Then you're getting every fucking word."

He kisses me again, brutal and perfect, and suddenly we're past the point of teasing, past the point of slow. He's everywhere, overwhelming, dragging every filthy sound out of me while muttering in my ear how I begged for this, how I wanted him unhinged, how I'm never getting away from him now. I love how uncontrolled he can be in these moments between us.

Harley's still crushing me into the mattress, eyes dark and hungry, but when he shifts lower, his tone changes. Rougher, yes, but deliberate.

"You think you can just strip naked, crawl into bed, and expect me to slide inside you like I'm not built to split you in half?" His voice is low, dangerous, almost taunting. "Nah, baby, you know better."

I open my mouth to answer, but then his hand is between my thighs, fingers dragging slow and firm over me, and all I can do is whimper.

He smirks against my throat. "That's it, wet already, knew you would be." Two fingers tease me, not inside yet, just circling, coaxing, making my hips jerk up against his hand. "But not wet enough, not for me."

"Harley."

"You wanted me unhinged, you wanted filthy?" His teeth graze my ear, sending shivers down my spine. "Then take it. Feel how hard I am, and know you're not even close to me fitting inside you yet."

He grinds against me, cock straining against the fabric.

"See?" he says, almost cruel, sliding one finger into me, then another, stretching me slow. "You're still tight as fuck, and I've barely touched you. Gonna open you up, pretty girl. Gonna make you drip all over my hand before I even think about giving you cock."

I cry out, nails raking his shoulders, but he doesn't let up. His fingers curl, finding that spot that makes me sob, and he watches me unravel, chest heaving, sweat slick at his temples.

"Look at you," he rasps, working me harder. "Begging without words, soaked, desperate, all because I said I'd wreck you."

"Please," I choke out. "Please, Harley."

"Not yet," he growls, shoving his fingers deeper, thumb circling my clit until I'm shaking. "You'll take every second of this, because I'm not risking hurting you.

I'm crying his name now, thighs trembling around his wrist, pleasure building sharp and unbearable.

"Come on then," he commands, voice hoarse. "Come for me. Show me you're ready to take me."

And when I break apart on his hand, shuddering, nails carving red down his back, his smile is wicked and reverent all at once.

"Good girl."

He pulls his fingers out of me, slow, deliberate, like he's making sure I feel every inch leaving. I'm still twitching, still catching my breath, when he grabs a condom from the drawer by the bed and tears it open with his teeth.

I lick my lips. "You're not touching me bare," he growls, sliding it down his length with one hand, the other holding my hip down because I can't stop squirming toward him. "Not tonight. Not when I'm this close to losing my mind."

I whimper at the sight of him, thick and heavy, the condom rolled tight.

That smirk of his is lethal. "Yeah, and you're gonna take every fucking inch."

I gasp when he drags the head of his cock through my slick

folds, teasing, coating himself. He pauses at my entrance, pressing just enough for me to feel the stretch, then pulling back again. My nails claw his chest in frustration.

"Harley!"

"You think I'm rushing this?" His voice is gravel, low and dangerous. "I told you, baby, once I'm inside, I'm not stopping."

And then he pushes inside me, slow at first, the thick crown breaching me, stretching me wider than his fingers ever could. My body clenches hard around him, and he grits his teeth, sweat beading at his temple.

"Fuck, I always forget how tight you are," he snarls, pressing in another inch. "Relax for me, Lo, let me in, I've got you."

I pant, head thrown back, overwhelmed by the burn and the fullness. My legs shake around his hips, and he bends down, mouth on my ear, whispering filth.

"Feel that? That's just the tip, you've got so much more to take."

I moan, and he groans with me, inching deeper, stretching me slowly but relentlessly. His control is razor-thin, I can see it in the way his jaw flexes, in the way his hands tremble against my thighs.

"Fuck, baby," he grits out. "You're swallowing me whole."

When he finally bottoms out, buried to the hilt, we both cry out. He stays there, deep inside me, chest pressed to mine, letting me feel every inch of him, letting my body adjust.

"Holy fuck," I breathe, nails digging crescents into his skin.

He grins, feral. "You know why I have to get you ready. You're perfect around me, Lola, made for me."

And then he starts to move, not slow, not gentle, not anymore. He pulls nearly all the way out, leaving me empty and gasping, then slams back in with a force that makes the bed creak.

"Harley!" I scream, and he shoves his mouth into the crook of my neck, muffling his own groan.

"That's it, scream my name."

His thrusts are brutal, filthy, each one hitting so deep I see stars. He pins my wrists above my head with one hand, his other gripping my hip so hard I'm sure I'll have bruises tomorrow.

"You love it," he snarls against my mouth. "You love how I ruin you."

"Yes," I sob, arching under him, desperate for more. "Don't stop, please don't stop."

"Not a chance."

He pounds into me, pace rough and relentless, sweat dripping down his chest, hair falling into his eyes. I'm clinging to him, body stretched and undone, drowning in the feel of him everywhere.

"Say it," he demands, voice jagged. "Say you're mine."

"I'm yours," I cry. "Always yours."

I'll never want anyone else like this. This man is going to ruin me for anyone who isn't him. God, I think I'd let him break me a thousand times just to feel this again.

When I do break, it's not just my body, it's every thought, every breath. I sob his name, raw and wrecked, and he follows, burying himself deep, shuddering like I just tore the ground from under him.

We're still clinging, still gasping, hearts pounding out of sync as he collapses on top of me, breath hot against my neck.

The room is nothing but ragged breaths, slick skin, and the faint creak of the mattress beneath us. He stays inside me, trembling, chest heaving against mine.

Then he tilts my chin up, eyes dark and reverent all at once.

"You'll be the death of me Lola Maxwell," he whispers, voice breaking. "And I'll thank you for it."

We're both still panting, my body wrecked, trembling from head to toe and he's still buried inside me, holding me down with his weight like he's afraid I'll vanish if he lets go.

My laugh comes out shaky, half-broken. "Jesus, Harley... you're insane."

He lifts his head, hair damp and plastered to his forehead, that wolfish grin cutting through the wreckage. "Took you like you asked, didn't I?"

I slap his chest, weak and giggling. "You didn't just 'take' me, you tried to break me in half."

His laugh is rough, deep. "You loved it."

I bite my lip, trying not to look smug. "Yeah. I really fucking did."

He kisses me quick, still grinning. "Knew it."

I squirm under him, feeling him still thick inside me, twitching. "I told you why I started this."

He raises a brow. "Because you like to torture me?"

"No." I grin, because you're hot."

His eyes go darker if that's even possible. He shifts his hips, dragging another moan out of me. "So my girl gets wet when I play businessman?"

I giggle, caught. "Apparently."

He leans in, lips brushing my ear. "You're in trouble then. Because when I've got all this nailed down, I'm gonna look a hell of a lot more dangerous."

I shiver, clinging tighter to him. "Good. I want the world to see you like that. My sexy millionaire with tattoos."

His laugh rumbles against my skin, and he nips my neck before finally pulling out, both of us groaning at the loss. He strips the condom off, ties it at the end and tosses it in the bin, then flops onto the mattress beside me.

"Christ," he mutters, dragging me to his chest.

"Worth it," I say smugly, kissing his jaw.

We lie there for a while, sweat cooling, bodies tangled. His thumb strokes lazy circles into my hip, grounding me. Then he sighs, stands up, and hauls me up over his shoulder upside down. A little scream leaves my mouth.

"Shower," he says simply.

"You have an epic backside Harley Nash," I tell him as he dumps me on my feet in the tiny bathroom.

"I also could have walked here myself, babe."

"Now where's the fun in that?"

He turns on the tap, smirks, pushes me gently into the cubicle under the hot spray, steam curling around us. And presses me to the wall, rinsing the mess from my skin with a gentleness that makes my throat ache.

No dirty talk, no snapping, no growling, just Harley's big hands smoothing shampoo into my hair, kissing the slope of my shoulder like he can't get enough of touching me.

When he's done, he just holds me under the water, chin resting on the crown of my head.

"Lola," he murmurs, voice low, raw. "You know I love you, right?"

I tilt my head back, blinking up at him through wet lashes. "I know. And I love you too. So much."

His chest heaves, like he's taking those words into himself. He kisses me, slow and deep, nothing rushed, love bleeding through every touch.

Later, back in bed, we curl up beneath the sheets and he tucks me tight against him, my face pressed into the solid warmth of his chest, his arm banded around me like a shield.

"You fit here," he whispers into my hair. "Always."

I hum, eyes fluttering shut, wrapped in Harley's bigger body, safe in the cocoon of his heat.

And that's how we fall asleep. Tangled, spent, still damp from the shower, hearts beating in sync.

CHAPTER 24

Mountains Meets Hollywood

HARLEY

Harley created the group "DBDL"

Harley: Zane just confirmed. Dan Bailey arrives tomorrow. 2PM.

He's bringing someone with him. Lucy Taylor. Keep it quiet. Just us four.

Imogen: WAIT. *The* Lucy Taylor???

Ash: Who's Lucy Taylor? And what is DBDL?

Lola: Dan Bailey's PA. Single mum. Left her ex, took her daughter, rebuilt her whole life. They're engaged now.

Ash: Right. No pressure then.

Imogen: I love her. She's a *force.* Also her shoes are always perfect. How does she do that with a ten-year-old?

Harley: Focus, Ash, DBDL is 'Dan Bailey, Down-Low'.

Ash: You invited the blueprint of emotional survival and now you want us to be chill?

Harley: Ash, gear room. Imogen, strip the doc. Key stats only.

Lola, you stay close.

Lola: What, to Lucy or to you?

Harley: Yes

Lola: 

Harley: Babe...

Lola: 👀 Yes.

Imogen: Do we act like we haven't memorised her outfits from that Tatler spread?

Harley: Just... no screaming.

Ash: What if I scream internally?

Harley: Muted the group.

I didn't bother asking how Zane knew Dan Bailey. Zane knows everyone. Investors, athletes, half of London's nightlife, if there's a back door into a circle, he's already got the key. So when he said Dan and his fiancée were flying out, it didn't even sound strange. Just inevitable.

Still, knowing it and seeing it aren't the same thing. The Red Frog's our place, scarred tables, beer rings that never come out, Niko mouthing off while propping up the bar. It's not where you expect to find an A-list actor and the woman who rebuilt his life from scratch.

But Zane set it up, and if Zane says "they're in," you don't argue. You just sit with the nerves buzzing under your ribs and wait for the door to open.

❄

Lola

Zane gets to the door first. Of course he does.

I'm behind the Red Frog's bar, polishing a bottle that doesn't need polishing in an effort to focus my nerves when a black Range Rover pulls up. That kind of car isn't just built to survive the snow, it's built to make an entrance in it.

The driver's door opens and Dan Bailey climbs out. The *Dan Bailey.* He doesn't pause or wait for attention, just moves around to the passenger side and opens the door, like this is all completely normal.

It's fucking surreal. Not because he's famous, though he is. Not because he's stunning, though he definitely is. But because he's here. At the Red Frog. In our world.

Dan helps Lucy down like it's instinct. Her coat's long and black, her hair's a halo of thick brown curls. Confident. Effortless. But not untouchable. She looks like someone who's had to fight for her place. There's a steel in her stance that doesn't need volume to be noticed.

Zane greets her first, arms out, grinning. She hugs him without hesitation, like they've known each other forever. Then Dan gets a handshake, a shoulder-clap, the kind of warmth Zane usually saves for old teammates.

"Welcome to the Red Frog," Zane calls out, loud enough for the rest of us to hear through the open door.

I glance at Harley. He's watching them closely, jaw set, but his hand brushes mine under the counter, quick and grounding. I straighten up and tuck a curl behind my ear. Not for Dan. Not for Lucy. For Harley.

Zane walks them through the bar like royalty. Harley trails behind, casual but sharp-eyed. The main space is quiet, we closed it for this. Just the back booths and the firelit table.

Ash is already there, lounging like he's not ready to explode from nerves. Imogen's got her laptop open, notes queued, files ready. The room hums with that nervous, hopeful energy we've all been living in for weeks.

Lucy clocks it straight away. "It's cosy," she says.

"It's strategic," Zane replies smoothly. "No distractions."

Dan nods. He gets it.

They sit. Dan takes the corner booth, Lucy beside him. She removes her gloves and rests one hand on his knee, casual, intimate. Present. I'm nearly blinded by the massive rock on her left hand, third finger, and have to make a concerted effort to look away.

Harley takes the seat opposite them. Ash drops in beside him. I stay behind the bar, not sure if I'm supposed to be part of this or just scenery.

Zane claps his hands once.

"Dan. Lucy. Meet the team behind Break Line. Harley, he's

the founder, the fire starter, the one who wouldn't shut up long enough for me *not* to invest."

Harley grins, and Zane continues.

"This is Ash Morgan, logistics, safety, structure. Ex-Army. Now keeps the rest of us alive."

Ash gives a nod, smirk in place.

"Imogen Vale, operations, heart, mind, spreadsheets. Basically runs the show while Harley broods in corners."

Lucy laughs. It's soft, but real.

"And Lola Maxwell," Zane finishes, nodding toward me.

I meet Lucy's eyes. Then Dan's. I don't shrink, don't overdo it. Just a nod. A small, crooked smile.

"She's been at the centre of it more than she realises," Harley adds. "Come and sit with us, babe," he tells me, holding his arm up gesturing towards me.

Ash scoots over so I slip out from behind the bar and drop in next to him, his arm casually coming up to rest on the back of the booth behind me.

Lucy tilts her head, eyes still on me. "I can see that."

Then Dan leans forward. "Tell me what you've built."

Harley begins.

And somehow, he's calm. Voice steady. None of the muttering, none of the nerves I see when we're alone. This is Harley locked in. Holding the room, not performing, just *being*. Clear. Powerful. True.

He walks Dan through everything. The vision. The structure. The why. The kids who fall through the cracks. The ones written off too soon. How Break Line pulls them back into something worth holding on to.

He doesn't say *his* story. But it's there. In every word.

Imogen slides in with the data, the strategy. Timelines. Projections.

Then Dan's eyebrows furrow and he asks Harley, "Why you? Why this? What makes you believe you can reach them?"

Harley looks at him. Not evasive. Not dramatic. Just... honest.

"Because I was one of them. Foster homes. Suspension by

fourteen. Sleeping rough at fifteen. Nobody expected anything from me except failure. Until someone did."

"Ash met me at a skatepark. I was twelve. He brought me food. Told me I was good enough to compete. I only entered skateboarding competitions because he said it like he meant it."

Harley takes another beat to take a breath.

"Break Line exists because someone like him believed in someone like me. And now... it's our turn to pay it forward."

And in this moment, I'm so fucking proud of Harley I could burst because it's him who holds Dan's attention like a wire pulled tight. He's telling it. The part of himself he only ever whispers in the dark. And he's doing it like it doesn't hurt. Like he's not terrified he'll be dismissed. And I hate that I can't hug him right now.

And Lucy.

She watches all of us. But mostly me.

Not with judgement. Not curiosity, even. With... recognition.

Like she's looking at a version of herself.

It unsettles me more than it should.

Harley finishes and sits back slightly.

Dan doesn't speak right away. He just nods, slow, once. "It's good," he says. "Really fucking good."

Harley blinks. That's it.

Ash lets out a breath he's clearly been holding for ten minutes. Imogen calmly shuts her laptop. Zane practically glows.

"What's next?" Imogen asks, already flipping to logistics.

And Lucy turns to me.

"I can see why he needs you," she says softly.

I freeze.

Her voice is warm, sure. There's no play in it. No flattery.

"You remind me of someone," she adds.

My mouth moves before my brain does. "Who?"

She tilts her head. That small, reflective smile again. "Me. Before everything sharp. Before life knocked me around."

And then she looks away. Just like that.

But something lingers. Like a thread caught between us.

Something quiet.

And very, very real.

The meeting's wound down now. Laptops closed. Glasses empty. Zane and Dan are still in discussion near the fireplace, hands moving, heads low, already onto next steps. Harley's standing beside them, quiet, unreadable, but I know the signs. He's keyed up. Running through every beat again in his head. He'll replay it tonight and still find ways he could've said it better.

Lucy steps away first.

I'm standing near the front edge of the bar, arms folded. Watching, but trying not to look like I'm watching.

She sees me. Doesn't hesitate.

"Got a second?" she asks, stopping just a little off to the side. It's casual. Easy. Like she's done this before, walked up to women younger than her who think they've got the world handled and offered them something they didn't ask for.

I nod.

She glances over her shoulder, then leans lightly against the edge of the bar, not too close.

"You've built something solid here," she says. "Break Line. It's rare. You can tell when something's been earned the hard way."

"Harley earned it," I say before I can stop myself.

She raises an eyebrow. "You didn't?"

I shift my weight. "I just... support. He's the one with the vision."

Lucy gives a small smile like she's heard that line before. Like she once said it herself.

"Let me guess," she says. "You think being the glue isn't as important as being the spark."

I don't answer.

"Yeah," she says softly. "I used to think that too."

"I was nineteen when I had Grace. Her dad was... complicated. The kind of man who makes you feel chosen and small all at once. And I thought if I could just keep things steady, keep things clean and running and calm, I could build a life from it."

Her eyes meet mine, not pitying. Just real.

"But calm doesn't mean safe. And clean doesn't mean kind. And being the one who holds it together doesn't make you weak, it makes you dangerous. Especially when you finally stop doing it for the wrong people."

I don't know what to say to that.

She doesn't wait for a response. Just lets it hang there, soft and sharp and exactly the kind of thing I'll think about later when it's three am and I can't sleep.

She nods once. "You're doing more than you think, Lola. I see it."

And then she turns and walks back toward Dan, who's already watching. He smiles when she reaches him, like nothing in the room matters more than the fact that she came back.

And I just stand there, pulse thrumming stupidly, wondering why the hell I suddenly feel seen.

❄

Harley

Dan Bailey's leans forward by the fireplace like he didn't just watch me pour my whole fucking soul out across a table and call it strategy.

He reaches for his glass of red wine but doesn't drink it. Just rolls it between his palms.

"That was one of the best pitches I've ever sat through," he says grinning.

I blink. Not because I don't believe him. Because I do. That's the part that's messing with me.

Zane leans forward slightly, smiling, like he's known what was coming and he's just been waiting for me to catch up. "Told you," he says.

Dan gives a small nod, then shifts his gaze back to me. "I'm in."

Two words. No fanfare. No handshake. No dramatic contract pulled from a leather satchel. Just I'm in.

And still, my stomach clenches like I'm going to throw up.

Not because I don't want this.

Because I do.

Because I want this more than I've ever let myself admit out loud.

Because now it's real.

I nod once, trying not to look like I'm gripping the edge of the table under my palm.

"Okay," I say, even though it's not even close to what I mean.

Ash claps a hand on my shoulder, firm. "Mate."

Imogen looks up. "There'll be legalities. Contracts. Timeline markers."

Dan raises a hand, already tracking ahead. "I've got a lawyer I trust. We'll arrange a sit-down in London. Zane can coordinate it."

He glances at Zane, who gives a slight, knowing tilt of his head like they've already discussed this.

Dan turns back to me. "I know this stuff can get heavy fast. I'd rather walk you through it, step-by-step. Clear, slow. You set the pace."

I don't know what the hell to say to that.

I've never had someone say you set the pace and mean it.

Imogen's watching me carefully, her expression unreadable. She knows what this means. She knows how fast this can spiral in my head if I let it. So does Ash. So does Zane.

And somehow... I think Lucy saw it before any of them.

"Thanks," I say, throat thick. "That helps."

Dan nods once. No pressure. No timeline. Just steady.

He pushes the empty glass aside, eyes flicking around the room like he's absorbing the space in full before he leaves.

"I've got a shoot starting in LA soon," he adds. "But we can squeeze the meeting in before I go. I'd like to get the ball rolling before the end of the season."

Zane grins. "We'll lock it in."

There's a stretch of silence after that. Not awkward. Just full.

I glance toward the bar where Lola's talking to Lucy again.

Quiet voices. Her head tilted, eyes soft, like she's actually letting herself hear something.

That alone could undo me.

Dan follows my gaze. "She's strong."

I look back at him. He doesn't mean it like a compliment. He means it like a fact.

"She is," I say.

"She remind you of you?"

I shake my head. "She's got more guts."

Dan smiles slightly. "It's a good match."

I don't answer. Because if I say what I'm thinking, I'll fall apart in front of two A-listers and a fucking fireplace.

Imogen starts talking again, thank God, and we shift into logistics. Next steps. Data-sharing. Permissions. Ash pulls out the mapped risk assessments for the mountain phase. Zane references a contact in London who can help with venue space. The meeting tightens, sharpens, gets business-like, but my mind's still spinning.

Because everything's changing.

And for the first time in my life... that doesn't feel like a threat.

It feels like the start of something that might actually hold.

❄

The second the door clicks shut behind us, the silence drops heavy. Not the kind that suffocates. The kind that strips you bare.

I stand there for a moment, back against the wood, trying to pull a breath deep enough to fill my chest. My head's still wired, buzzing so loud I swear I can hear it in my ears. Adrenaline still clings to me like smoke, sharp and restless.

It doesn't feel real. None of it.

Dan Bailey said yes.

Lucy looked at me like I wasn't a fraud.

And now I'm standing here, in this room that's supposed to feel familiar, but the air's thicker, charged, like it knows everything's shifted.

Lola sits on the bed without a word. Not with that usual flop she does after a shift, not the dramatic collapse onto the mattress with a groan about her feet. She lowers herself slowly, deliberately, like she knows if she moves too fast, the thin thread I'm holding onto will snap.

She doesn't ask me anything. Doesn't press. Just sits there, her coat sliding from her shoulders, slips her boots off, hair falling out of whatever knot she had it in. And she watches me.

Her eyes aren't heavy with expectation. No demand in them. Just... steady.

I walk to the bed before my legs give in. I pull my own boots off and drop beside her. The mattress dips under my weight, springs creaking, and the familiar sound should ground me but it doesn't. Not yet.

My hands cover my face, then drag back through my hair, elbows braced on my knees. My chest's too tight, breath ragged. I've been in fights calmer than this. I've stood on rooftops looking down and felt steadier.

But sitting across from Dan Bailey, laying out Break Line like it wasn't stitched together from scraps of my past, I've never felt more exposed.

And then he said yes.

And it's like my brain can't catch up.

"Hey."

Her voice is soft. The kind of soft that makes the noise in my head falter.

I turn my head. She's watching me, chin tipped, eyes dark in the lamplight. She leans closer, her arm brushing mine, and doesn't add anything else. Just waits.

I blow out a shaky breath. "I don't even know what the fuck just happened."

Her lips twitch, a small smile breaking. "You pitched your dream. And he said yes."

When she says it like that, stripped bare, no extra layers, it hits harder.

I let out a laugh, sharp, rough. "Yeah. That."

She shifts, folding her legs up cross-legged so she faces me. Then her hand slides into mine, certain, fingers weaving through like they belong there.

It anchors me so fast my chest aches.

"You okay?" she asks, quietly.

I swallow. My throat's tight. "Thought I'd fuck it up. Thought I'd sit there, forget everything, or say something stupid that'd make him look at me like I wasn't worth his time."

Her thumb drags slowly across my knuckles. "You didn't."

"Felt like I could've. Every second."

"You didn't." Stronger this time, no space for argument. Then she leans in, knee pressing my thigh. "Harley, you owned it. You showed him *you*. That's why he said yes."

I look down at our hands. Safer than her eyes.

But she doesn't let me hide. Her other hand slips under my chin, gentle but insistent, coaxing me back until I'm staring into her again.

"I'm proud of you," she says.

The words crack me open. I didn't even know I needed them until they're right there, and suddenly I can't breathe around them.

My voice is raw. "Yeah?"

"Yeah." She presses her lips to my temple, lingering. "So proud."

I close my eyes, forehead leaning into hers, our joined hands a lifeline.

Didn't think I'd get here. Didn't think this was possible.

Didn't think anyone would ever say that to me and mean it.

"Didn't think it'd feel like this," I whisper.

"Like what?"

I open my eyes. She's waiting. Always waiting.

"Like the start of something."

Her smile is small, sure. "It is."

And that's when it sinks in. This isn't mine anymore. Not just scraps in my head. It's ours. Real.

I can't sit still with it. My hands are already moving, catching her waist, tugging.

She doesn't hesitate. Just shifts, easy as anything, swinging her legs over until she's straddling me. Knees braced either side of my hips, chest pressed to mine, arms looping my shoulders.

The weight of her lands and something inside me finally unclenches.

Her body fits against me like it's meant to be here. Solid, steady. I bury my face against her neck and inhale. Her heartbeat drums fast but steady under my chest, and I lock onto it.

She whispers against my ear, "Better?"

I nod, breath catching. "Yeah. That's better."

Her fingers thread through my hair, nails grazing my scalp, and I almost lose it. Everything that meeting dragged out of me, the fear, the fight, the need, it all crashes against me at once. But her heartbeat's there. Her warmth's there. And I can carry it.

I whisper, "Don't let go."

Her hold tightens instantly. "Never."

I stay like that, clinging, pressing closer, until I can breathe again.

When I pull back, her face is right there, eyes shining. And I kiss her. Not rushed. Not greedy. Just slow, soft, grounding.

She kisses back the same way, like telling me I don't need to prove a thing.

When we part, I rest my forehead against hers, breathing her in. "You're staying close, yeah?"

"Always," she says, like it's not even a question.

Something eases inside me then. The last knot loosens.

I hold her tighter, her chest pressed to mine, heartbeat still steady under my ribs.

And I realise, this is it.

Not just surviving anymore.

We're building.

Together.

CHAPTER 25

Cold Tea and Clarity

LOLA

The toaster's jammed again. I stare at it like the sheer force of my exhaustion might make it pop. Niko's left a trail of croissant crumbs across the table and Tyler's mug still has lipstick on the rim, even though I'm ninety-nine percent sure he wasn't wearing any last night. Imogen's already gone. Morning meetings. Lip gloss. World domination. And Sophie's... quiet.

She's sitting across from me, cup of tea going cold between her palms. No bar banter. No sarcastic jabs. Just this strange, thoughtful silence.

I wait.

Then I crack first. "Are you okay?"

She blinks. "Yeah. Just... thinking."

I nod, expecting that to be the end of it. But then she speaks again.

"Ash told us everything. About Harley. About Break Line. About you."

My stomach tightens. "Okay."

Sophie looks up, and there's no heat in her eyes. No claws. Just something quieter.

"I didn't get it, at first," she says. "You and him. I thought it was just a phase. A rebound. You were new, and he's always had a weakness for beautiful things he thinks he can't have."

I flinch, slightly.

"But," she continues, "I saw him last night. Saw the way he looked when your name came up."

Her voice softens, almost surprised by its own honesty.

"It's not bravado with him. Not with you. He's different."

I say nothing.

Sophie gives a small, lopsided smile. "I used to think I knew him. That sleeping with someone meant knowing them. But I never saw that look on his face. Not once."

There's a long pause. Just the hum of the fridge and the distant thud of boots in the hallway.

Then she adds, "I don't hate you, you know."

I blink.

"I don't like you all the time," she says wryly. "But I don't hate you."

That draws a shaky laugh from me. "Thanks?"

Sophie shrugs and finally sips her tea. "Just don't hurt him. Because if you do, he'll still forgive you. But I won't."

Before I can respond, the door creaks open and Imogen breezes in, her long dark ponytail swinging behind her. She's in all black again, turtleneck, tailored trousers, heeled boots with a click that announces her before she speaks.

She pauses when she sees us.

"Well," she says, arching a brow, "this looks civilised. No blood on the floor."

Sophie rolls her eyes but doesn't bristle. "Calm down, Vogue."

Imogen crosses to the table, plucks the now-cold toast from the broken toaster with surgical precision, and drops it in the bin like it personally offended her.

"Should I ask?" she says.

"About what?" I croak, still catching up emotionally.

Imogen levels me with that steel gaze. "About the fact that you look like you've just been emotionally steamrolled."

Sophie rises. "That one's on me."

Imogen blinks. "Are we... apologising now?"

"Don't get used to it," Sophie mutters, brushing past and out the door. She pauses halfway through. "Just don't screw it up, Maxwell."

Then she's gone.

Imogen watches the door close, then turns to me with a dry smile. "Well. If that wasn't a plot twist, I don't know what is."

I shake my head slowly. "I think I need to lie down."

"You probably do," she says, softer now. "But not until you've had something stronger than caffeine."

She reaches into her coat pocket and pulls out two miniature bottles of Baileys.

"Not for now," she says with a grin. "Emergency rations for later."

Then. "Go," she orders, glancing at the window where a pale slice of sky shows through the glass. "He'll be waiting."

"He didn't say he was."

"He never has to."

I pull on my jacket and scarf and step into the corridor that smells like wet wool and lemon cleaner. My phone buzzes as I push through the side door.

Harley: Button lift or straight to the chair?

I smile.

Me: Chair. I like the view.

Harley: Thought you'd say that. I'm by the green run. Bandage on?

Me: Yes, coach. I can tie my own shoes too.

Harley: You don't have laces, menace.

Me: You know what I meant.

Harley: I know everything you mean xx

He's there, where the piste opens out, leaning one shoulder against the lift corral barrier, skis crossed at the tips. White jacket, black trousers, dark hair shoved back like he ran a hand through it on his way out the door. When he sees me, that unreadable look flickers over his face, the one that says he's feeling too much and trying not to show all of it at once. His mouth softens anyway.

"Hi," I say.

"Hi," he says back, and it's more than a greeting.

He pushes off to meet me halfway. His gloved fingers find my hip for a second, nothing anyone else would notice, everything I notice. He looks down at my boots.

"Support bandage?" he asks.

"Yes." I lift my trouser cuff to show the beige line above my boot. "Still wearing it."

"Good." He taps the plastic with his knuckles. "Any pain today?"

"Not yet."

"Tell me if that changes."

I roll my eyes. He smiles like I've just agreed to something serious.

"Alright," he says, nodding toward the queue. "You ready to graduate?"

"I thought I graduated last time."

"Last time you stayed upright. Let's see if we can add 'less terrified' to the list."

"Rude."

"Accurate."

We shuffle into the line. There's that mild chairlift chaos, kids lifting their poles at the wrong moment, someone dropping a glove and swearing softly as it slides under the barrier. My stomach does a nervous little flip as the bullwheel hums overhead. Harley slips his pole straps off and nudges my elbow.

"Okay," he says, voice low. "Keep your poles in one hand. Sit when the chair taps the backs of your knees. Don't look at your skis on the way in. Look straight ahead. When we get to the top, you'll stand when the snow meets your boots and just glide forward. I'll be right beside you."

"You always are," I say without thinking.

His eyes jump to mine. The world blurs for a second into

something warm. He clears his throat, then grins like he needs to deflect before he says something that will level me.

The barrier gate opens. We slide to the line, pause, and the chair sweeps in behind us. I sit. The seat lifts us clean off the ground. My stomach swoops and then settles. The resort falls away below at a steady, soothing pace.

The view opens like a held breath finally letting go. Pine trees crusted white. A run curling off into the distance with tiny bright jackets threading back and forth. Far beyond that, mountains stacked on mountains, blue-grey and endless.

His arm settles behind me, not touching, just there, steady. His knee presses into mine, quiet and constant. He speaks low, like the rest of the world doesn't exist right now.

"What did Sophie want this morning?" he asks. "You sounded off in your text."

I pick a spot on the horizon and hold it so my voice comes out steady. "She said she doesn't hate me."

His mouth curves. "High praise."

"She also said if I hurt you, you'd forgive me. But she wouldn't."

He doesn't flinch. Doesn't pretend it's a joke. "She's probably right."

I turn toward him. "Which part?"

He exhales, slowly. Looks away. "Both."

"Harley."

He drags a hand over his face. "I don't have a track record. Haven't done this before. But if I did..." He swallows. "If it were you, yeah. I think I would."

I stare at him. His eyes are on the horizon like it's safer than looking at me.

"I hate that," he adds, voice lower now. "Not because of you. Just... what it says about me. That I'd bend like that for someone. That I already know I'd let you wreck me if it came to it."

Something inside me pulls tight and quiet.

"I'm not planning to test that," I say.

He finally looks at me. "Good. Just needed to say it. Out loud. While I still have the choice."

The chair jerks slightly as we pass over the tower, cables groaning overhead. A gust slips under my collar and I shiver.

Harley tilts his arm, pulls me closer without saying a word. His gloved fingers brush the edge of my scarf where it meets my jaw, just a quick touch, almost nothing.

But it lingers.

"What do I do if I panic?" I ask.

"Breathe. In through your nose, out through your mouth. Then look where you want to go. Don't overthink it, your body will catch up."

"And what do I actually do?" I ask, needing something real, something simple.

He nods. "Start with a wedge to keep the speed down. Turn, then let the skis run for a second before you set the next edge. That's it."

"That's it?"

"No overthinking. Keep your shoulders still. Let your legs move under you. Pressure goes into the outside ski. Just feel for it."

I nod, trying to picture it.

"You'll get it," he says, quiet but certain.

I look at him. "You always sound so sure."

"That's because I am." He smiles, not cocky. Just solid.

The offload ramp comes into view. He points with his chin. "Poles in one hand. Tips up. Stand when the snow meets your boots. Glide straight. We'll pull off to the right and regroup."

We do it. Clean. I don't stumble. He doesn't need to catch me.

At the top there's a small flat stretch where a few families are faffing with gloves and goggles. Harley guides us off to the side.

He takes my poles and checks the strap at my wrist before handing them back.

"How's the ankle?"

I pause. "Still attached."

His mouth twitches. "That's not an answer."

I shrug. "It's fine enough."

He watches me for a second, then nods. "You say something hurts, we stop. Deal?"

"Deal."

He shifts, planting his own poles. "Ready?"

I blow out a breath. "Show me."

He clicks his goggles down. "I'm going to ski backwards in front of you for the first bit. Don't think, just follow my cues. If I say eyes up, eyes up. If I say outside ski, you put pressure where I tell you. Got it?"

"Got it."

He pushes off and I follow. He carves a smooth line just below me, then flips to face uphill, gliding backwards like it's easy. Like breathing.

His arms are out, steady, tracking me. Not grabbing, just there.

"Start with the wedge," he calls up. "Eyes on me. Not your skis."

I lift my gaze.

Something in my body lets go.

"Okay," he says, tone steady, calm. "We're going to the left. Press a little more on the inside edge of your right ski. Outside ski, right big toe. Yes. Let the left knee soften in. Hips stay facing down the hill. Don't twist your shoulders."

The turn comes late, but it sticks. One ski catches and holds, slicing through the snow with a sound I haven't heard before, softer, cleaner.

I let out a breath I didn't know I was bracing for.

"Better," he says. "Now let them flatten for a beat. Feel that? Skis go quiet. There. New turn. Press the left big toe. Right knee softens in. Hips steady. Keep your hands forward like you're carrying that tray you hate."

"I hate the tray," I say through a laugh.

"You love my tray."

"Never say that again."

He grins, still gliding backwards, still watching me, eyes flicking between my skis and my face, tracking everything.

The slope levels a little. I'm still moving. Still up. But my legs are burning.

"Shake it out," he calls. "Quick reset. Then we go again, three turns, no wedge between. You're ready."

"I'm not."

"You are. Trust me."

I do. Stupidly, fully. Somehow when he says it, my body listens.

We go again. Three turns. No wedge.

Somewhere in the middle, my skis drift into parallel without me even trying, it just happens, and for a second it feels like flying.

I squeak, an actual squeak, and wobble so hard I almost sit down.

Harley laughs, gliding closer. He reaches out and straightens my hands with a quick tap.

"Eyes up," he says. "Where you look, your feet follow."

I glance at him, grinning. "And if I'm looking at you?"

He doesn't miss a beat. "Then I hope you hit me hard enough that I have to marry you."

My heart skips. I wasn't expecting him to say that. Not like that. Not so easily.

"Already planning on that," I mutter, too fast.

His mouth softens, not a full smile, just the start of one. The kind you don't mean to give away.

And for a second, I feel everything at once: shaky and strong, seen and so seen, like I've just stumbled into something real without knowing where the edge was.

By halfway down he's turned and started skiing beside me instead of backwards. He gives fewer cues. He doesn't hover. When I wobble again he lets me fix it alone. He doesn't rush to catch me. Just watches, quiet and sure. It shouldn't turn me on, but it does.

We stop off to the side where the piste narrows and trees close in a little. He steps closer and brushes snow out of my hair with careful fingers. The intimacy of that simple touch makes my chest ache. I tilt my face up. He kisses me, slow and warm, nothing showy. It tastes like trust. Like something I've never had but always needed.

"Good work," he says against my mouth.

"You're a decent teacher."

He hums. "Don't tell anyone. I've worked hard to cultivate a reputation."

"What, as a menace?"

"As a menace you trust."

"Unfortunately."

He laughs. Then he nods toward the slope. "One more run. This time I want you to ski ahead of me. I'll hang back and watch. If you need me, call. If you don't, you won't hear a word."

"Harley..."

"It's time," he says gently. "Pick your line."

Something opens under my ribs. Not fear. Not quite. It's that weird, weightless feeling you get when something good actually happens, and you don't know what to do with it.

I push off. He doesn't follow straight away, just hangs back like he trusts me. Or wants me to feel like he does. Either way, I know he's there, not hovering, just keeping watch.

I cut across the slope, knees soft, weight forward. Let the skis run flat for a beat, then tip onto the new edge. They respond. Not perfectly. But enough.

The snow hisses under me. It's not magic. It's me.

I don't look back. I don't need to.

By the bottom I'm flushed and breathless. I skid to a stop near the lift corral, heart thudding. When I turn, he's already slowing, eyes locked on me like I'm something he's never seen, and somehow always known. He glides in close, plants his pole, and leans in, lips brushing the space just beneath my beanie, warm and sure.

"Proud of you," he says, quiet. No show. No audience. Just truth.

We shuffle into the line again. The chair hums overhead. I'm not scared of it now. My legs are shaking and my ankle's a little sore, but it's the kind of sore that proves I did something hard.

On the ride up, we don't talk. Just sit close, breathing steady, watching skiers weave below like it's the most normal thing in the world.

The second run I still ski first. He trails, then pulls ahead for the last third and sets a playful pace. I keep up. He cuts a small turn across my line and throws a spray of snow at my shins. I squeal and aim one back. He laughs. It feels easy. It feels like us.

We call it after that. My legs are shot, my ankle's twinging, and I'm starting to ski like a drunk baby deer. Harley unclips both my skis, kneels to pop the bindings like he did that first week, then stands and slips two fingers into the collar of my jacket, tugging me in.

He kisses me once, warm and sure, and I smile back at him.

"Food," he says. "Then rest."

"Yes, coach."

He grins like I've just dared him. "You're a menace."

"And you like it."

"Unfortunately."

We carry our gear back through the side corridor. In the boot room, he drops everything by the rack and leans against the wall. I sit, tugging off my gloves one finger at a time. He doesn't say anything, just watches me like I'm still mid-run, like he's not ready to look away yet.

"You didn't crowd me," I say.

"I wanted to," he admits. "Every second. But I wanted to see you choose your own turns more."

"You did," I say. "And it was better."

Harley kneels to unclip my boots. I brace one hand on the bench, the other on his shoulder to steady myself. For a second, we just stay like that, me catching my breath, him watching me like he already knows the next thing I'm going to say.

"I nearly stacked it halfway down," I mutter.

"You didn't."

"No, but I could've."

"You didn't," he says again, quiet this time.

I look at him. "You didn't jump in."

"I knew you'd save it."

"I wasn't sure I would."

His eyes don't move. "I was."

And something in me settles. Not because I was perfect. But because he let me try.

"I love you," he says.

"I love you more."

He smiles, doesn't look away. "Tomorrow, no wedge. Straight into parallel. Easy slope. You'll hate it. You'll nail it."

"Sounds like me."

"Exactly like you."

We put our gear away. The room warms with the dryers and the smell of wet wool. People move in the corridor, voices stacking over each other, laughter spilling around corners. He reaches for my hand as we step out and I let him have it, not because I need it to stay upright, but because I like the way it feels when he links our fingers and doesn't let go.

Outside, the light's different, flatter, softer. My legs ache and my trousers are soggy, but I don't care. We walk in sync, hands still joined, swing-soft between us. I don't say it, but I'm proud of myself. Not just for skiing. For not backing out. For not flinching.

Imogen's at the end of the path with a clipboard and a look that says she's been waiting for a report she won't admit she wants. She glances down at our linked hands and lifts one brow.

"Well?" she asks.

I lift my chin. "Parallel."

Her mouth twitches like she is trying very hard not to grin. "Of course."

Harley squeezes my hand once, then lets go. But the feeling doesn't. It lingers, quiet, certain, like he's still holding on in ways I can't shake.

"Lunch?" he asks.

"Starving," I say.

We walk toward the dining room together. Somewhere behind us the chairlift hums, steady as a heartbeat. I don't look back. I don't need to. I know I'll be on it again tomorrow, and the day after that, and the day after, carving a line I chose with a boy who loves me enough to let me ski it first.

CHAPTER 26

21 and Surprises

HARLEY

Zane texts me while I'm still in the shower.

Zane: Break Line chat? Pop by the Frog before dinner, about six pm. Got someone for you to meet.

I stare at the screen, water dripping off my hair onto the tiles. Last time we talked about Break Line, I'd mentioned getting locals on board. Maybe he's found someone. I fire back

Me: Be there.

Back in the bedroom, I towel off and drag on some clothes.

Lola's already dressed. Black trousers tucked into boots, the kind that crunch against the snow. That green top doesn't belong in this weather but she wears it anyway, and her hazel eyes catch the light, sharp and impossible to ignore.

She's taming her curls in the mirror, the tiny lines between her brows pucker while she bites her lip. The second she sees me, her whole face lights up.

"You look hot," she says, walking over to stand in front of me. Her hands fly up to my neck and she smooths my collar like she's been waiting to put her hands on me since breakfast.

I kiss her, quick, because if I start I won't stop. "You look unreal. I'm looking forward to some alone time with my gorgeous girl later."

"Zane pinged, I said we'd pop by before dinner. He wants me to meet someone for Break Line. You mind?"

"Of course not," she says, too bright, too fast. The smile reaches her eyes, and there's a fizz behind it, secret electricity.

I watch her a beat too long. "What's that smile about?"

"Nothing," she says, way too quickly.

"Mm." I hook an arm around her waist, mouth to her ear. "Keep looking shifty and I'll throw you over my knee when we get back."

Her breath hitches. She tries for coy and lands on wrecked. "You wouldn't."

"Wouldn't I?" I give her arse a light slap. Her cheeks go pink. Good. "Come on."

There's a tug at the back of my mind, but her fingers lace through mine and she pulls me out into the cold, so I let the feeling slide.

❄

Lola's too quiet, and the snow crunches louder because of it. Boots on hard packed snow. Breath fogging the air. The chalet windows glow warm behind us, the village ahead is all fairy lights and murmurs. Lola swings our hands once, then twice, like she can't bottle whatever's fizzing under her skin.

"You sure he said six?" she asks.

"Yeah."

She nods too hard. "Great. Perfect."

I cut her a look. "You're terrible at lying."

"Lying about what exactly? We have a table booked at seven pm at the Brasserie."

"That, right there," I say, pointing at her mouth, "is your lying smile."

She bites it back and fails. "What, no I'm not?"

I stop walking, just to look at her. She takes two more steps before she realises I'm not beside her, then turns. Her hair's tucked into her coat, lips glossy, eyes wide like I might pounce.

"Baby," I say, soft. "Whatever this is, you're cute. And if you keep giving me that sly little smile, I swear to God I'll warm your arse so thoroughly when we get home you won't sit through Scarlett's morning briefing."

She actually sways. "Stop."

"Not a chance."

She laughs, then gets serious, stepping into me until we're chest to chest. "Trust me?"

I do. Against sense, against habit, against every muscle memory that taught me to need an exit. "Yeah."

"Good," she says, and tugs me the last stretch.

❄

The Red Frog looks closed. The shutters are half down, the lights aren't on. I glance from the door to Lola. "Maybe I got the time wrong," I say, taking out my phone to check the text again. "Nope, he said six pm."

"It's early and he probably hasn't fully opened yet, you know this place doesn't really start getting busy until at least nine" she says, tiny smile back on her mouth. "Go on."

I push and the door creaks. Inside's pitch black. The kind of black that makes your hearing go feral.

"Zane?" I call.

The lights hit like a snowball to the face.

POP!

Confetti, poppers, a cheer that knocks the air out of me. Stevie Wonder's 'Happy Birthday' bursts from somewhere behind the bar. A banner stretches across the back wall in unapologetic vinyl, **HAPPY 21st, HARLEY!** Balloons in a lopsided arch. Streamers, the works.

My body goes statue-still. I blink and try to compute.

Everyone's here. Imogen, already glassy-eyed, Niko's standing on a chair, whooping. Ash is at the edge of the room, smirk easy, like he's just waiting to say I told you so. Tyler and Sarah flanking a chalet chef with a chocolate cake topped with twenty-one in gold letters. Jesus, the cake is obscene. Sophie's by the bar with a drink and a surprisingly genuine smile. Locals too, a pair of returning guests raise their glasses like we've shared seasons.

I turn because I need an anchor.

Lola's right behind me, hands fisted in her coat, eyes shining and her teeth worrying her lip. Maybe she thinks I'll bolt.

I don't, I walk into her and bury my face in her neck. She smells like her coconut shampoo.

"You little shit," I murmur, voice shredded.

She laughs and squeezes. "Happy birthday, babe."

I've had birthdays before, technically. Ash bought me a beer last year. Niko once sang off-key and called it a present. But this is the first one that feels...noticed. Like someone cared enough to remember the date, not just the guy attached to it.

It hits like an avalanche, every year nobody gave a toss, every house where birthdays meant nothing, every time the calendar rolled over and I pretended it didn't sting. At ten, when I stole a cupcake from a church bake sale and ate it in a park on my own. At thirteen, when the woman whose couch I was sleeping on forgot my name, let alone a date. At Sixteen, when they celebrated the other kid because he had a "proper" family now and I had... the bus pass and a social worker who couldn't look me in the eye.

And now this. Banner, music, noise. Friends, Lola's arms. My name shouted like it belongs to people.

My throat burns, my eyes sting.

"You did this?" I croak.

She leans back enough to see me, smiling like she's been waiting to tell me for weeks. "Everyone chipped in, obviously Zane let us take over the bar, Scarlett got the chef to make the cake and do the food. Imogen bullied half the valley. It wasn't hard."

"I didn't see this coming." The words scrape on the way out. "Not after... the last one. Thought I'd fucked it up. Thought I'd ruined any chance you'd ever try something like this for me again."

Her eyes are sharp and soft all at once. "You could never ruin anything not with me."

Something in my chest gives and doesn't hurt when it does.

Ash's hand finds my shoulder and then I'm yanked into a hug that knocks the air out of me. "You look like you're about to cry, mate."

"Shut up."

Imogen wipes under one eye. "He totally is."

"Get a picture," Tyler says. "Before he cries and someone has to fetch tissues."

I flip them off, but they cheer anyway. Someone shoves a pint in my hand, Niko bangs the bar twice like a judge approving chaos. Sophie lifts her glass without snark. The noise swells and rises and wraps around me until the part of my brain that thinks about exits goes quiet.

I catch Jack at the back, arms folded, jaw clenched, staring at Lola. His expression is unreadable. But the look is wrong and for some reason it crawls up my spine like cold.

Lola touches my side like she feels me go tense, so I brush the back of my knuckles against her cheek and give her quick soft kiss.

"Alright," Zane calls, clinking a glass from behind the bar. The room hushes in a way you only get when people are actually listening. "Wasn't going to say anything, then I saw that face Harley just made and thought, yeah, this needs freezing."

Cue laughter. I keep my eyes on Lola because if I look anywhere else I'll crack.

"To the guy who gives more than he takes," Zane says, voice easy but steady, "fights harder than he has to, and shows up even when he's been let down a hundred times. You've changed this place, Nash. You've changed us. And we're better for it."

Lola's crying now too, soft, quiet tears that don't demand a scene. They undo me more than a sob would.

"Happy birthday, Harley," Zane finishes.

"Happy birthday Harley!" the room roars back.

Glasses clink too loudly, someone's cranked the music again, and the chef makes a whole show of sliding the cake onto the counter like it's the crown jewel. Chocolate, ganache so thick it could glue Niko's mouth shut, a small mercy. I'm half-listening, half-scanning the room out of habit, until my eyes land on Lola.

"Best fucking birthday of my life," I tell her, slipping an arm around her waist and kissing her temple because if I aim for her mouth I'll forget the rest of them exist.

"I love you so much."

"I love you too," she says, glowing like she built the sun. "You deserve every second of it."

We're swallowed by people, hands on my shoulder, sloppy kisses on my cheek from tipsy locals. Niko leans over the bar to announce, "Now he's legal in America, girls, hide your grandmas," and gets a tea towel to the face from Zane.

Imogen hugs me properly when there's a gap, no quip, just arms around my neck and a muffled, "Don't you dare get used to going without this." She pulls back, swipes at her eyes like she's furious they betrayed her. "God, you're a pain."

"Love you too," I tell her, quietly. She nods like we've decided something important and goes to boss the chef about napkins.

Sarah appears with a plate that absolutely no one asked for and everyone needs, indecent slabs of cake, slices shoved sideways, ganache fingerprints on the rim. "Eat," she orders. "Sugar's cheaper than therapy." She kisses my cheek. "Happy birthday, sweetheart."

"Cheers, Sar."

Tyler, who almost never says more than two words when a nod will do, clears his throat. "He's... he's a good one," he says to the table more than to me, like he's rehearsed it and can't look at the person it's for. "Fixed the bloody espresso machine last week without making me feel like an idiot." He shrugs, embarrassed by his own sincerity. "Anyway. You're alright, Harley."

The whole table laughs. I elbow him. "You too, mate."

Sophie slides over, unexpected and unsharp. "Don't let it spook you," she says, eyes sincere. "Being loved loudly, you earned it." She clinks my glass and is gone before I know how to answer.

Lola tugs at my hand. "Dance with me."

"It's a bar, babe."

"Exactly, and I seem to remember lots of dancing my first time here."

I roll my eyes and give into her, because ultimately I'm always going to give her exactly what she wants. We sway near the bar like idiots, her arms loop behind my neck. My hands settle at her waist. The music's too loud for romance, but she mouths the words at me anyway. There are crumbs on her mouth and I can't stop staring. It's a stupid thing to want, but I want to brush them away with my tongue. I want to take her home now.

"You okay?" she asks, voice low like we're alone.

"More than okay. Didn't think you could surprise me anymore."

"Arrogant," she says, smugly. "Zane helped. Ash kept you busy. Remember when he made you ski with toddlers for two hours so you'd be too tired to snoop?"

"Bastard."

"It was worth it."

We do a lap so I can shake hands with people who apparently decided somewhere along the line I'm worth coming out for. An old liftie I've only ever seen in oil-stained overalls splits a grin and says, "About time somebody shouted your name in lights." A ski school mum thanks me for teaching her kid to be brave. My throat is a mess of gravel and sugar and something I don't have a word for because it feels like standing in sun after a long winter and remembering you have skin.

When it gets loud again, we find a sofa. I sit, drag Lola down so she ends up half on my lap, half under my arm. My fingers fall into her hair like they've got muscle memory for it.

"You really got me," I say.

She leans back to look at me, smug like a cat who found the cream and a bank card. "I know."

"I didn't think birthdays mattered. But this... this mattered." I swallow.

Her mouth softens. "It's mattered because it's yours, because it's ours, not borrowed." She nudges my chin with her knuckle.

"You're the one who made this family, Harley, you're just the last person to realise it."

I kiss her, slow and long because I can, because no one's going to take her away from me tonight, because for once I don't feel like I need a door to my back. The room blurs around us into gold and laughter and the clink of glasses.

Towards the end of the evening goodnights are shouted, hugs are stolen and the chef packs the last of the cake like contraband into a box and shoves it at Sarah for safe keeping. Zane wipes the bar with that slow look of satisfaction he gets when the night did what he wanted. He catches my eye and tips his chin.

"I didn't see it coming," I tell him when I step within earshot. "Not after... last time." The jealousy, the public fuck-up, the way I accused the girl I love of the one thing that would wreck her. I let the shame pass through me without hooking in. "Thought I'd blown any chance she'd ever try again."

Zane's eyes do that kind thing they sometimes do when he forgets to play the lad. "Some people'll give you one chance. Good people'll give you two. The right person doesn't count." He flicks a glance at Lola. "You've got the right one."

"I know," I say, and it doesn't feel like superstition to say it out loud.

Everyone's drunk and emotional, and we're one of the last couples to leave. Meanwhile Imogen herds a pair of locals out with the efficiency of a bouncer in couture and Ash lingers, pulls me in so our foreheads touch for a beat, much like an old soldier's blessing. "Happy birthday," he says. "Make a wish you're prepared to work for."

I laugh because of course he'd ruin a wish with labour. "I am."

Lola and I step into the cold. The door swings shut behind us and the night snaps quiet. Snow squeaks under our boots. The village hum is a low, a feeling of contentedness settles in my stomach as she tucks her hand into my coat pocket

"You okay?" she asks again, because she has a habit of asking on repeat until I tell the truth.

"Yeah," I say. Then, more honestly, "I'm... good." The word

feels huge. Like borrowing a coat two sizes too big and finding it fits anyway. "Didn't know I'd need this. Didn't know I could have it."

"You can have it," she says. "And I'm going to give you a thousand more."

We climb the last little hill to the staff entrance and I don't need to look over my shoulder for once, no exit plans, no old reflexes, no itch under my skin that I can't scratch. Just birthday cake in a box, a mouth I get to kiss in the dark, friends who didn't let me go, a bar that shouted my name without laughing, and the girl who made sure the banner had my age printed right.

We barely make it up the stairs before Lola's tugging at my hand, laughing at how many people tried to shove cake at me on the way out. My head's still buzzing, my chest still too full. The door clicks shut behind us, and for the first time tonight, it's just us.

I drop onto the bed, scrubbing a hand down my face. "I still can't believe you pulled that off. Thought I'd sussed it the second Zane texted me, but... Christ, I didn't see that coming."

She perches on my lap, straddling me easily like it's the only place she belongs. My hands go to her arse and pull her impossibly closer to me reflexively. "That's because you were too busy sulking about Jack and my 'secret plans' last time." Her eyes glint, teasing. "Thought you'd ruined birthdays forever."

I groan, burying my face in her neck. "Don't remind me. I was a jealous prick."

"Mm, you were," she says, smug. "But you're my jealous prick."

She presses a soft kiss to my nose, then slides off me and rummages in her bag. When she turns back, there's an envelope in her hand. She looks suddenly shy, nervous even, which sets every nerve in me on edge.

"What's this?"

"Your real present." She pushes it toward me. "The party was just for everyone else. This is for you."

I tear it open and find the hotel booking inside. London. Two nights. The date circled, right between seasons.

I stare at the paper, then at her. My throat locks. "Lola..."

Her voice is barely a whisper. "So you can visit her. Your mum. With me there. Because you shouldn't have to do it alone anymore."

Something in me breaks wide open. All the years I've shoved that part of me into a corner, convinced no one could ever care enough to stand beside me in it. And here she is. Offering not just a trip, but her heart.

I swallow hard, blink fast, but it's useless. "You'd do that for me?"

She cups my face, steady as anything. "Babe, I'd do anything for you. You're not just where I sleep, Harley. You're where I live. I gave up my room weeks ago, didn't I? Because I don't just live in your bed. I hope I also live in your heart."

That's it. I haul her against me, crushing her to my chest like I'll never let her go. My voice is wrecked when I manage, "I love you so much, Lo."

Her smile's wet and shaky, but brighter than anything I've ever seen. "I love you too. Happy birthday, my dangerous, stupidly sexy, tattooed millionaire."

I laugh, broken and raw, and kiss her like she's the air in my lungs. Because she is.

CHAPTER 27
The Storeroom
LOLA

I'm humming to myself as I dig through a crate of battered Powder White flyers, half singing, half mumbling nonsense lyrics under my breath. I still feel flushed from last night, my thoughts tangled in Harley's mouth on my neck and the way he whispered mine makes me feel giddy.

The storeroom is cold. Same as always. The light flickers above me, casting weird shadows on the walls, but I don't care. Everything's been good lately. Better than good. I'm still not used to how soft Harley's become with me. How he looks at me like I matter.

I smile, alone with the damp walls and metal shelves. I'd never say it out loud, but I'm happy. Really, properly happy. It still feels like wearing someone else's life, like I'm going to wake up back in my dad's house with his rules and his grief and his silence. But I'm not. I'm here. With him. With all of them.

The door clicks.

I look up.

It's Jack.

He closes it behind him. Quietly. No hello.

I straighten. "Scarlett said we were done for the night. I was just grabbing these."

Jack doesn't answer right away. His face is unreadable, jaw clenched too tight.

"You shouldn't be in here alone," he says finally, voice flat.

I frown. "I'll be out in a sec."

He steps further in. I feel the shift immediately, like something turning sour in the air. My shoulders go tense.

"You've changed," he says. "Since Harley. You walk around like you're someone now."

I grip the edge of the crate. "What are you talking about?"

He moves closer. I can smell the beer on him now. Sharp. Familiar.

"You think you're better than everyone because Harley picked you."

My stomach drops. I take a step back. "Jack, don't..."

"He's not who you think he is. You think he actually loves you? You're just another girl to him. You'll see."

I glance toward the door, then shift to move around him. Jack steps in front of me, blocking the path. I try again. He cuts me off. Again.

I back into a metal shelf, the cold biting through my thin jumper. "You need to go."

His face twists. "You never even looked at me. Not once."

I shift again, trying to edge past him. He blocks me. His eyes are glassy. Wild.

"I don't want this," I say, louder now, heart hammering. "You're drunk. You don't mean this."

"Don't I?" he snaps. "I see the way you look at him. Like he's the answer to everything. You never looked at me like that. Not even once."

I try to push past him again.

He lunges.

His hand clamps around my wrist, yanking me sideways. I stumble, hitting the shelving hard, my shoulder scraping along the edge. I cry out, kicking back, trying to shove him off, but he's strong. Too strong.

"Let go!"

He slams me against the shelf again. One arm bars my chest, the other grabbing at the hem of my jumper, pulling it up.

"You think he's the only one who wanted you? You think you're untouchable now?"

"Get off me!" My voice cracks. I twist, thrashing, but I can't get free. Panic explodes through my chest.

He presses closer. His breath is foul. I turn my face, scream, scream louder, but the walls eat the sound.

"Stop! Please!"

His hand clamps over my mouth.

Then he bites my shoulder.

Pain shoots through me. I cry out, trying to twist away, heart pounding so hard it hurts. The world narrows. My head spins.

The door slams open.

"GET THE FUCK OFF HER!"

Harley's voice. Snarling. Loud.

Jack is ripped away. I collapse to the floor, shaking, my jumper twisted, shoulder burning. I can't breathe. Can't see. Just Harley's voice. Loud. Terrifying.

He slams Jack into the wall, fist flying. There's the crack of bone, a grunt, another punch.

"You touch her again and I swear to God I will end you."

Jack spits blood. "She was into it...."

Another punch.

I sob. Loud and broken.

Harley stops. Spinning toward me.

He crouches, voice breaking. "Lo. Look at me. Did he... did he get inside your clothes?"

His eyes flick over me, taking in the lifted hem of my jumper, the bruises blooming on my wrist, the torn fabric where Jack grabbed, the red mark on my shoulder.

I shake my head hard, chest heaving. "No. He tried. He tried, but he didn't. Just the bite. I swear."

Harley freezes. His whole body goes still.

Then. "He fucking bit you?"

I flinch as he rises, fury snapping off him in waves. He turns like he's about to go back in there.

"Don't!" I grab at his arm, desperate. "Please. Don't go. Don't leave me."

That stops him. Dead in his tracks. Breathing like it hurts.

"I can't let him walk."

"You already stopped him," I whisper. "You already did."

His hands shake. But he doesn't argue. Doesn't push. Instead, he shrugs out of his jacket and wraps it around me, gentle now. Focused. As if staying still takes more strength than swinging again ever could.

"I've got you," he says, voice torn raw.

Then he lifts me, carries me out of there like it's the only thing that matters.

❄

Harley

Ash answers on the second knock. He takes one look at Lola in my arms and goes still.

"What the fuck happened?"

"She was attacked," I say, pushing past him into the room. "Jack. Storeroom. He bit her and..."

Ash's face shifts into something I haven't seen since his army days, all restraint and calculation, the kind of stillness you see before a bomb goes off.

Lola's trembling now. I set her down gently on the edge of Ash's bed and kneel in front of her. Her hand flutters at the bite on her shoulder, but she winces when she touches it.

"I need Scarlett," I say.

Ash's jaw ticks. "Already calling."

He grabs his phone off the bedside table and steps into the hallway.

I stay with her.

"Lo," I whisper, brushing her hair off her face. Her curls are matted, one cheek swollen. "I've got you. You're safe now."

She doesn't speak. Just leans into my palm like she's holding herself up on my touch.

Scarlett arrives ten minutes later. Eyes wide with horror when she sees Lola's state.

"What the hell happened?"

"I found her in the storeroom," I say, voice low, barely holding. "Jack had her pinned. He bit her."

Scarlett's already pulling out her phone. "I'm calling the police."

"Good."

The officers arrive within twenty minutes. Élise Fournier, sharp-eyed and calm, separates me from Lola; Scarlett stays with her.

A younger officer, Lieutenant Julien Rousseau, asks me to come to Scarlett's office to give a statement.

"Tell me exactly what happened. No detail is too small."

I tell him everything. How I found the door ajar. How I heard her scream. How I got Jack off her. How I hit him.

"Did you witness the assault itself?"

"No, but I saw him on top of her. Her clothes were torn. She was screaming."

He nods, professional. "We'll need your statement typed and signed. Jack's already been detained by the local police. We're treating this as an attempted sexual assault."

When I arrive back at Ash's room, Fournier is sitting quietly with Lola. She offers her a drink, asks questions gently, doesn't push. "I know this is hard, mademoiselle. But we are here for you. You're safe now."

She answers in whispers. Keeps repeating, "He didn't get far."

"Would you like to press charges?" She asks.

She nods. Once. Small but sure.

Scarlett hands over CCTV footage of Jack entering the storeroom alone and provides her written statement. It's enough to hold him.

Fournier speaks to me again. "She's going to need a hospital check-up. The bite mark could be infected, and we'll need photos for evidence."

❄

The emergency clinic is twenty minutes away. Ash is driving the roads are icy. I can feel the slight slip of the tyres on the road. It's dead quiet. I'm with Lola in the back seat, her head is resting against the cold window, my jacket still pulled tight around her frame.

Every muscle in my body still tense. My knuckles ache from how hard I hit Jack. I can still feel the moment I yanked him off her. The sound she made.

Once we're inside and she's taken back by the nurse, the weight of it all finally hits me. I sink into a hard plastic chair beside Ash in the waiting room, elbows on my knees, head down.

"You need to talk to me," he says, low. "You're not okay."

"I nearly killed him."

Ash doesn't flinch.

"If I didn't get there in time...." I drag a hand through my hair, as I get up and start pacing, feeling sick with the fear of what could have happened.

"Something in me snapped, Ash. Proper snapped. I wasn't thinking. I wasn't there. Not like me. Not even close."

Ash studies me. "And what stopped you?"

"She did." My throat tightens. "The second I heard her voice, I felt it. The fear. The way she was shaking. It was like I came back into my body and realised, fuck, she needed me calm. She needed me safe."

"You were," Ash says firmly. "You were what she needed."

I nod once, jaw tight.

"I've never been scared of myself before," I murmur. "But for the first time... I didn't know what I was capable of. All I knew was that someone was hurting her. And I'd have done anything to stop it."

Ash leans back in his chair. "You're in love with her."

"Yeah, I fucking am," I say.

❄

Lola's quiet all the way back to the chalet. Too quiet.

Ash drops us off without asking questions, just squeezes my shoulder before we step out. Scarlett's promised to keep the others distracted, and Jack's still at the police station. But that doesn't stop Lola from flinching every time we pass a dark hallway.

I unlock my room. She steps in first, arms locked tight around her middle.

"Do you want to lie down?" I ask, keeping my voice low. She shakes her head.

Her skin's pale, scraped at the collarbone. I can see the bite through the open neckline. Purple, ragged. Brutal. It's all I can do not to put my fist through the fucking wall.

"I need to shower," she says.

"Okay."

She tries to undress, but her fingers are shaking and she fumbles.

"Let me help you, baby," I say, reaching out for her. She nods giving me permission to touch her.

I help her, slowly and carefully.

She steps into the shower and looks back at me. "Get in with me?"

I undress quickly, step in behind her reaching for the body wash. I pour some onto a flannel and wash her like she's glass. She turns so I can wash her back, her forehead presses to my chest, tears mixing with the water.

"I feel broken," she whispers.

"You're not, baby. You're the strongest person I know."

She blinks up at me, eyes wide and hollow.

"You survived losing your mum and brother all by the time you were sixteen. You lived under a man who never saw you, who shut you down at every turn. You walked out of that house and came here. Alone. No backup. No lifeline. Just you. And not only did you survive, you made something of yourself. You show up every damn day with your head held high. Most eighteen-year-olds wouldn't have the guts, let alone the strength to do that. But you did."

She clings tighter.

"I was happy," she says. "Before that. For the first time. I thought I was safe."

"You are. You're with me. No one's touching you again," I promise.

She nods. But she doesn't believe it yet. I can tell.

Later, dressed in one of my oversized T-shirts and tucked into the bed, against me, she holds onto me like a life vest.

"I love you," she says. Quietly, like she's scared of it.

"You're it for me," I tell her. "You always were."

I lie beside her all night. Awake. Guarding.

Because she's mine. And I'll never let anyone hurt her again.

CHAPTER 28

Escaping Traumaville

LOLA

When I wake, it takes me a second to remember where I am.

The first thing I feel is pain. A dull, throbbing burn in my shoulder, like something had sunk its teeth into the muscle and didn't let go.

Because it did.

I wince, shifting slightly. The movement sends a flare through the bruise, but I grit my teeth and push past it. That's when I notice the warmth beside me. The weight. Harley's hand is curled gently at my waist.

We're facing each other. His eyes are closed, lashes dark, mouth parted like he's barely started to dream. One of his arms is tucked under the pillow between us, the other resting lightly against my stomach like he's been holding me there all night. Not tight. Just close. Just his.

I'm wearing his T-shirt. It hangs loose on me, the cotton soft and warm against my skin. I don't remember putting it on, only that his hands were shaking when he helped me out of my torn clothes.

My throat closes. Last night comes rushing back in pieces. The storeroom. Jack. The shelf against my back. His disgusting breath on my skin.

And Harley. His fists. His voice.

Me, falling apart in his arms.

I shift again, trying not to wake him, but his eyes flutter open almost instantly, like he's been hovering on the edge of sleep, waiting for me to move.

"Hey," he says softly, voice hoarse with sleep.

"Hey."

He looks at me like he's checking every part of me, like I might vanish if he blinks.

"How's your shoulder?"

"Sore," I admit. "But I'm okay."

His hand brushes the hem of the T-shirt, his fingers barely touching my side. "You don't have to be."

I nod, throat tight. "I want to see Imogen."

He blinks, and I watch the flicker of hesitation cross his face.

"Right now?"

"Yeah. If she's up."

"You sure you don't want to stay in bed a little longer?"

"I'm sure."

He nods slowly. "Alright."

He doesn't say anything at first. But I see it, the way his fingers tighten slightly on the duvet, like he's bracing for something. I hate that I'm the one making him feel like that.

I shift to sit up, and his hand moves to help me before I even ask. He watches me carefully as I swing my legs off the bed, walk to the en suite and wash my face and clean my teeth. When I'm done, I walk to his dresser, to the drawer he cleared out for my clothes weeks ago. He'd presented it with a flourish like it was some grand romantic gesture. It was. It made me fall even more in love with him.

I grab some leggings but keep his T-shirt on. It smells like him, and it calms me.

"Can I wear your fleece?" I ask, already grabbing it from the chair.

When I glance back at him, he's already standing, running a

hand through his hair like he doesn't quite know what to do with himself.

"Of course, baby. I'll walk you."

"You don't have to."

"I want to."

His voice is calm. Gentle. Not pushing, just... steady. Like he's trying not to hold too tightly but can't bring himself to let go.

I nod again, and he grabs his door keys.

I squint. The hallway is too bright. My feet are cold even against the carpeted floor as we walk past doors I've never paid attention to before. I've worked here for months, but I've only ever really known the reception, the bar, the kitchen. Not the spaces people sleep in. Not the place I'd been carried after being pulled out of a storeroom by the boy everyone warned me about.

Harley walks beside me, close enough that our shoulders brush, and laces one of his hands through mine, keeping pace, head on a swivel like he's ready to throw himself at something. Someone.

He stops outside Imogen's room, jaw clenched. Then knocks.

When the door opens, Imogen's already dressed. Hair in a loose bun, sleep still in her eyes. She looks between us and frowns slightly. "Everything okay?"

Harley doesn't answer at first. Then he clears his throat. "She wants to talk. Can you..."

"I've got her," Imogen says before he finishes.

He nods, but doesn't move.

"Harley," I say quietly, reaching up to touch his cheek.

He glances at me, and something in his expression falters. Like he's battling every instinct in his body. Then he leans in and presses a kiss to my temple, light, but lingering.

"Don't go anywhere without her," he says, a hint of finality in his tone to Imogen. "Please."

"I won't."

He hesitates a beat too long, jaw tight like he's biting back something he won't say. Then turns, shoulders rigid, and walks away.

I don't look back, but I feel it.

He let me go. Even when it hurt.

"Come on," Imogen says gently. "Let's get coffee."

"Okay, but can I borrow some shoes? I didn't wear any," I say pointing down at my naked feet.

She smiles, turns picking up her brown UGGs and passes them to me. They're a little big for me, but they'll work for now.

We walk in silence. I don't even realise I'm shaking until she links her arm through mine.

When we reach the staff lounge, it's empty. Chairs are scattered like they were left mid-conversation. A half-finished jigsaw lies abandoned on the coffee table. I breathe in slowly, grounding myself in the quiet, the stillness. Not the smell. Not the space. Just this moment.

I curl up on the sofa, knees to my chest. The fleece still wrapped around me like armour. It still smells like him. Still makes me feel safe.

He gave it to me when I couldn't stop shaking. Just wrapped it around me and sat beside me like he didn't know what else to do.

I didn't sleep properly. I woke up heart pounding, breathing shallow, like I was still trapped in that storeroom. Harley comforted me, told me I was safe, got me a glass of water. He hasn't let himself rest, not really. Not when I'm still shaking.

I trace the bite on my shoulder through the fabric, fingers brushing the curve of bruised skin. A pulse of nausea rises in my throat. I see flashes. His breath against my neck. My own voice breaking. The way the shelf dug into my back as I tried to shrink into it, disappear.

The residual fear coils in my lungs. In my ribs. Tight and hard and constant.

Imogen notices the panic on my face when she comes back to the sofa with our coffees, placing them on the table in front of us. She drops beside me and pulls me into a hug, her head resting gently on the shoulder that doesn't hurt.

And I crack. I don't sob. I don't make a sound. I just cry silent tears soaking into her jumper, my shoulders convulsing so hard I nearly choke on the silence. Her cheek rests on the top of my head, and she doesn't say a thing. Just holds me.

Like she knows. I think about pulling away. For a second, I almost do. The instinct to retreat is still stronger than it should be. But I stay with her.

Eventually, I pull back. Not far. Just enough to look up.

Her own eyes are glassy. "He told me," she says softly. "Ash. Not everything. Just... enough."

I nod, throat closed, breath shaky.

She wipes her nose on her sleeve. "You're not alone, you know."

Something in her voice makes me pause. She's looking at her hands now, fingers twisted tight in her lap. Her leg bounces once, then stills.

"I left uni early," she says, quieter. "Year two. After..." Her lips press together. "A man followed me home from a club. I thought I was just being paranoid. That I was overreacting. But he waited. Until I was unlocking my door."

Her voice breaks. "He tried."

She blinks hard, jaw tight. "I screamed bloody murder. Kicked him as hard as I could. Matt, my neighbour, came out, and ran after him. He didn't catch him, unfortunately."

My breath catches.

"It didn't matter. Everything after that just... collapsed. I couldn't sleep. Couldn't stay in my flat. I couldn't look at my own reflection without..." She exhales, quick and sharp, and shakes her head.

"Imogen," I whisper, voice barely there.

She shakes her head again. "I get it. The not sleeping. The flinching. The way people start speaking to you like you might shatter."

I nod, eyes burning again. My throat feels raw. My spine aches from how tightly I'm holding myself together.

"This place, Powder White?" she adds with a wry smile. "It's full of us. The runners. The rebuilders. We should rename the resort Escaping Traumaville or something."

Despite everything, I laugh, a sharp, messy snort. She grins, and I see it then, the fracture behind her perfect cheekbones, the fight in her eyes.

The door opens again.

I tense instinctively. Then relax when I hear the voices.

Niko and Tyler stroll in, mid-conversation. Niko spots me instantly and changes direction without a word. He walks straight to me and pulls me into a bear hug, warm and tight, his cheek pressed against mine.

I let myself fall into it. No hesitation this time. No pulling away.

I smell his aftershave, citrus and something warmer, and it hits me. I feel safe.

"You cry on my hoodie and I'm charging rent, bébé."

Tyler hovers awkwardly by the door, rubbing the back of his neck. "Hey, Lo," he says gently. "I didn't wanna... I mean, didn't want to freak you out."

I glance at him. There's a beat, then I smile. Small, but real. "You're fine," I manage. "Really."

He smiles, relieved. "Just glad to see you, mate."

Imogen squeezes my hand once, firm. Silent reassurance.

Niko sits on the arm of the sofa beside me and offers me a banana from his pocket with a sheepish grin.

"I stole it from the breakfast buffet."

I take it. I don't even like bananas. But I take it.

"Where's Nash? I'm surprised he's not attached to your hip," Niko asks, eyebrow raised.

"Harley gave strict instructions to keep her safe," Imogen says lightly.

"Yeah, and no one's taking you on, Im," Tyler confirms.

And for the first time today, I don't feel like I'm surviving.

I feel like maybe I've got my people.

I know it'll come back. The shaking. The noise. The dark corners. But for now, this moment, I'm not alone in it.

CHAPTER 29

Apres Bliss.... Finally

LOLA

I don't know when night ended, or if it ever did. I've been watching the light change behind the curtains for what feels like hours. Harley's asleep beside me, warm and quiet, the rise and fall of his chest the only thing steady in me right now. I haven't moved, not really, not since he wrapped himself around me and whispered that I was safe.

His T-shirt hangs off one shoulder, soft and oversized against my skin. My shoulder aches beneath it, bruised, bitten, and still tender to the touch. Every breath feels like I'm borrowing time from a body that used to be mine. It's foreign, it's fragile.

He shifts in his sleep, nuzzles a little closer, his hand slides across my waist his fingers digging in, like he's checking I haven't disappeared. I close my eyes for a moment.

He stirs again, eyelashes fluttering as he surfaces. "Hey," he whispers, voice sanded down by sleep.

"Hey."

His hand lingers at my hip, his thumb starts brushing slow, steady circles. "You alright?"

"Sort of," I admit.

He tips my chin up with his hand and watches me like I'm the most complicated equation he's ever had to solve. "How's your shoulder, baby?"

"Honestly… it still hurts a bit."

His jaw tightens. "I wish I could take it from you."

"You stayed and that's helped me more than anything."

He exhales softly, then lifts my hand to his chest and presses it over his heart. "Then I'll keep staying, however long it takes."

We stay tangled like that for a while, breathing in sync, until I finally say, "I need to shower, to feel clean."

He sits up a little, brushing hair from my face. "Want company?"

I pause, touching his wrist lightly. "I think I can manage solo."

His hand cups the side of my face, thumb brushing beneath my eye. "Okay. I'll be right here, just shout if you need me."

He presses a kiss to my forehead, slow and reverent, like the act itself is sacred.

I pad into the en suite, pain flaring as I move. The heat from the water scalds, but I don't turn it down, I let it burn, let it sanitise me and remind me I'm still here.

When I'm done, I see him sitting on the edge of the bed, fiddling with a thread on the duvet, like he's waiting to be told what part of me is broken now. I catch the way his foot taps once, then stills. He wants to fix it. But this isn't a bruise he can ice or a jacket he can wrap me in. He just has to stay. And he is.

I linger in front of the mirror, towel wrapped tight around me, steam curling against the glass. My reflection stares back, eyes bruised with exhaustion, skin blotched from heat. I press my fingers to the bite mark on my shoulder, wincing slightly. It still looks raw and angry. Like it's trying to remind me of something I'd rather forget.

I force a breath, comb through my damp hair, and dress slowly. Piece by piece, like maybe pulling on my uniform will anchor me. I don't feel normal. Not really. But I'm learning to pretend again. It's easier when he looks at me like I'm still whole. Like he doesn't see what's missing. Or maybe he does, and loves me anyway.

When I wander out, the mirror's fogged. It's his turn, and his voice carries through the steam, tuneless and loud, some godawful remix of "Ain't No Mountain High Enough" that he's butchering on purpose.

I lean against the sink, cleaning my teeth, watching the water bead down the glass. "You do realise you're tone deaf, right?" I call through the open door.

The water cuts off, a second later, and the door creaks until it's fully open and Harley emerges, towel slung low on his hips, wet hair dripping down his temples like something out of a Levi's ad.

He smirks. "You love it."

I try not to choke on my toothpaste. "I love you, not your crime against Motown," I tell him.

He crosses the room in one step, plucks the toothbrush right out of my mouth, and kisses me, minty, wet and slow. "Still counts," he murmurs, then swats my arse on the way out. I roll my eyes, but I'm grinning like an idiot. I don't know what I did to deserve this brilliant, intense, beautiful man, but I'm grateful anyway.

Downstairs, the lobby is already buzzing. The scent of fresh coffee drifts through the air, and the hum of conversation pulses like background music I'm still tuning back into.

"Morning, Mrs Nash," Niko calls out as I walk past reception.

His name on me still feels like armour, even as a joke.

"Shut it," I say without breaking stride.

Tyler leans over the counter. "He's still in his room, then? Knew it. You've got that smug, just-shagged strut."

I pause, raise an eyebrow. "Would you like me to ask Imogen to assign you toilet cleaning for the rest of the week?"

He clutches his chest dramatically. "She's drunk on power."

Niko snorts. "And orgasms."

I flip them both off as I pass. "Classy as always, boys."

It feels weird, being okay. Like I'm playing a version of myself from before. But their teasing makes me smile anyway, and I let it.

It's a smooth morning, no guest meltdowns, no broken lifts

or food mix-ups. Imogen's in a good mood, compliments my bun and tells me she likes my new boots.

Sophie swings by reception before her shift and drops two takeaway coffees on the desk without comment, then lingers.

"I've got you in the poker sweep tonight," she says, eyes flicking toward my lanyard. "You, me, Imogen, and Sarah versus the boys."

"You think I'm lucky?"

"I think Harley's good at poker, and you're good at distracting him."

I raise a brow. "Is that a compliment or a warning?"

Sophie smiles, slow and dry. "Bit of both."

Then she's gone, coat swinging behind her, espresso in hand.

At lunch, Harley appears at reception, grinning like he hasn't just terrorised his advanced group on the mountain all morning.

"Want to sneak out after shift?" he asks, draping himself over the counter, relaxing into the hot, tattooed boy he was before he became my number one protector.

I glance at the clock. "Where?"

"Into town, dinner? Or just a walk, just us."

I hesitate, only for effect. "Will there be wine?"

"There'll be me."

"Then I'll bring the wine." I smile.

He grins. "I love you."

"I know, I'm irresistible."

❄

Harley

Our shifts are finally over, and someone's queued up a playlist that swings between French pop, Arctic Monkeys, and aggressively horny reggaeton. The long wooden table in the staff lounge has been cleared of menus and rotas, now buried under a green felt mat, a pyramid of Pringles, and a suspiciously battered deck of cards.

Lola's curled up in the crook of the sofa, legs tucked under her, chips balanced on her knee.

And I am officially, stupidly obsessed with her.

"So what's the prize tonight?" Tyler asks, flopping down between Sarah and Niko.

"Winner gets to assign cleaning duties for the week," Imogen announces, eyes sharp behind her winged eyeliner. "Loser gets a back to back shift with Sophie on Sunday brunch."

Sophie groans. "That's a threat, not a punishment."

Lola raises a hand. "What happens if we catch Harley cheating?"

I grin across the table. "You'll have to prove it first."

"Oh, I'll prove it," she says sweetly. "And then I'll make you clean the guests' boots."

Ash deals the first round like he's spent time in Vegas. "Alright, misfits, time to play."

Half an hour in and Niko's singing along to a song no one else knows, Tyler's accusing Sarah of hiding cards in her bra, and Sophie's made it her mission to out-drink everyone in the room.

Imogen's deadly calm, stacking her chips like a Bond villain, while Lola's bluffing so badly I'm starting to worry she thinks the goal of poker is not to win.

She meets my eyes from across the table, tongue pressed to her cheek, and raises the pot again.

I narrow my gaze. "You're bluffing."

"You sure about that?"

"Nope." I fold.

The table erupts.

"You let her win!" Tyler cries, pointing an accusatory crisp at me.

"I did not," I protest.

"You absolutely did," says Imogen, sipping her rosé.

"You're whipped," Sarah grins.

"You're all jealous," Lola purrs, sweeping the chips into her pile.

I shoot her a look that promises consequences later. She bites back a smirk, then takes a long, victorious sip of wine.

By midnight, we're draped across chairs and cushions, laughter echoing off the chalet walls. Imogen's half-asleep, head on Ash's shoulder, while Sarah and Lola are deep in conversation about who would die first in a horror movie.

"I'd sacrifice you," Lola says solemnly. "But I'd cry."

I'm Harley. Calm, controlled, reserved. That's who I used to be.

But now she's got me grinning like an idiot in front of everyone. Now she's got me dreaming about things I never used to let myself want. Peace, love and a life that doesn't end when the snow melts. She catches me looking.

"What?" she mouths.

"You wreck me," I mouth back.

She doesn't blink. "You love it."

And leans across the table, steals a chip from my pile, and smirks like she owns me, and maybe she does.

CHAPTER 30

Calm Before the Storm

LOLA

"What's this mean?"

My finger traces the faded black ink on Harley's ribs, the broken compass. We're still tangled in the sheets, his arm slung over my hip, my cheek pressed to the warm skin of his chest.

He exhales through his nose. "It was supposed to mean direction. But I got it using a fake ID when I was sixteen, drunk on cider, pissed off at the world."

"Do you still feel lost?" I ask.

His eyes meet mine, sea-glass blue in the soft amber light of the lamp by the floor. "Not when I'm with you."

The weight of it settles over me. Heavy, but in a good way.

The first thing I'd noticed when I woke up wasn't the light or the quiet or even the comfort of the bed, it was him. Wrapped around me like a second skin, his body curved protectively along mine. His hand on my stomach, the heat of him. Safe, even before I opened my eyes.

His thumb strokes lazy circles just beneath my ribs. "You slept through."

"First time in a while," I whisper.

"Good." He kisses the top of my shoulder, over the bruised

skin. The bite mark Jack left, a gentle acknowledgment that he sees it and that he hasn't forgotten.

We don't move for a long time, there's no rush, no guests to greet. No chaos to wade through. Just this, just us.

Eventually, I turn to face him. He shifts too, hand coming to rest between my shoulder blades. He studies me in that quiet way he has.

"You alright?"

"Yeah." I touch his face, thumb brushing his jaw. "Are you?"

He nods slowly. "Better now."

A beat of silence, then he asks, "You heard from your dad lately?"

I blink, the question settling like a stone in my chest. He says it so gently, like it matters, like I matter.

"He messaged me after the storeroom… thing. Said he was proud of me, that I was braver than he gave me credit for."

Harley's brows knit. "How'd he even know about that?"

"My aunt. She reads everything Mum's old friends post on Facebook, and someone from home shared a guest's rant about 'Powder White staff dealing with dangerous situations.'" I sigh. "Small-town gossip chain."

"Right," he mutters, jaw tight.

"Did you reply?"

I shake my head. "Not yet."

Harley waits, not pushing, just holding space.

"I keep writing drafts then deleting them. It's like… if I say the wrong thing, he wins. But if I say nothing, I'm still carrying it."

"You don't owe him forgiveness," Harley says. "But if you need closure, you get to decide what that looks like."

"I might talk to him. One day soon, on my terms."

"I'll be there with you, if you want."

"I know."

We lay like that for a while, quiet and close, lazy kisses peppering the quiet.

"You were going to tell me something," I say. "About the

meetings with Zane now he and Dan Bailey have agreed to back you."

His mouth tips up. "They're going well, better than I thought. He's serious about it, wants to put his money where his mouth is, but he also wants to be involved hands-on. Says it's personal for him, too."

"That's huge."

"It is."

"You should be proud."

He shrugs, but I see the flicker of it, the quiet pride he doesn't know how to hold.

"I am. I just... never thought I'd be the guy building something instead of running from everything."

"You are that guy. You've always been that guy. You just needed space to be seen."

He kisses my forehead. "You make me want more, of everything."

"Good. Because I want it too, all of it."

Another pause, I trace the lines of his compass again.

"You ever think about next season?" I ask.

"I think about a lot of things. But yeah. You and me, working together. Starting fresh in the sun."

"Sounds like a dream."

His voice softens. "With you, it's real."

I curl into his chest, feeling his heartbeat under my palm.

"I think this is what peace feels like."

He strokes my back. "Then let's stay in it a little longer."

A beat passes, quiet but full. Then his voice, barely above a whisper. "There was this one placement, right before I aged out, I was seventeen. They called it a short-term foster setup, but I knew better. It was the last stop."

I say nothing, just wait.

"The dad... he wasn't violent with me. But the little ones, yeah. He threw things. Shouted. Broke plates near their heads. I tried to stop it once, grabbed his wrist and got labelled aggressive and moved the next morning."

I feel the tension in his body like the old hurt wearing a familiar face.

"You weren't aggressive," I say. "You were brave, you protected them."

"I still think about them," he admits. "Wonder if they're okay, if I should've done more."

"You were a kid too."

His fingers tighten slightly at my hip. "Doesn't feel like enough."

"It was."

"I want to build Break Line for kids like them. So they never feel like I did, like help was always one room out of reach."

"And you will," I whisper. "You already are."

His breath hitches again. We stay tangled in silence, skin to skin, breath syncing slowly. And in that quiet, something roots itself. Deeper than fear, stronger than doubt. Love that doesn't ask to be proven, only lived. Wrapped in warmth, in each other, in a calm that feels almost sacred, the kind that comes right before everything changes.

❄

Harley's grin is pure mischief when he pulls the chairlift safety bar down. "Blue run today."

My stomach does a swoop that has nothing to do with the height. "You're serious?"

"You're ready," he says, leaning back on his poles, as casual as if we're about to grab coffee instead of point ourselves down a slope. "Parallel turns only today. No more snowploughing into it, you've outgrown it."

The chairlift sways as we rise, the mountain unfolding below in clean, endless white. Harley glances over like he's checking the view, but it's me he's scanning. Always is. I don't say anything, just nudge my knee against his and let it rest there. He lets it stay.

"And if I fall?" I ask. Not because I think I will, but because part of me still needs to know he'll be there if I do.

"I'll be right behind you."

I smirk. "So you can laugh?"

"So I can catch you before you hit a tree."

I roll my eyes, but the warmth in my chest is impossible to hide. At the top, he guides me over to the slope's edge, where the blue run opens up, wider than the nursery slope, steeper, dotted with confident skiers carving smooth arcs. My breath fogs in front of me.

"Alright," Harley says, planting his poles. "You're linking turns now, so let's build on that. Focus on your edge changes, smooth transitions, let the skis do the work. Keep your hands forward, core steady, eyes up. Trust yourself."

I nod, focusing.

He pushes off first, carving slow, exaggerated turns so I can copy. I follow, knees flexing, edges biting into the snow. The speed is quicker up here, more alive. My heart hammers, part nerves, part thrill.

"Nice!" he calls over his shoulder. "Now hold that edge. Don't rush the finish. Just feel it through."

I shift my weight, more instinct than thought now, and the skis glide clean under me. No wedge. No wobble. Just me, balanced and moving like I finally belong here. The turn comes smooth, low and steady, and a grin pulls at my mouth before I can stop it.

"That's the girl," Harley shouts, pride thick in his voice. "That's a carve."

By the time we reach the bottom, I'm breathless, flushed from more than the cold.

"That was amazing," I pant.

"You were amazing." His gaze lingers, and it's the kind of look that makes the whole mountain fade to nothing. "One more run?"

"Always."

We queue again for the chairlift. When the bar comes down, his gloved hand finds mine. Just rests there, warm and solid. He doesn't say anything. Doesn't need to. My chest does that weird achey thing and I stare straight ahead, pretending it's no big deal. But it is.

Because I don't want to let go.

We slide off the chair and skate to the lip where the blue peels away into two lines. One swings wide and looks easier. The other cuts steeper for the first third before easing out.

Harley nods at the steeper start. "Pick your line."

I smirk. "You're gonna hate it."

His grin flickers. "Only if you half-ass it."

I push off. The snow's colder up here, slick just under the surface, but it holds. My first turn is slow and steady, more instinct than instruction. I find a rhythm. Not perfect, but mine. Behind me, I hear Harley's breath. Then nothing. He's giving me space. Letting me own it.

He pulls up beside me, eyes tracking my turns.

"You look good on a blue."

I snort. "Better than crying on a green?"

"Miles better."

He grins and drops back again. I link three turns without thinking and feel the inside ski glide to parallel, smooth and sure. My thighs burn, I need to work out more.

We pull off where the piste narrows between a crooked line of trees. He slows, leans on his pole, nods at the snow just ahead.

"That patch's slick. Wind's scraped it smooth."

I eye it, nerves twitching. "Ice?"

"Maybe. Just don't fight it. Stay loose. Float it, then set your edge after."

I bite my lip, nod.

He tips his head. "What do you do if it catches you?"

"Panic. Flail. Cry."

He grins. "Try breathing instead. And maybe keep your hands where they belong."

"Which is where exactly?"

He moves in closer, drops his voice. "On me, eventually. But for now? Forward."

I laugh. That shaky, charged kind of laugh that always happens when he gets too close.

"Show me," he says. Not demanding. Just... knowing.

I take the chute and just... do it. No overthinking. No panic. I glide over the shine like he said, let my legs do the rest.

When it opens up again, I stop, turn, catch him watching me.

He doesn't say anything. Doesn't need to.

It's all over his face, like I surprised him, like he's proud, like he wants me bad.

And I want him to look at me like that again.

And again.

"Again," I shout.

"Greedy looks good on you," he says, and pushes off.

We drop into a wide bowl where the snow's soft and quiet. Harley glides toward a sloped patch off to the side and nods for me to follow.

"Garlands," he says, flicking his pole toward the hill. "Half turns. Tap the edge, pull it back. It's like flirting, not dating."

I arch a brow. "With skis?"

"Exactly. You're just getting to know them. No commitment."

I groan. "Drills on a date?"

"Date?" He pretends to think. "That why you're trying to impress me?"

"Always."

I do the drill. It's boring for two seconds and then not at all, because the feedback is immediate, a little pressure here and the ski hums, a little less there and it drifts. Harley watches with his head tipped, that coach look he can't help, then skis in close enough that his knee brushes mine as we pause.

"Parallel again from the top on the next pitch," he says, voice low. "No wedge start. You've got it."

"Bossy."

"Confident."

I pull my goggles down tighter and go. The slope tilts and my body meets it cleanly. Skis flat for a beat, then edges roll, hands steady, hips quiet, eyes ahead. It isn't perfect. It doesn't need to be, it's mine.

Harley shadows me for the first two turns and then drops further back. I feel it like sunshine on my spine, warm, present, not pressing. When I check speed with a little hockey stop at the edge, snow sprays him on purpose. He coughs theatrically and laughs, coming in hot to kick a spray back that splashes my shins.

"War, is it?" he calls.

"Only if you think you can win."

He closes in, toe to toe for a few metres, faces me, skis backwards just to show off while I hold my arc. "Eyes up," he says, softer this time. "Look where you want me."

"Already there."

His mouth does that helpless curve again, the one that ruins me.

We cut over to a quiet shoulder of the run that hugs a line of trees. It's calmer here, sound muffled by the pines, just the hiss of our skis and the scrape of snow. Harley nods toward a small crest ahead.

"It drops quick, then flattens out. Most people lose momentum there because they back off too soon."

He glances at me. "You're not most people. Keep your speed through the rise, then set your edge once you're over it. Commit early and you won't have to push to recover."

"Commit," I repeat, because it applies to everything that's got his name on it.

I stay loose and let the speed come. The crest passes under me before I even think about it, and I'm already on the far side, balanced, steady, no wobble, no panic, just moving.

At the bottom of the stretch there's a viewpoint pullout, a small wooden fence and a map board nobody's reading. He glides in and taps his pole to the fence post. "Break."

I unclip one boot and rest, chest heaving, thumbs pressed into my thighs. He steps close and brushes snow from my hair, the backs of his fingers grazing my cheek. It's nothing and everything at once.

"Talk to me," he says.

I look up. "I'm not dead."

He smirks. "I can work with that."

We stand side by side and look out at a valley that looks painted. The light is soft and the clouds are starting to stack somewhere far off, the kind of formation that makes the air feel electric without knowing why. He notices it too. I feel it in the way his hand finds the small of my back and settles there.

"Last top section," he says, voice back to business but softer. "Then an easy glide to the base. You lead all of it, I'll keep an eye on you. If I need you, I'll shout. If you need me, you call my name."

I don't answer with words. I just point my skis downhill.

The top looks easier than it is. My legs burn but settle as I fall into rhythm. Left. Right. Left. The skis hold. The snow gives. Someone crosses in front of me and I adjust without thinking. A tighter turn. More weight on the outside ski. No panic. Just flow. Behind me, Harley whistles low. It's not a warning. It's pride.

I reach the last third and open the turns a little wider to let my legs breathe. The piste is busier here, a mix of confident locals and holidaymakers who don't know what their own skis are doing yet, but the line I pick threads through cleanly. When a kid sits down unpredictably near a roller, I steer early and give them a wide berth. Harley doesn't say a thing, he doesn't need to.

By the base my lungs are on fire and my smile hurts my face. I plant my poles and turn. He's already sliding towards me, eyes bright, mouth open like he's about to say something reckless and decided against it.

"I'm so fucking proud of you Lo," he says, just like that. No build, no show. "Properly proud."

I don't hide the way it lands. He sees all of it and steps into me, one hand curling at my jaw, thumb skimming the edge of my beanie. He kisses me slow and sure in the cold air, the kind of kiss that steadies rather than steals. Heat blooms under my skin and settles everywhere.

"Food?" he asks when he pulls back. "Then nap. Coach's orders."

"Yes, coach," I say, and he groans like I've done it on purpose, which I have.

We shuffle toward the lift line to ski home, but he stops me with a light tug on my sleeve. "One more thing."

"What?"

He gestures at the run we just did. "You led, I followed, that's not nothing."

I let it in, the fact of it, the way it sits right at the place where fear used to live. "It's everything."

We start gliding again. The mountain sounds normal now. Lifts clatter. Poles click. Someone laughs and the wind steals it before it settles. In the distance, the light shifts in that strange way that makes you check the sky and wonder if something's coming. Harley glances up once, then looks back at me like he's made a decision about what matters most.

He squeezes my hand where it's tucked into his. "Parallel," he says. "On snow, in life."

"Cheesy."

"True."

We share a quick grin behind our goggles and head back toward the chalet. Side by side. No need to speak. Our skis match pace without trying. It's easy now, the kind that sneaks up after you've worked for it.

❄

Harley

That night after we ski home, and shower, she's curled up against me. I shouldn't touch her. Not tonight when she's tired from our last ski lesson. I was so fucking proud of my girl. From Bambi to a student I'd have no issue with adding to my advanced ski group. Okay, I might not want to take her down any blacks, but that says more about me than it does about her ability.

She's curled up against me, soft and warm, her breath even where it brushes my throat.

But I can't not wake her. Not when she's lying here in my shirt, bare thighs tangled with mine, her hair spilling over the pillow, smelling like me. Not when every inch of her presses against me like she was made to fit there.

I tighten my arm around her waist, dragging her closer, and she stirs, humming softly. Then her hand slides up my chest, slow and sleepy, and rests over my heart. Like she knows. Like she can feel it hammering beneath her palm.

"Harley?" she whispers, voice rough with sleep.

I breathe her name back, low and quiet. "Yeah, baby."

She blinks up at me, half-awake, lips swollen, cheeks flushed. Christ, she's beautiful. I can't even look at her without wanting to lose my mind.

"Why aren't you asleep?" she murmurs.

"Because I can't stop looking at you."

Her breath catches, the faintest hitch, and she bites her lip like she's not sure what to do with that.

I roll us so she's beneath me, my weight braced on my forearms, her hair fans across the pillow like a halo. She stares up at me, wide-eyed, like she's not sure if I'm about to kiss her or ruin her entirely. Probably both.

"Harley," she whispers again, like she's trying to ground me.

I lower my head until my lips hover above hers. "You wreck me, Lola."

Her breath stutters. "I do?"

"You have no fucking idea." My voice is raw. Gravelly. "You're not like any girl I've met before... this... this is different. You're different."

Her hand slides up to cup my jaw, thumb stroking my cheekbone, and she whispers, "Show me."

I don't kiss her right away. I just look at her like I've got a lifetime of memorising to do. Then I lower my mouth to hers, slow and deliberate, and the second we connect, it's over for me.

I kiss her like I've got nowhere else to be. Like this is the only thing that matters. Because it is.

Her hands pull at the back of my neck dragging me closer until there's no space left between us. She sighs into my mouth, this soft, broken sound that punches straight through my ribs, and I swear I'll chase that noise for the rest of my life.

"Take this off," I murmur against her lips, tugging lightly at the hem of my shirt she's wearing.

She lifts her arms and I pull it over her head, slow, careful, dropping it onto the floor without breaking eye contact. My hand skims down her side, reverent, like she'll vanish if I touch her too roughly.

She shivers under my palm.

"Harley," she breathes, and fuck, the way she says my name, low and wrecked, makes me harder than I can stand.

"I've got you," I whisper, kissing the corner of her mouth, her jaw, her throat. "Always."

I trail lower, kissing down her chest, between her breasts, across her stomach. Every inch of her gets my mouth, my breath, my hands. I'm not rushing this. I want her begging, not because I pushed her there, but because she feels me there.

By the time I slide between her thighs, she's trembling, soft whimpers spilling from her lips.

I look up at her once, just once, to make sure, and she nods frantically, reaching for me.

"Harley, please..."

I drop my head, my tongue parting her slowly, deliberately, and her entire body jolts beneath me.

I hold her hips down, groaning into her, devouring her like I'll never get the chance again. Every sound she makes, every soft gasp, every whispered please pulls me deeper under.

"You taste so good, baby," I murmur against her, voice rough and wrecked. "Mine."

She comes hard, thighs shaking around my head, crying my

name, I keep licking her through it until she collapses back against the pillow, spent, beautiful and ruined for anyone but me.

I crawl back up her body, kissing her as she tastes herself on my tongue, and settle between her legs. I line myself up, rubbing the tip of my cock against her slowly, teasing, because I want her breathless when I finally push inside.

"Look at me," I whisper.

She does. Wide eyes, parted lips, pupils blown so dark they swallow me whole.

I move up onto my knees, reach over to our bedside table, grab a condom and roll it on to my throbbing cock. I push inside her slowly, deep, until I'm fully buried, and fuck. The sound she makes nearly undoes me right there. My body shudders with the effort it takes to hold back. My forehead drops against hers, breaths tangling, heart pounding like it's trying to crawl out of my chest.

Her nails dig into my shoulders, her hips lifting to meet mine, pulling me deeper. Her lips brush my jaw, her breath hot and shaky against my skin.

I start to move, slow and deliberate, rolling my hips until I feel her gasp, until she clenches around me and moans my name like it's the only word she knows.

"Lola..."

The sound of it rips out of me. Rough. Uncontrolled. Like a prayer and a curse wrapped into one.

She whispers my name back, soft and broken, and I swear it brands itself into my bones.

"Look at me," I rasp, pulling back just enough to make her meet my gaze. She does.

And it wrecks me. Those wide, hazel eyes, full of everything she isn't saying, trust, need, love, and all I can do is give it back, push deeper, grind slower, worship her like she's the only thing I'll ever need.

I kiss her like I'm starved. Like I'm dying for air and she's the only thing keeping me alive. When I pull back to breathe, the words rip out of me without thought, without hesitation, raw and brutal and true: “I love you so fucking much.”

Her hands cradle my face, pulling me closer, her voice shaking when she whispers, “I know… because, Harley, you’re my whole heart.”

Something snaps inside me. I kiss her harder, deeper, my thrusts losing rhythm as the heat builds, consuming me from the inside out. She’s gripping me everywhere, my back, my neck, my arm, holding on like she feels it too, like she’s right here with me in this free fall neither of us can stop.

Every little sound she makes pushes me closer, the soft, broken whimper when I hit deep, the breathless moan when my mouth drags along her throat.

And then there’s this one. a low, desperate, “Please, Harley.”

And fuck, I’m gone. That sound tears me in half.

“Again,” I growl, barely breathing. “Say it again.”

She does, whispering it into my ear, softer this time, almost shy, but I feel it vibrate down my spine.

The heat coils low and sharp, curling tight until I’m seconds from losing it. My rhythm falters, my body takes over, hips snapping forward harder, deeper, desperate to be as far inside her as I can go.

And then she clenches around me, crying my name, shattering beneath me, and it drags me straight over the edge with her.

I come with a raw, hoarse groan, my entire body locking up, pleasure tearing through me so hard it borders on pain. Every muscle tightens, spine arching, vision blurring until the whole world narrows to the sensation of her around me, her hands gripping me, her voice whispering my name.

It’s overwhelming. Full-body. Consuming. Like falling. Like burning.

Like every wall I’ve ever built collapsing in one brutal, beautiful second.

I spill into the condom, hips jerking against hers, desperate to stay inside her, to give her everything, to never let this end.

By the time I slow, I'm shaking, chest heaving, forehead pressed to hers, my breath ragged and uneven.

I pull her into me, sliding my arms under her, holding her so tight I don't know where I end and she begins.

"I love you," I whisper against her damp skin. "So fucking much."

She kisses me softly, her lips trembling against mine. "I love you too," she breathes.

She's my undoing. And I'm hers.

CHAPTER 31

Avalanche

HARLEY

The lobby's busy for an early morning, staff weaving around guests in layers of down and fleece, that low hum of voices rising every time someone stamps snow off their boots. I'm by the boot racks, already geared up, running over the plan in my head when the group starts to appear one by one.

Max is first, of course. The guy's built for entrances, broad shoulders, grin like he's permanently on the cover of his own LinkedIn profile. Fintech. Says it in the first five minutes every time. Today's flex is a sleek navy jacket with a logo I don't recognise but can tell cost more than my first car. He gives me a chin lift like we're old mates.

"Ready to see if you can keep up this time, Nash?"

I smirk. "You buying the beers you owe me from last run first?"

He laughs. "Only if you give me a head start."

Chloe arrives right behind him, all white-on-white ski gear that probably came straight from a luxury magazine shoot. Goggles perched on her head so her blow-dry can be properly appreciated. She sidles up, trailing a gloved finger along my arm like it's a reflex.

"So," she says, voice pitched low enough to make it private

even in the crowd, "are you taking me somewhere dangerous today?"

"Depends," I say, checking my watch. "You planning to listen to instructions this time?"

Her smile says no.

Rachel comes in last, with Oliver in tow. She's in simple black gear, no fuss, no frills, a helmet already buckled. Early forties, confident stride, not a single part of her screaming for attention like Chloe, but she gets it anyway. Oliver's practically bouncing, goggles already down, gloves half on. He's got that public school polish, skis since birth, the kind of kid who can drop into a black run without thinking but still tries to impress.

"Morning," Rachel says, nodding at me. Her voice is warm, clipped in a way that makes you pay attention.

"Morning," I reply. "We're doing a few reds and blues to warm up before the main event."

Chloe sighs dramatically. "Main event. I like the sound of that."

Rachel cuts her a look. "We're here to ski, not audition for GQ, Chloe."

That earns her a glare from Chloe and a suppressed laugh from Max.

We head out to the lift, boards and skis clattering, boots crunching. The air is knife-sharp, the kind that stings your lungs in a good way. The sun's bouncing off every surface, so bright you can almost hear it.

The first run is an easy blue, wide, forgiving, perfect for the warm-up. Max tries to overtake me halfway down, and I match him turn for turn until he's puffing and pretending he's not. Chloe follows close, always just a little too near, like she's waiting for me to stop so she can "accidentally" crash into me. Rachel is further back, skiing like she's been doing it for decades, precise, controlled. Oliver weaves between them, showing off just enough to earn an eye-roll from his mum.

We knock out a couple of reds next, the pace picking up, legs working into the rhythm. Max keeps challenging me, Chloe keeps flirting, and I keep half an eye on the tree line where we'll head later. The snow's decent, a little more give than I like this early, but nothing on the advisory says we should change the plan.

By the time we hit the mid-mountain lodge for lunch, the group's buzzing. We claim a table outside in the sun, helmets and gloves piled in the middle. Max orders two pitchers of beer 'for the table', and then claims the first pint for himself. Chloe takes the seat next to me, Rachel opposite like she's deliberately playing buffer.

Banter flows easy. Max is telling some story about closing a deal in a chalet in Verbier, Oliver chimes in with his own tales of skiing with the school team, and Chloe keeps trying to turn every comment into something suggestive. Rachel keeps her in check with these perfectly timed little jabs that make me want to laugh out loud.

While they're talking, I pull my phone from my jacket pocket and check it under the table.

Three new messages from Lola.

The first one is a photo, just her legs, bare, tangled in my sheets, sunlight spilling across her skin.

The second: Wish you were here. Not at work. Here.

The third: When you get back, I want your mouth on me before you even take your boots off.

I suck in a breath through my teeth, before I can stop it.

"Everything alright?" Rachel asks, eyebrow raised.

"Yeah," I say, pocketing the phone quickly. "All good."

Max grins. "Sounds like someone's got a reason to ski faster this afternoon."

Chloe leans in, syrup-sweet. "Oh? Do tell."

Rachel cuts in before I have to. "Leave him alone, Chloe. We'll get better runs if he's not distracted."

Max laughs into his beer. Oliver looks mildly horrified.

I just shake my head and pour myself some water, but my pulse hasn't slowed since I opened that first message.

After lunch, the air feels different. The sun's dipped just

enough to harden the snow in places, shadows stretching long across the runs. Perfect time to push them a little.

We take the chairlift higher, the air thinning, colder, that deep quiet settling in over the upper slopes. The group chatters on the ride, Max with another story, Oliver hanging on his every word, Chloe laughing too loud, but I'm scanning the ridge line, watching the tree line below. Snowpack looks fine from here, but the wind's picked up a fraction. I clock it. Adjust the mental plan.

At the top, I swing my skis around and plant them. "Alright, listen up. We're going to take this red down to the turnoff for the black. Once we hit the split, we stop and regroup before we drop in. Stay behind me until then."

Chloe sidles closer, eyes wide like she's on some exotic safari. "And if I… accidentally end up in front?"

Rachel snorts. "Then you'll accidentally end up in the trees."

Max grins. "I'd pay to see that."

"Eyes forward," I say, though it's hard not to smile.

We push off. The red is wide and smooth at first, then narrows with a few steeper pitches that make Oliver's competitive streak flare. He takes off after Max, the two of them carving tight turns, spraying snow. Chloe's right behind me, still too close, but Rachel hangs back enough to keep her in sight.

Halfway down, Oliver catches an edge. One second he's up, the next he's tumbling sideways toward the netting.

"Oliver!" Rachel's voice is sharp.

I'm already braking hard, cutting across to grab him just before he slides too far.

"You alright?" I ask, steadying him by the jacket.

He's breathless, cheeks flushed. "Yeah. Was trying to…."

"Don't," I cut in, my tone flat. "Save it for the bottom."

Max slows to wait for us. "Close one, mate."

Oliver grins sheepishly. "Guess you do need to pay attention."

"Guess you do," Rachel says pointedly.

We regroup at the split. The black run drops away below us, steep and shaded, the kind of slope that demands your full respect. You can hear it even from here, the change in snow texture, that faint crackle where wind meets powder.

"Alright," I say, scanning their faces. "This is your final run of the week. Black-rated, steep sections, some chopped-up patches, a tree run at the end. Follow my line exactly. If you get into trouble, sit down and wait. Don't try to recover on the steep."

Max gives me a mock salute. Chloe looks like she's about to eat the mountain whole. Rachel's calm, Oliver's buzzing.

Chloe leans in again. "And if I make it down without falling?"

"You'll do exactly what I tell you for the rest of the day," I say before I can stop myself. Her eyes light up like I just handed her the keys to the bar.

Rachel mutters, "Not if I get to her first."

I take one last look up at the ridge line. Wind's still light. Sky's still clear. Snow's holding. We're good.

I drop in first.

The black run drops hard off the ridge, a sharp, narrow start that demands commitment. I cut a clean first turn, then another, letting the edge bite into the cold-packed surface. The group follows, a staggered line of movement behind me.

The sound changes here, the soft, even hiss of skis on snow giving way to a crunchier bite, sharper, like tearing paper. My legs adjust automatically, knees absorbing the chatter.

We cut into the shadow of the pines. The air drops a couple of degrees. It's quieter here, the sound dampened by the trees, but every now and then you hear the wind rush through the top branches like a warning.

Max is keeping up well, athletic and confident, though he keeps throwing little flourishes into his turns like he's auditioning for that GQ shoot. Oliver follows his line, and Rachel shadows her son with a hawk's precision. Chloe... she's not reckless yet, but she's letting her skis run just a fraction too long before turning. I file it away.

Halfway through, the slope flattens for a short stretch before the final pitch. I pull up, signalling for them to stop.

Max slides in beside me, breathing steady. "Hell of a view," he says, glancing down through the trees to the valley.

Oliver whistles. "Worth the whole week."

Chloe edges closer, lifting her goggles just enough to flash me a look. "So... what happens if we beat you down?"

Rachel answers before I can. "You buy the first round."

Max smirks. "I'll take that bet."

I'm about to answer when I hear it.

A low, deep whumpf, somewhere above. Subtle, but it vibrates under my skis. The kind of sound you feel more than hear.

My eyes go up. The upper ridge looks fine at a glance, no obvious fractures, no plume of snow drifting, but the hairs on my neck rise.

I take a slow breath. "Alright. Last pitch. Same rules. Follow my line exactly, and stay alert."

They nod, still riding the high.

We drop in. The final stretch is steeper, tighter. The trees crowd close on either side, sunlight flickering through the branches. The snow here is deeper, softer. It swallows the skis a little more than before.

Then there's another sound. Louder this time. Sharper.

A crack.

It doesn't echo. It rolls.

My stomach knots. Every muscle goes rigid.

I glance uphill.

The ridge above us shifts. Just a breath, a shiver through the snowpack, but I know what it means.

"MOVE! HARD RIGHT! TREE LINE! NOW!" My voice is already raw.

Max reacts first, cutting hard toward the pines, spraying a wall of powder as he powers into the turn. The guy might be cocky, but he's quick. Behind him, Rachel's already calling for Oliver, but the kid's eyes are locked uphill, body stiff.

"Oliver! Go!" I push every decibel I've got into it, but he doesn't move.

Chloe's just ahead of him, stock still, mouth open. "Harley."

"RIGHT, CHLOE! NOW!"

She jolts like I've slapped her, edges in, and disappears between two trunks.

The snow groans above. The pitch under my skis goes weightless for half a heartbeat, then settles again, like the mountain's inhaling.

I skate toward Oliver, heart pounding. "Let's go, kid!"

He tries, pushes off, but catches an edge and crashes sideways, one ski popping loose and spinning away.

"Shit." I'm on him in seconds, grabbing a fistful of his jacket.

Up close, I can hear it. The slide. Not just a sound, a living thing, tearing free, gaining speed.

"On your feet! Now!" I haul him upright, shove his remaining ski straight. We push off together, legs driving, but the slope's turning into quicksand under us. The avalanche is coming in high and wide, spilling between the trees, a boiling wall of snow and debris.

Something hits the back of my legs, pressure, then lift. My skis are gone before I know they've left. Oliver's yanked sideways, his arm wrenched from my grip.

The sound is everywhere now, a freight train swallowing the world. Snow slams into my chest, wraps around my shoulders, hauls me off my feet.

It's not falling, it's being taken. The mountain has me, and it's not letting go.

I tumble, smash into something solid, tree, rock, I can't tell, then I'm under. Snow packs into my mouth, my nose, my ears. My body spins, flips, slams again.

I fight to get my hands up toward my face, to make a pocket, but the weight crushes down like wet cement. My right arm's pinned. My left moves a few inches before the snow sets like concrete.

Up, down, sideways, it's gone. There's no direction. Only dark. Only cold.

Lola's face hits me hard. That little furrow between her

brows, the way she tilts her head when she's trying not to smile. Her laugh in my bed this morning. The warmth of her skin.

Not like this.

I force my breath shallow, counting, one, two, three, because every second I keep my head means another chance they find me. My chest burns. My fingers go numb. The roar fades to a dull, pressing silence.

❄

Lola

The front desk is running on autopilot, or it was until my phone rings. I swipe to answer so fast I almost drop it. "Ash?"

"There's been an avalanche." His voice is steady in that awful, deliberate way that tells me he's choosing every word.

My grip on the counter tightens. "Where?"

"Pine ridge, western drop. Harley's group."

The floor tilts under me. "Is he..." My throat closes before I can finish.

"Some guests made it out. Harley's beacon's active. Patrol's on him, but... they haven't got to him yet."

I press my palm flat to the desk, like that can hold the world still. "He's under?"

"They're searching. They're good, Lo. But it's bad."

The phone nearly slips from my hand. Imogen's suddenly at my side, reading my face like she's flipping straight to the ending of a book she already hates. She takes the phone from me without asking.

"It's Imogen. Tell me exactly what's happening," she says, voice like steel wrapped in velvet.

Niko's head snaps up from behind the brochure stand. "What the hell's going on?" He's already moving closer, his accent thickening with panic. Tyler swivels away from the printer, brows pulled low.

"Ash, mate, talk to me, what happened?" Tyler calls, like sheer volume can reach through the phone.

Imogen flicks a sharp look at both of them, not cruel, just a silent order to let her handle it.

"How many buried?... Okay. Any injuries?... Right. Call me the second you know," she says, her tone clipped, measured. But I can see the pulse hammering in her neck.

There's a pause before Ash answers something I can't hear, and something shifts in her face. Softer. More human. "You come back in one piece too, yeah?" she says, low enough that only I catch it.

She hangs up and exhales through her nose like she's pushing the emotion out before it cracks her voice. Then she passes the phone back to me, her hand lingering over mine for a beat.

"Harley's in there," she says quietly. "They've got eyes on his beacon. They're digging now."

Niko mutters something in French, harsh and ugly. Tyler scrubs a hand over his face, eyes darting to mine. "We're just standing here? We can't just.."

"What exactly are you gonna do?" Imogen cuts in, still calm. "You go up there without gear, without training, you make more work for the people trying to get him out."

The staff door bangs open before anyone can answer. Scarlett strides in, Zane right behind her, both scanning the lobby like they've already felt the shift in the air.

"What's going on?" Scarlett's voice slices through everything.

"Avalanche," Imogen says, keeping one arm tight around my shoulders. "Harley's group. He's missing."

Scarlett's face drains but her movements are precise, already pulling her phone from her blazer. "I want ski patrol on the line in ten seconds. Tyler, Niko, clear the lobby. No guests wandering in here until we know what's what."

Zane plants a big hand between my shoulder blades, grounding me. "Harley's a fighter. Don't start writing him off yet."

But I've stood in this air before. With Mum. With Liam. That suspended moment where life can tilt either way and you're powerless to stop it.

I can't lose him. Not him.

The helicopter comes first.

We hear it before we see it, the deep, chopping thud of rotor blades moving through the valley air. It rattles the lobby windows, and everyone goes still.

Scarlett's on the phone at the front desk, Zane pacing with his mobile pressed to his ear. His voice is low, quick, in French. The words blur, but the tension in them carries.

Imogen hasn't left my side. Tyler's sunk into one of the lobby armchairs, elbows on his knees, eyes fixed on the carpet like he can burn a hole in it. Niko's stalking from window to window, swearing in French every time he catches sight of the chopper banking over the ridge.

Zane ends the call, turns to us. "They can't get a line straight to the beacon. Snow's too deep. They think there's rock or debris in the way."

My throat tightens. "So what now?"

"They dig. Fast." He pauses. "They've got maybe... fifteen minutes before oxygen becomes the real problem."

Fifteen minutes.

Scarlett ends her call and tosses the phone onto the desk. "They've pinged a signal," she says, voice sharp. "But it's not Harley's. Wrong location. They're moving to the next reading."

The blood drains from my face. "They're wasting time?"

"Not on purpose," Zane says, trying to be gentle but failing. "It happens. Avalanche scatters everything. Signals bounce."

I grip the edge of the counter until my knuckles go white. The pressure in my chest rises until it's a physical ache. My stomach heaves.

"I'm..." I don't even finish the sentence. I lurch sideways, make it to the bin behind reception just in time. Acid burns my throat as I retch, the sound ugly and raw in the quiet. Imogen's hand is on my back instantly, murmuring something low I can't catch.

When I straighten, shaking, the room feels smaller. Tighter. The air tastes stale. Imogen reaches into the mini fridge behind reception and hands a bottle of water to me. "Drink, please," she orders. I do as I'm told and tell her thanks.

Zane's phone rings again. He snatches it up. "Ouais. Putain... okay. Where exactly?... Shit." His gaze flicks to me, and for a second I think he's going to lie. "They're on his signal now. It's deep."

"How deep?" Tyler asks, voice tight.

"Two metres. Maybe more."

The lobby feels too small. I can hear my own pulse, loud in my ears.

❄

Harley

I'm going to die.

Before I even open my eyes, I know it. My chest won't move. My arms are dead weight. There's a crushing silence pressing down on everything, so absolute it roars.

I try to move. Nothing. My body's locked, buried in snow. Heavy. Cold. Claustrophobic.

Not snow. Not even light. Just... nothing. Like limbo.

Panic hits fast. My lungs scream for air that isn't there. My jaw clenches, trying to force a breath. Still nothing. I'm not just stuck, I'm trapped. Buried alive in a freezing tomb.

The white behind my eyelids is blinding. Too bright to be dark, too dead to be alive. The kind of brightness you get just before you pass out.

I should be calm. Logical. I've done the training. I've led enough drills. But nothing prepares you for this. The stillness. The weight. The fucking silence.

Then she hits me.

Lola.

Her laugh, too loud when she finds something funnier than it is. Her curls, wild and impossible to tame, framing her face like they've got their own idea of where to fall. Her fingers tracing slow lines across my skin like she's memorising me.

I see her face. Clear. Present. Real.

God, Lo.

No. Not like this. Not now.

I promised I'd protect her. Promised I'd come back. Told her I loved her. I meant it. Every word.

Who's going to keep her safe if I don't make it out?

Jack's gone. But fear like hers doesn't vanish. Not with the abuser. Not with time. It lingers. It haunts. I've seen it in the way she startles, the way she stiffens when someone walks too close behind her. The way she doesn't always realise she's bracing for impact.

She needs someone who sees her. Who never lets go. And that's me.

I can't leave her. I won't.

But I'm losing ground. Cold creeps deeper. My fingers are already numb. My thoughts slowing, fraying at the edges. Each second longer in this icebox, and my chances shrink.

Then, her voice.

Not real, but real enough.

"Don't you dare give up on me."

It's her voice. Sharp. Fierce. The kind that gets through even the worst of it.

I focus. Fight the urge to let go. I try to move something. Anything. A finger. A twitch.

Then I hear it.

A beep. Distant. Then closer.

Another beep.

Muffled voices.

"There. Signal's close. Right beneath us."

"Go. Dig."

The pressure above me shifts. A gust of cold air brushes my cheek. Then hands. Heavy, gloved, yanking snow away from my face. Rough fingers pressing into my neck.

"He's alive!"

"Harley Nash. Can you hear me?"

I try to answer. Only a broken rasp escapes. My throat's sand. My chest burns. But I'm still here.

A face appears. Goggles. Helmet. A voice shouting into his comms.

"Stay with us. I will. For her, my Lola.

Her name pulses like a drumbeat behind my eyes. She's the only thing I can see now. The only thing I care about.

Someone presses an oxygen mask over my mouth. The air rushes in, icy and sharp. Relief comes fast, followed by the dizzy crash of adrenaline giving way to shock.

Everything blurs.

And now that I'm safe, now that someone else has me, I finally let go.

❄

Lola

The lobby is too bright. Too warm. The hum of the heater in the corner is a low, constant drone, but it might as well be silence.

Nobody's talking. Not really.

Tyler's pacing a slow, restless loop from the fireplace to the door, running a hand over his jaw like he can keep himself from saying the wrong thing. Niko's wedged into the armchair nearest the phone, elbows on his knees, staring at the floor like he can see straight through it to the mountain. Imogen hasn't moved from my side, her hand locked around mine so tight my fingers are numb.

I can feel my own heartbeat in my throat. Every time the main doors shift against the wind, my head snaps up, hoping it's..

Zane's phone goes off.

The sound makes all of us jump. He's on it in a heartbeat, stepping away from the group, his deep voice switching instantly into rapid French. Too fast for me to follow. His tone isn't loud, but it's sharp, urgent.

I can't breathe. I'm trying to read his face, but it's impossible.

He's listening more than he's speaking, jaw tight, shoulders bunched. The seconds stretch like they're mocking me.

Then I see Niko's head lift. He's tuned in, processing every word, and I watch the change in him, tension breaking, shoulders loosening. His eyes dart to me, wide, almost disbelieving, before he's on his feet.

He crosses the space in two strides and yanks me into a hug so fierce it knocks the air out of me. "Il est vivant," he says against my hair, his voice breaking. "He's alive."

For a second, my brain refuses to catch up. Then it hits, a rush so violent I have to grab his jumper just to stay upright.

"Oh my God." My voice cracks, my knees threatening to give.

Niko's still holding me, but over his shoulder I see Zane ending the call, giving a short nod that confirms it. The kind of nod you don't fake. Relief is in the set of his mouth, even if the rest of him is still wired tight.

I pull back enough to look at Niko. "I swear to God, I'm learning French," I say, my voice shaking, trying for a laugh but failing. "It's the only language that matters right now."

He smiles at me, but it's sad around the edges. "You wouldn't have wanted to understand the first part."

I don't ask. I can't.

Scarlett finally exhales, running a hand down her face, and Zane starts speaking again, low and steady, like he's briefing a team before a mission. I only half-hear the words. All I can think is that he's alive.

Alive.

The only thing that matters.

CHAPTER 32

When Snow Stills

LOLA

The woman who walks in isn't wearing a white coat. Just pale green scrubs and the tired look of someone who's been awake longer than I've been alive. Her dark hair is pulled back in a bun that's coming loose, and there's a faint accent when she says my name.

"You are Harley's family?"

Ash answers before I can, his voice flat but firm. "Yes."

She nods once. "Then I tell you both, yes?"

We stand too quickly. My legs feel like they're made of wet paper, and I have to grab the back of the plastic chair to keep upright. Ash shifts closer, his shoulder a wall beside mine.

"He is stable now," she says, hands clasped in front of her like she's holding something still.

The word stable barely lands before she adds, "But..."

It slices through whatever breath I'd managed to take.

"We have finished surgery for the fractures. His right leg was broken in two places, his arm in three. Several ribs were moved from position but not broken, these we have stabilised. All the breaks are fixed with metal. He is intubated, sedated. His body needs to rest before we wake him."

Something caves in my chest. "Wake him?"

She looks straight at me. Patient, kind, but unflinching. "Yes.

The coma, it is not... natural coma. It is medical. We give him medicine to keep his brain quiet, so it can heal. If we wake him too fast, the swelling can cause damage."

My stomach twists. I grip the edge of the chair so tight my nails bend. "So... he's not just... gone?" My voice cracks halfway through.

Her gaze softens, but her words don't falter. "Non. He is here. But we keep him sleeping while his body repairs itself. When the swelling in the brain is less, when his lungs are stronger, we remove the medicine. We see how he wakes."

I blink. My head can't keep up. "So you can choose... to keep him asleep? For as long as you need?"

"Not want," she corrects gently. "Need. It protects him. Think of it like... putting the body in pause. A safe pause."

Beside me, Ash finally speaks, his voice low and rough. "How long?"

"Six, maybe seven days. We lift the sedation slowly. This is not exact science." She glances between us, making sure neither of us misses it. "He is young. Strong. The beacon meant we found him quickly. These are good signs."

They don't feel like enough.

I hear movement further down the corridor. Zane steps out from the shadows by the vending machine, arms folded, his tall frame a silent sentinel. He must've been waiting the whole time. The doctor sees him too, but she keeps her eyes on me.

She takes a small step closer, switching her English to something slower, cleaner, so even my panic-clogged brain can't miss a single word. "There is risk, yes. Always. But we do all we can. He is not alone."

Her gaze flicks past me to Zane for the first time, then back to Ash. Like she knows none of us are letting go of Harley, not now.

When she leaves, the corridor feels colder.

Ash drags a hand down his face. "Bloody hell."

Zane finally moves, his voice a low rumble. "Stable means alive. That's what matters tonight." His accent makes it sound firmer, heavier, like the words are weighted down with iron.

I want to believe him. I do. But all I can see is Harley lying somewhere behind those doors, metal rods holding him together, machines keeping him breathing. A pause button on the only boy I've ever loved.

Ash notices the way I'm swaying. "Lo." He steadies me with a hand on my arm. "You want to see him?"

Do I? My throat closes around the thought. I nod anyway.

The door clicks open, and the sound of the machines hits me first. Steady beeps, the quiet hiss of oxygen. Then the sight.

Harley.

What's left of him.

His face is swollen, bruises blooming purple and black across his jaw and temple. A tube snakes from his mouth, taped at the edges, the steady rise and fall of his chest belonging more to the ventilator than to him. Needles and wires sprout from his arms, disappearing into machines that blink and hum like something out of a nightmare.

My knees buckle. For a second the room tilts, the white walls swimming. I don't even realise I'm falling until both Ash and Zane grab me, one on each side.

"Easy," Ash mutters, voice rough.

"You're okay," Zane adds, his arm a solid bar across my back, keeping me upright.

But I'm not okay. Seeing Harley like this feels like my chest's been torn open.

I clutch at the rail on the side of his bed, fingers curling around the cold metal. "That's not him," I whisper, though he's right there. "That's not my Harley."

"He's here," Ash says firmly. "Doesn't look it, but he's here."

Zane's voice is quieter. "Machines make it worse than it is. They keep him alive, that's all."

I want to crawl into the bed, curl up beside him, shield him from all of it. Instead, I sink into the chair beside the rail, both hands gripping his, ignoring the tape, the IV line. His skin is warm. Not gone.

Ash leans against the wall, arms crossed tight, but his jaw

flexes like he's one word away from breaking. Zane stays by the door, silent, watchful. They're both holding themselves together, but it's costing them.

❄

Hospitals make time fold in on itself.

It's been seven days since the avalanche. Seven days of counting the rise and fall of Harley's chest. Seven days of bad coffee, stiff chairs, and pretending the cot they gave me is anything but decoration.

I haven't left.

Ash comes and goes. Tried once to talk me into sleeping at the chalet hotel, but I told him I'd rather cut my own arm off with a rusty knife than have Harley wake up without me here in this room with him. He didn't bring it up again.

Zane too. He doesn't say much, just slips in with his long stride, sets a fresh coffee on the table, sometimes sits in the chair opposite me without a word. His calm fills the room in a way I can't explain. Not a distraction, not comfort exactly. Just a presence that says: you're not carrying this alone.

Imogen came first. Arms full of a bag with joggers, my hoodie, enough dry shampoo to keep me human. She set it down, pulled me into her arms without asking. I sagged into her, and she smelled like the chalet bar, perfume and spilled wine and the faint tang of citrus from the lemons she always slices.

"Ash told me you're not eating. You can't starve yourself, Lo," she whispered into my hair. "You're no good to him if you burn out."

I nodded, but it wasn't enough. My throat was too tight for words. She held me tighter. Her own body started to shake. I didn't notice at first, but when she pulled back her mascara was streaked.

"Sorry," she muttered, swiping at her face. Then she bolted, head ducked, pushing through the door like she couldn't breathe in here anymore. I knew she'd gone to find Ash, because a minute later I heard his voice low in the corridor, the sound of her crying muffled against him.

Sarah came next, cheeks flushed from rushing straight from the hotel, and marched to my side, eyes wet, mouth firm.

"Don't you dare think he won't make it, Lola." Her voice cracked but she pushed on, fierce as I'd ever seen her. "That boy loves you too damn much to give up. You hear me? He's gonna claw his way out of this bed if it kills him, because he can't stand the thought of you being alone. Not now. Not ever."

Her tears slid down her cheeks as she said it, but her grip on my shoulders was iron. I believed her. Or at least, I let her believe for both of us when I couldn't.

Niko breezed in like a storm, loud at first, trying to fill the air with too much energy. He perched on the end of Harley's bed, ignoring the way the nurses frowned, and launched into a story about some German guest who tried to ski in a wetsuit. Or the time Tyler got trapped in the coffin lift with a tray of oysters and a half-naked Sophie.

His hands flailed, his grin was wild, and for a second it almost worked.

But then his voice wavered. Just once. And when he looked at Harley, really looked, the bravado cracked. His shoulders curled in, and he pressed the heel of his hand to his eyes.

"Fuck," he muttered. "I hate this, Lo."

I reached for him without thinking. He clutched my hand back harder than I expected, his palm sweaty, desperate. Then he pulled away quick, swiping his face, mumbling something about needing to get back to work.

Tyler came last. Quiet. Steady. He stood at the foot of the bed, arms folded, eyes fixed on Harley like he was trying to will him awake through sheer force. He didn't say much, just rested a hand on my shoulder before leaving, a warm, grounding weight that lingered long after he was gone.

It's weird, laughing in a hospital. But between Niko's stories, and Imogen's dry wit when she managed to come back in, there were moments the tightness in my chest eased.

Underneath it, though, the fear never moved.

They left eventually. The quiet came back.

Why me? Why him? Why anyone?

Mum. Liam. And now maybe... Harley.

Ash reappeared with two vending machine coffees and warm bottles of water. "Still here," he said.

"Still here," I answered.

Movement in the corridor caught my eye, Imogen again, arms crossed, head lowered. Ash went to her without hesitation. They spoke low. I saw her grip his jacket, his hand graze her cheek. She rested her forehead on his shoulder. He pressed a kiss to the top of her head. Both of them still, like moving might break something.

I looked away.

Twice I thought Harley moved, once his fingers twitched around mine, once his head turned just slightly when I spoke.

The doctors started easing the sedation two days ago, he's breathing by himself now, this gives me hope.

"You may see signs soon," they'd told me. "It will be slow. Not dramatic."

Last night, I curled onto the edge of his bed, hand on his chest, counting breaths until I drifted off.

Now it's morning. The light through the blinds is thin and grey.

And his hand is moving.

At first, I think I'm dreaming.

"Lo?" Barely a whisper, but it's him.

I jerk upright so fast the bed frame groans. "Harley?"

His eyes are open. Clouded. Unsteady. But awake.

"You're... here, baby," he breathes.

"Where else would I be?" He exhales, shaky and uneven.

"Thought I... dreamed you."

"You didn't."

His thumb brushes over my hand like he's checking I'm real.

"Am I... okay?"

"You broke your leg, your ribs, your arm. But you're here. You're alive."

His brow furrows. "I remember the snow. The sound. You. Thought I was dying thinking about you."

The words hit so hard I can't breathe. Tears spill before I can stop them.

"You scared the hell out of me."

"Sorry," he whispers. "Didn't mean to."

"I know." My voice cracks. "I love you so much, Harley."

He smiles, small but certain.

"Love you too, baby."

He swallows, and for a second, I think that's it, but then his brow tightens.

"Lo," he murmurs, barely audible. "The others... Max, Oliver... Chloe, Rachel, did they make it?"

My throat closes. I shift higher, press my forehead to his.

"They're safe," I whisper. "You kept them safe. They all made it down. Everyone's okay."

His whole body lets go of something. I feel it in the way his hand loosens, the breath he releases like it's the first clean one he's taken in days.

"Good," he says. Quiet. Final.

His eyes flutter closed again, but it's just sleep this time. I lie down beside him properly, my head on his shoulder, arm across his chest like I could keep the world off him if I held on hard enough. For the first time in a week, my heart unclenches. Harley came back to me.

CHAPTER 33

Coffin Lift and Crutches

LOLA

Ash pulls into the car park and lets the van idle. The chalet's tucked behind the trees, windows lit, warm and familiar. No one speaks.

Harley leans forward, taking it in, a small smile pulling at his mouth.

"Why does this place always smell like burnt cheese and wet socks?"

Ash doesn't look back. "Because you're home, sunshine."

Harley looks out at the building, that small curve to his mouth that means he's already judging it.

I laugh before I mean to. Harley's sling cuts across his chest, the strap digging into his neck where he wouldn't let me pad it. His face is still bruised, yellow fading to green around his jaw. The cast on his leg is hard to ignore. He's leaning on me more than he'd admit, warm and solid at my side. His long-sleeved T-shirt's too plain, ironed flat because Imogen insisted.

The sliding door rumbles. Cold air knifes in, clean and sharp. Outside, they're already there.

Imogen, scarf wrapped tightly, eyes steady, hands tucked into coat sleeves like she is containing herself. Niko shifting his weight, gloves on, gloves off, the human equivalent of a spark. Tyler at the rail, shoulders set, watching the door the way people watch for news. No one's pretending this is a normal arrival. Up in the window of the lobby, Sarah has a toddler on her hip, the child's socked feet bouncing against her stomach. She lifts her free hand and waves, a small steady motion, then taps the glass twice with two fingers, a quiet you're seen. Harley looks up, and smiles back at her.

Ash stays still for a beat, the kind of pause that says he knows this next part is going to be hard. He twists, meets Harley's eyes, and speaks like a promise.

"We've got you."

Harley's jaw works. He wants to say he can do it himself. He also wants to get out of this van without collapsing in front of his team. Pride and pain have always been neighbours in him. He nods, once. That's the truce.

Tyler's already at the door, voice calm. "Alright. One thing at a time."

Niko pops his head in, grin too wide, voice too loud, the mask he wears when he's about to feel something big. "You planning to winter in here or are we doing the heroic exit now?"

Imogen steps in closer, no performance, one hand to Harley's forearm, a touch that says here, not holding, not crowding, simply here.

They move together with the easy choreography of people who have hauled furniture, drunk friends, and broken hearts through this car park in every weather. Ash takes the casted leg, both hands under the calf, careful and precise, his face all focus. Tyler slides an arm around Harley's back and another under his good shoulder. Niko braces the doorway, then leans in to take a share of weight like he is the third corner of a triangle.

"On three," Ash says, voice even. "One. Two. Three."

Harley's breath punches out of him as his foot finds the snowy ground. It's not a sound he wants to make. It is one his body makes anyway. For one beat nothing else exists. Not the mountain, not the warm windows, not even me. Just four men breathing together so nobody falls.

His good foot steadies. The crutches are there, Tyler already adjusted them earlier because of course he did. Harley takes one, then the other. He tests them. He nods. The shake in his hand is not dramatic. It's real.

Niko clears his throat too loudly because silence is starting to feel like a cliff edge. "Well then. Ten out of ten. Graceful as a baby giraffe with excellent hair."

"Shut up," Harley says, and the bite in his voice is not anger. It's gratitude wrapped in something he can survive.

The spell loosens. We move.

Inside the boot room, the air changes to the muffled heat of wet gear, disinfectant and snow that's lost the will to be anything but water. The dryers hum, low and constant. A pair of tiny mittens hang from their string over a bench, forgotten or left as a marker that a small person exists in this world and will be back for them. I want to cry about mittens. Instead I put a hand to the back of Harley's ribs, the lightest of anchors, and breathe slow and loud enough that he can match it if he needs to.

He stops. The staff lift waits with its dented doors and its reputation. The name is older than any of us.

"The coffin lift," Tyler says, because we always say it out loud, like a ritual.

Harley glares at it. "No."

"It's this or four flights," Ash says. "You're not doing stairs today."

"Tomorrow either," Imogen adds.

Niko reaches past everyone with theatrical flourish and presses the call button. "Coffin lift chooses the brave."

"Shut up," three voices say at once. It makes me smile in a way that's not about amusement.

The doors slide open with a metal scrape. The interior is narrow and unforgiving. There is no way to keep elbows from knocking something. They manoeuvre him in with a lot of breath and six hands and a muttered warning from Ash when Harley tries to insist on turning himself. Tyler gets the crutches squared. Niko jams himself in at an angle like a clown in a tiny car.

“Pray to the Gods of hydraulics,” Ash calls as he leans over the stairwell to watch them go.

The motor complains and hauls and works. The light flickers once, then holds. I stay at the bottom. Imogen stands beside me and presses two fingers briefly to my wrist before dropping her hand like it meant nothing. We listen to the lift climb. Somewhere above, a door opens. A guest laughs. A child yells something triumphant about socks.

Imogen and I take the stairs, counting the hum between the floors.

By the time we reach the top, the doors are open and they’re all standing there, ugly and beautiful in equal measure, the way real things are. Harley’s got his shoulders back like defiance is the only way he knows how to stand. Niko’s hair is crooked. Tyler looks like he just negotiated a treaty with the lift and won it by one vote. Ash is already near the stairwell, hands still half-raised, like he hasn’t stopped bracing for impact.

“I’m suing,” Harley says, which is poetic.

“You would have to survive a second use,” Niko says cheerfully. “Jury is still out.”

We’re two steps into the corridor when Scarlett comes into view. Arms crossed, eyes sharp, mouth flat. She takes in the scene in a single sweep that misses absolutely nothing.

“Well then,” she says. “Our resident drama magnet returns.”

Harley lifts his chin, not quite smile, not quite dare. “You miss me?”

“Not even a little,” she says, then decides to be honest. “You scared the living daylights out of all of us.”

He swallows. “Sorry.”

“Don’t be sorry,” she answers. “Be smart. No slopes, no lifting, no heroics. Bed here until season ends, medical still covered, your job is yours when you can do it without breaking anything that’s already fixed. Understood?”

“Yes,” he says simply.

Her eyes flick to me. She considers my face the way she

considers a rota. "You're with him tonight, but back on tomorrow." She holds my gaze. "That is not a suggestion."

"Thank you," I say, and it lands more like relief than gratitude.

Scarlett nods once then is gone, already moving toward the next thing that needs her. The echo of her boots is a comfort. It means someone else is steering for a while.

We take Harley the last stretch. The staff corridor is warmer. Inside our room, it's clear Imogen's been through already. The bed's made too neatly for how we usually leave it, with two extra pillows stacked at the head and water on both sides. A quiet island of calm. The curtains are drawn just enough to keep the dark out and the warmth in. There's a small stack of books on the bedside table, business titles, probably Zane's influence, but also the worn paperback I saw Harley reading in hospital. A room waiting for him. For us.

Getting him onto the bed is a patience test. It's a dance in slow motion. Tyler manages crutches and clearance. Niko talks too much because silence still feels like something that could tip. Ash takes the brunt of the weight when the cast needs that final lift to get onto the mattress without banging. Harley sets his jaw and breathes with the measured concentration of someone who's decided not to yell today. When he finally sinks back against the pillows, his exhale is so soft it almost is not sound. I feel it anyway. He closes his eyes for three breaths, then opens them again because he hates not seeing what's happening.

"Water," Imogen says. She presses the glass to his good hand, watches him drink, nods in a way thats also a note to herself. "We're outside if you need us."

Niko hovers like a balloon someone forgot to tie down. "Do you want me to fluff a pillow? Tell a story? Perform a small dance?"

"Leave," Harley says, but there's zero heat in it.

Tyler squeezes Harley's shoulder once, brief and careful. "Good to have you back."

"You too," Harley says, which makes no literal sense and is exactly right.

Ash and I are last. He checks the angle of the sling strap without touching it, then looks at me instead of Harley.

"Shout," he says. "Anything goes weird, you shout."

"I will."

He gives me a small nod that reads like, I'm still here, and disappears.

We're alone.

I sit on the edge of the bed and slide my hands under the strap of his arm sling to adjust it where I saw it rubbing his neck earlier. He watches me with that focused softness that has replaced bravado in him lately. He's not used to being tended to.

"There," I say.

"Thanks."

"Always."

I go to the mini fridge, expecting emptiness and a sad bottle of water.

I open it.

It's full.

Bottles of apple and orange lined like soldiers. Two small boxes of cranberry juice tucked at the back. A can of Irn-Bru front and centre, orange and blue as if it is dressed up for a party. On the shelf beside the kettle someone has arranged herbal tea sachets in a row like a tiny parade. A packet of good biscuits sits next to them, not the cheap kind we get for guests, the kind Sarah buys for people she cares about. There is also a plate under foil with a note stuck to it in her looping hand.

Homemade carrot cake. Don't you dare complain it's too sweet.

Propped against the kettle there's a plain card. Inside, her handwriting spills quick and certain.

So happy you are getting better. Make the most of the quiet with Lola. The rest can wait.

S x

My throat burns. It's stupid to cry over tea and a drink in a tin and cake under foil. It's also not stupid at all. These are the things that hold people together when big things try to break them.

I take the card to Harley and hand it over without speaking because if I try I might squeak. He reads it, the muscle jumping in his jaw. He presses his tongue to his molars like he's stopping words from coming out that are not ready to be said. He sets the card on the table with much more care than a piece of paper usually receives from him.

He looks at the Irn-Bru and snorts once, a broken little laugh. "Of course."

"She waved," I tell him. "From the lobby window. Toddler on her hip. She had to work, but she waited here to see you pull in."

"I saw, but couldn't wave back because.... Well you know." He says, looking down at his body. "But I did give her a smile."

"Open the cake," he says, roughly.

I do. The foil peels back with a crackle and the smell is immediate, warm spice and sugar and the faint citrus of icing. I break off a corner, small enough that he'll not cough around it, and put it into his palm. He eats it like he's tasting something for the first time. He licks a smear of icing off his thumb and closes his eyes while he does it, which should be ridiculous, but is not. It is reverent.

"Better than hospital jelly," he says.

"That's a seriously low bar."

"My favourite kind."

I set a juice on the table and push the straw in for him. He takes a sip, grimaces at the sweetness, then drinks again anyway. He nods at the Irn-Bru. I roll my eyes, take it on myself, and set it down next to the juice with the tab already pulled.

He watches my hands. It calms him. It calms me.

"You need to pee," I say, because romance here is logistics, and honesty.

"God," he mutters. "I hate this."

"I know."

We do it with dignity and quiet. It's not a big thing except it is a big thing, because this is what it is to help someone heal, the thousand small domestic kindnesses that feel like love because they are love. When he's settled again I re-smooth the sheet near his hip and he doesn't tell me to stop.

He tips his head to look at me. "You alright?"

"Yeah."

"Liar."

"Partial liar."

He smiles real now, the kind that lights his eyes, not his mouth. "Come here."

I sit again. He slides his good hand out palm up and I lay mine in it. We rest like that, both of us looking at our joined hands the way you look at something you worked hard for and finally own.

Silence isn't empty in this room. It is full of small sounds. The hum of the fridge. The central heating ticking as it adjusts. Boots on the hallway carpet somewhere far away. The faintest rise and fall of his breathing. I match mine to his without deciding to. I think we have both learned to do that now.

"I love you," I say, because there's never a wrong time to put that in the air."I love you too," he says quietly, just for me. Like it always has been.

He slides his thumb along the inside of my wrist, like he's memorising a map he has no intention of forgetting again.

There's a soft knock and the door eases open a fraction. Imogen's voice stays at the crack so as not to break whatever is in here. "You two need anything?"

"We have cake," I call back. "And Sarah's smuggled a national treasure into his fridge."

"Good," she says. "Eat. Sleep."

"Boss says I'm back on tomorrow."

"She told me too. I can run first hour at the desk so you don't have to show your face until after morning transfers."

"Thank you."

"You're welcome," she says.

The door snicks closed.

Harley sighs, “Back on tomorrow. I wish you could stay with me forever in our little bubble.”

“I’ll come up in breaks,” I say. “Bring you proper food. Check your temperature with the back of my hand and announce findings in a serious voice.”

“Hot,” he says.

“Always.”

He lifts our hands and kisses my knuckles, one by one. It’s not sexual and somehow it’s the sexiest thing I’ve ever seen him do. He doesn’t look away while he does it. That’s new. He used to hide when he felt too much. Now he lets me watch. I think that is the difference between surviving and actually living. You let someone see you when you want to hide.

We watch five minutes of muted football, he dozes, those little dips and rises of near-sleep. Every time his breathing stutters I whisper his name and he steadies. Every time I shift, he tightens his fingers so I can’t forget I am tethered to him.

It gets quieter in the building as the night moves on. The last of the dinner plates will be stacked. The bar will drop into low voices and glass clinks. The printer will threaten another tantrum. I know the rhythm now. It’s a drum behind the walls.

I get up once to turn off the main light and leave the lamp on low. I check the card again because I want to read those words one more time before sleep blurs them. The rest can wait. I think that might be the kindest sentence I have ever seen written down.

When I lie back down I’m careful, sliding onto the outside edge where I won’t jostle him, my head near his shoulder, my arm across his ribs without weight. He angles his body that fraction so I fit. I stare at the ceiling for a while and count the beats I can feel in him. I stop counting when my body knows them without trying.

“Lola,” he says when he is almost under.

“Yeah.”

“Thanks for bringing me home.”

“You did the hard part,” I say.

"Still," he whispers.

Outside, the snow's still falling. The lamp hums. His chest rises and falls. I close my eyes.

He's here.

I'm not letting go.

CHAPTER 34
It Gave Me You
LOLA

It starts with a lie.

Harley thinks we're going for a "quiet drink." One pint. Maybe two. Just to mark that he's finally out of the last cast and walking without crutches. He even joked earlier that his physiotherapist cried when she saw him manage stairs again. I told him she probably cried because he did it shirtless and my man is a tattooed god.

And now, as we're walking down the icy slope toward the Red Frog, I'm wondering how on earth I managed to keep my face straight when he said it.

The bar's windows glow against the dark, throwing streaks of amber light across the snow. The familiar hum of bass carries through the door, not loud, but enough to buzz in my chest. I tug my coat tighter, trying to hide how jittery I am.

Harley notices anyway. Of course he does.

"You're twitchy," he says, eyes flicking down at me as he adjusts the scarf I practically forced around his neck. "You nervous about having a pint now? Or is this about me?"

"About you," I shoot back, because if I try to play it off, he'll see straight through me. "You still walk like Bambi on ice. I'm just bracing for a dramatic re-broken leg."

His mouth quirks, but it doesn't quite make it to a smile. "You're hoping I'll fall so you can laugh at me, admit it."

That makes me laugh, which I can tell he wanted. But beneath it, I can feel the nerves creeping off him. He hasn't said it, but I know this is his first real night out since everything. Since the avalanche a month ago. Since hospital beds and nightmares and the sound of machines beeping in sterile rooms.

And the truth? I'm nervous too. Because walking into that bar with him feels bigger than just a drink. It feels like proof that he's still here. That I didn't lose him.

We reach the door. His hand lingers on the handle, fingers curling tight, knuckles pale. He doesn't push it open right away.

"You sure about this?" he asks.

"Are you asking me if I'm sure about having a drink?" I murmur, "or are you asking if you're ready to be seen?"

That earns me a side-eye so sharp it could cut glass. "You're a pain in the arse."

"And yet," I say, nudging his shoulder, "here you are."

His hand finally presses the handle down.

But when we step inside the Red Frog, it isn't quiet.

Not a surprise party, not exactly. No one jumps out. No one yells. There's no confetti this time. But the place is full of our people, gathered around tables pushed together, glasses already clinking, laughter bouncing off the walls. The music is low, the lights softer than usual. A celebration without being loud about it.

And I feel Harley freeze beside me.

He stops dead in the doorway, shoulders going tight. He's not suspicious, not this time. Just... stunned. Like he doesn't know what to do with the sight of it.

I can feel it in the way his grip on my hand tightens, almost to the point of pain. The air leaves my lungs, and for a second, I think he might bolt.

So I squeeze back. Hard. A silent message: You're safe. You're wanted.

His eyes scan the room, taking in every familiar face, every grin and raised glass. And I swear, for a second, he looks younger. Not the Harley who's been through hell, not the Harley who carries scars inside and out, but just a boy being reminded that people love him enough to show up.

And my heart nearly caves in.

Niko spots him first, waving an arm from the bar like he's hailing a taxi in central London. "About bloody time! We were starting to think you'd crawled back to hospital for the free morphine."

Everyone at the table erupts with laughter. Tyler slaps the table so hard beer sloshes over the rim. Sarah nearly chokes on hers, coughing into her sleeve.

Harley doesn't move. His jaw tightens, and I can feel the old reflex, the one where he wants to snap something sharp back, keep people at a distance. But then Sarah lifts her glass high, her grin fierce, all edges and warmth at once.

"Look at you, Nash," she calls out, voice carrying over the music. "Standing. Breathing. Almost handsome again."

That does it. Harley huffs out a laugh, shaking his head, and some of the tightness in his body unwinds.

Even Sophie, yes, Sophie, is leaning against the bar with a small smile, like she's letting the night be bigger than her pride. I don't miss the way her eyes soften when they catch Harley's, just for a beat, before she takes another sip of her drink and looks away.

Harley mutters, "What the hell is this?"

I lace my fingers through his. "Not dying deserves a pint. Sit down before they make a toast without you."

He doesn't argue. He lets me tug him forward, and the crowd shifts to make space.

Tyler is first, rising to clap him on the back, sliding a pint into his hand like it was waiting there all along. "Good to see you vertical, mate."

"You say that like I haven't been vertical for weeks," Harley deadpans, though the corner of his mouth betrays him.

"Yeah," Niko cuts in, grinning from ear to ear, "but now you're vertical with dignity."

That sends everyone off again, the kind of easy, full-bellied laughter that doesn't happen when you're waiting for the next disaster.

Harley rolls his eyes, but he's smiling now, and this one's real. The kind that softens him. Makes him look younger. The kind that makes my ribs ache in the best way.

I watch him take a sip of his beer, his throat working, and it hits me all over again. He almost wasn't here. He almost didn't make it back to this table, this banter, this moment.

And now he is.

The sound of it all, friends shouting over one another, glasses clinking, the thrum of bass under it, wraps around me like armour. For the first time in weeks, the air doesn't feel heavy. It feels alive.

The night moves easily after that. Drinks, banter, too much noise spilling out of all of us at once. For the first time in months, it doesn't feel like surviving anymore. It feels like living again.

Later, I catch sight of Imogen and Ash tucked into a booth in the corner.

It shouldn't stand out. The Red Frog is chaos by now, Niko's on a chair leading some sort of drinking chant, Sarah's arguing with Sophie about who makes the stronger cocktail, Tyler's disappeared outside. Noise, movement, mess everywhere.

But my eyes snag on them. Imogen, leaning in close, glass cradled between both hands like it's something delicate. Ash, shoulders relaxed for once, voice low, his hand brushing hers as he murmurs something that makes her laugh into her drink.

It's quiet. Private. Unspoken. But it's charged, electricity caught in that small space between them, waiting for lightning to strike.

Ash says something I can't catch, and Imogen tips her head back, laughing harder than I've seen her all season. Her hand slips, landing on his wrist for balance, but she doesn't move it. And he doesn't flinch.

Then Sophie drifts past with a cocktail in hand, casual as you like, her words dropping like a lit match. "Careful, Imogen. Someone might think you've got feelings."

Imogen's laugh dies in her throat. Colour floods her cheeks. Ash's eyebrow arches, sharp, amused.

"Someone's jealous," he says flatly, eyes flicking to Sophie's retreating figure.

"Please," Sophie tosses over her shoulder without missing a beat. "I'm not jealous. I'm observant."

She disappears into the crowd, leaving the air heavier than before.

Imogen's shoulders are tight now, her smile frayed at the edges. Ash doesn't look fazed, if anything, he looks like he's waiting. Watching her carefully.

I slide into the booth beside Imogen, nudging her knee under the table. "So... you and Ash?"

Her eyes dart toward him, then back to me. "We've always been close."

"Close like friends? Or close like... if this were a movie, you'd already be making out in the linen cupboard?"

Her laugh sputters out, half-shy, half-exasperated. "Lola..."

"What?" I grin, but softer. "It's obvious. And I think it's cute."

She shakes her head, glass turning in her hands. "Honestly? I don't know. But..."

There's a beat where she lets that sit, like even saying it out loud is terrifying. Her fingers tighten around her glass, but her gaze flicks across the table to Ash, who's pretending not to listen and failing miserably.

That's enough for me. I squeeze her hand under the table, giving it a quick, sure squeeze. "Then that's all that matters. The rest will sort itself out."

Her lips twitch, like she wants to argue, but instead she nods. And I mean it, I'm rooting for them. They've carried enough of this season's weight. They deserve something light.

❄

Near midnight, the Red Frog spills onto the patio. People pour out like the walls gave up holding us in. Cold air hits warm skin, wakes everyone up. Laughter climbs higher, boots crunch over packed snow, glasses fog in our hands. Fairy lights hang loose above us, flickering against the dark, smoke curling from nearby chimneys.

Harley slides up behind me, arms wrapping tight around my waist, his chin settling into the curve of my shoulder like it belongs there. His warmth anchors me against the cold, the steady thrum of his chest pressed against my back a reminder that he's really here. Not broken, not buried, alive.

"You look happy," he murmurs, voice low and rough for me alone.

"I am."

His arms tighten, the shift subtle but desperate, like he's still bracing for me to say something else, something darker. "Even after this hellscape of a season?"

I twist in his hold until we're face-to-face. His breath curls white in the air between us, his scars catching in the fairy light, his eyes blue enough to split me wide open. "Especially because of it," I say. "It gave me you."

His breath stutters, a crack through the armour he always wears. "Say that again."

"You," I whisper, my thumb tracing the line of his jaw. "It gave me you."

The kiss he pulls me into is slow, deep, and weighted with everything unspoken. Not frantic, not greedy, but deliberate. A seal. A vow. Relief threads through it too, like he didn't realise until right now how badly he needed me to say it.

A dramatic cough cuts through, shattering the quiet bubble we'd built.

"Right," Niko says, smirking as the group drifts closer. "Before you two start dry-humping in the snow, we've got a vote to call."

Groans, laughter, the shuffle of boots. Sarah takes charge, naturally, snagging an empty pint glass from the outdoor table and plonking it down like a gavel.

"Alright," she says, sharp grin in place. "It's been one fucked-up winter. Broken bones, avalanches and drunken disasters..." She raises her glass toward Harley, then me. "But we made it through. Together. So, who's going to Ibiza for the summer season with Sunship?"

Hands fly up. Mine. Harley's. Niko's. Tyler's. Imogen's. Even Sophie, who lifts her drink in a silent toast, her eyes softer than I've seen in months.

Ash doesn't raise a hand. He just nods once, solid, like the decision was made long ago the second Imogen smiled at him tonight.

The circle buzzes with it, the weight of what we're agreeing to. This isn't just about flights or jobs or contracts. It's about choosing not to let this winter be the only thing that defines us. Choosing more, more nights, more chaos, more living.

Snow crunches as we shift closer, shoulders bumping, hands brushing. And in that messy, crowded circle, I see flashes of everything that's come before, the hospital waiting room, the falls on the slopes, fights that cut too deep, laughter that stitched us back together.

We've survived avalanches, heartbreak, bruises you can't see and bruises you can't hide. And now we're choosing what comes next.

It's unanimous.

We're doing this. Together.

Because away from the mountain, life keeps moving, indifferent and fast.

But in here, in this circle, under the fairy lights, with snow beneath our boots and hope thick in our chests, we have the quiet between.

CHAPTER 35

Epilogue - Four Years Later

HARLEY

The fire crackles, slow and steady, casting a golden glow over the thick fur blanket we're tangled in. Outside, the snow is falling again, quiet and unbothered, the way it only ever falls in the Alps. This cabin's been ours for a week now, a break we swore we'd take and never did, until four years passed and we finally let ourselves stop. No noise up here. No calls. No guests. No team to rally. Just us.

Lola's curled against my chest, bare feet tucked beneath the throw, her hair damp from the hot tub and fanned across my shoulder. She smells like pine and peppermint oil, and I can feel the weight of her breath when she exhales, deep and easy.

I cooked dinner. A decent one. Steak, potatoes, garlic butter everything. She pretended to be impressed, even though I burnt the edges and forgot the wine. It didn't matter, she drank beer with me instead. We laughed. We always do.

Break Line's taken off. What started as a scribble in my notebook is now a full-time mission. We work out of two offices, Ibiza in the summer, Le Deux Alpes in the winter. We've got partners, sponsors, a waitlist for intake. The thing is, I don't care about the numbers. I care that we kept our word. That we made something real out of nothing.

And that she's still here.

My Lola.

Her eyes flutter open, sleepy and soft. "You're staring," she murmurs, smiling.

I brush her cheek with the back of my hand. "Can you blame me?"

She lifts her chin and kisses me, slow and lazy, like we've got nowhere to be. Because we don't. For the first time in months, it's just us.

"You happy?" I ask.

"I'm always happy with you."

My throat tightens and I sit up a little, shifting her in my arms. She goes easily, blinking up at me with that look, the one that used to undo me back when she was still just a girl in a reception uniform who wrote in a journal late at night.

"I... My voice catches, and I laugh, nervous. Me. Nervous. "I don't say it enough."

Her brow furrows. "Say what?"

I reach into the pocket of my hoodie. It's not smooth or cool or any of the ways I imagined doing this. But then, Lola's never been about grand gestures. She's about truth. And this is mine.

I open the smooth black velvet box and pull out the ring. Her breath catches. Imogen helped me choose it. Told me if I didn't get Lola the best fucking ring in the world, she'd personally kick my arse on her behalf. Then she sent me about a hundred links to diamond rings with price tags that made me sweat. I picked the biggest one I could afford, an oval-cut diamond in a platinum band, simple, stunning, no frills. Just like her. Only the best for my girl.

I hold it up, heart thudding like it's trying to break through my ribs. "Lola Maxwell... you're my best friend. My soulmate. The love of my fucking life. I still wake up and can't believe it's you beside me. And I want it to be you. Every morning. For the rest of my life."

She covers her mouth with her hand.

"Will you marry me?"

She doesn't speak. Doesn't move. Just stares.

Shit.

My stomach sinks. My heart stops beating altogether.

"Lo?" I whisper, panic threading through my chest like ice water. "You okay?"

Her eyes fill and a sob breaks free.

"Fuck, baby, I...was it too soon? I thought maybe, we've talked about it, I mean, not seriously, but..."

She launches herself at me, tears falling in hot streaks down her cheeks. Her arms wrap around my neck so tight I can't breathe.

"Yes!" she cries into my shoulder. "Of course yes. There's no question, Harley."

I let out a breath that turns into a laugh, shaking and full of relief. I slip the ring onto her finger, and it fits perfectly. She holds her hand out and stares at it like it's the most precious thing she's ever seen.

"It's beautiful, thank you, but also you saved me," she whispers. "When I was lost, you saw me. And you stayed."

I kiss her so deep it feels like it could rewrite history.

"No," I say. "We saved each other."

❄

Epilogue: Seven Years Later - Ibiza

Lola

The beach is quieter in the late afternoon, the golden light softening every edge. The sea glitters like melted glass. Warm, lazy waves kiss the shore while the breeze tousles my hair just enough to remind me I'm alive. Nine months pregnant, and I still feel good. Heavy. Swollen, slightly feral with hormones. But good.

I sink a little deeper into the striped lounger, toes buried in the warm sand, trying not to fall asleep. Imogen is beside me, wearing an oversized hat and sipping an iced coffee that I am one hundred percent resenting her for.

"He hasn't got a shirt on again," I mutter, not even pretending to hide my stare.

Imogen follows my gaze.

Across the beach, Harley is sprinting barefoot through the sand, chasing a football and three shrieking kids who are clearly losing their minds with joy. Niko intercepts the ball with an overly dramatic dive. Ash howls with laughter, arms spread wide like he just won the World Cup.

But my eyes are fixed on Harley. Tanned. Shirtless. Muscles rippling under golden skin. Tattooed arms, and torso, wild grin, black curls damp with sweat.

Imogen sighs. "You're so obvious."

"I'm nine months pregnant and horny. Everything he does feels like foreplay."

She snorts, choking on her coffee. "Jesus, Lo."

"You asked."

"No, I didn't."

I shift on the lounger, trying to get comfortable, which is laughable at this point. There is no comfortable. There is only shifting between one semi-tolerable position and another.

I rest my hand on my belly, feeling the slow roll of movement beneath my palm.

"Any day now," Imogen says softly.

"I know."

My eyes stay locked on Harley. The way he lifts one of the kids, Leo, a new Break Line recruit, and swings him around until he's dizzy with laughter. The way his joy is real. Effortless. Like the boy he never got to be is finally alive in him.

My phone buzzes on the small table next to me. I glance down.

It's Dad. We made our peace the weekend we went back to England when Harley turned twenty one. Said he'd had a lot of time to think about his behaviour once I'd left for France. He's re-married now to Gemma, my wonderful, caring step-mum. Harley says he's punching and I wholeheartedly agree. She's a therapist and I strongly believe that she actually managed to coach him back into the man my mum must have seen all those years ago.

I smile faintly, then reach to pick it up, and freeze.

A strange wetness pools between my legs.

Oh fuck.

I look at Imogen.

"What?" she asks.

"My waters just broke."

Her coffee sloshes. "Are you serious?"

I nod, oddly calm. "Harley's not going to be, though."

She leaps up, yells toward the boys, waving her arms. "Nash!"

Harley glances over, eyebrows furrowed. Then he sees my face.

Everything changes in an instant.

He barrels across the beach like a man possessed, sand flying, kids scattering.

"Lola? Baby, what?"

I try to stand but he's already there, crouched, panicking, hands everywhere. "Are you okay? Is it happening? Are you in pain? Do we need the car? Is it too soon? Should I call an ambulance?"

"Harley."

He's spiralling.

I grab his face between my hands.

"We're having a baby. Right now. Breathe."

He blinks. Nods. Swears. Then lifts me effortlessly and starts barking orders at our friends like a military commander.

❄

Harley

Hospitals make me nervous.

Always have. They smell like endings, my ending and I'm immediately back in that side room in Grenoble after they pulled me out from under the avalanche all those years ago. I breathe in and out to steady my nerves. It's different this time. This place smells like beginnings.

Lola's asleep now, finally, after what felt like a hundred years of screaming and squeezing my hand until it went numb. And now he's here. Our boy.

Wrapped in a white blanket, sleeping against her chest like he's always belonged there.

I'm sitting beside the bed, shirtless, because she threw up on my clothes and I wasn't about to leave the room for anything. A nurse offered me scrubs. I said no. I wanted to be skin to skin with my son.

He's perfect.

Ten fingers, ten toes, little tuft of black hair.

And she's never looked more beautiful. Even wrecked. Even exhausted. She's everything.

She opens her eyes and finds me staring.

"What?"

I clear my throat. Try to speak and fail.

"I was thinking," I say finally, voice thick. "That maybe we should call him Liam."

Her eyes flood. Instantly.

Tears immediately spill down her cheeks as she stares at me, then at the baby, then back.

"You mean it?"

"For the brother you lost," I whisper. "And the boy I want him to grow into, brave, kind, and stubborn as hell."

She nods, crying harder now.

"Liam," she whispers, cradling him closer.

I lean in, pressing my forehead to hers.

"You did so good, Lo. You made him. You made us."

She kisses me, slow and salty and sweet, "We made him, Harley, two broken kids then, now we're whole."

And in that moment, in a quiet hospital room in the middle of the Ibizan night, with Liam breathing between us and the past nowhere in sight, I finally understand what family feels like.

Acknowledgments

Writing a book is never done alone, no matter how many late nights and quiet mornings it takes. I owe deep thanks to the people who held me steady and made this story sharper, louder, truer.

To my beta readers, thank you for lending your eyes, your hearts, and your honesty. You caught the cracks, you pushed me harder, and you reminded me what readers really feel when a story lands. This book is stronger because of you.

To my early readers and cheerleaders, you know who you are, thank you for the late-night messages, the encouragement, and for letting me talk endlessly about fictional people as if they were real. Your excitement carried me through every draft.

And to Summer, thank you for every eye-roll, every sigh, and every "Mum, not Harley Nash again." This book exists in part because winding you up about it became half the fun.

And finally, to everyone who has picked up this book, thank you for stepping into these mountains with me. I hope you see yourself somewhere in the snow.

About the Author

Emily Harrison writes slow-burn romance with sharp edges, stories that simmer with longing, crackle with tension, and never play it safe. Her work blends emotional depth with grounded realism, exploring what happens when flawed people fall into the kind of love that doesn't come easy... or quietly.

Peak Season is her second novel, set in a world of snowstorms, second chances, and the kind of chemistry you feel in your bones. When she's not writing, Emily somehow manages to be a mum, a newlywed, and a Nana, a walking contradiction with a full-time job, a loud mind, and a tendency to spill her guts onto the page. She's based in the UK, powered by wine, grit, and a refusal to write anything that doesn't bleed.

Follow her behind-the-scenes chaos.

www.ingramcontent.com/pod-product-compliance
Ingram Content Group UK Ltd.
Pitfield, Milton Keynes, MK11 3LW, UK
UKHW040710031125
8722UKWH00021B/93

9 781919 202914